ASK
FOR IT

مرشه

ASK FOR IT

SYLVIA DAY

BRAVA

KENSINGTON PUBLISHING CORP.
http://www.kensingtonbooks.com

BRAVA BOOKS are published by

Kensington Publishing Corp.
850 Third Avenue
New York, NY 10022

All Kensington titles, imprints and distributed lines are available at special quantity discounts for bulk purchases for sales promotions, premiums, fund-raising, educational or institutional use.

Special book excerpts or customized printings can also be created to fit specific needs. For details, write or phone the office of the Kensington Special Sales Manager: Kensington Publishing Corp., 850 Third Avenue, New York, NY 10022. Attn. Special Sales Department. Phone: 1-800-221-2647.

Brava and the logo Reg. U.S. Pat. & TM Off.

ISBN 0-7582-1472-3

First Kensington Trade Paperback Printing: August 2006
10 9 8 7 6 5 4 3 2 1

Printed in the United States of America

*To my mother, Tami Day, for fostering my love of
romance novels and being such an awesome PR person.
(She promotes my books like mad!)
I love you, Mom.*

Acknowledgments

Many thanks go to the judges of the 2004 IRW Golden Opportunity and the 2004 Gateway to the Rest contests for awarding this story First Place and Best of the Best rankings. Being named a winning finalist in the contests gave me confidence in both the story and my writing abilities.

Huge hugs go out to my critique partners—Sasha White, Annette McCleave, and Jordan Summers. Their assistance, support, and friendship helped me (and the story!) immeasurably.

My undying gratitude goes to my fabulous editor, Kate Duffy. She's absolutely wonderful. I'm so very, very lucky to write for her.

And to the Allure Authors (*www.AllureAuthors.com*), my friends and colleagues, for their support, encouragement, and ambition. You are an awesome group of women, and I'm so glad to be a part of Allure!

Prologue

"**A**re you worried I'll ravish the woman, Eldridge? I admit to a preference for widows in my bed. They are much more agreeable and decidedly less complicated than virgins or other men's wives."

Sharp gray eyes lifted from the mass of papers on the enormous mahogany desk. "*Ravish*, Westfield?" The deep voice was rife with exasperation. "Be serious, man. This assignment is very important to me."

Marcus Ashford, seventh Earl of Westfield, lost the wicked smile that hid the soberness of his thoughts and released a deep breath. "And you must be aware that it is equally important to me."

Nicholas, Lord Eldridge, sat back in his chair, placed his elbows on the armrests, and steepled his long, thin fingers. He was a tall and sinewy man with a weathered face that had seen too many hours on the deck of a ship. Everything about him was practical, nothing superfluous, from his manner of speaking to his physical build. He presented an intimidating presence with a bustling London thoroughfare as a backdrop. The result was deliberate and highly effective.

"As a matter of fact, until this moment, I was not aware. I wanted to exploit your cryptography skills. I never considered you would volunteer to manage the case."

Marcus met the piercing gray stare with grim determination. Eldridge was head of the elite band of agents whose sole purpose was to investigate and hunt down known pirates and smugglers. Working under the auspices of His Majesty's Royal Navy, Eldridge wielded an inordinate amount of power. If Eldridge refused him the assignment, Marcus would have little say.

But he would not be refused. Not in this.

He tightened his jaw. "I will not allow you to assign someone else. If Lady Hawthorne is in danger, I will be the one to ensure her safety."

Eldridge raked him with an all-too-perceptive gaze. "Why such passionate interest? After what transpired between you, I'm surprised you would wish to be in close contact with her. Your motive eludes me."

"I have no ulterior motive." At least not one he would share. "Despite our past, I've no desire to see her harmed."

"Her actions dragged you into a scandal that lasted for months and is still discussed today. You put on a good show, my friend, but you bear scars. And some festering wounds, perhaps?"

Remaining still as a statue, Marcus kept his face impassive and struggled against his gnawing resentment. His pain was his own and deeply personal. He disliked being asked about it. "Do you think me incapable of separating my personal life from my professional one?"

Eldridge sighed and shook his head. "Very well. I won't pry."

"And you won't refuse me?"

"You are the best man I have. It was only your history that gave me pause, but if you are comfortable with it, I have no

objections. However, I will grant her request for reassign-
ment, if it comes to that."

Nodding, Marcus hid his relief. Elizabeth would never ask
for another agent; her pride wouldn't permit it.

Eldridge began to tap his fingertips together. "The journal
Lady Hawthorne received was addressed to her late husband
and is written in code. If the book was involved in his death . . ."
He paused. "Viscount Hawthorne was investigating Christopher St. John when he met his reward."

Marcus stilled at the name of the popular pirate. There
was no criminal he longed to apprehend more than St. John,
and his enmity was personal. St. John's attacks against Ashford
Shipping were the impetus to his joining the agency. "If Lord
Hawthorne kept a journal of his assignments and St. John
were to acquire the information—bloody hell!" His gut tightened at the thought of the pirate anywhere near Elizabeth.

"Exactly," Eldridge agreed. "In fact, Lady Hawthorne has
already been contacted about the book since it was brought
to my attention just a sennight ago. For her safety and ours,
it should be removed from her care immediately, but that's
impossible at the moment. She was instructed to personally
deliver the journal, hence the need for our protection."

"Of course."

Eldridge slid a folder across the desk. "Here is the information I've gathered so far. Lady Hawthorne will apprise
you of the rest during the Moreland ball."

Collecting the particulars of the assignment, Marcus stood
and took his leave. Once in the hallway, he allowed a grim
smile of satisfaction to curve his lips.

He'd been only days away from seeking Elizabeth out. The
end of her mourning meant his interminable waiting was
over. Although the matter of the journal was disturbing, it
worked to his advantage, making it impossible for her to
avoid him. After the scandalous way she'd jilted him four

years ago she would not be pleased with his new appearance in her life. But she wouldn't turn to Eldridge either, of that he was certain.

Soon, very soon, all that she had once promised and then denied him would finally be his.

Chapter 1

Marcus found Elizabeth before he even set foot in the Moreland ballroom. In fact, he was trapped on the staircase as impatient peers and dignitaries sought a word with him. He was oblivious to those who vied for his attention, arrested by a brief glimpse of her.

She was even lovelier than before. How that was possible he couldn't say. She had always been exquisite. Perhaps absence had made his heart grow fonder.

A derisive smile curved his lips. Obviously, Elizabeth did not return the sentiment. When their eyes met, he allowed his pleasure at seeing her again to show on his face. In return, she lifted her chin and looked away.

A deliberate snub.

The cut direct, exactly administered but unable to draw blood. She had already inflicted the most grievous laceration years ago, making him impervious to further injury. He brushed off her disregard with ease. Nothing could alter their fate, however she might wish it otherwise.

For years now he'd served as an agent to the crown, and in that time he had led a life that would rival the stories written in any sensational novel. He'd fought numerous sword fights, been shot twice, and dodged more than any man's fair share of cannon fire. In the process, he had lost three of his own ships and sunk a half dozen others before he'd been forced to remain in England by the demands of his title. And yet the sudden fiery lick of awareness along his nerve endings only ever happened when he was in the same room as Elizabeth.

Avery James, his partner, stepped around him when it became obvious he was rooted to the spot. "There is Viscountess Hawthorne, my lord," he pointed out with an almost imperceptible thrust of his chin. "She is standing to the right, on the edge of the dance floor, in the violet silk gown. She is—"

"I know who she is."

Avery looked at him in surprise. "I was unaware that you were acquainted."

Marcus's lips, known widely for their ability to charm women breathless, curved in blatant anticipation. "Lady Hawthorne and I are . . . old friends."

"I see," Avery murmured, with a frown that said he didn't at all.

Marcus rested his hand on the shorter man's shoulder. "Go on ahead, Avery, while I deal with this crush, but leave Lady Hawthorne to me."

Avery hesitated a moment, then nodded reluctantly and continued to the ballroom, his path clear of the crowd that besieged Marcus.

Tempering his irritation with the importunate guests blocking his path, Marcus tersely acknowledged the flurry of greetings and inquiries directed at him. This melee was the reason he disliked these events. Gentlemen who did not have the initiative to seek him out during calling hours felt free to approach him in a more relaxed social setting. He never mixed business with pleasure. At least that had been his rule until tonight.

Elizabeth would be the exception. As she had always been an exception.

Twirling his quizzing glass, Marcus watched as Avery moved through the crowd with ease, his gaze drifting past his partner to the woman he was assigned to protect. He drank in the sight of her like a man dying of thirst.

Elizabeth had never cared for wigs and was not wearing one tonight, as most of the other ladies did. The effect of stark white plumes in her dark hair was breathtaking, drawing every eye inexorably toward her. Nearly black, her hair set off eyes so stunningly colored they brought to mind the luster of amethysts.

Those eyes had locked with his for only a moment, but the sharp shock of her magnetism lingered, the pull of it undeniable. It drew him forward, called to him on the primitive level it always had, like a moth to a flame. Despite the danger of burning, he could not resist.

She had a way of looking at a man with those amazing eyes. Marcus could almost have believed he was the only man in the room, that everyone had disappeared and nothing stood between where he was trapped on the staircase and where she waited on the other side of the dance floor.

He imagined closing the distance between them, pulling her into his arms, and lowering his mouth to hers. He knew already that her lips, so erotic in their shape and plumpness, would melt into his. He wanted to trail his mouth down the slim column of her throat and lick along the ridge of her collarbone. He wanted to sink into her lush body and sate his driving hunger, a hunger that had become so powerful he was very nearly mad with it.

He'd once wanted everything—her smiles, her laughter, the sound of her voice, and the view of the world through her eyes. Now his need was baser. Marcus refused to allow it to be more than that. He wanted his life back, the life free of pain, anger, and sleepless nights. Elizabeth had taken it away and she could damn well give it back.

His jaw clenched. It was time to close the distance between them.

One look had shaken his control. What would it be like when he held her in his arms again?

*   *   *

Elizabeth, Viscountess Hawthorne, stood for a long moment in shock, heat spreading across her cheeks.

Her gaze had locked on the man on the staircase for only a moment and yet during that brief time her heart had increased its rhythm to an alarming pace. She was held motionless, arrested by the masculine beauty of his face, a face which had clearly shown pleasure at seeing her again. Startled and disturbed by her reaction to him after all these years, she had forced herself to cut him, to look away with haughty disregard.

Marcus, now the Earl of Westfield, was still magnificent. He remained the handsomest man she had ever encountered. When his gaze met hers, she felt the spark that passed between them as if it were a tangible force. An intense attraction had always existed between them. She was profoundly disturbed to discover it had not abated in the slightest.

After what he'd done, he should repulse her.

Elizabeth felt a hand at her elbow, jolting her back into the conversation. She turned to find George Stanton at her side, his concerned gaze searching her face. "Are you feeling unwell? You look a bit flushed."

She fluffed the lace at the end of her sleeve to hide her unease. "It is warm in here." Snapping her fan open, she waved it rapidly to cool her hot cheeks.

"I think a beverage is in order," George offered and she rewarded his thoughtfulness with a smile.

Once George had departed, Elizabeth directed her attention toward the group of gentlemen who surrounded her. "What were we discussing?" she asked no one in particular. Truthfully, she hadn't been paying attention to the conversation for most of the past hour.

Thomas Fowler replied. "We were discussing the Earl of Westfield." He gestured discreetly to Marcus. "Surprised to see him in attendance. The earl is notorious for his aversion to social events."

"Indeed." She feigned indifference while her palms grew

damp within her gloves. "I had hoped that predilection of the earl's would hold true this evening, but it appears I am not so fortunate."

Thomas shifted, his countenance revealing his discomfort. "My apologies, Lady Hawthorne. I had forgotten your past association with Lord Westfield."

She laughed softly. "No need for apologies. Truly, you have my heartfelt appreciation. I'm certain you are the only person in London who has the sense to forget. Pay him no mind, Mr. Fowler. The earl was of little consequence to me then, and is of even less consequence now."

Elizabeth smiled as George returned with her drink and his eyes sparkled with pleasure at her regard.

As the conversation around her continued, Elizabeth slowly altered her position to better secure furtive glimpses of Marcus navigating the clogged staircase. It was obvious his libidinous reputation had not affected his power and influence. Even in a crowd, his presence was compelling. Several highly esteemed gentlemen hurried to greet him rather than wait for him to descend to the ballroom floor. Women, dressed in a dazzling array of colors and frothy with lace, glided surreptitiously toward the staircase. The influx of admirers moving in his direction shifted the balance of the entire room. To his credit, Marcus looked mostly indifferent to all of the fawning directed toward him.

As he made his way down to the ballroom, he moved with the casual arrogance of a man who always obtained precisely what he desired. The crowd around him attempted to pin him in place, but Marcus cut through it with ease. He attended intently to some, offhandedly to others, and to a few he simply raised an imperious hand. He commanded those around him with the sheer force of his personality and they were content to allow him to do so.

Feeling the intensity of her regard, his gaze met hers again. The corners of his generous mouth lifted upward as perception passed between them. The glint in his eyes and the warmth of his smile made promises that he as a man could never keep.

There was an air of isolation about Marcus and a restless energy to his movements that had not been there four years ago. They were warning signs, and Elizabeth had every intention of heeding them.

George looked easily over her head to scrutinize the scene. "I say. It appears Lord Westfield is heading this way."

"Are you quite certain, Mr. Stanton?"

"Yes, my lady. Westfield is staring directly at me as we speak."

Tension coiled in the pit of her stomach. Marcus had literally frozen in place when their eyes had first met and the second glance had been even more disturbing. He was coming for her and she had no time to prepare. George looked down at her as she resumed fanning herself furiously.

Damn Marcus for coming tonight! Her first social event after three years of mourning and he unerringly sought her out within hours of her reemergence, as if he'd been impatiently waiting these last years for exactly this moment. She was well aware that that had not been the case at all. While she had been crepe-clad and sequestered in mourning, Marcus had been firmly establishing his scandalous reputation in many a lady's bedroom.

After the callous way he'd broken her heart, Elizabeth would have discounted him regardless of the circumstances but tonight especially. Enjoyment of the festivities was not her aim. She had a man she was waiting for, a man she had arranged covertly to meet. Tonight she would dedicate herself to the memory of her husband. She would find justice for Hawthorne and see it served.

The crowd parted reluctantly before Marcus and then regrouped in his wake, the movements heralding his progress toward her. And then Westfield was there, directly before her. He smiled and her pulse raced. The temptation to retreat, to flee, was great, but the moment when she could reasonably have done so passed far too swiftly.

Squaring her shoulders, Elizabeth took a deep breath. The glass in her hand began to tremble and she quickly swallowed the whole of its contents to avoid spilling on her dress. She passed the empty vessel to George without looking. Marcus caught her hand before she could retrieve it.

Bowing low with a charming smile, his gaze never broke contact with hers. "Lady Hawthorne. Ravishing, as ever." His voice was rich and warm, reminding her of crushed velvet. "Would it be folly to hope you still have a dance available, and that you would be willing to dance it with me?"

Elizabeth's mind scrambled, attempting to discover a way to refuse. His wickedly virile energy, potent even across the room, was overwhelming in close proximity.

"I am not in attendance to dance, Lord Westfield. Ask any of the gentlemen around us."

"I've no wish to dance with them," he said dryly, "so their thoughts on the matter are of no consequence to me."

She began to object when she perceived the challenge in his eyes. He smiled with devilish amusement, visibly daring her to proceed, and Elizabeth paused. She would not give him the satisfaction of thinking she was afraid to dance with him. "You may claim this next set, Lord Westfield, if you insist."

He bowed gracefully, his gaze approving. He offered his arm and led her toward the dance floor. As the musicians began to play and music rose in joyous swell through the room, the beautiful strains of the minuet began.

Turning, Marcus extended his arm toward her. She placed her hand atop the back of his, grateful for the gloves that separated their skin. The ballroom was ablaze with candles, which cast him in golden light and brought to her attention the strength of his shoulder as it flexed. Lashes lowered, she appraised him for signs of change.

Marcus had always been an intensely physical man, engaging in a variety of sports and activities. Impossibly, it appeared he had grown stronger, more formidable. He was power personified and Elizabeth marveled at her past naiveté in believing she could tame him. Thank God, she was no longer so foolish.

His one softness was his luxuriously rich brown hair. It shone like sable and was tied at the nape with a simple black ribbon. Even his emerald gaze was sharp, piercing with a fierce intelligence. He had a clever mind to which deceit was naught but a simple game, as she had learned at great cost to her heart and pride.

She had half expected to find the signs of dissipation so common to the indulgent life and yet his handsome face bore no such witness. Instead he wore the sun-kissed appearance of a man who spent much of his time outdoors. His nose was straight and aquiline over lips that were full and sensuous. At the moment those lips were turned up on one side in a half smile that was at once boyish and alluring. He remained perfectly gorgeous from the top of his head to the soles of his feet. He was watching her studying him, fully aware that she could not help but admire his handsomeness. She lowered her eyes and stared resolutely at his jabot.

The scent that clung to him enveloped her senses. It was a wonderfully manly scent of sandalwood, citrus, and Marcus's own unique essence. The flush of her skin seeped into her insides, mingling with her apprehension.

Reading her thoughts, Marcus tilted his head toward her. His voice, when it came, was low and husky. "Elizabeth. It is a long-awaited pleasure to be in your company again."

"The pleasure, Lord Westfield, is entirely yours."

"You once called me Marcus."

"It would no longer be appropriate for me to address you so informally, my lord."

His mouth tilted into a sinful grin. "I give you leave to be inappropriate with me at any time you choose. In fact, I have always relished your moments of inappropriateness."

"You have had a number of willing women who suited you just as well."

"Never, my love. You have always been separate and apart from every other female."

Elizabeth had met her share of scoundrels and rogues but always their slick confidence and overtly intimate manners left her unmoved. Marcus was so skilled at seducing women, he managed the appearance of utter sincerity. She'd once believed every declaration of adoration and devotion that had fallen from his lips. Even now, the way he looked at her with such fierce longing seemed so genuine she almost believed it.

He made her want to forget what kind of man he was—a heartless seducer. But her body would not let her forget. She felt feverish and faintly dizzy.

"Three years of mourning," he said, with a faint note of bitterness. "I am relieved to see grief has not unduly ravaged your beauty. In fact, you are even more exquisite than when we were last together. You do recall that occasion, do you not?"

"Vaguely," she lied. "I have not thought of it in many years."

Wondering if he suspected her deception, she studied him as they changed partners. Marcus radiated an aura of sexual magnetism that was innate to him. The way he moved, the way he talked, the way he smelled—it all boasted of powerful energies and appetites. She sensed the barely leashed power he hid below the polished surface and she recollected how dangerous he was.

His voice poured over her with liquid heat as the steps of the minuet returned her to him. "I am wounded you are not more pleased to see me, especially when I braved this miserable event solely to be with you."

"Ridiculous," she scoffed. "You had no notion I would be here this evening. Whatever your purpose, please go about it and leave me in peace."

His voice was alarmingly soft. "My purpose is you, Elizabeth."

She stared a moment, her stomach churning with heightened unease. "If my brother sees us together he will be furious."

The flare of Marcus's nostrils made her wince. Once he and William had been the best of friends, but the end of her engagement had also brought about the demise of their friendship. Of all the things she regretted, that was paramount.

"What do you want?" she asked when he said nothing more.

"The fulfillment of your promise."

"What promise?"

"Your skin against mine with nothing in between."

"You're mad." She breathed heavily, shivering. Then her eyes narrowed. "Don't toy with me. Consider all the women who have graced your sheets since we parted. I did you a good turn by releasing you to—"

Elizabeth gasped as his gloved hand spun about beneath hers and his fingers squeezed with crushing force.

With darkened gaze, he bit out, "You did a great many things to me when you broke your word. A good turn is not one of them."

Shocked at his vehemence, she fought back. "You knew how I felt about fidelity, how strongly I desired it. You could never have been the type of husband I wanted."

"I was exactly what you wanted, Elizabeth. You wanted me so badly it scared you away."

"That's not true! I am not afraid of you!"

"If you had any sense, you would be," he muttered.

She would have retorted, but the steps of the dance led him away. He flashed a brilliant smile at the woman who minced steps around him and Elizabeth grit her teeth. For the rest of the dance he spoke not a word, even while he charmed every other woman he came into contact with.

Elizabeth's hand burned from Marcus's touch and her skin was flushed from the heat of his gaze. He'd never hidden the blatant sexuality of his nature. Instead he'd encouraged her to release her own. He'd offered her the best of both worlds—the respectability of her station and the passion of a man who could turn her blood to fire—and she'd believed he could make her happy.

How naive she'd been. With a family such as hers, she should have known better.

The moment the dance was over Elizabeth fled with rapid steps. A slightly raised hand caught her eye, and she smiled at the sight of Avery James. She cleared her thoughts, knowing immediately he was the man she awaited. Avery would only attend a social event such as this at Lord Eldridge's behest.

Eldridge had assured her that as the widow of a trusted agent if she ever required anything she was only to ask. Avery had been assigned as the man for her to contact. Despite his cynically world-weary appearance, he was in fact a gentle and considerate man who had been indispensable to her in the first few months after Hawthorne's death. The sight of him reminded her again of why she was here.

Elizabeth picked up her pace as, behind her, Marcus called out her name.

"The dance you requested is over, Westfield," she threw over her shoulder. "You are free to bask in the glow of your hard-earned reputation and the amorous attentions of your admirers."

She hoped he understood the obvious. Whatever the cost, she would not be seeing him again.

Marcus watched Elizabeth move gracefully toward Avery. With her back to him, he no longer had to suppress his grin. She had given him the cut direct. Again.

But alas, his sweet Elizabeth would soon discover that he was not so easily dismissed.

Chapter 2

"Mr. James," Elizabeth greeted him with genuine affection. "It is a pleasure to see you again." She held out her hands and they were swiftly engulfed in his much larger ones, his face lit with a rare smile. Tucking her hand under his arm, he led her through nearby French doors to an indoor atrium.

She squeezed his forearm. "I thought perhaps I had arrived too late and missed my appointment."

"Never say it, Lady Hawthorne," he replied with gruff fondness. "I would have waited all evening."

Tilting her head back, Elizabeth sucked in a deep breath of the lushly scented air. The heady redolence contained within the vast space was a pleasant and most welcome relief after the smells of smoke and burnt wax, powders and heavy perfumes that had overwhelmed the ballroom.

As they strolled casually through the paths, Elizabeth turned to Avery and asked, "Would I be correct in assuming that you are the agent assigned to assist me?"

He smiled. "I will be partnering another agent in this matter, yes."

"Of course." Her mouth curved ruefully. "You always work in pairs, don't you? As did Hawthorne and my brother."

"The order of things works well, my lady, and has saved lives."

Her steps faltered. Saves *some* lives. "I lament the exis-

tence of the agency, Mr. James. William's marriage and sub-
sequent resignation is a blessing I treasure. He almost died
the night I lost my husband. I eagerly await the day when the
agency is no longer a part of my life."

"We will do our best to resolve this with the utmost haste,"
he assured her.

"I know you will," she sighed. "I'm pleased you are one of
the agents Lord Eldridge chose."

Avery squeezed her hand where it draped over his forearm.
"I was grateful for the opportunity to meet with you again. It
has been several months since we last met."

"Has it truly been that long?" she asked, frowning. "Time
is running away from me."

"I wish I could say the same . . ." a familiar voice interjected from behind her. "Unfortunately, the last four years
have seemed an eternity to me."

Elizabeth tensed, her heart stopping before quickening its
pace.

Avery turned them both to face their visitor. "Ah, here is
my partner now. I understand you and Lord Westfield are old
acquaintances. Hopefully such a fortuitous arrangement will
expedite matters."

"Marcus," she whispered, her eyes widening as the import
of his presence struck her like a physical blow.

He bowed. "I am in your service, madam."

Elizabeth swayed on her feet, and Avery tightened his grip
to steady her. "Lady Hawthorne?"

Marcus reached her in two strides. "Don't faint, love. Take
a deep breath."

It seemed an impossible task as she gasped like a fish out
of water, her corset suddenly unbearably constricting. She
waved him off, his proximity and the scent of his skin making it even more difficult to expand her lungs.

She watched as Marcus shot a telling glance to Avery, who
then turned and walked away, suddenly finding interest in
the fronds of a distant fern.

Lightheaded but recovering, Elizabeth shook her head rapidly. "Marcus, you have truly lost your mind."

"Ah, feeling better, I see," he drawled with a sardonic tilt to his lips.

"Find your amusement in some other venture. Resign your commission. Leave the agency."

"Your concern is touching albeit confusing, after your own callous disregard for my well-being in the past."

"Save your sarcasm for another day," she snapped. "Have you no notion of what you've involved yourself in? It's dangerous to work for Lord Eldridge. You could be hurt. Or killed."

Marcus released a deep breath. "Elizabeth, you are overwrought."

She glared at him and glanced quickly at Avery, who maintained his discretionary study of the fern. She lowered her voice. "How long have you been an agent?"

His jaw tightened. "Four years."

"*Four years?*" She stumbled backward. "Were you an agent when you paid your addresses to me?"

"Yes."

"Damn you." Her voice was a pained whisper. "When were you planning on disclosing this to me? Or was I never to know until you came home in a coffin?"

He scowled and crossed his arms over his chest. "I don't see that it much matters now."

She stiffened at his icy tone. "All these years I feared reading the banns announcing your marriage. Instead I should have been perusing the obituaries." Turning away, Elizabeth sheltered her racing heart with her hand. "How I wish you had stayed far, far away from me." She gathered her skirts and hurried away. "I wish to God I'd never met you."

The sharp tapping of his heels on marble was the only warning she had before her elbow was caught and she was spun about.

"The feeling is bloody damn mutual," he growled.

He towered over her, his sensual mouth drawn taut with

anger, his emerald gaze sparkling with something that made her shiver.

"How could Lord Eldridge assign you to me?" she cried. "And why did you accept?"

"I insisted on taking this mission."

At her astonished gasp, his lips thinned further. "Make no mistake. You fled from me once. I will not allow it to happen again." He tugged her closer and the air sweltered between them. His voice turned rough. "I don't care if you marry the King himself this time. I *will* have you."

She struggled to escape, but his grip was firm. "Good heavens, Marcus. Haven't we inflicted enough damage on one another?"

"Not nearly." He thrust her away as if the feel of her against him was distasteful. "Now let us dispatch this matter regarding your late husband so Avery can retire."

Shaking, Elizabeth moved swiftly toward Avery. Marcus followed behind her with the predatory gracefulness of a jungle cat.

There was no doubt she was the one being hunted.

She stopped beside Avery and took a shuddering breath before turning.

Marcus watched her with an unreadable expression. "I understand you received a book written by your late husband." He waited for her answering nod. "Is the sender familiar to you?"

"The handwriting on the parcel was Hawthorne's. It was obviously addressed some time ago, the wrapping was yellowed and the ink faded." She had puzzled over the package for days, unable to determine its origin or its purpose.

"Your husband addressed a package to himself and it arrives three years after his murder." Marcus narrowed his gaze. "Did he leave any grilles[1], any cards with odd holes in them, anything written that struck you as unusual?"

---

[1]The grille method was developed by the French Cardinal Richelieu in the 1600s. Its purpose was to create secret messages that could only be deciphered by a special card punched with holes in strategic locations.

"No, nothing." She reached into her reticule, withdrawing the slim journal and the letter she'd received just a few days ago. She handed both to Marcus.

After a cursory perusal he tucked the book into his coat and then glanced through the letter, a frown gathering between his brows as he read. "In the history of the agency only Lord Hawthorne's murder remains unsolved. I had hoped to keep your involvement to a minimum."

"I will do whatever is necessary," she offered quickly. "Hawthorne deserves justice and if my involvement is required, so be it." Anything to finish this.

Marcus folded the missive carefully. "I dislike exposing you to danger."

Her emotions on edge, Elizabeth bristled. "So you seek to withhold me from harm while risking your own neck? I am more heavily invested in the outcome of this than you or your precious agency."

Marcus growled her name in warning.

Avery cleared his throat loudly. "It appears you two will not work well together. I would suggest bringing this difficulty to Lord Eldridge's attention. I'm certain there are other agents who—"

"No!" Marcus's voice cracked like a whip.

"Yes!" Elizabeth nearly collapsed in relief. "An excellent suggestion." Her smile was heartfelt. "Surely Lord Eldridge will see the sense in the request."

"Running again?" Marcus taunted.

She glared. "I am being practical. You and I quite obviously cannot associate with one another."

"Practical." He gave a derisive snort. "The word you seek is craven."

"Lord Westfield!" Avery frowned.

Elizabeth waved him off. "Leave us for a moment, Mr. James. If you would, please." Her gaze remained locked on Marcus as Avery hesitated.

"Do as she says," Marcus murmured, glaring back at her.

Avery grunted, then spun on his heel and moved away with angry strides.

Elizabeth cut straight to it. "If I'm forced to work with you, Westfield, I will simply refuse to share any further information with the agency. I will handle the situation alone."

"Like hell you will!" The muscle in Marcus's jaw began to tick. "I will not allow you to place yourself in jeopardy. Attempt something foolish and see what happens. You won't like the outcome, I assure you."

"Truly?" she goaded, refusing to cower in the face of a temper that frightened most men. "And how do you propose to stop me?"

Marcus approached her menacingly. "I am an agent of the Crown—"

"We've established that."

"—on an assigned mission. Should you think to hinder my investigation I will view your actions as treasonous and treat you accordingly."

"You wouldn't dare! Lord Eldridge would not allow it."

"Oh but I would, and he wouldn't stop me." He came to a halt before her. "This volume looks suspiciously like a journal of Hawthorne's assignments and it could be related to his death. If so, you are in danger. Eldridge will not tolerate that any more than I."

"Why not?" she challenged. "Your feelings toward me are obvious."

He stepped closer, until the tips of his shoes disappeared beneath the edge of her hem. "Apparently not. However, plead your case to Eldridge if you must. Tell him how I affect you and how you long for me. Tell him about our sordid past and how even the memory of your dearly departed husband is not enough to overcome your desire."

She stared, and then her mouth fell open as a dry laugh escaped. "Your arrogance is stunning." She turned away, hiding the way her hands shook. He could have the damn journal. She would seek out Eldridge in the morning.

His mocking laughter followed her. "*My* arrogance? You are the one who thinks this is all about her."

Elizabeth stopped and spun about. "You made this personal with your threats."

"You and I becoming lovers is not a threat. It is a foregone conclusion and has nothing to do with your late husband's journal." He held up his hand when she attempted to argue. "Save your breath. This mission is important to Eldridge. I insisted for that reason alone. Having you in my bed does not require working with you."

"But . . ." She paused, recalling what he'd said to her earlier. He never stated his insistence was about her. Her face heated.

Marcus strolled casually past her, heading in the direction of the ballroom. "So feel free to disclose to Eldridge why you cannot work with me. Just be certain he understands that *I* have no difficulty at all working with *you*."

Gritting her teeth, Elizabeth bit back every expletive that fought to blurt from her mouth. No fool she, she understood his game. She also understood he would not leave her be until he decided he'd had enough, mission or not. The only part of this debacle that was within her power to control was whether she survived this encounter with her pride intact.

Her stomach tightened. Now that she had rejoined society she would have to watch his seductions. She would be forced to associate with the women who caught his fancy. She would see the smiles he shared with them, but not with her.

Damnation. Her breathing quickened. Against every shred of self-respect and intelligence she had, she took the first step to follow him.

The soft touch upon her elbow reminded her of Avery's presence. "Lady Hawthorne. Is everything well?"

She gave a jerky nod.

"I will speak with Lord Eldridge as soon as possible and—"

"That won't be necessary, Mr. James."

Elizabeth waited until Marcus rounded the corner and disappeared from her view before facing Avery. "My role is simply to deliver the journal. Once that is accomplished the rest remains up to you and Lord Westfield. I see no need to change agents."

"Are you certain?"

She nodded again, anxious to finish the conversation and return to the ballroom.

Avery's look was clearly skeptical, but he said, "Very well. I will assign two armed outriders to you. Take them with you everywhere and send word to me as soon as you receive details about the meeting."

"Of course."

"Since we've finished here, I shall depart." His smile held a touch of relief. "I never cared much for these affairs."

He lifted her hand and kissed the back.

"Elizabeth?" William's booming voice rang through the vast space.

Eyes wide, she clutched Avery's fingers. "My brother must not see you. He'll suspect immediately that something is amiss."

Avery, appreciating her concern and trained to think on his feet, nodded grimly and ducked swiftly behind a rounded bush.

Turning, she caught sight of William approaching. Like Marcus, he didn't mince his steps. He walked toward her with casual grace, his leg bearing no outward sign of the injury that had almost taken his life.

Although they were siblings they could not have been more disparate in appearance. She had the raven hair and amethyst eyes of their mother. William had the fair hair and bluish-green eyes of their father. Tall and broad-shouldered he had the look of a Viking, strong and dangerous but prone to mirth as witnessed by the fine laugh lines that rimmed his eyes.

"What are you about?" he queried, casting an overly curious glance around the atrium.

Elizabeth tucked her hand in the crook of his elbow, and
steered him toward the ballroom. "I was merely enjoying the
view. Where is Margaret?"

"With her acquaintances." William slowed and then stopped,
forcing her to halt with him. "I was told you danced with
Westfield earlier."

"Gossip already?"

"Stay away from him, Elizabeth," he warned softly.

"There was no polite way to refuse him."

"Do not be polite. I don't trust him. It's odd that he is in
attendance tonight."

She sighed sadly at the rift she'd caused. Marcus made
poor husband material, but he'd been a good friend to
William. "The reputation he's established these last few years
has justified my actions of long ago. I'm in no danger of
being swept away by his charms again, I assure you."

Tugging William toward the ballroom, Elizabeth was relieved when her brother gave no further resistance. If they
hurried, she might be able to see where Marcus was headed.

Marcus stepped out from his hiding place behind a tree
and brushed a stray leaf from his coat. Kicking dirt off his
shoes, his gaze remained riveted on Elizabeth's retreating
back until she disappeared from his sight. He wondered if it
was obvious, this maddening desire he had for her. His heart
raced and his legs ached with the effort he exerted not to follow her and snatch her away for his pleasure.

She was infuriatingly stubborn and obstinate, which is
how he'd known she was perfect for him. No other woman
could arouse his passions thusly. Furious or consumed with
lust, only Elizabeth made his blood heat with the need to
have her.

He wished to God it was love he felt. That emotion faded

eventually, burning out once the fuel was gone. Hunger only grew worse with time, aching and gnawing until it was fed.

Avery appeared at his side. "If that is what you call an 'old friend,' my lord, I would hate to see what your enemies are like."

His smile held no humor. "She was to be my wife." Stunned silence was the reply. "Have I rendered you speechless?"

"Damnation."

"An apt description." Girding himself inwardly, Marcus asked, "Does she plan to speak with Eldridge?"

"No." Avery shot him a sidelong glance. "Are you certain your involvement is wise?"

"No," he admitted, relieved his ploy had worked and grateful that, despite the years, he still knew her so well. "But I'm certain I have no other choice."

"Eldridge is determined to catch Hawthorne's murderer. In the course of our mission we may be forced to deliberately put Lady Hawthorne in danger to achieve our aims."

"No. Hawthorne is dead. Risking Elizabeth's life will not bring him back. We will find other ways to carry out our mission."

Avery shook his head in silent bemusement. "I trust you know what you are about, even if I do not. Now if you will excuse me, my lord, I shall make my egress through the garden, before anything else untoward occurs."

"I believe I'll accompany you." Falling into step beside his partner, Marcus laughed at Avery's raised brow. "When engaged in prolonged battle, a man must be prepared to retreat on occasion so that he may return refreshed to seize the day."

"Good God. Battles and brothers and broken engagements. Your personal history with Lady Hawthorne will only lead to trouble."

Marcus rubbed his hands together. "I look forward to it."

Chapter 3

"I am under siege!" Elizabeth complained as another obnoxiously large display of flowers was carried into the sitting room.

"There are worse fates for a woman than being courted by a devilishly handsome peer of the realm," Margaret said dryly, as she smoothed her skirts and sat upon the settee.

"You are a hopeless romantic, you know." Rising to her feet, Elizabeth collected a tiny brocade pillow and tucked it behind her sister-in-law's back. She deliberately kept her gaze diverted from the gorgeous and obviously costly flower arrangement. Marcus had implied that his interest was both professional and carnal, and she'd been as prepared as possible for such engagement. This soft assault on her feminine sensibilities was a surprise attack.

"I'm *enceinte*," Margaret protested as she was arranged more comfortably. "Not an invalid."

"Allow me to fuss a little. It brings me such pleasure."

"I'm certain I will appreciate it later, but for the moment, I am quite capable of seeing to myself."

Despite her grumbling, Margaret settled into the pillow with a sigh of pleasure, the soft glow of her skin displayed to perfection by the dark red of her curls.

"I beg to differ. You look more slender at five months pregnancy than you did before."

"*Nearly* five months," Margaret corrected. "And it is difficult to eat when you feel wretched most of the time."

Pursing her lips, Elizabeth reached for a scone, set it on a plate, and offered it to Margaret. "Take it," she ordered.

Margaret accepted with a mock glare, then said, "William says the betting books are filled with wagers on whether Lord Westfield still has matrimony in mind or not."

In the process of making tea, Elizabeth gaped. "Good God."

"You are a legend for jilting him—an earl so handsome and desired that every woman wants him. Except for you. It is simply too juicy to ignore. A tale of a rake's love thwarted."

Elizabeth snorted derisively.

"You've never told me what Lord Westfield did that caused you to break off your engagement."

Her hands shook as she spooned the tea leaves into the steaming pot. "It was long ago, Margaret, and as I've said many times before, I see no reason to discuss it."

"Yes, yes, I know. However, he clearly is desirous of your company, as witnessed by his repeated attempts to call on you. I admire Westfield's aplomb. He does not even blink when he is turned away. He simply smiles, says something charming, and takes his leave."

"The man has charm in bushels, I agree. Women flock to his side and make fools of themselves."

"You sound jealous."

"I am not," she argued. "One lump or two today?" Nevermind. You need two."

"Don't change the subject. Tell me about your jealousy. Women found Hawthorne attractive as well, but it never appeared to bother you."

"Hawthorne was steadfast."

Margaret took the offered cup and saucer with a grateful smile. "And you've said Westfield was not."

"No," Elizabeth said with a sigh.

"Are you certain?"

"I could not be more certain if I'd caught them in the act."

Margaret's mossy green eyes narrowed. "You took the word of a third party over that of your fiancé?"

Shaking her head, Elizabeth took a fortifying sip of her tea before answering. "I had a matter of grave urgency to discuss with Lord Westfield, grave enough that I ventured to his home one evening—"

"*Alone?* What in heaven's name would goad you to act so rashly?"

"Margaret, do you wish to hear the tale or not? It's difficult enough to talk about this without you interrupting."

"My apologies," came the contrite reply. "Please continue."

"I waited several moments after I arrived for him to receive me. When he appeared, his hair was damp, his skin flushed, and he was attired in a robe."

Elizabeth stared into the contents of her cup and felt ill.

"Go on," Margaret prodded when she didn't speak.

"Then the door he'd come through opened and a woman appeared. Dressed similarly, with hair as wet."

"Good grief! That would be difficult to explain. How did he attempt it?"

"He didn't." Elizabeth gave a dry, humorless laugh. "He said he was not at liberty to discuss it with me."

Frowning, Margaret set her cup and saucer on the end table. "Did he attempt to explain later?"

"No. I eloped with Hawthorne, and Westfield left the country until his father passed on. Until the Moreland ball last week, we've never again crossed paths."

"Never? Perhaps Westfield has collected his error and wishes to make amends," Margaret suggested. "There must be some reason he's pursuing you so doggedly."

Elizabeth shivered at the use of the word "pursuing."

"Trust my judgment. His aim is nothing as noble as making amends for past wrongs."

"Flowers, daily visits—"

"Discuss something less distasteful, Margaret," she warned. "Or I will take my tea elsewhere."

"Oh, fine. You and your brother are a stubborn lot."

But Margaret was never one to be denied, which is how she'd convinced William to give up his agency life and marry her. Therefore, Elizabeth anticipated the moment when Margaret would return to the subject of Marcus and was not surprised when it came later that evening.

"He is such a beautiful man."

Elizabeth followed Margaret's gaze across the crush of guests at the Dempsey rout. She found Marcus standing with Lady Cramshaw and her lovely daughter, Clara. Elizabeth pretended to ignore him even as she studied his every move. "After hearing about our past, how can you be taken by the earl's pretty face?"

She'd deliberately avoided social events for the last week, but in the end had accepted the Dempsey invitation, certain the Faulkner ball up the street would be more likely to attract Marcus. The annoying man had found her anyway, and dressed so beautifully. His deep red coat fell to his thighs and was liberally decorated with fine gold embroidery. The heavy silk gleamed in the candlelight as did the rubies that adorned his fingers and cravat.

"Beg your pardon?" Margaret turned her head, her eyes wide with bemusement. She pointed her fan across the room. It was then that Elizabeth saw William and she blushed furiously at her mistake.

Margaret laughed. "They make a stunning couple, your Westfield and Lady Clara."

"He is not mine and I pity the poor girl if she's caught his eye." She lifted her chin and looked away.

The telltale swish of heavy silk skirts announced a new participant in their conversation. "I agree," murmured the elderly Duchess of Ravensend as she completed their circle. "She's just a child and could never hope to do that man justice."

"Your Grace." Elizabeth dipped a quick curtsy before her godmother.

The duchess had a mischievous gleam in her soft brown eyes. "Unfortunate that you are now widowed, my dear, but it does present you and the earl with renewed opportunities."

Elizabeth closed her eyes and prayed for patience. From the very beginning her godmother had championed Marcus's suit. "Westfield is a scoundrel. I consider myself fortunate to have discovered that fact before saying my vows."

"He is quite possibly the handsomest man I have ever seen," observed Margaret. "Next to William, of course."

"And attractively formed," added the duchess as she peered at Marcus through her lorgnette. "Prime husband material."

Sighing, Elizabeth fluffed her skirts and fought the urge to roll her eyes. "I wish you both would set aside the notion that I marry again. I will not."

"Hawthorne was barely more than a boy," noted the duchess. "Westfield is a man. You will find the experience to be quite different should you choose him to share your bed. No one said marriage was required."

"I have no desire to be added to that libertine's list of conquests. He is a voluptuary. You cannot deny that, Your Grace."

"There is something to be said for a man with experience," Margaret offered. "Married to your brother, I would know." She waggled her brows suggestively.

Elizabeth shuddered. "Margaret, please."

"*Lady Hawthorne.*"

Turning quickly, she faced George Stanton with a grateful smile. He bowed, his handsome face awash in a friendly grin.

"I would be pleased to dance with you," she said before he could ask. Eager to get away, she placed her fingertips upon his sleeve and allowed him to lead her away.

"Thank you," she whispered.

"You appeared to be in need of rescue."

She grinned as they took their places in line. "You are remarkably astute, my dear friend."

With a sidelong glance, she watched as Marcus bowed over the young Clara's hand and escorted her to the dance floor. As he moved toward her, Elizabeth couldn't help but admire his seductive gait. A man who moved as he did would be an expert lover, there was no doubt. Other women watched him as well, coveted him as she did, lusted for him . . .

When he lifted his head to catch her gaze, Elizabeth looked away quickly from his knowing smile. The man knew just how to rile her and was ungentlemanly enough to use that knowledge to his advantage.

As the steps of the *contredanse* brought the dancers together and then moved them apart she followed his progress out of the corner of her eye. The next step would bring them together. Heated anticipation coursed through her veins.

She withdrew from George and turned gracefully to face Marcus. Knowing the encounter would be fleeting she permitted herself to enjoy the sight and smell of him. She drew a deep breath and set her palms against his. Desire flared instantly. She saw it in his eyes, felt it in her blood. She retreated with a sigh of relief.

As the music for the dance concluded, Elizabeth rose from her low curtsy. She couldn't resist smiling. It had been so long since she'd danced, she had almost forgotten how much she enjoyed it.

George returned her smile and deftly moved them into position for the next dance in the set.

Someone stepped in front of them, blocking their way. Before she looked up, she knew who it was. Her heart rate quickened.

Obviously, she'd miscalculated the lengths Marcus would go to to achieve his ends.

He nodded curtly in greeting. "Mr. Stanton."

"Lord Westfield." George looked to Elizabeth with a frown.

"Lady Clara, may I present to you Mr. George Stanton?" Marcus asked. "Stanton, the lovely Lady Clara."

George collected Clara's hand and bowed. "A pleasure."

Before Elizabeth could guess his intent, Marcus had reached for her. "An excellent pairing," Marcus said. "Lady Hawthorne and I, being *de trop*, shall leave you two to finish the set."

Tucking her hand firmly around his arm, he pulled her toward the open doors that led to the garden.

Elizabeth offered an apologetic smile over her shoulder, while inside, her heart leapt at the primitive display. "What are you about?"

"I thought that would be obvious. I'm causing a scene. You goaded me into this course of action by avoiding me the last sennight."

"I have not been avoiding you," she protested. "I've yet to receive another demand for the journal, therefore there was no reason to see you."

Exiting to the balcony, they found several guests enjoying the cool night air. Held so closely to his side, the sheer force of Marcus's presence once again surprised her.

"Your behavior is atrocious," she muttered.

"You may insult me at your leisure when we are alone."

Alone. A ripple of awareness brushed across her skin.

His gaze traveled over her face and searched her eyes. His own narrowed and though she tried to discern his thoughts his handsome features were set in stone. As they took the stairs into the garden, his pace quickened. She followed breathlessly, wondering what he meant to do, what he meant to say, startled to discover an unknown remnant of girlish romanticism thrilling at his determination.

Tucking her into a small alcove off the bottom of the staircase, Marcus eyed their surroundings carefully. Seeing they were alone, he moved swiftly. With gentle fingertips, he lifted her chin.

A kiss, she thought too late as his mouth covered hers. Then she couldn't think at all.

His lips were unbelievably gentle as they melded with hers but the sensations they elicited were brutal in their intensity. Elizabeth could not move, arrested by the powerful response of her body to his. Only their lips touched. A simple step backward would have broken the contact but she could not manage even that. She stood frozen, her senses reeling from the taste and scent of him, every nerve firing to life at his bold advance.

"Kiss me back," he growled, his fingers circling her wrists.

"No . . ." She tried to turn her head away.

Cursing, he took her mouth again. He did not kiss her sweetly as he had a moment before. This was an assault driven by bitterness so sharp she could taste it. His head tilted slightly, deepening the kiss, and then his tongue thrust forcefully between her parted lips. The depth of his ardor frightened her, and then fear flared into something far more powerful.

Hawthorne had never kissed her like this. This was more than just the joining of lips. It was a declaration of possession, of unquenchable need, a need Marcus built within her until she could no longer deny it. With a whimper, Elizabeth surrendered, tentatively touching her tongue to his, desperate for the intoxicating taste of him.

He growled his approval, the erotically charged sound causing her to sway unsteadily on her feet. Releasing her wrists, he supported her waist while a warm hand gripped the back of her neck, holding her still for his ravishment. His mouth moved skillfully over hers, rewarding her response with deeper flicks of his tongue. Her fists clutched his coat, pulling and tugging, trying to win some control but in the end unable to do more than just take what he gave her.

Finally he tore his mouth away with a tortured groan and buried his face in her perfumed hair. "Elizabeth." His voice was thick and unsteady. "We must find a bed. Now."

She gasped out a laugh. "This is madness."

"It has always been madness."

"You must stay away."

"I have. Four bloody years. I've paid the price for my imagined sins." He pulled back and stared down at her with eyes so hot they burned. "I've waited long enough to have you. I refuse to wait any longer."

The reminder of their past was sobering for both of them. "There is far too much between us to ever enjoy a liaison."

"I damn well intend to enjoy one regardless."

Shaking, she pulled back and, to her surprise, was released immediately. She pressed her fingers to her kiss-swollen lips. "I do not want the pain you bring. I do not want you."

"You lie," he said harshly. His finger traced the edge of her bodice. "You have wanted me since the moment we met. You want me still, I can taste it."

Elizabeth cursed her traitorous body, still so enamored of him it refused to listen to the dictates of her mind. Hot and aching all over, she was no better than any of the other besotted women who fell so easily into his bed. She backed away, but was stopped by the cold marble railing. Reaching behind her, she wrapped her hands around the baluster, gripping it so tightly the blood left her hands.

"If you had any care for me at all you would leave me be."

Flashing a smile that stopped her heart, Marcus stepped toward her. "I will show you the same care you once showed to me." His gaze smoldered with seductive challenge. "Give in to your desire for me, sweet. I assure you, doing so will not be something you regret."

"How can you say that? Have you not already wounded me once? Knowing how I feel about my father, you still acted as you did. I loathe men of your ilk. It's despicable to promise love and devotion to bed a woman only to cast her aside when you weary of the sport."

Marcus stopped abruptly. "It was *I* who was cast aside."

Elizabeth backed up tighter against the railing. "For good reason."

His lips twisted in a cynical smile. "You will receive me when I come to call, Elizabeth. You will drive out with me in the afternoons and accompany me to events such as these. I will not be turned away again."

The cold marble baluster froze her hands through her gloves and sent shivers up her arms. Despite the chill she felt hot, flushed. "Are you not satisfied with the numbers of women who fawn over you?"

"No," he replied with his habitual arrogance. "Satisfaction will come when you burn for me, when I invade your every thought and every dream. One day your infatuation will be so consuming that every breath you take apart from me will sear your lungs. You will give me whatever I desire, whenever and however I desire it."

"I will give you nothing!"

"You will give me everything." He closed the small gap between them. "You will yield all to me."

"Have you no shame?" Tears welled and clung to her lashes. He was implacable and the direness of her situation struck home with cruel effect. "After what you did to me, must you seduce me as well? Is my utter destruction the only thing that will appease you?"

"Damn you." His head dropped down to hers, his mouth brushing across her lips in a feather-light kiss. "I never thought to have you," he breathed. "I never expected that you would ever be free of your marriage, but you are. And I will have what was promised to me long ago."

Releasing the baluster, Elizabeth placed her hands against his waist to ward him off. The firm ridges of his stomach beneath her palms brought a raw, sweet ache to her body. "I will fight you with everything I have. I urge you to desist."

"Not until I have what I want."

"Leave her alone, Westfield."

Sagging with relief at the sound of the familiar voice, Elizabeth glanced up and saw William descending the staircase.

Marcus backed away with a vicious curse. Straightening, he shot his old friend a fulminating glare. Elizabeth exploited his distraction, taking the opportunity to slip past him. Running into the garden, she disappeared around a corner of yew hedges. He stepped forward, determined to go after her.

"I wouldn't," William said with soft menace, "If I were you."

"Your timing is unfortunate, Barclay." Marcus swallowed a growl of frustration, knowing his old friend would relish any opportunity to fight with him. The situation worsened as spectators, alerted by the carrying tone of angry voices and the rigid set of William's body, lined the edge of the balcony anticipating noteworthy gossip.

"When you desire Lady Hawthorne's company in the future, Westfield, be aware that she is indisposed to you indefinitely."

A statuesque redhead pushed her way through the throng of curious onlookers and ran down the steps toward them.

"Lord Westfield. Barclay. Please!" She clutched William's arm. "This is not the venue for such private discourse."

William broke off eye contact with Marcus and glanced at his lovely wife with a grim smile. "No need to fret. All is well." Lifting his gaze, he gestured to George Stanton who left the balcony and moved quickly to join them. "Please find Lady Hawthorne and escort her home."

"I would be honored." Stanton inched his way carefully between the two angry men before picking up speed and melding into the garden shadows.

Marcus sighed and rubbed the back of his neck. "You intercede based on a false assumption, Barclay."

"I will not debate the matter with you," William countered, all trace of civility gone. "Elizabeth has refused to see you and you will respect her wishes." He gently removed

Margaret's hand from his sleeve and stepped closer, his shoulders taut with repressed anger. "This will be your only warning. Keep your distance from my sister or I will call you out." The crowd above erupted in a series of muted gasps.

Marcus steadied his breathing with effort. Level-headedness had seen him through many volatile situations, but this time he made no effort to defuse the tension. He had a mission, as well as his own agenda. Both would require a great deal of time spent in Elizabeth's company. Nothing could be allowed to stand in his way.

Meeting William's challenge head-on, he stepped the last few paces until they were only inches apart. His voice softened ominously. "Interfering in my association with Elizabeth would not be wise. There is much left to be resolved between us and I will not have you intruding. I would never deliberately harm her. If you doubt my word, name your second now. My position is firm and worth whatever risk you present to me."

"You would risk your life to proceed?"

"Without question."

A weighted pause fell between them as they each measured the other carefully. Marcus made his resolve clear. He would not be deterred, threats of death or otherwise.

In return, William's gaze penetrated with its intensity. Over the years they had managed an icy public association. With William's marriage a stark contrast to his own bachelor's life, they'd rarely had the occasion to exchange words. Marcus lamented that lack. He often missed the companionship of his friend, who was a good man. But William had passed judgment too easily and Marcus would not bruise his pride by pleading a case to deaf ears.

"Shall we return to the festivities, Lady Barclay?" William said finally, the set of his shoulders relaxing a tiny fraction.

"I believe the night has grown chilly," Marcus murmured.

"Yes, my lord," Lady Barclay agreed. "I was about to say the same."

Hiding his regret, Marcus nodded, and then turned on his heel and left.

Elizabeth crossed into the foyer of Chesterfield Hall with a silent sigh. Her lips still throbbed and tasted of Marcus, a heady flavor that was dangerous to a woman's sanity. Although her heart rate had slowed, she was left feeling as though she'd just run a great race. She was grateful when her butler removed her heavy cloak and, tugging off her gloves, she headed directly toward the stairs. There was so much to consider, too much. She hadn't expected Marcus to be so damned determined to have his way. How she would handle a man such as he would take careful planning.

"My lady?"

"Yes?" She paused and turned to face the servant.

In his hand he held a silver salver which supported a cream-colored missive. Innocuous though it appeared, Elizabeth shivered at the sight of it. The handwriting and parchment were the same as the letter demanding Hawthorne's journal.

She shook her head and released a deep breath. Marcus would call on her tomorrow, of that she was certain. Whatever demand the note contained could wait until then. Reading it alone held no appeal. She knew how dangerous the agency's missions were and she didn't take her new involvement lightly. Therefore, if Marcus was so determined to plague her, she would at least make use of him in some small way.

Dismissing the servant with a wave, Elizabeth lifted her skirts and ascended the stairs.

What a sad twist of fate it was that the man assigned to protect her was the very one who'd proven he was not to be trusted.

Chapter 4

Unlike Marcus's own townhouse in Grosvenor Square, Chesterfield Hall was a sprawling estate located a good distance from the nearest house. Standing in the visitor's foyer, Marcus handed over his hat and gloves to the waiting liveried footman, then followed the butler down the hall to the formal parlor.

The location of his reception was a slight not lost on him. At one time he would have been shown upstairs and received as a near family member. Now he was not considered worthy of such a privilege.

"The Earl of Westfield," the servant announced.

Entering, Marcus paused on the threshold and glanced around the room, noting with interest the portrait that graced the space above the fireplace. The late Countess of Langston stared back at him with a winsome smile and violet eyes like her daughter's. Unlike Elizabeth's, however, Lady Langston's eyes held no wariness, only the soft glow of a woman content with her lot. Elizabeth had witnessed only briefly the kind of happiness his own parents had fostered over a lifetime. For a moment, regret rose like bile in his throat.

Once he'd sworn to dedicate his life to making Elizabeth look that happy. Now he wanted only to be done with his craving and free of her curse.

Clenching his jaw, he looked away from the painful reminder and found the curvaceous form that afflicted his waking and sleeping thoughts. As the butler shut the door with a soft click behind him, Marcus reached around his back and turned the lock.

Elizabeth stood by the arched window that overlooked the side garden. Dressed in a simple muslin day gown and bathed in indirect sunlight, she looked as young as when they'd first met. As always, every nerve ending in his body prickled with the sharp current of awareness that arced between them. In all of his many encounters, he'd yet to meet a woman who appealed to him as deeply or as hotly as Elizabeth did.

"Good afternoon, Lord Westfield," she said in the low throaty voice which brought to mind tumbled silk sheets. She shot a pointed glance at his hand, which remained curved around the knob. "My brother is at home."

"Good for him." He crossed the broad expanse of Aubusson rug in a few strides and lifted her bare fingertips to his lips. Her skin felt exquisite, the scent of her arousing. His tongue darted out to lick between her fingers and he watched as her pupils widened and the irises darkened. Marcus brought her hand to his heart and held it there. "Now that your mourning is over, do you intend to return to your own residence?"

Her gaze narrowed. "That would ease matters for you, wouldn't it?"

"Certainly breakfast in bed and afternoon trysts would be facilitated by a more private arrangement," he replied easily.

Yanking her hand from his grip, Elizabeth turned her back to him. Marcus bit back his smile.

"Considering your obvious distaste for me," she muttered, "I cannot understand why you desire to become intimate."

"Physical proximity does not necessitate intimacy."

Her shoulders stiffened beneath the fall of her dark hair. "Ah yes," she sneered. "You have proven that fact again and again, have you not?"

Flicking an imaginary piece of lint from his ruffled cuffs, Marcus walked to the settee and adjusted his coat before sitting. He refused to show his irritation at the censure he heard in her tone. Guilt was something he didn't require, he felt it often enough on his own. "I became what you once accused me of being. What would you have had me do, love? Go mad thinking of you? *Longing* for you?"

He sighed dramatically, hoping to goad her into facing him. It was a simple pleasure, gazing upon her features, but after four years it was a delight he needed as much as air. "I am truly not surprised to learn that, given the choice, you would have denied me what little solace I could find, cruel-hearted creature that you are."

Elizabeth spun about, revealing cheeks stained bright with color. "You blame *me*?"

"Who else is there to blame?" He opened his snuff box and took a small pinch. "It should have been you in my arms all these years. Instead, every time I bedded another woman I hoped she would be the one to make me forget you. But they never did. Not one." He snapped the lid shut.

Her nostrils flared on a swiftly indrawn breath.

"Often I would turn down the lamps and close my eyes. I would pretend it was you beneath me, you with whom I shared sexual congress."

"Damn you." Her hands clenched into tiny fists. "Why did you have to become just like my father?"

"You would have me be a monk?"

"Better that than a libertine!"

"While you sated another man's needs and suffered not at all?" He strove to appear calm and unaffected while every fiber of his being stood tense and expectant. "Did you think of me, Elizabeth, in your marriage bed? Were you ever haunted by dreams of me? Did you ever wish it were my body covering yours, filling yours? My sweat coating your skin?"

She stood frozen in place for a long moment, and then suddenly her lush mouth curved in a come-hither smile that made his gut clench. He'd known when the butler allowed him entry that Elizabeth was no longer willing to hide or run.

He'd girded himself inwardly for a fight. A sexual assault, however, had never crossed his mind. *Would he never understand her?*

"Would you like me to tell you about my marriage bed, Marcus?" she purred. "Would you like to hear the many ways Hawthorne took me? What he liked best, what he craved? Hmmm? Or would you prefer to hear how *I* like it? How I prefer to be taken?"

Elizabeth strolled toward him with a deliberate sway to her hips that made his mouth dry. In all of his dealings with her she'd never been the sexual aggressor. He was profoundly disturbed at how it aroused him, especially considering the last four years had been spent indulging in liaisons instigated by his lovers and not the reverse.

It didn't help that his reluctant passion was engaged by her words and the images they evoked. He pictured her face down on the bed, spread and willing as another man thrust into her from behind. His jaw ached from the force with which he clenched it, primitive feelings of claiming and possessing nearly undoing him. Pulling open the flaps of his coat, Marcus revealed the straining length of his cock within his breeches. Her steps faltered and then, with a lift of her chin, she continued toward him.

"I am not an innocent to run screaming at the sight of a man's desire." Elizabeth stopped before him and set her hands on either side of his knees. Before him hung the voluptuous swell of her breasts, nearly spilling from the rounded cut of her satin-edged bodice. In evening attire, her bosom was pressed flat by her corset. In day wear, the restriction was far less severe and his gaze was riveted by the bounty displayed for his benefit alone.

Never one to miss an opportunity, Marcus reached up and cupped the upper swell with his hands, gratified to hear the sharp hiss of her breath through her teeth. Her body had changed from the virginal ripeness of a girl to the fully curved figure of a woman. Squeezing and kneading, he stared at the valley between her breasts and imagined thrusting his cock through it. He growled at the thought and looked up at her mouth, watching in an agony of lust as she licked her lower lip.

Then suddenly she straightened, turned her back to him, and reached down to the small table. Before he could order her return, she'd tossed a sealed missive at his chest and walked away. He knew already what he would find inside. Still, he waited for his breathing to slow and his blood to cool before turning his attention to it. He noted the paper, a popular weight and tint he'd seen before.

Breaking open the unmarked seal with care, he scanned the contents. "How long have you had this?" he asked gruffly.

"A few hours."

Marcus turned the paper over and then lifted his gaze to hers. Elizabeth's skin was flushed and her eyes glazed, yet her chin was lifted at a determined angle. He frowned and stood. "You weren't curious enough to open it?"

"I'm aware of what it must say. He is prepared to meet with me and retrieve the book. How he worded the demand doesn't much matter, does it? Have you perused Hawthorne's journal since I gave it to you?"

He nodded. "The maps were easy enough. Hawthorne had some detailed drawings of the English and Scottish coasts, as well as some colonial waterways I'm familiar with. But Hawthorne's code is nigh indecipherable. I was hoping to have more time to study it."

Refolding the missive, Marcus put it in his pocket. Cryptography was a hobby he'd acquired after Elizabeth's marriage. The task required intense concentration, which allowed him a brief respite from thoughts of her, a rare gift. "I know this spot he refers to. Avery and I will be close by to protect you."

Shrugging, she said, "As you wish."

He stood and stalked over to her. Grabbing her shoulders,

he shook her. Hard. "How the hell can you be so bloody calm? Have you any notion of the danger? Or have you no sense at all?"

"What would you have me do?" she snapped. "Fall apart? Cry all over you?"

"A little emotion would be welcome. Something, *anything* to tell me you have a care for your own safety." His hands left her shoulders and plunged into her hair, tilting her head to the angle he desired. Then he kissed her as hard as he'd shaken her. He backed her up roughly, forcing her to stumble until he'd pinned her to the wall.

Elizabeth's nails dug deeply into the skin of his stomach as she clutched at his shirt. Her mouth was open, accepting the thrusts of his tongue. Despite the lack of finesse, she trembled against him, whimpered her distress, and then melted into his embrace. She kissed him back with a frenzy that nearly undid him.

Suddenly unable to breathe, Marcus broke away. His forehead pressed to hers, he groaned his frustration. "Why do you only come alive when I touch you? Don't you ever tire of the façade you hide behind?"

Her eyes squeezed shut and she turned her face away. "And what of your façade?"

"Jesus, you are stubborn." Nuzzling against her without gentleness, he rubbed the scent of her onto his damp skin while leaving his own sweat upon her cheek. With a rough and urgent voice he whispered, "I need you to follow my instructions when I give them to you. You must not allow your feelings to interfere."

"I trust your judgment," she said.

He stilled, his fists clenching in her hair until she winced. "Do you?"

The air thickened around them.

"Do you?" he asked again.

"What happened . . ." She swallowed hard and her nails dug deeper into his skin. "What happened that night?"

He let out his breath in an audible rush. His entire frame relaxed, the tension of their past releasing its merciless grip. Suddenly exhausted, Marcus realized the cold fury he still carried over the demise of their betrothal was all that had fueled him these many years.

"Sit down." He pulled away and waited until she crossed over to the settee. Studying her for long moments, he relished the sight of her mussed hair and swollen lips. From the beginning, he'd pursued her with singular attention, stealing her away to quiet corners where he would take her mouth with rushed, desperate kisses, risking scandal for glimpses of the fire Elizabeth hid so well.

Her beauty was simply the wrapping on a complex and fascinating treasure. Her eyes gave her away. In them one could find no trace of a lady's expected docility or meekness. Instead there were challenges, adventures. Things to be explored and discovered.

He wondered again if Hawthorne had been fortunate enough to see all her facets. Had she melted for him, opened to him, become soft and sated by his lovemaking?

Clenching his jaw, Marcus thrust the torturous thoughts away. "You know of Ashford Shipping?"

"Of course."

"One year I lost a small fortune to a pirate named Christopher St. John."

"St. John?" She frowned. "My abigail has mentioned the name. He's quite popular. Something of a hero, a benefactor of the poor and underprivileged."

He snorted. "A hero he's not. The man is a ruthless cutthroat. He was the reason I first approached Lord Eldridge. I demanded St. John be dealt with. Eldridge offered instead to train me to manage the pirate myself." His lips curved wryly. "The prospect of exacting my own retribution was irresistible."

Elizabeth pursed her lips. "Of course. A normal life is so dreadfully boring after all."

"Some tasks require personal attention."

Crossing his arms over his chest, Marcus enjoyed this opportunity to have her undivided attention. The simple act of conversing with her was a pleasure he relished, regardless of her scornful remarks. He'd been fawned over and catered to his entire life. Elizabeth's refusal to treat him as anything other than an ordinary man was one of the traits he found most attractive in her.

"I will never understand the appeal of a dangerous life, Marcus. I want peace and quiet in my life."

"Understandable, considering the family in which you were raised. You've had no structure, left to do as you wished by male family members too preoccupied with the pursuit of pleasure to see to you."

"You know me so well," she said scathingly.

"I have always known you well."

"Then you admit how poorly we would have suited."

"I admit nothing of the sort."

She dismissed the topic with a wave of her hand. "About that night . . ."

He watched her chin lift, as if she awaited a punishing blow, and he sighed. "I learned of a man who offered potentially damning information about St. John. We agreed to meet at the wharf. In return for his assistance the informant had one request in return. His wife was with child and knew nothing of the activities he'd engaged in to provide for her. He asked me to see to her welfare should anything untoward befall him."

"That was his wife in the robe?" Her eyes widened.

"Yes. In the midst of the meeting we were attacked. The sounds of a scuffle drew her attention and she came closer to investigate, into harm's way. She was thrown into the water and I leapt after her. Her husband was shot and killed."

"You did not bed her." It was a statement, no longer a question.

"Of course not," he answered simply. "But we both were

covered in filth. I brought her to my home to bathe while I made arrangements for her."

Elizabeth stood and began to pace, her hands clenching rhythmically in the folds of her gown. "I suppose I have always known."

A humorless laugh broke from his throat. Marcus waited for her to say something further, wondering at his sanity in wanting her still. He'd long suspected his imagined infidelity was merely the excuse she'd sought to sever their ties. To his mind, this afternoon only proved that to be true. She did not run into his arms and beg his forgiveness. She did not ask for a second chance or make any attempt to reconcile, and her silence infuriated him to the point where he wished to do violence.

His hands clenched into fists as he fought the urge to grab her and tear her clothes from her skin, to press her to the floor and plunge his cock into her, making it impossible for her to disregard him. It was the one and only way he knew he could penetrate her protective shell.

But his pride would not allow him to reveal his pain. He would, however, effect some change in her, a tiny crack in her reserve at least.

"I was as stunned as you when she entered, Elizabeth. She assumed you were the woman assigned to care for her. There was no way for her to know that my betrothed would visit at such an hour."

"Her dishabille . . ."

"Her garments were soaked. She had nothing aside from the robe lent to her by my housekeeper."

"You should have followed me," she said in a low, angry tone.

"I attempted to. It took me a moment, I admit, to recover from your slap to my face. You were too quick. By the time the widow was settled and I was free to come for you, you had departed with Hawthorne."

Elizabeth stopped her fevered pacing, her skirts settling

slowly as she stilled. Her head turned, revealing eyes that hid far too much from him. "Do you hate me?"

"Occasionally." He shrugged to hide the true depth of his bitterness, a bitterness that gnawed at him from the inside and tainted everything in his life.

"You want revenge," she stated without inflection.

"That is the least of it. I want answers. Why the elopement with Hawthorne? Do the feelings you have for me scare you that much?"

"Perhaps he was always an option."

"I refuse to believe that."

Her lush mouth curved grimly. "Does the possibility prick your ego?"

He snorted. "Play whatever game you like. You may hate wanting me, but you *do* want me."

Moving toward her, Marcus was stopped by her outstretched hand. She appeared calm, but her fingers shook badly. Her arm dropped.

There was far more to their differences than he'd yet discerned. They were strangers, bound by an attraction that defied all reason. But he would learn the truth. Despite his fear that she would elude him again, his need for her outweighed his instinct for self-preservation.

She'd asked if he hated her. At moments like this, he did. He hated her for making him care, hated her for remaining so beautiful and desirable, hated her for being the only woman he had ever wanted in this manner.

"Do you remember your first Season?" he asked in a hoarse voice.

"Of course."

He walked to the intricately carved sideboard and poured a small libation. It was too early for alcohol, but at the moment, he didn't care. He felt cold inside and as the fiery beverage splashed down his throat he relished the warmth it brought.

Finding a bride had not been his aim that year or any year

thereafter. He'd made it a point to avoid debutantes and their marriage machinations, but one look at Elizabeth and his intentions had changed.

He'd arranged an introduction and she'd impressed him with a confidence that belied her age. Securing permission to dance with her, he'd been delighted when she accepted despite his reputation. The simple contact of her gloved hand on his elicited a powerful sexual awareness, one he had never experienced before or since.

"You impressed me from the first, Elizabeth." Staring at his empty glass, he rolled it back and forth restlessly between his palms. "You didn't stammer or look faint when I was overbold with you. Rather you teased me and had the temerity to scold me as well. You shocked me so deeply the first time you swore at me I missed a step. Do you remember?"

Her voice was soft as it floated across the room. "How could I forget?"

"You scandalized every matron there by making me laugh aloud."

After that memorable first dance, he'd made it a point to attend the same events she did, which sometimes necessitated stopping at several houses before finding her. Society dictated that he could claim only one dance per evening and every moment spent with her had to be chaperoned, but despite these restrictions they'd discovered a mutual affinity. He was never bored with her, was instead endlessly fascinated.

Elizabeth was genuinely kind but had a quick temper that rose in an instant and dissipated as rapidly. She had in abundance all of the things that made a girl a woman but retained a childishness that could be at once endearing and frustrating. He admired her strength, but it was the fleeting glimpses of vulnerability that pushed him far past infatuation. He longed to protect her from the world at large, to shelter her and keep her all to himself.

And despite the years and the misunderstandings between them he still felt that way.

Marcus cursed under his breath and then jumped as her hand touched his shoulder.

"I know your thoughts," she whispered. "But it can never be that way again."

His laugh was harsh. "I've no desire to have it that way a second time. I want simply to be rid of the craving I have for you. You won't suffer in the slaking, I can promise you that."

Turning, he stared into her upturned face, seeing the violet eyes so unfathomable and sad. Her lower lip quivered and he stilled the betraying movement with a soft stroke of his thumb.

"I must go and make preparations for the meeting tomorrow." He cupped her flushed cheek and then lowered his hand to her breast. "I will speak with the outriders Avery assigned to you. They'll follow at a discreet distance. Wear neutral colors. No jewelry. Sturdy shoes."

Elizabeth nodded and held still as a statue as he lowered his head and brushed his lips across hers. Only the racing of her heart beneath his palm told him how he affected her. He closed his eyes at the painful tightening of his loins and chest. He'd give up his fortune to be rid of this longing.

Sick with self-disgust he stepped past her and departed, hating the hours between now and the moment when he could see her again.

Chapter 5

Marcus stared through the cover of bushes, his jaw clenching as a droplet of sweat trickled between his shoulder blades. Elizabeth stood a few feet away in the clearing with her husband's journal clutched tightly in her tiny hands. The grass beneath her feet was trampled by her pacing, releasing the scent of spring into the air, but it didn't soothe him as it normally would.

He hated this. Hated leaving her out there, exposed to whoever it was that wanted Hawthorne's book. She shifted nervously from one foot to the other and he longed to go to her, longed to soothe her and take the burden of waiting from her slight shoulders onto his own.

He'd had precious little time to prepare. Surrounded by trees, the specified location made surveillance frustratingly difficult. There were too many places to hide. Avery and the outriders, who stood nearby watching the worn paths that led to the meeting place, were completely undetectable to him. He couldn't signal them, nor they him, and he felt helpless. Waiting patiently was not in his nature and he gripped the hilt of his small sword with barely restrained ferocity. What in hell was taking so damn long?

This mission was the most important of any he'd previously been assigned to; it required the presence of mind and unflappable calm that marked all of his dealings. But to his dismay, he was as far from level-headedness as he'd ever been in his life. Failure was never an option, but this . . . *this* was Elizabeth.

As if she sensed his turmoil, she glanced around furtively, searching for him. She chewed her bottom lip between her teeth and his breath caught in his throat as he watched her. It had been so long since he'd had the opportunity to study her at his leisure. He drank her in, every detail, from the uplifted chin that defied the world, to the restless way she shifted the journal. A slight breeze ruffled the curls at her nape, revealing the slender white column of her throat. Distracted momentarily by her courage and the fierce protectiveness it engendered, Marcus failed to see the dark-clad body dropping from the tree until it was too late. He leapt to his feet as the realization hit, his blood roaring so loudly he could scarcely hear past it.

Elizabeth was knocked to the ground, the book flying from her hands to land a few feet away. She cried out, the startled sound cut short by the crushing weight of the man atop her.

With a low growl of fury, Marcus lunged over the bushes and tackled the assailant away from her, his fists striking before they rolled to a halt. A quick blow to the man's masked face subdued him and Marcus continued pummeling him with punishing blows, his rage such that he couldn't think beyond the instinct to kill anyone who threatened Elizabeth. He fought like a man possessed, snarling with the need to ease the fear that gripped him.

Elizabeth lay immobile, her mouth agape. She'd known Marcus was a physically powerful man, but he had always controlled himself with a confident air of self-mastery. She had romanticized him in her thoughts, imagining the self-assured rogue brandishing a sword or a pistol with careless arrogance, taunting his opponents with a few cutting remarks before making quick work of the matter with nary a bead of sweat on him. Her imagination had not pictured the Marcus before her—a vengeful beast, easily able to kill a man with his bare hands and at this moment quite willing to do so.

She scrambled to her feet, eyes wide, as he wrapped his hands around the man's throat, a man who was their only clue to the importance of Nigel's book. "*No!* Don't kill him!"

Marcus loosened his grip at the sound of Elizabeth's voice, the haze of bloodlust retreating. With amazing strength after such a beating, the assailant bucked upward, effectively garnering his release by throwing Marcus to his back.

Rolling quickly to his stomach, Marcus pushed himself up, prepared to fight, but the attacker scooped up the book and fled.

There was the barest glint of sunlight off the muzzle of a gun as the fleeing man turned and took aim, but it was warning enough. Marcus rose from the ground, his only goal to reach Elizabeth and shield her from harm. But he couldn't move fast enough. The report of the pistol bounced off the trees around them. He yelled a warning and turned, his heart stopping at the sight that greeted him.

Elizabeth stood by her mount, her hair in disarray about her shoulders. In her outstretched hands was the smoking muzzle of a gun.

Realizing where the shot originated, he turned his head and watched in confounded wonder as the assailant stumbled to his feet from where he'd fallen, his dropped gun skittering away across the dewy grass. The man's left hand was limp, the red journal abandoned, while his right hand pressed against a wound to his shoulder. Swearing, he ducked between two bushes and disappeared into the trees.

Stunned by the series of events, Marcus was startled as Avery ran past him in pursuit.

"Bloody everlasting hell," he snapped, furious at himself for allowing the situation to go so awry.

Elizabeth took his arm, her voice shaky and urgent. "Are you hurt?" Her free hand drifted over his torso.

His eyes widened at her obvious concern.

"Damn you, Marcus. Are you injured? Did he hurt you?"

"No, no, I'm fine. What the devil are you doing with that?" He stared, dazed by the sight of the pistol she held at her side.

"Saving your life." Her hand to her heart, she released her breath in a rush and then walked to the fallen journal to retrieve it. "You may thank me when you recover your wits."

Marcus sat silently in the sitting room of his London townhouse. Divested of his coat and waistcoat, he lounged with his feet propped up on the table, and watched the play of light from the window behind him as it moved through the brandy in his snifter.

To say the morning had been a disaster would be an understatement, and yet Elizabeth had retained the book and wounded her attacker. Marcus was not surprised. His friendship with William had given him rare insight.

Her mother lost to illness, Elizabeth had been raised by a father and older brother who were both notorious voluptuaries. Governesses never lasted long, finding the young Elizabeth to be incorrigible. Without the calming influence of a woman in the house, she'd been allowed to run wild.

As children, William had taken his sister with him everywhere—galloping neck-or-nothing through the fields, climbing trees, shooting pistols. Elizabeth had been blissfully unaware of the societal rules women were expected to follow until introduced to them at boarding school. Years of rigorous training in deportment had given her the tools she used to hide herself from him, but he paid them no mind. He would know her, all of her.

The mystery of the book was proving to be far more dangerous than any of them had previously realized. Steps had to be taken to ensure Elizabeth was kept safe.

"Thank you for allowing me to repair myself here," Elizabeth said softly from the doorway that led to the bedroom.

She'd used the room that was meant to be hers—that of the lady of the house. Turning to face her, he saw her staring down at her clasped hands. "William would have known something was amiss if I'd returned home looking a mess."

Marcus studied her, noting the dark circles that rimmed her eyes. Was she having trouble sleeping? Was he tormenting her dreams the way she tormented his?

"Is your family not in residence?" she asked, looking about as if she could find them. "Lady Westfield? Paul and Robert?"

"My mother writes that Robert's latest experiment is delaying their arrival. So that leaves you and me quite alone."

"Oh." She bit her lower lip.

"Elizabeth, this matter has become extremely dangerous. Once the man who attacked you recovers, he will come after you again. If he has associates, they won't wait."

She nodded. "I'm aware of the situation. I will be on my guard."

"That's insufficient. I want you to be guarded night and day, not just outriders when you go out. I want someone with you at all times, even when you sleep."

"Impossible. William will grow suspicious if I have guards at the house."

Marcus set the glass down. "William is more than capable of making his own decisions. Why don't you allow him to decide if he can be of assistance to you?"

She rested her hands on her hips. "Because *I* have made the decision. He is finally free of that damned agency. His wife is with child. I refuse to risk his life and Margaret's happiness for nothing."

"*You* are not nothing," he growled.

"Consider what happened today."

He stood. "I cannot stop considering it. It rules my thoughts."

"You were almost killed."

"You don't know that."

"I was there . . ." Her voice broke and turning on her heel, she strode toward the door.

He moved swiftly to block her egress. "I've not finished speaking, madam."

"I am finished listening." She attempted to step around him, but he sidestepped quickly into her path. "Damn you. You are so bloody arrogant."

She poked him in the chest with her finger and he stilled the movement with his hand. It was then he noticed her trembling.

"Elizabeth . . ."

She stared up at him, so tiny and delicate, yet formidable in her fury. The thought of her injured made his stomach clench. Deep in her eyes, he saw fear and his heart went out to her.

"Spitfire," he murmured, pulling her toward him. His fingertips tingled from the touch of her ungloved hand. Her skin was so soft, like satin. His thumb brushed over the pulse at her wrist and it leapt to match his own quickened heartbeat. "You were so brave today."

"Your charm won't work on me."

"I'm sorry to hear that." He tugged her closer.

She snorted. "Despite everything I say, you still insist on attempting to seduce me."

"Merely attempting? Not succeeding?" He laced his fingers with hers and found her hand cold. "I must try harder then."

Violet eyes glittered dangerously, but then he'd always liked a bit of danger. At least she was not thinking about the assailant anymore. Her hand was quickly warming within his. He intended to warm the rest of her as well.

"You are trying quite hard enough." Elizabeth took a step back.

He followed, directing her backward steps toward his bedroom, which waited on the other side of the private sitting room.

"Have women always fallen all over themselves for you?"

Arching a brow, he replied, "I'm not certain how I should answer that."

"Try the truth."

"Then yes, they have."

She scowled.

He laughed and squeezed her fingers. "Ah . . . Jealousy was always the emotion most easily inspired in you."

"I am not jealous. Other women can have you with my blessing."

"Not yet." He smiled when her scowl deepened. Stepping nearer, he slipped their joined hands around her back and tugged her to him.

Her gaze narrowed. "What are you about?"

"I'm distracting you. You are overwrought."

"I am not."

Her lips parted as his head lowered. He smelled gunpowder and her heady vanilla rose scent beneath that. Her palm grew damp within his and he nuzzled his nose against hers.

"You were magnificent this afternoon." He brushed his mouth across hers and felt her sigh against his lips. He nibbled gently. "Although it disturbs you to have shot a man, you don't regret it. You would do it again. For me."

"Marcus . . ."

He groaned, lost in the sound of her voice and the sweetness of her taste. His entire body was hard and aching from holding her so closely. "Yes, love?"

"I don't want you," she said.

"You will." He sealed his mouth over hers.

Elizabeth sank into Marcus's hard chest with a sob. It was not fair that he could overwhelm her—by touching her, caressing her, seducing her with his low, velvety voice and rich masculine scent. His emerald gaze burned, half-lidded with a desire she'd done nothing to arouse.

Against her will, her hands slipped around his lean waist

and caressed the powerful length of his back. "You're horrid to be so tender."

His sweat-misted forehead rested against hers. He groaned, his fingers slipping under the long hem of her riding jacket. "You're wearing too many damned clothes."

He took her mouth again, his tongue caressing with lush, deep licks. Lost in his kiss, she didn't realize he'd lifted and moved her until he kicked the door to his bedroom closed behind them, shutting them away from the world.

Protesting, she attempted to pull away. Then his hand cupped the curve of her breast, bringing aching pleasure even through the barrier of her garments. She moaned into his mouth and he tilted his head in response, deepening an already drowning kiss.

Elizabeth stood rigid, her arms at her sides, her thoughts warring with the dictates of her body. Her blood was on fire, her skin hot and painfully tight.

"I want you." His voice was a rough-edged caress. "I want to bury myself inside you until we forget ourselves."

"I don't want to forget."

His tone deepened. "I must think of this mission and the events that took place today, but I cannot. Because all I can think of is you. There isn't room for anything else."

Placing her fingers over his lips, Elizabeth silenced the seductive words that should have sounded practiced and confident, but didn't.

He tossed the counterpane back, revealing decadent silk sheets. With soft, tender kisses, he attempted to distract her from his fingers, which worked with deft skill to free the row of buttons that barred him from her skin. Slipping his hands under the open flaps, he pushed the jacket to the floor. She shivered even though she was flushed and he crushed her to his chest.

"Hush," he murmured against her forehead. "It's just you and me. Leave your father and Eldridge out of our bed."

She buried her face in the linen of his shirt and breathed him in. "I hate it when you leave me no privacy at all."

Turning her head to rest her cheek against his chest, Elizabeth took a shuddering breath. The bed was massive, easily big enough to sleep four large men side by side with room to spare. It waited . . . *for them.*

"Look at me."

Her gaze found his again, discovering a deep needy emerald hunger. Her lips quivered softly and Marcus leaned over, brushing his mouth across hers. "Don't be afraid," he whispered.

Remaining in a bedroom with him was the worst sort of danger. Far more dangerous than the attacker in the park. That man struck swiftly, like a viper. Marcus was more of a python. He would wrap himself around her and squeeze the life from her slowly until nothing of her independence remained.

"I'm not afraid." She shoved him backward as her stomach clenched tight. Caring nothing for her jacket, longing only to be away from him, she walked quickly to the door. "I am leaving."

Escape was seconds away when he grabbed her roughly and threw her face down upon the bed. "What are you doing?" she cried.

Marcus held her down, his grip tight as he bound her hands together with his cravat. "You would leave here half-dressed," he growled, "in your eagerness to put distance between us. This fear you have of me must be banished. You have to trust me implicitly, in every way, without question or you could be killed."

"This is the way you win trust?" she snapped. "By holding me against my will?"

He came over her, his knees straddling her hips, his large body caging hers to the bed. His teeth nipped her ear and his voice, low and angry, made her shiver all over. "I should have done this years ago. But I was lost in your charms and failed to see the signs. Even until this moment, I thought you so skittish that a gentle hand was necessary not to frighten you. Now I realize you need a good, hard riding to be broken properly."

"Bastard!" Heart pounding, Elizabeth struggled beneath him. In response he sat on her, effectively crushing her protest.

Nimble fingers tugged at the fastenings to her skirts and bustle. Then his weight left her. Standing at the edge of the bed, Marcus yanked the garments down. She briefly considered rolling on her back to conceal her buttocks, clearly visible beneath the thinness of her chemise, but didn't, deciding the front of her was far more needy of protection. "You won't get away with this," she warned. "You cannot keep me bound forever and when you release me, I'll come after you. I'll—"

"You won't be able to walk," he scoffed.

He reached for her boots and she lashed out at him, kicking with all her might. She screamed at the sudden sharp sting to her arse. The first spank was quickly followed by several more, each drop of his hand burning more than the last until she buried her face in the counterpane and cried with the pain of it. Only when she stopped flailing, and took the abuse without movement did he cease.

"Your father should have taken you over his knee long ago," he muttered.

"I hate you!" She turned her head to look at him, but couldn't reach around far enough.

Marcus's sigh was loud and resigned. "You protest too much, love. You will thank me eventually. I've given you the freedom to enjoy me. You can fight all you want and still get what you desire. All the pleasure and none of the guilt."

His hands cupped the flaming curves of her derriere and stroked gently, soothingly. The gentleness of his touch aroused her, the contrast startling after his previous treatment. "So beautiful. So soft and perfect." His voice deepened, became cajoling. "Let yourself go, sweet. If you must be forced, why not relish the experience?"

When his hands moved lower to the hem of her chemise and then slipped under it, she moaned in anticipation, her skin prickling with goosebumps at the feel of bare skin on bare skin. Her blood heated, her anger melting into something intoxicating as his thumbs moved higher, massaging either side of her lower back. Deep inside, her body softened at his skillful touch. The feel of air directly on her burning flesh coaxed a whimper of relief from her.

"You would fight me to the death, my stubborn temptress, if you were able, but tied up for my needs brings unexpected rewards, does it not?" He rolled her to her back before gripping her shoulders and pulling her into a seated position.

Elizabeth bit her lower lip to hide the pout of disappointment she felt at the unwanted distance between them. Her nipples ached, peaked hard and tight, eager for the pinch of his fingers to ease their torment. Marcus's dark green gaze narrowed on her flushed face. There was no tenderness, no sign of possible mercy, just stark intent and she knew he would not be swayed. Her stomach flipped as moisture pooled between her thighs at her helplessness.

He assisted her to her feet and moved her to the nearby chair whose wooden arms curved so beautifully. Pressing her down to the seat, he then tugged his shirt from his breeches, before pulling it over his head.

Elizabeth stared, arrested by his virility which was displayed so beautifully by rippling muscles beneath golden skin. His left shoulder was marred by a circular scar left by a bullet and silver ribbons on his flesh betrayed nicks from the sharp edge of a sword. As magnificent as he was, the sight of his past injuries reminded her that he was not meant for her. Even as her blood heated, her heart chilled.

"The agency has left its mark on you," she said snidely. "It's revolting."

Marcus arched a dark brow. "That explains why you cannot take your eyes from me then."

Peeved, she forced herself to look away.

He crouched before her and cupped the backs of her knees, spreading her legs wide and hooking them over the carved arms of the chair. Her face heated in embarrassment as the damp lips of her sex were opened to his view. "Close the curtains."

Frowning, he stared at the apex of her thighs. "God, no." He brushed across her curls with his fingers. "Why would you wish to hide this? It's heaven you hold here. A sight I've longed to see for far too long."

"Please." She squeezed her eyelids tightly together, her body tense and then trembling.

"Elizabeth. Look at me."

Tears accompanied the lifting of her lids.

"Why are you so frightened? You know I would never hurt you."

"You leave me nothing, you take everything."

He ran a blunt fingertip through her cream and then dipped a bit inside. Against her will, she arched into the caress, despite the painful tension the angle placed on her arms.

"You shared this with Hawthorne, but you won't with me? Why?" His voice was rough and abrasive. "Why not me?"

Her reply was shaky, betraying the depth of her distress. "My husband never saw me like this."

The wicked finger stilled, just barely entering her. "What?"

"Such things are done at night. One must—"

"Hawthorne made love to you in the darkness?"

"He was a gentleman, one who—"

"Was certifiable. Good God." Marcus snorted and removed his finger. He stood. "To have you for his own, to fuck as he wished, and not appreciate your beauty? What a waste. The man was an idiot."

Elizabeth lowered her head. "Our marriage was no different from any other."

"It was completely different than it would have been with me. How often?"

"How often?" she repeated dumbly.

"How often did he take you? Every night? Every few days?"

"What does it matter?"

His nostrils flared on a deep breath, his frame taut beside her. Running an agitated hand through his hair, he was silent for a moment.

"Release me, Marcus, and forget this." Her shame was complete, there was no more he could do to her.

Hard fingers lifted her chin to meet his gaze. "I'm going to touch you everywhere. With my hands, my mouth. In the light of day and long into the night. I'll take you in whatever manner I choose, wherever I choose. I will know you as no one else in your life has known you."

"Why?" She struggled again, completely at his mercy and unbearably aroused. Spread for him, she felt the emptiness inside her and hated how badly she needed him to fill it.

"Because I can. Because after today you will crave me and the pleasure I can give you. Because you'll trust me, damn you." He growled low in his throat. "All these years, married to him and then mourning him, when you could have been mine."

Dropping to his knees, he held her hips and dropped his head. Elizabeth held her breath as he closed his mouth full upon her breast, soaking through the fabric of her shirt and chemise. Startled at first, she was soon moaning and arching her back in silent encouragement. Sharp pangs of sensation radiated outward, moving in rhythm with his suction, her womb contracting in spasms of need.

Marcus's warm fingertips stroked from her waist to the ebony curls below. Painful tension seared her senses and Elizabeth gasped in surprise.

"I will touch you here," he warned. "With my fingers, my tongue, my cock."

She bit her bottom lip, eyes wide.

"You will enjoy it," he promised, his thumb tugging her lip free from her teeth.

"You want to treat me like a whore. That is your revenge."

His smile was devoid of humor. "I want to give you pleasure, I want to hear you beg me for it. Why should you be deprived?"

Marcus stood and freed the placket of his breeches. Reaching inside, he withdrew his cock, and a heretofore unknown level of wanting had her writhing in the chair. He was long and thick, the head broad and dark with the blood that engorged it. He jerked his hand along the length and creamy moisture leaked from the tip.

"See what the sight of you does to me, Elizabeth? How much power you wield? You are tied and helpless, yet it is *I* who is at *your* mercy."

Swallowing hard, her gaze was riveted to his display.

"Trust, Elizabeth. You must trust me, in all ways."

She looked up and ached at the sight of him. So beautiful, and yet harsh and rugged as only a man could be. "Is this about your mission?"

"This is about *us*. You and me." He stepped closer, and then closer still. "Open your mouth."

"*What?*" Her lungs seized.

"Take me in your mouth."

"No . . ." She recoiled.

"Where is the minx who said she was not one to run from the sight of a man's desire?" Marcus widened his stance until his powerful thighs bracketed the side of the chair and the glistening head of his cock rested directly before and slightly below her mouth.

"This is trust," he whispered. "Think how you can hurt me, how vulnerable I am. You can bite me, love, and unman me. Or you can suckle me and bring me to my knees with pleasure. I ask this of you, knowing the risk, because I trust you. Just as I expect you to trust me."

Elizabeth stared at him, fascinated by the abrupt change in the balance between them. She met his eyes again and saw the longing there, the need. For now there was no bitterness. He looked so much as he had before, when they'd been promised to one another and free of past injuries. He was so breathtakingly handsome, appearing younger without the burden of his enmity.

It was that openness that decided her mind. Taking a deep breath, Elizabeth followed the urging of her heart and opened her mouth.

Chapter 6

Marcus stood in an agony of lust as Elizabeth's lips parted and she leaned forward to take him into her mouth. As she scalded him with wet heat, his breath hissed out between his teeth. His knees buckled and he gripped the high back of the chair with his free hand to remain upright.

She pulled away with wide-eyed horror. "Did I hurt you?"

Incapable of speech, he shook his head rapidly. She swallowed hard and his cock leapt in his hand. Licking her lower lip, she opened her mouth and tried again, this time engulfing the whole of the crown.

"Suck," he gasped, his head falling so that he hovered over her, watching as her cheeks hollowed and she tugged with soft suction. His legs trembled and he groaned a low, tortured sound.

Encouraged, she took him deeper, her tongue swirling in tentative exploration. Her mouth was stretched wide to accommodate his girth and the sight was enough to wipe his brain of any rational thought.

"I'm going to move," he bit out. "Don't be frightened." His hips began to thrust forward, fucking her mouth with gentle, shallow strokes. Her eyes widened, but she didn't pull away or protest, instead she responded with less and less hesitation.

Watching her, Marcus was certain he'd passed on to his

reward and been given the realization of his deepest longing. He was afraid to believe it was Elizabeth who serviced him so well.

"God, Elizabeth . . ."

Releasing his cock, he dropped his hand between her legs and caressed her through the open folds of her sex. She moaned and he stroked with more intent, determined to concentrate on her in an effort to hold off his own imminent release. Slick and hot, she melted into his touch. She felt so good, like satin, and he grit his teeth as he slipped a finger inside her. Tight as she was, she'd be a snug fit. His chest ached. His sac weighed heavily, then drew up. He stepped back on shaky legs, his cock slipping from her mouth with a soft, wet pop.

She worked her jaw and licked her lips, her violet eyes dark and questioning.

His voice like gravel he whispered, "It's time."

Elizabeth shivered. Marcus had always looked at her as if she were a meal laid before a starving man. At the moment however, his gaze was . . . *desperate*. The tip of his cock leaked profusely, and she swallowed, her mouth flavored with his essence.

He'd felt so different from what she'd expected. She'd thought herself beyond the innocence of a virginal girl. Now she realized how little she knew. With the thick, pulsing roping of veins that etched his erection she'd imagined he would be hard, textured. Instead the skin had been as soft as the finest silk, slipping over her tongue in a rhythm that awakened a matching pulse between her legs.

The act was not what she had expected, not at all. She'd thought she'd feel used, nothing more than a receptacle for his lust. But he was devastated, she could see it and she'd felt it in the way he trembled. The way his voice had grown so hoarse. There was power to be had in possessing a man's passion.

"Release me," she ordered breathlessly, wanting to see how far she could take this.

He shook his head and pushed the back of the chair onto its hind legs. Caught off balance, she screeched until he stopped. It was then she understood his aim. Resting the top of the chair against the nearby damask-covered wall angled her perfectly, presenting her spread sex to his cock. His grin stole her breath, filled as it was with wicked promises. He reached between them and pressed his erect shaft down, bending his knees until he breeched her. He stroked up and down, coating her with the semen that continued to dribble from the flushed head.

She couldn't hold back the half-sob of anticipation. The blatant, deliberate teasing had her sweating and gasping for air. She ignored the voice that urged her to fight, choosing instead to enjoy him . . . just this once.

"Do your arms pain you?" he asked, never ceasing his movements, soaking her with the evidence of his excitement.

"*You* pain me."

"Should I stop?" From the catch in his voice, she knew the thought was torturous.

"I shall shoot you if you stop."

With a groan, he positioned and thrust deep, forging through her in a relentless drive. She writhed against the invasion, the size of him far too much for her long unused flesh. The tip of him rubbed inside her, stretching her, stroking her far better than his magical fingers had done.

Both hands to the wall, Marcus gasped as he slipped deep. "Ah, Christ." He shuddered. "You're hot as hell and tight as a fist."

"Marcus . . ." She whimpered. There was something undeniably erotic in the way he took her, still partially dressed with his boots on. It should have offended her. But it didn't.

All these years she'd spent consoling the women discarded by her father and listening to the gossip of women left disillusioned by Marcus's inconstancy. How had they failed to see their own influence? Marcus had nearly killed a man with his bare hands, yet here he stood before her, weakened in his need.

He pulled out, his head down bent. "Watch me fuck you, Elizabeth." His powerful thighs flexed beneath his breeches as he pressed back inside. She gazed, eyes riveted to the sight of the thick, proud shaft slick with her cream withdrawing, only to return in a painfully slow glide.

Her arms ached, her legs stretched uncomfortably, and her tailbone was growing numb from bearing the brunt of her weight, but she didn't care. Nothing mattered beyond the apex of her thighs and the man who rutted there.

"This is trust," he said, his hips pumping his cock into her with a precise, unfaltering rhythm.

Trust. Tears slipped past her lashes as the divine torment continued, his skill undeniable. He knew just how to stroke her, dipping with bent thighs to rub his cock in just the right spot to pleasure her to madness. She was panting with it, and then begging for it. Her blood roared, her nipples peaked so tightly beneath her garments they ached. "Please . . ."

Marcus was panting too, his chest heaving so forcefully it shook the sweat from his hair to drip onto her face. Her heart swelled at the intimacy.

"Yes," he growled. "Now." He dropped one hand between her legs and rubbed gently. Like a spring coiled too tightly, she broke free with a sharp cry. Her back bowed and Marcus moved in slow, deep strokes, drawing out her pleasure, keeping her taut and breathless and tearful beneath him.

"No more . . ." she cried, unable to bear another moment.

He thrust his cock deep and held it there, allowing the fading ripples of her orgasm to milk him. He sucked in a sharp breath and then began to shudder with such force the chair back tapped against the wall. He groaned, a long, low, pained sound as his cock jerked inside her filling her with his seed.

Gasping, he finally stilled. He tilted his head and stared

into her eyes. The frank bemusement in the emerald depths soothed her somewhat, lost as she was in her own devastation.

"Too fast," he muttered. One of his hands left the wall and cupped her cheek, his thumb following the curve of her cheekbone.

"Are you mad?" She swallowed hard to ease the hoarseness of her voice.

"Yes." He pulled away slowly, carefully, but she still winced from the loss. With great care he unhooked her legs from the arm of the chair and helped her to her feet. Weakened, she crumpled against him. He caught her up, and carried her to the bed.

Laying her on her side, Marcus untied her hands, rubbing her shoulders and arms when they tingled as the blood returned. Then he reached for the bow at her throat.

Elizabeth pulled back. "I must leave now."

Chuckling, Marcus took a seat next to her. He bent low to tug off his boots, removing a blade hidden there and setting it on the nightstand. "You are exhausted, and can barely walk. You are in no condition to seat a horse."

Elizabeth's hand drifted across his back, a finger swirling curiously around the bullet wound scar that marred his hard flesh. Turning his head, he kissed her fingertips as they traveled over the top of his shoulder, stunning her with the tender gesture. He stood, quickly doffing his breeches and she looked away as heat flared within her, staring out the window at the afternoon sky partly-hidden behind filmy sheers.

"Look at me," he said gruffly, a plea hidden under a rough command.

"No."

"Elizabeth, there is no shame in wanting me."

Her mouth curved ruefully, the view of the window fading from her perception. "Of course not. Every woman does."

"I am not thinking about other women, you shouldn't be

either." He sighed with the exasperation one would display over a recalcitrant child. "Look at me. Please."

She turned her head slowly, her heart hammering in her chest. Impossibly broad shoulders tapered to a rippled stomach, lean hips, and long, powerful legs. Marcus Ashford was perfection, the scars that marred his torso only serving to make him human and not some ancient god.

She'd intended to keep her gaze high, but she was unable to stop herself from looking lower. Long and thick, his impressive erection made her swallow hard.

"Heavens. How can you . . . ? You're still . . ."

He gave her a wicked smile. "Ready for sex?"

"I am exhausted," she complained.

Marcus tugged at the tie at her neck, using her distraction with his cock to lift her shirt over her head. "You don't have to do anything." But when he reached for her chemise she slapped his hand away, needing some barrier, however sheer, between them.

He strolled with casual ease to the corner and went behind the screen, returning a moment later with a damp cloth. He pushed her back into the pillows and reached for her knee. She rolled away.

"It's a little late for modesty, wouldn't you say, sweet?"

"What are you about?"

"If you come back here, I'll show you."

Elizabeth thought for long moments, guessing his intent and not certain if she could grant him that level of intimacy.

"My body has been inside yours." His voice was low and seductive. "Can you not trust me to bathe you?"

The hint of challenge in his tone decided her. She turned onto her back and spread her legs with more than a hint of defiance. His lopsided smile made her blush.

Gently he swept the cloth across her curls before parting her with reverent fingers and cleansing her folds. Sore as she was, the cool dampness felt wonderful and she breathed a soft sound of pleasure. She forced herself to relax, to close her eyes and release the tension brought on by Marcus's proximity. On the verge of drifting to sleep, she shot up with a startled cry when molten heat drenched her sex.

She stared down the length of her torso with wide eyes, her heart racing to see Marcus's dark smile.

"Did you just . . . *lick* me?"

"Oh yes." Tossing the washcloth carelessly to the rug, he crawled over her with potent grace. "I see I've scandalized you. Since you've already suffered enough today, I shall grant you a short reprieve. But be prepared to accept my future attentions in whatever manner I choose."

Shivering as his furred chest brushed across her chemise-covered nipples, Elizabeth sank farther into the pillows, overwhelmed by the sheer force of his presence.

This she knew—the feeling of a hard male body atop hers. But the feelings that rioted within her were all new. She had welcomed Hawthorne to her bed as she should, she'd appreciated his haste and solicitousness. Aside from the first painful time, the rest had not been unpleasant. He'd been quiet, clean, careful. Never had it been raw and primitive as it was with Marcus. Never had it caused this gnawing, aching need and heady desire. Never had it resulted in a blinding flash of pleasure that left her sated to her soul.

"Easy," he murmured against her throat as she rubbed impatiently against him.

Her husband's body had been a mystery, known to her only as a shadowy form that ventured into her room under the cover of darkness and a warm hand that pushed up her night rail. Marcus had begged her to look at him, had wanted her to know him and see him as he was, in all his glory. He was magnificent naked. The mere sight of him was enough to make her wet between her legs.

She refused, however, to be the only one left shaken from this afternoon dalliance.

"Tell me what you like, Marcus."

"Touch me. I want to feel your hands on my skin."

Her hands roamed across his back, down his arms, discovering scars and lengths of muscle so hard they felt like stone. Marcus moaned as she found especially sensitive areas, urging her to linger. His body was a tapestry of textures—soft and hard, fur and satin. He closed his eyes, his arms supporting his weight above her, allowing her to explore him at her leisure. The rigid length of his cock pulsed against her thigh, the warm trail of moisture it leaked telling her how much he enjoyed her unschooled touch.

This was power.

Groaning, he lowered his head, his silky hair drifting across her breasts filling the air around her with his scent. "Touch my cock," he commanded gruffly.

Taking a breath of courage, Elizabeth reached between their bodies and stroked the silken length, amazed at the hardness and the way it jumped under her touch. It was obvious he found pleasure in the caress, the crests of his cheekbones flushing, his lips parting with panting breaths. Encouraged, she experimented. Rough and soft, quick and teasing, she attempted to find the rhythm that would drive him to madness.

"Do you want me?" he asked. He stayed her hand by covering it with his own and she frowned in confusion. Then his hand drifted lower, catching her knee and spreading her wide.

"I'm surprised a libertine such as yourself needs to ask," she retorted, refusing to give him the capitulation he requested.

With no further warning he thrust into her, sliding through swollen tissues until there was no farther he could go.

She whimpered in surprise. Lovemaking in the bright light of day was something she wondered if she could ever learn to accept. She looked up at him, eyes wide.

Pinning her with his hips, Marcus gripped the straps of her chemise and rent the garment in half to the waist.

"You think you can build barriers between us with words

and clothing?" he asked harshly. "Every time you attempt it, I will take you just like this, become a part of you so that all your efforts will be for naught."

There was no place to hide, nowhere to run.

"This will be the last time," she vowed.

She was stunned that she had allowed him this close, a man whose beauty and charm had always weakened her. Then he lowered his mouth to hers, kissing her with a ravenous hunger. Gripping her hips possessively, Marcus held her still as he withdrew and then thrust again, shuddering as she did at the exquisiteness of it.

Elizabeth shifted restlessly, awed that her body had stretched to accommodate him, was even now stretching to hold him more comfortably. It was amazing, his hardness inside her, filling her completely, bringing a feeling of connection so deep she couldn't breathe.

"Elizabeth." His voice was deeply sexual as he wrapped his arms beneath her, pulling her tightly against him in a full body embrace. He nuzzled against her throat. "Only when I'm sated will you be rid of me."

With the ominous threat he began to move, a sinuous glide of his body upon and within her own.

"Oh!" she cried, startled as the sensations built higher with every slide. She'd meant to withhold her pleasure from him, meant to lie there and deny him what he wanted. But it was impossible. He could melt her with a heated glance. To fuck him, as he so crudely called it, was an act she was helpless to resist.

She tried to increase the pace, wrapping her legs around his hips, her hands grasping his buttocks and pulling him into her, but he was too strong and too determined to have his own way.

"Fuck me," she gasped, trying to regain the feeling of control by stealing some of his. "Faster."

Marcus groaned as she writhed beneath him. His voice

came, slurred with pleasure. "I knew it would be this way with you . . ."

In response, Elizabeth dug her nails into the flesh of his back. She loved feeling his damp skin against hers, his warm scent surrounding her. Slipping a little in his control, he slammed into her, hard and impossibly deep. Her toes curled.

Liquid heat traversed her veins, pooled in her core, and then convulsed in climax. She tightened around his thrusting cock, crying out his name, holding onto his flexing body as the only anchor in a swirl of incredible sensation.

And Marcus held on, drenched in sweat, heat radiating from every pore. He growled her name as he spilled into her and the brand of possession burned deep.

Closing her eyes, she cried.

Elizabeth felt as if her limbs were weighted with lead. It took all the effort she had to turn her head and look at Marcus sleeping next to her. His long, black lashes cast peaceful shadows upon his cheeks, the austere beauty of his features soft in repose.

She managed to roll onto her side, which was no easy task with his heavy arm thrown casually across her torso. Lifting onto one elbow, she studied him silently. Boyishly innocent while sleeping, he was so gorgeous she could hardly breathe.

Slowly, she traced her finger along the generous curve of his mouth, then his eyebrows and the length of his jaw. She squealed in surprise as his arm tightened, drawing her body over his.

"What do you think you are doing, madam?" he drawled lazily.

Sliding off him, Elizabeth sat on the edge of the bed, struggling for the nonchalance she was certain she should display. "Is this not when lovers part ways?" She needed to think and she couldn't do that with him lying naked beside her.

"There is no need for you to go." Leaning back against a

pillow, Marcus patted the space next to him. "Come back to bed."

"No." She slid off the mattress and gathered up her clothes. "I am sore and tired."

As she came around, his arm shot out and grabbed her, hauling her closer. "Elizabeth. We can take a nap and have tea later. Then you can go."

"That's not possible," she murmured without looking at him. "I must go home. I want a hot bath."

He rubbed her arm and grinned playfully. "You can have a bath here. I'll attend you myself."

Standing, Elizabeth hastily pulled on her stockings. She struggled with the tapes of her skirts, having difficulty tightening them. Marcus rose from the bed, heedless of his nakedness and crossed the room to her, brushing her fingers aside.

She turned away quickly, her face flushed. *Lord, he was handsome!* Every part of him was perfect. His muscles rippled with power just beneath golden skin. Recently sated, she still felt the renewed stirrings of desire.

He made quick work of dressing her, adjusting her garters, and securing her tapes. Jealous at his obvious experience, she stood stiffly until he turned her to face him.

He sighed, pulling her against his bare chest. "You are so determined to keep to yourself, to allow no one to get close to you."

She rested her head against his chest for a moment, savoring the smell of him now mixed with her own scent. Then she pushed him away.

"I gave you what you wanted," she replied, irritably.

"I want more."

Her stomach clenched. "Find it elsewhere."

Marcus laughed. "Now that I've shown you pleasure, you'll crave it, crave me. At night, you will remember my touch and the feel of my cock in you, and you will ache for me."

"You conceited—"

"No." He caught her wrist. "I will be craving you as well. What happened today is singular. You won't find the same elsewhere, and you will need it."

She lifted her chin, hating the idea that, deep inside, she suspected he was right. "I am free to look."

His fingers tightened painfully. "No. You are not." He tugged her hand down to his rampant erection. "When you need this, you will come to me. Don't doubt that I would kill any man who touches you."

"Does such forced fidelity work both ways?" She held her breath.

"Of course."

Marcus stood for a moment in the tense silence, before turning away to retrieve his discarded breeches.

Expelling the air from her lungs in a silent sigh of relief, Elizabeth took a seat in front of the mirror and attempted to fix her hair. She was amazed at the visage that stared back at her. Cheeks flushed, lips swollen, eyes bright—she looked nothing like the woman she'd been that morning. Looking away, she caught Marcus's reflection. She watched him dress, weighing his words and damning her foolishness. He was even more determined now than he'd been before bedding her.

When she was ready, she stood quickly, a little too quickly for legs still shaky from the afternoon's events. She stumbled, but Marcus was there, his arms warm bands of steel around her. He had been observing her as well.

"Are you all right?" he asked gruffly. "Did I hurt you?"

She waved him away with her hand. "No, no, I'm fine."

He stepped back. "Elizabeth, a discussion is in order."

"Why?" She fluffed her skirts nervously.

"Bloody hell. You and I. Just made love. In that bed." He gestured with an impatient thrust of his chin. "And the chair. And the floor in a moment, if you don't cease irritating me."

"We made a mistake," she said softly, icy fear settling in her stomach.

"Damn you." His sidelong glance was scathing and she flinched. "Play your games and bury your head in the sand if you must. I will have my way regardless."

"It was not my intent to play games, Marcus." She swallowed hard and moved toward the door. He made no move to stop her so she was startled when she turned and found him directly behind her.

"Don't be frightened about what happened in the park today," he murmured, once again all charm and honeyed drawl. "I will protect you from harm."

Her eyes slid closed. Suddenly the thought of leaving held less appeal. "I know you will."

"Where will you be this evening?"

"The Dunsmore musicale."

"I shall meet you there."

She sighed and opened her eyes. His determined gaze and dogged persistence warned her that he would not allow the matter between them to rest.

He brushed his mouth softly across hers before stepping back and offering his arm. Wary at what she perceived to be his far too easy capitulation, she took it and allowed him to lead her to the main floor.

The butler stood ready with her hat and gloves. "My lord, a Mr. James has called."

"The study? Excellent. You need not wait."

The butler bowed and retreated.

Elizabeth searched Marcus's face as he settled her hat on her head and deftly tied the ribbons. "I pray I can leave here unseen."

His mouth moved to her ear, and he spoke in a seductive whisper. "Too late. Even now the servants are watching us. It won't be long before every household in London knows we're lovers. Avery will learn of us, whether you are seen or not."

The color drained from her face. She hadn't considered that. Servants were the worst gossips. "I would think a man with a secret life such as yours would have discreet servants in his employ."

"I do. However, this is one bit of news I suggested they spread."

"Are you mad?" Then her eyes widened. "Is this about the wager?"

Marcus sighed. "You wound me. Losing is odious, love, but I would never use you in such a callous manner."

"Lose?" she cried, her mouth agape. "You didn't!"

"I did." He shrugged with nonchalance. "How foolish to avoid a bet in which the outcome is decided by my own actions."

She frowned. "Which way did you lean?"

His grin was blinding and made her heart skip a beat. "As if I'd tell you."

His hand at her elbow, Marcus escorted her through the rear garden and out a side gate that led to the stables beyond. He looked on grimly as she mounted her horse. The two armed outriders waited a discreet distance up the mews.

He sketched a quick bow. "Until this evening."

The burning between her shoulder blades told her he watched her until she rounded the corner and blended into the street beyond. The ache in her chest made breathing difficult and she knew it would only get worse the more time she spent with him.

And she knew what must be done about it.

Chapter 7

"Why does it smell like a perfumery in here?" William grumbled as he walked the upstairs hallway of the Chesterfield mansion with Margaret.

"The scent comes from Elizabeth's rooms."

He glanced at her with a frown and saw her eyes shining in mischievous anticipation.

He paused at the open doorway of his sister's sitting room and blinked rapidly. "It looks like a damned florist shop!"

"Isn't it sweet?" Margaret laughed, her fiery hair swaying softly with the movement.

William could not resist touching one of the swinging curls. His sweet, wonderful wife. Those who did not know her well thought her a rare redhead of even temperament. Only he knew how she saved the wild, passionate side of her nature just for him. As desire tightened his loins, he sucked in a breath, and was assaulted with the overpowering smell of flowers.

"Romantic?" he barked. Entering the room he dragged Margaret behind him. Riotous bouquets of expensive, richly scented floral arrangements covered every flat surface in the room. "Westfield," he growled. "I'll kill him."

"Calm yourself, William," she soothed.

He surveyed the scene grimly. "How long has this been going on?"

"Since the Moreland ball." Margaret sighed, the soft sound making him scowl. "And Lord Westfield is so handsome."

"You are a hopeless romantic," he grumbled, choosing to ignore her last comment.

Stepping closer, she wrapped her arms around his lean waist. "I have a right to be."

"How so?"

"I have found true love, so I know it exists." She stood on tiptoe, brushing her lips across his. William immediately increased the pressure, kissing her until she was breathless.

"Westfield is a scoundrel, love," he warned. "I wish you would believe me."

"I believe you. He reminds me of you."

He pulled back with a grunt. "And you would want that for Elizabeth?"

Margaret laughed. "You are not so wicked as all that."

"Because you have reformed me." He nuzzled against her.

"Elizabeth is a stronger woman than I. She could easily bring Lord Westfield to heel, if she were of the mind to do so. Allow her to handle him."

William backed out of the room, pulling her with him. "I have duly noted your opinion."

She attempted to dig in her heels, but he lifted her easily and turned in the direction of their bedchamber.

"You don't intend to listen to me, do you?"

He grinned. "No, I don't. I will handle Westfield and you will cease talking about it." He kissed her soundly as they reached their room. It was only by a twist of fate that he turned his head at that moment and saw Elizabeth reach the top of the stairs. He frowned, and lowered Margaret to her feet. She gave a soft murmur of protest.

"Give me a moment, sweet." He started off down the hall.

"You're meddling," she called after him.

Something was wrong with Elizabeth. That was obvious even from a distance. Flushed and mussed, she looked feverish. His stomach clenched as he neared her. The color of her cheeks deepened upon seeing him, and she looked for a moment just as their mother had before she died, burning with fever. The brief flash of remembered pain quickened his steps.

"Are you unwell?" he asked, placing a hand to her forehead.

Her eyes widened, and then she shook her head quickly.

"You look ill."

"I'm fine." Her voice was low and huskier than usual.

"I will send for the doctor."

"That's not necessary," she protested, her spine straightening.

William opened his mouth to speak.

"A nap, William. It's all I need. I swear it." She sighed and placed her hand on his arm, her violet eyes softening. "You worry too much."

"I always will." He placed his hand over hers, and then turned to escort her to her room. Since their mother had passed on and their father withdrew emotionally, Elizabeth had been all he'd had for most of his life. She'd been his only emotional connection during the time before Margaret when he'd been determined never to fall in love and risk the same misery as their father.

As they neared her room, his nose reminded him of the organic eruption that awaited them. "Why didn't you tell me Westfield was harassing you? I would have dealt with him."

"*No!*"

Her abrupt cry gave him pause, the fierce protectiveness he'd always felt for her rearing up in suspicion. "Tell me you are not encouraging him."

Elizabeth cleared her throat. "Haven't we had this discussion before?"

Closing his eyes, William released a deep breath and prayed for patience. "If you assure me that you will come to me for assistance if you have a need, I will refrain from asking you questions you don't want to answer." He opened his eyes and looked down at her, frowning at the sight of the high color of her skin and glazed eyes. She didn't look well at all. And her hair was disheveled. The last time her hair had looked like that . . .

"Have you gone racing again?" he barked. "Did you take a groom with you? Good God, what if you were thrown—"

"William." Elizabeth laughed. "Go see to Margaret. I'm tired. If you insist on interrogating me, you can do so once I've rested."

"I am not interrogating you. I just know you well. You are stubborn to a fault and refuse to listen to good sense."

"Says the man who worked for Lord Eldridge."

William released a frustrated breath, recognizing from her sudden rigid tone that she was finished talking. All well and good. He intended to manage Marcus on his own terms anyway. "Very well. Find me later." He bent and kissed her forehead. "If you still look flushed when you wake, I'm sending for the doctor."

"Yes, yes." Elizabeth shooed him away.

William went, but his concern would not be dismissed so easily, and they both knew it.

Elizabeth waited in the hallway just outside the office of Lord Nicholas Eldridge, pleased with herself for having snuck out of the house while William was occupied. Because she arrived unannounced, she anticipated cooling her heels. To his credit, Eldridge did not keep her waiting long.

"Lady Hawthorne," he greeted her in what she imagined to be a customarily distracted manner. Rounding the desk, he gestured to her to have a seat. "To what do I owe the pleasure of your visit?" Though the words were polite, the tone held an undercurrent of impatience. He resumed his seat and arched a brow.

She'd forgotten how austere he was, how serious. Yet despite the drabness of his attire and the gray of his wig, his presence was arresting. He bore the weight of his power with consummate ease.

"I apologize, Lord Eldridge, for the importunate nature of my visit. I've come to offer you a trade."

Gray eyes assessed her sharply. "A trade?"

"I would prefer to work with another agent."

He blinked. "And what are you offering in return?"

"Hawthorne's journal."

"I see." He leaned back in his chair. "Has Lord Westfield done something in particular, Lady Hawthorne, which would cause you to seek his replacement?"

She could not prevent her blush. Lord Eldridge pounced on the telltale sign immediately. "Has he approached you in some manner that would not befit his duties? I would take such an accusation seriously."

Elizabeth shifted uncomfortably. She did not want Marcus reprimanded, simply removed from her life.

"Lady Hawthorne. This is a personal matter, is it not?"

She nodded.

"I had valid reasons for assigning Lord Westfield to you."

"I'm certain you did. However, I cannot continue to work with him, regardless of your motives. My brother is growing suspicious." That was not her only reason, but it would suffice.

"I see," he murmured. He remained silent for a long time, but she did not waver under his intimidating scrutiny. "Your husband was a valuable member of my team. Losing him and your brother has been difficult. Lord Westfield has done an excellent job of shouldering a great deal of responsibility despite the demands of his title. He is truly the best man for this assignment."

"I don't doubt his ability."

"Still, you are determined, are you not?" He sighed when she nodded. "I will consider your request."

Elizabeth nodded, understanding he had conceded as much as he was going to. Standing, she smiled grimly at his assessing gaze. He escorted her to the door, pausing a moment before turning the knob.

"It is not my place, Lady Hawthorne, but I feel I should point out to you that Lord Westfield is a good man. I am aware of your history, and I'm certain the ramifications are uncomfortable. However, he is genuinely concerned for your safety. Whatever happens, please keep that in mind."

Elizabeth studied Lord Eldridge silently, and then nodded. There was something else, something he was not telling her. Not that she was surprised. In her experience, agents were always tight-lipped, sharing little of themselves with others. She was greatly relieved when he opened the door and allowed her to escape. While she held no ill will toward Eldridge, she nevertheless looked forward to the day when he and his damned agency were no longer a part of her life.

Marcus entered the offices of Lord Eldridge just before ten in the evening. The summons had arrived just as he prepared to depart for the Dunsmore musicale. While he was impatient to see Elizabeth, he had some thoughts to share about the investigation and this unexpected audience was highly opportune.

Marcus adjusted his tails and dropped into the nearest chair.

"Lady Hawthorne came to see me this afternoon."

"Did she?" Settled, Marcus took a pinch of snuff.

Eldridge continued to work without looking up, the papers before him lit by the candelabra on his desk and the shifting glow from the nearby fireplace. "She offered Viscount Hawthorne's journal in exchange for removing you from your duties."

The enameled snuff box snapped shut decisively.

With a sigh, Eldridge set aside his quill. "She was adamant about it, Westfield, even threatening to become uncooperative if I refused her."

"I'm certain she was most persuasive." Shaking his head, he asked, "What do you intend to do?"

"I told her I would look into it, and so I have. The question is—what do you intend to do?"

"Leave her to me. I was on my way to her when I received your summons."

"If I discover you are using your position with the agency to further your own personal agenda, I will deal with you harshly." Eldridge's expression was grim.

"I would expect nothing less," Marcus assured him.

"How is the journal coming along?"

"I'm making headway, but the going is slow."

Eldridge nodded. "Soothe her concerns then. If she comes to me again, I will have no choice but to honor her request. That would be lamentable since you are making progress. I would prefer you to continue."

Marcus pursed his lips and said what was on his mind. "Avery related today's events to you, yes?"

"Of course. But you have something to add, I see."

"I've thought of this situation ceaselessly. Something is amiss. The assailant was too aware of our preparations, as if he'd gained the knowledge beforehand. Certainly he would have expected her to contact the agency considering her husband's involvement and the relevance of the book, but the way he'd hidden himself, the escape route he had planned . . . Damn it, we were not incompetent! Yet he evaded four men with little effort. He *knew* how the men were arranged. And Hawthorne's journal. How did he learn of it?"

"You suspect internal perfidy?"

"How else?"

"I trust my men implicitly, Westfield. The agency couldn't exist otherwise."

"Consider the possibility. It's all I ask."

Eldridge arched a gray brow. "Avery? The outriders? Who can you trust?"

"Avery bears an obvious fondness for Lady Hawthorne. So you, Avery, myself—that is the extent of my trust at this moment."

"Well, that certainly negates Lady Hawthorne's request, does it not?" Eldridge pinched the bridge of his nose and sighed wearily. "Let me reflect on who might have been told about Hawthorne's journal. Return tomorrow and we'll discuss this further."

Shaking his head in silent commiseration, Marcus departed, gazing about the empty outer offices before moving down the hall with its towering ceilings and dimly lit chandeliers. For a brief moment, he'd been furious with Elizabeth and then the feeling passed. She would never have involved Eldridge unless she felt the need was dire. She'd been affected this afternoon, shaken enough to set aside her formidable pride.

A crack had appeared in her armor. He hoped it wouldn't be long before the shell was removed and he could once again see the vulnerable woman who hid inside.

"You look the fittest I've seen you in years," Margaret said, her sweet smile revealing a charming dimple. "You are radiant this evening."

Elizabeth flushed and fluffed the pale blue silk of her overskirts. She looked ravished. There was no other way to describe it. "It is *you* who is radiant. Every woman here pales in comparison. Pregnancy agrees with you."

Margaret's hand moved to cover the slight protrusion of her lightly corseted stomach. "I'm pleased you are making the effort to socialize and be seen. Today's ride in the park did wonders for your complexion. William is concerned about those formidable looking outriders you hired, but I explained how difficult it must be for you, reemerging alone after the death of your spouse."

Elizabeth bit her bottom lip. "Yes," she agreed softly. "It has been difficult."

Just then, the tiny hairs on the back of her neck began to rise. It was not necessary to turn around to discern why.

Marcus had arrived. She refused to face him. Her blood

still thrummed with the pleasure he'd given her, and a man as perceptive as he was would know it.

Margaret leaned closer. "Heavens. The way Lord Westfield looks at you could start a fire. Fortunate for you that William did not attend this evening. Can you imagine if he had? I'd wager they'd come to fisticuffs. You should have heard Westfield say you were worth the risk of death in a duel. Every woman in London is green with envy."

Elizabeth could feel the burning emerald gaze from across the crowded room. She shivered, her senses acutely attuned to the man who approached her.

"Here he comes." Margaret arched a copper brow. "The gossips will go mad over this, crazed as they've been over that row with William at the Morelands'. This will only add fuel to the fire." Her voice tapered off.

"Lady Barclay," purred the velvet voice, as Marcus bowed low over Margaret's proffered hand. His shoulder brushed deliberately against Elizabeth's arm, leaving goose bumps in its wake.

"Lord Westfield, a pleasure."

He turned and the intensity of his gaze robbed her of breath. Dear heaven. He looked as if he meant to toss up her skirts at any moment. Dressed in a dark blue coat and breeches, he made every other man fade to insignificance.

"Lady Hawthorne." He captured her hand, which hung limply at her side, and lifted it, meeting it halfway with the descent of his mouth. His kiss was anything but chaste, melting through her glove as his fingers caressed the center of her palm.

Instantly she was aroused, on edge, wanting those fingers to caress her everywhere as they'd done mere hours ago. He watched her with a knowing smile, well aware of her reaction.

"Lord Westfield." She tugged her hand, but he would not release it. Her stomach fluttered as his fingertips continued their gentle stroking.

Her Grace, the Dowager Duchess of Ravensend, announced the start of the musicale, and all the guests left the formal parlor to move into the ballroom where chairs had been assembled to face the musicians. Marcus tucked her hand around his arm and led her out to the foyer, deliberately falling behind.

"The man escaped," he said for her ears only.

She nodded, unsurprised.

He stopped, and turned to face her. "More must be done to protect you. And I will not be handing this assignment over to someone else, so your efforts this afternoon were for naught."

"This entanglement offers no benefit to either of us."

His hand reached up to touch her face, and she stepped back quickly.

"You forget yourself," she scolded. She shot a wary look around the foyer.

With one warning glance, Marcus sent the attending footman fleeing with haste. Then he turned all of his attention upon her. "And you forget the rules."

"What rules?"

His gaze narrowed and she took another step back. "I can still taste you, Elizabeth. I can still feel the silky clasp of your cunt on my cock and the pleasure you gave me still warms my blood. The rules haven't changed since this afternoon. I can have you however and whenever I wish."

"To hell with you." Her heart racing, her chest tight, she stumbled backward until the wall prevented further escape.

He bridged the gap between them, enveloping her in his rich, warm scent. Music poured from the ballroom and she shot a startled glance toward the sound. When she looked back at Marcus, he stood directly before her.

"Why do you insist on driving us both to madness?" he asked gruffly.

Her hand went to her throat, nervously fingering the pearls that rested there. "What can I do to satisfy your interest?"

she asked bluntly. "There must be something I can do or say, that will cool your ardor."

"You know what you can do."

She swallowed hard, and stared up at him. He was so tall, so broad of shoulder that he dwarfed her until she could see nothing around him. But her fear did not come from that. In fact, it was only when she was with Marcus that she felt truly safe. No, her fear came from inside, from a cold and lonely place she preferred to forget existed. And there he stood, so damn confident and predatory. He felt none of the uncertainty that she felt. Libertines never did, shielded as they were by the knowledge of their undeniable charm and appeal. If only she could boast such assured sexuality.

A slow smile curved her lips as the solution to her dilemma presented itself in a flash of comprehension. How could she have missed the obvious? Here she'd been floundering and unsure how to respond in the face of such an overwhelming sensual onslaught when she'd grown up with the best examples of how to manage these situations in her own household. She would simply do what William or her father or Marcus himself would do.

"Very well, then. You can meet me in the bachelor quarters of Chesterfield Hall for your fuck." The crude word stumbled over her tongue and she lifted her chin to hide her discomfort.

He blinked. "Beg your pardon?"

She arched a brow. "That's what I can do, correct? Spread my legs until you sate your lust? Then you'll tire of me and leave me in peace." Just speaking the words reignited the heat in her veins. Images from the afternoon filled her mind, and she bit her lower lip against the sudden rush of desire.

The intense predatory look of his features softened. "Christ, when you present it in that manner—" His brows drew together in a rueful frown. "What an ogre I must seem to you at times. I cannot remember the last time I felt so chastened."

The faintest trace of a smile touched her lips. She took a step closer, her hand coming up to press against the elaborately embroidered silk of his waistcoat before drifting down, caressing the rippling expanse of his stomach beneath. Her hand tingled through her glove, reminding her of how delicate the balance of power was.

Marcus caught her wandering fingertips and tugged her closer. Staring down into her face, he shook his head. "I presume you've conceived of some mischief."

"Not at all," she murmured, stroking his palm with her fingers and watching his gaze darken. "I intend to give you what you want. Surely you won't complain about that?"

"Hmmm. Tonight then?"

Her eyes widened. "Good heavens. Again today?"

Laughing, he relented, his mouth curving in a smile that made her breathless. The change in him was startling. Gone was the brutish arrogance, replaced by a boyish allure she found hard to resist. "Very well then." He stepped back, and offered his arm. "And you are correct, I surely won't complain."

Chapter 8

Marcus paced before the fire in the Chesterfield guest-house and tried to recollect his first sexual encounter. It had happened a long time ago and the rushed tumble in the Westfield stables had passed in a blur of sweaty skin, prickly hay, and gasping relief. Still, despite the less than clear remembrance of that afternoon, he was certain he'd never been as anxious as he was at the present moment.

Having escorted Elizabeth home from the Dempsey Ball over an hour ago, he'd rushed home and changed, only to return on horseback. He'd been waiting ever since.

Doubt twisted his stomach into knots, a sensation wholly unfamiliar to him. Would Elizabeth come to him, as she'd promised? Or would he wait here all night, desperate to taste her and feel her beneath his hands?

Standing, Marcus tossed more coals into the grate before glancing around the beautifully appointed bachelor quarters. While he would have preferred to have Elizabeth once again in his own bed, he would take what he could get and gladly.

The Aubusson rug was soft under his bare feet as he moved back to the chair facing the fire. He'd removed every garment but his breeches, astonished and not a little disconcerted by his haste to press his bare skin to Elizabeth's.

The outer door opened, and then shut quietly. Marcus stood, and moved to the hallway, lounging against the jamb in an effort to appear nonchalant and less needy than he felt. Then Elizabeth turned the corner and his breath caught. Against his will, his feet moved, one in front of the other. She paused, her luscious bottom lip caught between her teeth. Dressed in simple muslin, her hair free of its previous evening elaborateness, her face scrubbed clean of both powder and patch, she was a vision of casual youthful beauty.

"Where have you been?" he growled as he reached her, his hands gripping her waist and lifting her against him.

"I—"

He crushed her response with a kiss. She stiffened at first, and then suddenly she opened for him. A groan escaped, as the heady taste of her flooded his mouth. Fierce but sweet, her kisses had always driven him to madness.

A loud thump momentarily distracted him, and he pulled back to discern the source of the sound. Lying at their feet was a small volume covered in red leather.

"Your returning Hawthorne's journal?"

"Yes," she said, in the breathy voice that betrayed her arousal.

As he gazed at the book on the floor, Marcus was surprised at the jealousy that rose up within him. Elizabeth carried another man's name. She had once been physically joined to someone else. He still stung from the pain of it, much to his chagrin. He was not some foolishly besotted lad, selfish in his desire for the affection of a fair maid.

But he felt like one.

Marcus linked his fingers with hers, and tugged her into the bedroom.

"I came as quickly as I could," she said softly.

"Liar. You debated internally for a moment, at least."

She smiled, and his entire body hardened. "Maybe a moment," she conceded.

"But you came, regardless." He wrapped his arms around her, and fell back into the bed.

She laughed, the cold wariness of her features instantly

transformed. "Only because I knew if I didn't, you would probably come up and collect me yourself."

Burying his face in her neck, he chuckled and groaned at the same time. Under other circumstances, as painfully aroused as he was, he would have rolled his lover over and mounted her. In this instance, however, he was determined to find a way past Elizabeth's defenses. Sexual satisfaction was not his only aim.

Not any longer.

"You are correct." He stared up at her. "I would have fetched you."

Her hand touched the side of his face, one of the rare tender gestures she bestowed on him. Any touch of hers, any melting look, stunned him and moved him.

"You are far too arrogant. You do realize that, don't you?"

"Of course." He sat up and settled her against the pillows. Then he reached for the bottle of wine he'd set on the nightstand, and poured her a full glass.

Elizabeth licked her bottom lip and her lashes lowered, hiding her gaze as she accepted the libation. "You are half naked. It's . . . disconcerting."

"Perhaps if you disrobed it would be less so," he suggested.

"Marcus . . ."

"Or drink. That should relax you." It was why he'd brought two bottles with him. He remembered her giddy on champagne during their courtship, laughing and mischievous. He was eager to see her that way again.

As if she thought the same, Elizabeth lifted the goblet to her lips and took a large swallow. Normally, he'd chastise such an abuse of excellent vintage, but in this case he was pleased. A small droplet clung to the corner of her lips and he leaned forward and licked it away, closing his eyes briefly in contentment. He was startled when she turned her head and pressed her lips more fully to his.

Eyes wide, she pulled back and drank the rest of the wine down. She thrust the empty glass at him. "More, please."

Marcus smiled. "Your wish is my command." He studied her furtively as he poured, noting the way her fingers brushed restlessly over her thighs. "Why are you so nervous, love?"

"You are accustomed to this sort of . . . arrangement. For me, however, sitting here with you half-dressed and knowing the entire purpose of being here is for . . . for . . ."

"Sex?"

"Yes." She opened her mouth and then closed it, shrugging delicate shoulders. "It makes me nervous."

"That's not the only reason we are here."

Elizabeth frowned, and took another large drink. "It's not?"

"No. I'd like to talk with you as well."

"Is that how these things are normally done?"

He chuckled ruefully. "Nothing about this is like anything in my experience."

"Oh." Her shoulders sagged just a little.

Catching her free hand, he laced his fingers with hers. Her cheeks were already flushed, betraying the effects of the wine. "Could you grant me one small favor?" he asked, even though he had promised himself he wouldn't.

She waited expectantly.

Tamping down the sudden apprehension he felt, he rushed ahead. "Could you find it in your heart to tell me what happened the night you left me?"

Her gaze lowered to stare into the contents of her glass. "Must I?"

"If you would be so kind, love."

"I'd really rather not."

"Is it so dreadful?" he coaxed softly. "The deed is done and cannot be undone. I ask only to be relieved of my confusion."

Elizabeth released a deep breath. "I suppose I owe you that much."

When her silence stretched out he prodded, "Go on."

"The tale starts with William. One night, about a month before the start of my first Season, I couldn't sleep. I often had that trouble over the years after my mother died. Whenever I was restless I would visit my father's study and sit in the dark. It smells like old books and my father's tobacco—I find the combination soothing.

"William entered shortly after, but he failed to see me lying on the settee. I was curious so I remained quiet. It was very late and he was dressed in dark clothing, he'd even covered his golden hair. It was obvious he was going somewhere where he didn't wish to be seen or recognized. He carried himself so strangely, all chained up-ferocity and energy. He left and did not return until dawn. That was when I first suspected he was involved in something dangerous."

Elizabeth paused to take another drink. "I began to watch him when we were out. I studied his activities. I noticed he sought out Lord Hawthorne with regularity. The two of them would detach themselves from the gathering and have heated discussions in quiet corners, sometimes trading papers or other items."

Marcus sprawled across the counterpane and rested his head on his hand. "I never noticed. Eldridge's expertise at subterfuge never ceases to amaze me. I certainly never suspected William was an agent."

"Why would you?" she asked simply. "Had I not been watching them so closely, I would never have suspected anything either. But eventually William began to look exhausted, drawn. I was worried about him. When I asked him outright to tell me what he was doing, he refused. I knew I needed help." She glanced at him then, her violet gaze tortured.

"That is why you came to me that night." The bitter irony was not lost on him. He took the glass of wine from her fingers and washed the taste of it from his mouth. "Eldridge keeps the identities of his agents a closely guarded secret. In the event one of us is captured or compromised we have little information to share. I personally know very few."

The tight line of her normally lush mouth betrayed her distaste for the agency. Right now he was not feeling too charitable toward Eldridge himself. William's assignment, as well as his own, had contrived to bring his engagement to such a tragic end.

Elizabeth breathed a forlorn sigh. "When I returned from your home I was too upset to retire, so I went to my father's study. Nigel called for William later that morning and he was shown into the room, unaware I was there. I vented my rage on him. I accused him of leading William on a path to destruction. I threatened to tell my father."

Marcus smiled, imagining the scene. "I have learned to respect your temper, sweet. You become a veritable termagant when angered."

She returned a weak smile, devoid of life or humor. "I had assumed their activities were degenerate. I was shocked when Nigel explained that he and William were agents for the Crown." Her eyes shone with withheld tears. "And it was all suddenly too much . . . what I thought you had done, the danger William was in. I told Hawthorne about your infidelity in a moment of weakness. He said marriages of high passion were not the stuff of longevity or true happiness. I would have been discontented eventually, he said. Best I learned your true nature when I did, rather than after it was too late. He was so kind, so gentle in my distress. He provided an anchor at a time when I was adrift."

Marcus rolled onto his back and stared at the red velvet canopy above him. After her mother's death and her father's decline into emotional apathy, Hawthorne's words must have sounded like the veriest wisdom to Elizabeth. Tense and frustrated, his anger toward a dead man had no outlet. It should have been *he* who was her anchor, not Hawthorne. "Damn you," he swore vehemently.

"When I returned from Scotland I inquired about you."

"I had left the country by then." His voice was distant, lost in the past. "I called on you that morning, once I'd settled the widow. I wanted to explain, and make things right between us. Instead, William met me at the door and threw your note in my face. He blamed me for your rashness. I blamed him for not going after you."

"*You* could have come after me."

Marcus turned his head to meet her gaze. "Is that what you wanted?"

When Elizabeth shrank back into the pillows, he knew his rage and pain must be evident on his face.

"I . . ." Her voice choked off.

"Part of me held on to the hope that you would fail to go through with it, but somehow I knew." His eyes narrowed. "I *knew* you had done it—married someone else. And I couldn't help but wonder how it was that he was there for you, when the events of that night could not have been predicted. Perhaps, as you said, he was always an option. I could not remain in England after that. I would have stayed away longer if my father had not passed on. When I returned, I discovered you were widowed. I sent you my condolences so you would know I was home. I waited for you to come to me."

"I heard about your liaisons, your endless string of women." Her spine stiffened and she swung her legs over the side of the bed.

"Where in hell do you think you're going?" he growled.

He set the empty glass on the nightstand and yanked her into a sprawl across his chest. Holding her instantly soothed the restlessness that was his constant companion. Despite everything, she was his now.

"I thought the mood was ruined," she said with a pout.

He arched his hips upward, pressing his erection into her thigh. Her gaze darkened, the irises fading as desire quickened her breathing.

"Don't think," he said gruffly. "Forget the past."

"How?"

"Kiss me. We'll forget everything together."

She hesitated only a moment before lowering her head and pressing her moist lips to his. Frozen, he lay aching beneath her, the soft pressure of her curves burning his skin, her vanilla scent intoxicating him. He tightened his grip on her hips to hide the trembling of his hands. Why she affected him like this, he couldn't guess, though he'd spent endless hours trying.

She lifted her head, and he groaned at the loss.

"I'm sorry," she murmured, color washing across her cheeks. "I'm not good at this."

"You were doing beautifully."

"You're not moving," she complained.

He gave a rueful laugh. "I'm afraid to, love. I want you too badly."

"Then we are at an impasse." Her smile was sweet. "I don't know what to do."

Capturing her hand, he placed it on his chest. "Touch me."

She sat up, straddling his hips. Several curls framed the beauty of her face. "Where?"

Marcus doubted he could survive it, but he would expire a contented man. "Everywhere."

Smiling, her finger drifted tentatively through the hair on his chest leaving tingling paths in their wake. Her fingertips swirled around the scar that marred his shoulder and then brushed across his nipples. He shivered.

"You like that?"

"Yes."

Elizabeth hummed, her palms coming to rest against his stomach, which tautened in response. "Fascinating."

Choking out a laugh, he said, "I pray your interest is more than curiosity."

She giggled, a bit tipsy he suspected. "You are quite the handsomest man I've ever seen." Reaching up, she caressed the tops of his shoulders and then down his arms to entwine her fingers with his. The moment was simple and yet achingly complex. On the surface, they appeared to be two lovers, hopelessly smitten with one another, but the heavy undercurrent of wariness ran both ways.

"I'd hoped you would think so."

"Why? So you can seduce me with ease?"

He brought their joined hands to his lips and kissed her knuckles. "You are doing the seducing."

Elizabeth snorted. "There is no help for you, Lord Westfield. You are a rogue through and through. When this affair is over—"

With a firm tug, he yanked her down and kissed her breathless. He didn't want to hear about the end or even think of it.

Releasing her hands, his fingers moved along her spine, loosening her dress. He murmured his pleasure at finding nothing beneath it, no corset or chemise. As frightened as she was of the way he made her feel, she'd still come prepared. He'd also say she was eager, if the near frantic way she was caressing him was any indication. Parting the back of her gown, he tugged down the front and exposed her breasts, full and heavy with arousal. They were lovely, so pale, tipped with rosy nipples. He hadn't had the pleasure of fondling them before, a neglect he planned to correct posthaste.

When she lifted her hands, he brushed them away. "No. Don't hide, sweet, I enjoy looking at you as much as you enjoy looking at me."

"After all the women—"

"No more," he admonished. "No more talk of that." Sighing, he dropped his hands to her thighs. "I cannot change my past."

"You cannot change what you are." All the softness in her face fled. Only Elizabeth could sit bare breasted on a man and be so remote.

"Damn it, my sexual history is not who I am. And if I were you, I would think twice before complaining, since without my experience I would not be able to pleasure you so well."

"Grateful?" she snapped. "I would have been more grateful had you turned your attentions elsewhere."

She attempted to slip away, but he restrained her. Marcus pumped his hips upward, pushing the heated length of his erection into the burning dampness between her thighs. When she gasped, he did it again, watching as she ground herself onto his cock. Her immediate helpless response cooled his irritation.

"Why does my past anger you so?"

A finely arched brow rose.

"Tell me," he urged. "I truly want to know." He would get nowhere with her if she kept these barriers between them. Certainly he could have her body, but he wanted more than that during the length of their affair.

She wrinkled her nose. "Do you really care nothing for the women whose hearts you break?"

"Is that what this is about?" He held his exasperation in check. "Elizabeth, the women who entertain me are vastly experienced."

Her look was clearly disbelieving.

Sliding his hands beneath the hem of her gown, he caressed the lithe length of her thighs, his thumbs coming to rest against the soft curls of her sex. His cock hardened further at the realization that only the material of his breeches separated his torment from her sweet relief.

"Women are a bit more susceptible to elevated feelings after a pleasurable sexual encounter," he admitted. "But in all honesty, rarely has a woman become overly attached to me and even then, I doubt it was love."

"Perhaps you simply didn't notice the extent of their attachment. I vow, William was always taken aback when one of my female acquaintances would no longer receive me because of their unrequited feelings for him."

Marcus flinched. "I'm sorry, love."

"You should be. I suffer from a deplorable lack of companionship because of men like you and William. Thank heavens he married Margaret."

He brushed the tips of his thumbs across the soft, damp lips of her sex and her hips canted forward in unmistakable invitation.

"I shall be like your jaded paramours," she said suddenly.

Moving his hands, he spread her with his fingers and brushed against her clitoris. It hardened as he circled it. "In what way? I can conceive of no way you are like any woman I've ever met."

"*I* will discard *you*."

Gently, he pressed his thumb against the gathering slickness and slipped inside her. This was his. She would not deny him the pleasure of it. "Perhaps I'll overwhelm you, drench you in rapture until you cannot conceive of a night passing without my cock here, deep inside you."

Her soft plaintive moan was the death of him. Reaching between them, he tore open the placket of his breeches. Glancing up, he watched Elizabeth's eyes melt. Discard him, indeed. She would surrender that icy control that chilled him, he would see to it.

"I wanted to savor you, Elizabeth."

She stiffened when he gripped her hips and positioned her over his cock. "What—" Her voice strangled to silence as he pulled her down, sheathing himself.

He groaned as the molten heat of her clasped him like a velvet fist. Twisting rapture coiled in his loins and stiffened his spine, causing Marcus to grit his teeth and arch off the bed.

"Christ," he gasped. If he breathed wrong, he would come.

Elizabeth writhed around him, finding a position of comfort that lodged him more securely within her. Sweat beading his brow, he relaxed his hold on her waist and sank back into the pillows.

With her lovely face flushed, eyes huge and hot with need, she stared at him in silent inquiry.

"I'm all yours, love," he encouraged, needing to see her make the effort. Wanting to lie still and be fucked mindless by the woman who'd jilted him so long ago.

Biting her lower lip, she rose, lifting herself from his cock until only the tip remained inside. When she lowered again, her movements were awkward, tentative, but devastating nonetheless. His hands fell to the bed and fisted in the counterpane. Elizabeth moved again, panting, and the cool air on his cock followed by the heated grip of her cunt tore a groan from him.

She paused.

"Don't stop," he begged.

"I don't—"

"Faster, sweet. Harder."

And to his delight, she obliged, moving over him with her natural grace. The sight of her, barely dressed, with breasts bouncing, arrested him. He watched her, eyes half lidded with drugging pleasure, remembering her standing across the Moreland ballroom, a vision of regal unattainable beauty. Now she was his, in the basest way possible, her whimpered cries betraying how much she enjoyed him despite everything.

When he couldn't take any more, when the need to come was so overwhelming he feared leaving her behind, he held her in place and lunged his hips upwards, fucking her suspended body with rapid impatient drives.

"Yes . . ." Her hands covered his and her head fell back, the gesture one of blatant surrender. "Marcus!"

He knew that cry, understood the command, *Take me.* And rolling, he did just that, thrusting into her so hard he shoved her up the bed. Still he couldn't get deep enough. He growled, frustrated that even this primal act was not enough to slake the need that grew stronger the more he tried to satisfy it.

Elizabeth arched her neck, her breasts lifting to press hard nipples into his chest. With a sharp broken cry she tightened around him before dissolving into the rippling caresses that felt like nothing he'd ever experienced before.

He fucked through them like a mad man, forcing his cock into grasping depths, dipping into the scalding cream that bathed her inner thighs and lured his seed. He roared when he came, his semen spewing until he thought he would die of it. Lowering his head he bit her shoulder, punishing her for being the bane of his existence, the source of his highest pleasure and deepest pain.

The soft sound of pages turning woke her. Elizabeth sat upright, startled and a bit embarrassed to find herself completely unclothed and uncovered by the sheets. Searching the room, she discovered an equally naked Marcus seated at the small escritoire with Nigel's journal open before him. His gaze was riveted on her.

Bared and far too vulnerable, she pulled the sheet over her. "What are you doing?"

Giving her a heart-stopping smile, he stood and moved to the bed. "I'd intended to puzzle out Hawthorne's code, but was repeatedly distracted by the view."

She bit back a smile. "Lecher. There should be a law forbidding the ogling of sleeping women."

"I'm certain there is." He leapt onto the bed. "But it does not apply to lovers."

The way he said the word "lovers" made her shiver. Staking a claim to his passion, however briefly, made her blood heat. And then chill. It was too much, too fast.

"You say that so smugly." Glancing briefly into fire, her fingers picked restlessly at the eyelet work bordering the sheets. "No doubt you are pleased with your easy conquest of me."

"Easy?" he scoffed, flopping backward into the pillows and tossing his arms wide. "Was bloody damn difficult." Turning his head to look at her, he frowned and his voice lost its teasing edge. Rolling to his side, Marcus propped his head in his hand. "Tell me about your marriage."

"Why?"

"Why not?"

She shrugged, wishing she could find the control she'd felt earlier. "There's nothing of note to relay. Hawthorne was an exemplary spouse."

Pursing his lips, Marcus stared pensively into the fire. Before she could resist the impulse, she reached over and brushed a tumbled lock from his forehead.

He turned to press a kiss into her palm. "You had an accord then?"

"We enjoyed similar activities and he was content to allow me my freedom. He was so preoccupied with his agency work, I rarely saw him, but the distance suited us both."

He nodded, appearing deep in thought. "You didn't mind the agency so much then?"

"No. I hated it even then, but I was naïve and had no notion that anyone would be killed."

When he said nothing, Elizabeth looked at him under her lashes, wondering what he was thinking and why she was staying. She should go.

Then he said, "I believe some of what is written in that journal is about Christopher St. John, but until I have an opportunity to peruse the volume at leisure, I won't be certain."

"Oh." She twisted the edge of the sheet around her finger. Here was her opportunity to depart without awkwardness. "I'm sorry to have disturbed you." Sliding her legs to the edge of the mattress, she attempted to leave the bed and was stopped by his hand at her elbow. She glanced over her shoulder.

Emerald eyes filled with banked fire met hers. "You are a distraction I welcome," he murmured in the deeply sexual voice she'd come to anticipate.

Marcus pulled her back, crawling over her, pressing her down, his mouth nuzzling her stomach through the bedclothes. "You have no notion of how it affects me to be in your company like this, to work in the moments when you are otherwise occupied."

Gasping as his mouth surrounded her nipple through the sheet, Elizabeth's hand drifted to the warm skin of his shoulders and arms, feeling the power within them as they held his weight from her. With rhythmic laps of his tongue, he abraded the stiff peak, intuitively knowing how to make her mad for him.

"Marcus . . ." She struggled, knowing it was wrong to give in, fighting to regain control.

With a low growl, he released her breast and yanked the sheet out of the way. He covered her body with his, his mouth claiming hers, the heat and hardness of his frame causing her to melt into him helplessly. His hands moved with tender skill, knowing her so well, ravishing her senses, coaxing away her tension.

Until she dissolved in pleasure, falling from grace with a cry of surrender, knowing even as she did so that the climb back up grew longer by the moment . . .

Chapter 9

Elizabeth entered the main house through the study's garden doors. Although not yet dawn, the kitchen staff would already be preparing for the day's meals and she didn't want to chance crossing paths with one of them. Not with her hair a fright and her skin so flushed.

"Elizabeth."

Startled, she jumped. Finding William in the open doorway, her stomach tightened.

"Yes, William?"

"A moment, if you please."

Sighing, she waited as he stepped into the room and closed them inside. She braced herself.

"What in hell are you doing with Westfield? In our guesthouse? Have you lost your wits?"

"Yes." There was no point in denying it.

"Why?" he asked, clearly confused and hurt.

"I don't know."

"I'll kill him," he growled. "To treat you like this, to use you so callously. I told you to stay away from him, that his intentions were dishonorable."

"I tried, truly I did." Turning away, Elizabeth sank into a nearby chair.

Muttering an oath, William began to pace in front of her.

"You could have had anyone. If you were so set against marriage, you could have chosen a more suitable companion."

"William, I love you for your concern, but I am a grown woman and I can make my own decisions, especially about something as personal as taking a lover."

"Good God," he bit out. "To have to speak of such matters with you—"

"You don't, you know," she said dryly.

"Oh yes, I do." He rounded on her. "After suffering through your endless lectures about my licentious behavior—"

"Yes, you see, I learned from the best."

William stilled. "You've no notion. You are in over your head."

Elizabeth took a deep breath. "Perhaps. Or perhaps it is Westfield who is out of his depth." If not, he soon would be.

He snorted. "Elizabeth—"

"Enough, William, I'm tired." She stood and moved toward the hallway. "Westfield will call this evening to escort me to the Fairchilds' dinner." She'd tried to argue, but Marcus insisted her safety was in question. It was either with his escort or she couldn't attend. He'd been adamant, in his charming, drawling way.

"Fine," William snapped. "I'll have a word with him when he arrives."

She waved her hand nonchalantly over her shoulder. "Be my guest. Send for me when you're done."

"This is odious."

"I gathered you think so."

"An abomination."

"Yes, yes." She moved out into the hallway.

"I will thrash him if he hurts you," William called after her.

Elizabeth stopped and turned to face him. As meddling as he was, he was acting out of love, and she adored him for it. With a tender smile, she returned to him and hugged his waist. He crushed her close.

"You are the most vexing sibling," he said into her hair. "Why could you not be more pliable and even-tempered?"

"Because I would bore you to tears and drive you insane."

He sighed. "Yes, I supposed you would at that." He pulled back. "Be careful, please. I couldn't bear to see you hurt again."

The sadness evident on his handsome features tugged at her heart, and reminded her of the precariousness of her situation. Playing with Marcus was playing with fire.

"Don't worry so much, William." Linking her arm with his, Elizabeth tugged him toward the staircase. "Trust me to take care of myself."

"I'm trying, but it's damned difficult when you engage in stupidity."

Laughing, Elizabeth released his arm and ran up the stairs. "First one to the vase at the end of the gallery wins."

Easily reaching the vase first, William escorted Elizabeth to her bed chamber. Then he returned to his own room and wasted no time changing. He left a bewildered Margaret still abed and traveled into town to the Westfield townhouse. Taking the steps two at a time, he pounded the brass knocker that graced the door.

The portal opened, revealing a butler dripping in chilly hauteur as he gazed down the length of his nose.

Handing over his card, William barreled his way through the doorway and entered the foyer. "You may announce me to Lord Westfield," he said curtly.

The butler glanced at the card. "Lord Westfield is from home, Lord Barclay."

"Lord Westfield is abed," William snapped. "And you will rouse him and bring him to me or I will seek him out myself."

With a disdainful arch of his brow, the servant led him to the study, and then retreated.

When the door opened again, Marcus entered. William lunged at his old friend without a word.

"Bloody hell," Marcus cursed as he was tackled to the rug. He cursed again when William's, fist connected with his ribcage.

William continued to rain blows as they rolled across the study floor, bumping into the chaise and knocking over a chair. Marcus made every effort to deflect the attack, but not once did he fight back.

"Son of a bitch," William growled, made more furious by being denied the fight he'd come for. "I'll kill you!"

"Damned if you're not doing an admirable job of it," Marcus grunted.

Suddenly, there were more arms in the fray, intervening and pulling them apart. Yanked to their feet, William fought off the unyielding grip that held his arms behind him. "Damn you, Ashford. Release me."

But Paul Ashford held tight. "In a moment, my lord. No offense intended. But Mother is home, and she does not care much for brawls in the house. Always made us go outside, you see."

Marcus stood opposite him and a few feet away, shrugging off the helping hand of Robert Ashford, the youngest of the three brothers. The resemblance between the two was uncanny. Only Robert's gold-rimmed spectacles and slighter frame distinguished the two. Unlike the brother behind William, who was raven-haired and dark-eyed.

William ceased his struggles, and Paul released him.

"Truly, gentlemen," Paul said, straightening his waistcoat and wig. "Much as I love a good fracas in the morning, you should at least be dressed for the occasion."

Holding a hand to his side, Marcus ignored his brother and said, "I trust your spirits have improved, Barclay?"

"Slightly." William glared. "It would have been more sporting if you'd participated."

"And risk angering Elizabeth? Don't be daft."

William snorted. "As if you have a care for her feelings."

"No doubt of that."

"Then why this? Why use her in this manner?"

Robert pushed up his spectacles, and cleared his throat. "I think we're done here, Paul."

"I hope so," Paul muttered. "Not the type of conversation I prefer to have at this time of morning. Now be good, gentlemen. Next time, it may be Mother who intercedes. I would pity you both then."

The brothers shut the door behind them as they retreated.

Marcus ran a hand through his hair. "Remember that chit you dallied with when we were at Oxford? The baker's daughter?"

"Yes." William remembered her well. A young, nubile thing. Beautiful and worldly, she was free with her favors. Celia loved a good hard fuck more than most and he'd been hot to give it to her. In fact, they'd once spent three days in bed, taking time only to bathe and eat. She'd been enjoyable with no strings.

Suddenly he caught the implication.

"Do you *want* to die?" William growled. "You are talking about my sister for God's sake!"

"And a woman grown," Marcus pointed out. "A widow, no innocent maid."

"Elizabeth is nothing like Celia. She hasn't the experience to engage in fleeting liaisons. She could be hurt."

"Oh? She seemed able to jilt me well enough and she shows no remorse for her actions."

"Why would she? You were an absolute cad."

"We are both to blame." Marcus moved to one of the wingbacks that flanked the dark fireplace and lowered himself into a weary sprawl. "However, things appear to have worked out for the best. She was not unhappy with Hawthorne."

"Then leave well enough alone."

"I cannot. There is something remaining between us. We've both agreed, as consenting adults, to allow it to run its course."

William moved to take the seat opposite. "I still cannot understand that Elizabeth could be so . . ."

"Nonchalant? *Laissez faire?*"

"Yes, exactly." He rubbed the back of his neck. "She was devastated at what you'd done, you know."

"Ah yes. So devastated she married another man post-haste."

"What better way to run?"

Marcus blinked.

"You think I don't know her?" William asked, shaking his head. "Have a care with her affections," he warned as he stood and moved toward the door. He paused on the threshold and looked back. "If you hurt her, Westfield, I'll see you on a field at dawn."

Marcus tilted his head in acknowledgment.

"In the meantime, come early this evening. We can await the women together. Father still has a fine collection of brandy."

"An irresistible invitation. I will be there."

Somewhat mollified, William made his egress. He also made a mental reminder to clean his pistols.

Just in case.

The ball was a massive success, as witnessed by the overflowing ballroom and the beaming face of the hostess, Lady Marks-Darby. Elizabeth wove her way through the crush, escaping onto a deserted balcony. From her vantage point, she could see couples wandering through the intricate maze of hedges in the garden below. She closed her eyes and took a deep, cleansing breath.

The last week had been both heaven and hell. She went to Marcus every night in the guesthouse and while he'd never promised anything in return, she'd had her own expectations.

When she suggested the affair, she assumed he would pounce on her immediately upon her arrival, carry her off to bed, and when finished with her body take his leave. Instead, he drew her into conversation or fed her sumptuous cold suppers he brought with him. He encouraged discourse on a variety of topics and appeared genuinely interested in her opinions. He asked her about her favorite books and purchased the ones she mentioned that he had not yet read. It was all so very strange. She was completely unaccustomed to such intimacy, which seemed much more pervasive than their physical connection. Not that Marcus ever allowed her to forget that.

He held her in a constant state of physical turmoil. An erotic master, Marcus used the entirety of his formidable skill to make certain he never left her mind for even a moment. He found ways to surreptitiously brush against her shoulder or slip his hand down the curve of her spine. He bent far too close when speaking, breathing in her ear in a way that made her quiver with longing.

Laughter from the maze below brought a thankful respite from her thoughts. Two women came to a halt directly beneath the balcony, their melodious voices floating up to be heard clearly.

"The marriageable men are slim in number this Season," said one to the other.

"That is unfortunately true. And it's hideous luck that Lord Westfield should be so determined to win that wager. He practically hovers over Hawthorne's widow."

"She seems not to care much for him."

"Fool is unaware of what she is missing. He is glorious. His entire body is a work of art. I must confess, I am completely besotted."

Elizabeth gripped the railing with white-knuckled force as one of the women giggled.

"Lure him back, if you miss him so keenly."

"Oh, I shall," came the smug reply. "Lady Hawthorne may be beautiful, but she's a cold one. He's merely in it for the sport. Once he has redeemed himself, he'll want a little more fire in his bed. And I'll be waiting."

Suddenly, the women gasped in surprise.

"Excuse me, ladies," interrupted a masculine voice. The two women continued further into the maze, leaving Elizabeth to fume on the balcony.

The unmitigated gall! She grit her teeth until her jaw ached. The damned wager. How could she have forgotten?

"Lady Hawthorne?"

She turned at the sound of her name murmured in a deep, pleasantly raspy voice behind her. She eyed the gentleman who approached, taking in his appearance in an effort to identify him. "Yes?"

The man was tall and elegantly dressed. She could not know his hair color, covered as it was by a wig that was long in the back and tied at his nape. He wore a mask that wrapped around his eyes, but the brilliant blue color of his irises refused to be contained by it. Something about him arrested her gaze, tugging at her memory in a vaguely familiar way, and yet she was certain she had never met him before.

"Are we acquainted?" she asked.

He shook his head and she straightened, studying him closely as he emerged from the shadows of the overhang. What she could see of his face was well deserving of such beautiful eyes. He was, quite frankly, beyond handsome.

His lips, though thin, were curved in a way that could only be described as carnal, but his gaze . . . his gaze was coldly intent. She sensed he was the type of man who trusted no one and nothing. But that observation was not what caused her shiver of apprehension. Her misgiving was due entirely to the way he approached her. The subtle cant of his body toward hers was decidedly proprietary.

The raspy voice came again. "I regret I must be importunate, Lady Hawthorne, but we have an urgent matter to discuss."

Elizabeth shielded herself in her iciest social deportment. "It is the rare occasion, sir, when I find myself discussing urgent matters with complete strangers."

He showed a leg in a courtly bow. "Forgive me," he replied, his voice deliberately low and soothing. "Christopher St. John, my lady."

Elizabeth's breath halted in her throat. Her pulse racing, she took a preservative step backward. "What is it you wish to discuss with me, Mr. St. John?"

He took the position next to her, resting his hands on the wrought iron railing as he looked out over the maze. His casual stance was deceptive. Much like Marcus, he used an overtly friendly demeanor to reassure those around him, subtly urging others to lower their guard. The tactic had the opposite effect on Elizabeth. She tried not to tense visibly as her insides twisted.

"You received a journal that belonged to your late husband, did you not?" he asked smoothly.

The color drained from her face.

"How do you know of it?" Her eyes widened as her gaze swept over him. "Are you the man who attacked me in the park?" He did not appear to be suffering from any injury.

"You are in grave danger, Lady Hawthorne, as long as that book remains in your possession. Turn it over to me, and I will see to it you are not disturbed again."

Fear and anger blended inside her. "Are you threatening me?" Her chin lifted. "I take leave to tell you, sir, I am not without protection."

"I am well aware of your prowess with a pistol, but that skill is no proof against the type of danger you find yourself facing now. The fact that you have involved Lord Eldridge only complicates matters further." He looked at her and the barrenness in the depths of his eyes chilled her to the bone. "It is in your best interests to give me that book."

St. John's voice was laced with soft menace, his eyes piercing from behind the mask. His casual pose was unable to hide the vibrant energy that distinguished him as a dangerous man.

Elizabeth couldn't stop her shudder of fear and revulsion. He cursed under his breath.

"Here," he murmured gruffly, reaching into a small pocket that graced his white satin waistcoat. He withdrew a small object, and held it out to her. "This belongs to you, I believe."

Refusing to take her eyes from his face, she closed her hand around it.

"You must—" He stopped and swiveled quickly. She followed his gaze and relief flooded her to find Marcus standing in the doorway.

Pure ferocious rage radiated from him in waves. The lines of his face were harsh, reflecting murderous intent. "Back away from her," he ordered. His tension was palpable, coiled like a tight spring, ready to lash out at the slightest provocation.

St. John faced her unperturbed, and bowed again. His casual deportment fooled no one. A profusion of ill will and resentment poisoned the air around the two men. "We will continue our conversation some other time, Lady Hawthorne. In the meantime, I urge you to consider my request. For your own safety." He walked past Marcus with a taunting smile. "Westfield. Always a pleasure."

Marcus sidestepped, halting St. John's escape to the ballroom. "Approach her again, and I'll kill you."

St. John grinned. "You've been threatening me with death for years, Westfield."

Marcus bared his teeth in a feral smile. "I was merely biding my time until the proper excuse presented itself. I have it now. Soon I shall have what I need to see you hanged. You cannot evade justice forever."

"No? Ah, well . . . I await your convenience." St. John glanced at Elizabeth one more time before circumventing Marcus and melting into the crowded ballroom beyond.

She looked down at the object in her hand and the shock

of recognition forced her to grip the railing for support. Marcus was beside her instantly.

"What is it?"

She held out her open palm. "It's my cameo brooch, given to me by Hawthorne as a wedding gift. I broke the clasp. See? It is still broken. He offered to return it to the jeweler's for repair the morning of his death."

Marcus plucked the pin from her hand, and examined it. "St. John returned it? What did he say? Tell me everything."

"He wants the journal." She stared up at his grim features. "And he knew of the attack in the park."

"Bloody hell," Marcus growled under his breath, pocketing the brooch. "I knew it." Wrapping her hand around his arm, he led her from the balcony.

Within moments, Marcus had retrieved their cloaks and called for his carriage, assisting her inside as soon as it rolled to a halt. Ordering the outriders to guard her, he turned back toward the manse, his stride lengthening with purpose.

Leaning out the window, Elizabeth called after him. "Where are you going?"

"After St. John."

"No, Marcus," she begged, her fingers gripping the sill, her heart racing madly. "You said yourself he's dangerous."

"Don't worry, love," he called over his shoulder. "So am I."

Elizabeth waited endlessly, devastated to her very soul. For the first time since starting the affair, she acknowledged how little control she had. Marcus cared nothing for her worry or her distress. Knowing how she must feel, he'd left anyway, deliberately courting danger. And now she waited. He'd been gone so long. Too long. What was happening? Had he found the pirate? Had they exchanged words? Or fought? Perhaps Marcus was hurt . . .

She gazed sightlessly out the window as her stomach roiled. Certain she was about to cast up her accounts, Elizabeth thrust open the door and stumbled down. The outriders moved to her side just as Marcus appeared.

"Sweet." He pulled her close. The heavy silk of his coat was cold from the night air, but inside she was far more chilled. "Don't be frightened. I will protect you."

Elizabeth gave a choked, half-mad laugh. The most pressing peril came from Marcus himself. He was a man who thrived on reckless behavior and lived for the thrill of the chase. He would forever be placing himself in jeopardy, because taking risks was ingrained in his nature.

The agency . . . St. John . . . Marcus . . .

She had to get away from them all.

Far, far away.

Chapter 10

Marcus paused in his prowling of the guesthouse foyer to stare at the Persian rug beneath his feet. He searched for signs of wear caused by his relentless tread.

This damned affair was beyond frustrating. His desire for Elizabeth showed no signs of waning, his body constantly hard and aching for her touch. His physical reaction alone was irritating, but even more troubling was her ceaseless occupation of his every thought.

In all of his other affairs, he'd never spent the night with his paramours. He never brought women to his home, never shared his bed, never gave more than a brief use of his body. He'd never wanted to.

The situation with Elizabeth was entirely different. He had to tear himself away from her, waiting until the cursed rising of the sun forced him to leave. He returned to his home with her scent on his skin, to lie in the bed she had once occupied and relive the memories of her, naked and begging beneath him. It was torture of the most delicious kind.

And it was not just when he was alone that he was maddened by his need. When he'd stepped onto the balcony and recognized the man with whom she conversed, his heart had stopped beating altogether. Then it had raced with the primitive instinct to protect what was his.

He wanted to be closer, damn it all. Elizabeth wanted dis-

tance. She was perfectly happy to keep things simple and un-
complicated by feelings or emotions. In past entanglements,
he would have been pleased. This time, this affair, he was
not.

Elizabeth was not immune. Her gaze lingered when she
thought he was not aware, and when he held her in his arms,
he could feel the racing of her heart against his chest. She
curled around him when she slept and sometimes murmured
his name, telling him he invaded her dreams as surely as she
invaded his.

As the door opened and Elizabeth entered, Marcus spun
about quickly. She offered a half-hearted smile, and then
glanced away.

Evasion, façades, shields—he despised all of the tools she
used to keep him at bay. Anger quickened his blood.

"Hello, my love," he muttered.

She frowned at his tone.

His eyes raked her from head to toe. When his gaze returned to hers, she was blushing.

Good. Better than indifferent.

"Come closer," he ordered arrogantly. There were some
barriers between them he could remove, her clothing being
one of them.

"No." Her voice was threaded with steel.

"No?" He arched a brow. There was something different
about her, a stiffness to her demeanor that caused his stomach to tighten.

Her eyes softened. Wondering what she saw, Marcus
glanced over her head to the mirror that hung on the wall behind her and was startled by the fierce longing that was reflected in his face. His hands clenched into fists.

"Marcus. I will not be staying tonight. I've come only to
tell you that our affair is over."

He felt as though all of the oxygen had been sucked from
the room. To be so easily discarded . . . *Again.*

"Why?" was all he could manage to say.

"There is no need for us to continue seeing each other."

"What about the passion between us?"

"It will fade," she said with a careless shrug.

"Then remain my lover until it does," he challenged.

Elizabeth shook her head.

He moved toward her, his heart thundering in a desperate rhythm, drawn to her scent and the need to feel her skin beneath his hands. "Convince me why we should end the affair."

Violet eyes widened, melting, and she backed away from him. "I don't want you anymore."

Stepping closer, Marcus didn't stop until he had her pressed against the wall, his thigh between hers, his hand curling around her nape. Burying his face in her neck, he breathed in her fragrance of warm, aroused woman.

She trembled in his arms. "Marcus . . ."

"You could have said anything else and I might have believed you. But to say you don't want me is so blatant a lie, I cannot credit it." He tilted his head and brought his lips to hers.

"No," she said, turning her head. "A physical response means nothing, as you well know."

Licking her lips, Marcus waged a battle of seduction, attempting to penetrate the defenses she'd erected against him. "Nothing?" he breathed.

She opened her mouth to retort and his tongue slipped inside, thrusting slow and deep, drinking in the taste of her. A moan escaped her. Then another.

His hand held her head still when she tried to pull away, his other wrapped around her hip, molding her into the heat of his erection. Marcus groaned, his body aching for her, his insides twisting as her hands remained at her sides, rejecting him silently even as her body responded helplessly to his touch. With a curse, he pulled away.

He didn't want her like this, bent to his will against her own. He wanted her warm and willing, as eager for him as he was for her.

"As you wish, Elizabeth," he said coldly, his gaze hard. He reached for his greatcoat, which hung on the rack beside the mirror. "You will crave me soon enough. When you do, come to me. Perhaps I'll still be available for your pleasure."

When she flinched and looked away, Marcus hardened his heart. He was hurting, a new and vastly unwelcome turn of events.

He left with a slam of the door, vaulting onto the back of his horse in his haste to leave. With a curt movement of his hand, he ordered the guards watching the guesthouse to remain behind.

As he rode away, his thoughts stayed with Elizabeth. Finding her on the balcony with St. John had nearly brought him to his knees. She had stood so bravely, with her spine straight and proud. She was no fool; he'd warned her of the danger, but she would not be cowed.

Damn her! Was there no way to rattle her? The still surface of her deportment was deceptive. The depths of her nature roiled with currents he longed to explore, yet he could never reach them.

She was tortured, he knew, and yet it was he who trolled the streets of London while she lay safe in Chesterfield Hall. It was he who suffered, and he had only himself to blame.

Why was it whenever she should be reaching for comfort, like tonight, she chose instead to turn away? Mere hours ago, she had been warm and passionate, her body arching beneath his, her thighs spread to welcome the thrusts of his cock. He could still hear the sound of his name on her lips and feel the bite of her nails in the flesh of his back. She'd been on fire, burning with passion. Over this last week together, he could have sworn the intimacy he felt with her went both ways. He refused to believe he was mistaken.

Feeling the chill of the late night air, he forced his mind

away from thoughts of Elizabeth to catch his bearings. Dazed, he was startled to see the front of Chesterfield Hall. Unconsciously, he had returned, driven by a part of him that was screaming to be recognized.

He ignored it.

Drawing to a halt before the now darkened guesthouse, Marcus glancing around, spotting the mounts of the guards tied nearby. They were either patrolling on foot or had followed her to the manse. He faced the guesthouse and wondered if the door remained unlocked, if Elizabeth's wonderful scent of vanilla and roses still lingered in the foyer. He dismounted and tested the knob, which turned easily. Entering, he closed his eyes to sharpen his sense of smell and inhaled deeply.

Ah, there it was—the faint alluring smell of Elizabeth. Slowly, he followed it, his eyes closed and stinging, his memory of the place guiding him through the darkness.

As he wandered silently through the house, Marcus allowed his mind to wander, replaying bits and pieces of their stolen moments together. He remembered her laughter, the throaty sound of her voice, the silken touch of her skin . . .

He paused, listening.

No, he was not mistaken. He heard the muffled sounds of crying. Tense, he walked cautiously toward the bedroom. With eyes now open, he could see the faint light of a fire dancing through the gap under the door. He turned the knob and stepped into the room. Elizabeth was there, seated in front of the grate. In much the same state as he was.

She was right—it was time to end the affair. He'd been a fool to press for one to begin with.

They were not meant to be lovers.

He couldn't think, could barely function, his work suffered along with his sleep. It was no way to carry on.

"Elizabeth," he called softly.

Her eyes flew open, and she brushed furiously at the wetness on her cheeks.

His heart softened. The crack in her shell was open wide and he could see the woman she hid so well, fragile and very much alone. He longed to go to her and offer the comfort she so obviously needed, but he knew her too well. She would have to come to him. Any overture on his part would only force her to flee. And he didn't want that. In fact, he couldn't bear the thought. He wanted to hold her, care for her. He wanted to be what she needed, if only just this once.

Saying nothing more, Marcus removed his clothing, his movements deliberately casual. He threw aside the counterpane and slipped into the bed. Then he watched her, waiting. As she did every night, she gathered his garments and folded them neatly. She was biding her time, collecting herself, and his chest tightened with his understanding.

When she came to him and presented her back, he said nothing, simply loosened her dress in response to her silent command. His cock twitched and then hardened as she shrugged out of it, revealing her body naked, as always, beneath. Sliding over, he allowed her the room to slip into the bed next to him, into his arms. Marcus tucked her against his chest and gazed at the gilt-framed landscape that hung above the mantel.

This is contentment, he thought.

Her face pressed against his chest, Elizabeth whispered, "It must end."

Marcus caressed the length of her spine with long soothing motions. "I know."

And as simple as that, their affair was over.

Marcus entered Lord Eldridge's offices a little past noon. Sinking into the worn leather chair in front of the desk, he waited for Eldridge to acknowledge him.

"Westfield."

"Lady Hawthorne was approached by St. John at the Marks-Darby ball last night," he said without preamble.

Gray eyes shot up to his. "Is she well?"

Marcus shrugged, his fingertips rubbing across the brass tacks along the arms. "By all outward appearances." Other than that he couldn't say. He'd been unable to coerce her into speaking about the subject. Despite his most passionate persuasion, she'd said not another word to him the rest of the night. "He knew of the book and the meeting in the park."

Eldridge pushed away from the massive desk. "A man matching St. John's description was treated for a bullet wound to the shoulder the same day."

Marcus released a deep breath. "So your assumptions about St. John's involvement in Lord Hawthorne's murder appear to be correct. Did the physician relate anything of value?"

"Nothing beyond the description." Eldridge stood, and stared out the window at the thoroughfare below. Framed by the dark green velvet of the curtains and the massive windows, the agency leader seemed smaller, more human and less legend. "I'm concerned for Lady Hawthorne's safety. To approach her at such a crowded event is an act of desperation. I would never have considered St. John would be so bold."

"I was surprised as well," Marcus admitted. "I intend to call on her now. Frankly, I'm afraid to leave her alone. St. John had a brooch of Elizabeth's, a piece she says Hawthorne had upon his person the night he was killed."

"So it's that way, is it?" Eldridge sighed. "The pirate has never lacked for boldness."

Marcus grit his teeth, remembering the vastly unpleasant encounters he'd had with St. John over the years. "Why do we tolerate him?"

"A reasonable question. I've often considered the alternative. However he is so popular I'm afraid his disappearance might make him a martyr. Hawthorne's work was a secret. We cannot reveal it, even to justify a criminal's death."

Cursing, Marcus stood.

"It chafes, Westfield, I know. But a public trial and hanging will do much to dispel his myth."

"You hope." He began to pace. "I've worked on the journal every day. The cryptic code changes with every paragraph, sometimes every sentence. I cannot find a pattern and I've learned nothing of value."

"Bring it to me. Perhaps I can be of assistance."

"I would rather continue my examination. I think I've learned enough to continue."

"Maintain a level head," Eldridge warned, turning around as Marcus growled low in his throat.

"When have I not?"

"Whenever Lady Hawthorne is involved. Perhaps she has information of import. Have you discussed any of this with her?"

Marcus sucked in his breath, not wanting to admit that he disliked talking about her marriage.

Eldridge sighed. "I had hoped it wouldn't come to this."

"I am the best agent to protect her," Marcus retorted.

"No, you are the worst, and I cannot tell you how it pains me to say so. Your emotional involvement is affecting this mission, just as I warned you it might."

"My personal affairs are my own business."

"And this agency is mine. I'm replacing you."

Marcus stopped and turned so swiftly the tails of his coat whipped about his thighs. "My services are required. Or have you forgotten? You have very few agents in the peerage."

Eldridge stood with both hands clasped behind his back. The somber tones of his garments and wig were matched by his grim features. "I admit, when you walked into my office that first time and knew what it is I do here, I was impressed. Brash, headstrong, certain your father would live forever and you could do as you pleased, you were perfect to send after St. John. The youthful delusion of immortality has never left you, Westfield. You still take risks others refuse. But never doubt there are more like you."

"Be assured, it has never once left my mind how expendable I am."

"Lord Talbot will take over."

Marcus shook his head and gave a wry, humorless laugh. "Talbot takes orders well enough, but he lacks initiative."

"He does not need initiative. He simply has to walk in your footsteps. He works well with Avery James, I've paired them often."

Cursing, Marcus spun on his heel and moved toward the door. "Replace me if you like. I won't leave her to the care of another."

"I am not giving you a choice, Westfield," Eldridge called after him.

Marcus slammed the door behind him. "I'm not giving you a choice either."

Marcus mounted his horse and headed straight to Chesterfield Hall. He'd planned to go there regardless, but now his need was more urgent. Elizabeth was certainly in the spirit of having nothing to do with him. He had to convince her otherwise and quickly. The affair was over, and good riddance. Now it was time to manage the rest of it.

He was immediately shown into the study where he forced himself to sit rather than pace in agitation. When the door opened behind him, he stood and turned with a charming smile for Elizabeth, only to scowl when he faced William.

"Westfield," came the terse greeting.

"Barclay."

"What do you want?"

Marcus blinked and then released a frustrated breath. Two steps forward and one back. "The same thing I want every time I call here. I wish to speak with Elizabeth."

"She does not wish to speak with you. In fact, she left specific instructions that you were no longer welcome."

"A moment of her time and all will be well, I assure you."
William snorted. "Elizabeth is gone."

"I will await her return, if you don't mind." He'd wait out by the street if he must. He had to talk with her before Eldridge did.

"No, you misunderstand. She has left Town."

"Beg your pardon?"

"She's gone. Packed up. Left. She came to her senses and realized what a cretin you are."

"She said that?"

"Well," William hedged. "I didn't actually speak with her, but Elizabeth mentioned her desire to leave London to her abigail this morning, although she left without the girl. Which is a good thing considering the mess she left behind."

Warning bells went off in Marcus's head. One of the many things he'd learned about Elizabeth in their short time together was that she was fastidiously tidy. Marcus strode toward the door. "Did she state her destination?"

"She mentioned only that she needed distance from you. Once she's calmed and sent word, I will go after her if she does not return on her own. This isn't the first time something you've done has goaded her into acting rashly."

"Show me to her rooms."

"Now see here, Westfield," William began, "I'm not lying to you. She's gone. I will see to her, as I always have."

"I will locate her boudoir myself, if I must," Marcus warned.

With a great deal of grumbling, cursing, and complaining, William led him upstairs to Elizabeth's suite of rooms. Marcus's gaze lifted from the rugs which were wildly askew and strewn with crushed flowers, to the armoire doors which were flung open and the contents scattered. Drawers were pulled out and the bed linens tossed about in a scene that came straight out of a nightmare.

"Seems she was in high temper," William said sheepishly.

"So it appears." Marcus kept his face impassive, but inside

his gut was clenched tight. He turned to the abigail. "How many of her garments did she take with her?"

The girl dipped a quick curtsy and replied, "None that I can tell, milord. But I've not finished yet."

Marcus wouldn't wait to find out. "Did she say anything of import to you?"

"No need to bark at the poor chit," William snapped.

Marcus raised a hand for silence and pinned the servant with his stare.

"Only that she was restless, milord, and eager to travel. She sent me into town on an errand and left whilst I was gone."

"Has she traveled without you often?"

The girl gave a jerky shake of her head. "It's the first time, milord."

"See how eager she was to flee you?" William asked grimly.

But Marcus paid him no mind. This was not the scene of a flared temper. Elizabeth's room had been ransacked.

And she was missing.

Chapter 11

"Sit down, Westfield," Eldridge ordered curtly. "Your frenzied pacing is driving me mad."

Marcus glared as he took a seat. "*I am* going mad. I need to know where Elizabeth is. God only knows the ordeal . . ." He choked, his throat too tight to speak.

Eldridge's normally stern features softened with sympathy. "You mentioned the outriders you assigned to her are gone as well. It's a good sign. Perhaps they were able to follow and will report her whereabouts when the opportunity presents itself."

"Or else they are dead," Marcus retorted. He stood and began pacing again.

Eldridge leaned back in his chair and steepled his fingers together. "I have agents checking all possible roads leading from Chesterfield Hall and questioning everyone who lives near enough to have seen or heard anything. Information is bound to surface."

"Time is a luxury we don't have," Marcus growled.

"Go home. Wait for word."

"I'll wait here."

"Your outriders may attempt to contact you. Perhaps they've already tried. You should return to your home. Keep yourself occupied. Pack and make preparations to leave."

The thought of a message waiting for him gave Marcus a sense of purpose. "Very well, but if you hear anything—"

"Anything at all, yes, I will send for you posthaste."

For the all too brief ride back to his home Marcus felt productive, but the moment he arrived and discovered nothing new had been reported his near ferocious agitation returned in full measure. With his family in residence, he could not give vent to his feelings, and was forced instead to retreat from their curious eyes.

He prowled the lengths of his galleries in his shirtsleeves, his skin damp with sweat, his heart racing as if he were running. Constant rubbing at the back of his neck left the skin raw, but he couldn't stop. The pictures in his mind . . . torturous thoughts of Elizabeth needing him . . . hurting . . . afraid . . .

His head fell back on a groan of pure anguish. He couldn't bear it. He wanted to yell, to snarl, to tear something apart.

An hour passed. And then another. Finally he could take the waiting no more. Marcus returned to his room, shrugged into his coats, and moved to the staircase, his intent to hunt St. John down. The pressure of his knife sheathed in his boot fueled his bloodlust. If Elizabeth were harmed in any way there would be no mercy.

Halfway down the stairs, he spotted his butler at the door and a moment later it opened, revealing one of the outriders. Covered in dust from his rapid return, the man waited in the foyer and bowed as Marcus's boot hit the marble floor.

"Where is she?"

"On the way to Essex, my lord."

Marcus froze. *Ravensend.* Seat of her late godfather, the Duke of Ravensend.

Elizabeth was running. Damn her.

He grabbed his packed valise, and turned to Paul who stood in the doorway of the study. "I will be in Essex."

"Is everything all right?" Paul asked.

"It will be shortly."

Within moments, Marcus was on the road.

The wheels of the Westfield travel coach crunched through the gravel on the final approach to Ravensend Manor before reaching the cobblestones that lined the circular driveway. The moon was high, its soft glow lighting the large manse and the small cottage beyond.

Marcus stepped down wearily and ordered his men to the livery. Turning away from the main house, he took rapid strides toward the cliff edge where the guesthouse and Elizabeth waited. He'd make his presence known to the duke in the morning.

The small residence was dark when he entered through the kitchen. He closed the door quietly, shutting out the rhythmic roar of the waves that battered the coast just a few yards away. Making his way through the house in darkness, Marcus checked every bedroom until he found Elizabeth.

Leaving his valise on the floor by the door, Marcus undressed silently and crawled into the bed next to her. She stirred at the feel of his cold skin beside hers.

"Marcus," she murmured, still fast asleep. She spooned into his chest, unconsciously sharing her warmth.

Despite his anger and frustration, he snuggled against her. Her trust while sleeping was telling. She had become accustomed to spending the nights next to him during the short duration of their affair.

He was still furious with her for running away, but his relief in finding her well and out of danger was foremost on his mind. Never again would he go through this torment. There could be no doubt that she was his. Not in Eldridge's mind, or hers.

Exhausted by worry, he buried his face in the sweetly scented curve of her shoulder and fell asleep.

*   *   *

Elizabeth woke and burrowed deeper into the warmth of the bed. Slowly rising to consciousness, she stretched out fully, her legs brushing along Marcus's hair-dusted calf.

With a sudden flare of awareness, she sat upright and shot a startled glance at the pillow beside her. Marcus slept peacefully on his stomach, the sheet and counterpane straddling his hips, leaving his muscular back exposed.

She jumped out of the bed as if it were on fire.

His eyes opened sleepily, his lips curving in a languid smile, and then he fell back asleep, obviously finding her angered surprise to be of no danger.

Grabbing her clothes, Elizabeth retreated to the next room to dress, wondering how he'd found her so quickly. She'd deliberately avoided any of her own family holdings so that it would be difficult, if not impossible to locate her. But Marcus had found her before even a day had passed.

Furious and flustered at finding him in her bed, Elizabeth left the house and made her way to the roped path on the cliffs that led to the beach below.

She picked her way carefully down the somewhat steep and rocky decline. The cliff rose some distance above the shore and Elizabeth ignored the stunning view in favor of studying the ground at her feet. She didn't mind the concentration it took. Instead she relished the temporary distraction from her confusion.

Finally reaching the beach, she dropped onto the damp sand and hugged her knees to her chest. She prayed for the sound of the waves lapping on the beach to soothe her.

She vividly recalled the first moment she'd laid eyes on Marcus Ashford, then the Viscount Sefton. She remembered how her breath had caught in her throat and how hot her skin had suddenly become, how her breathing and heart rate had quickened until she thought she might swoon. Those had not been singular reactions. She had felt them many times since then and even just that morning when he had smiled at her, all sleep-tousled masculine beauty.

She couldn't live like that, couldn't see how anyone could live consumed by a lust that seemed insatiable. Unschooled as she was, she hadn't known a body could crave the touch of another the way it did food or air. Now, finally, she understood an inkling of the hunger her father must feel every day. Without her mother he would always be ravenous, always searching for something that could appease the emptiness left by her loss.

Tilting her head, Elizabeth closed her eyes and rested her cheek against her knees.

Why couldn't Marcus simply stay away?

Marcus paused on the small porch and took in his surroundings. The bite of the salty morning air was sharp. He wondered if Elizabeth had collected a wrap before venturing out. To say she'd looked horrified to discover him in her bed would be an understatement. Knowing her as he did, he suspected she'd run out without forethought.

Where the devil had she gone?

"She's gone down to the beach, Westfield," came a dry tone to his left. Marcus turned his head to greet the Duke of Ravensend.

"Your Grace." He dipped his head in a bow. "It was my intent to present myself this morn and explain my presence. I trust you don't find my stay an imposition."

The duke led a black stallion by the reins and came to a halt directly before him. They were of an age, His Grace being the youngest after four older sisters, but Marcus was nearly a head taller. "Of course not. It's been too long since we last exchanged words. Walk with me."

Unable to refuse, Marcus reluctantly left the shadow of the guesthouse.

"Watch the horse," the duke cautioned. "He's a biter."

Heeding the warning, Marcus took the opposite side. "How fares Lady Ravensend?" he asked as they fell into step. He cast a longing glace over his shoulder at the roped path that led to the beach.

"Better than you. I thought you wiser than to chase more abuse. But I concede the appeal. Lady Hawthorne remains one of the most beautiful women I've ever had the fortune to cross paths with. I fancied her myself. As did most peers."

Nodding grimly, Marcus kicked a pebble out of his path.

"I wonder who she'll take up with once she's finished with you? Hodgeham, perhaps? Or Stanton again? A young one, I'm certain. She's as wild as this brute." The duke gestured to his horse.

Marcus grit his teeth. "Stanton is a friend in the chastest sense of the word and Hodgeham . . ." He snorted in disgust. "Hodgeham couldn't manage her."

"And you can?"

"Better than any other man."

"You should marry her then. Or perhaps that's your intent. Either you or some other poor chap. You leapt into that cage once before."

"She has no wish to marry again."

"She will," Ravensend said with a confident nod. "She has no children. When she's of the mind, she'll pick someone."

Marcus came to an abrupt stop. Eldridge, William, and now Ravensend. He'd be damned if another individual meddled in his affairs. "Pardon me, Your Grace."

He spun on the heel of his boot and made rapid strides toward the roped walk. He would put a stop to all their intrusions once and for all.

Elizabeth prowled the coastline restlessly, picking up small pebbles and stones along the way. She tossed them over the water, trying to skip them and failing miserably. William had once spent an entire afternoon attempting to teach her how to skip rocks. Although she'd never acquired the skill, the repetitive swing of her arm was calming. The music of the English coastline—the lapping waves and the cries of seagulls—brought her a measure of peace from her fevered thoughts.

"A calm surface is required, love," came the deeply luxurious voice behind her.

With shoulders squared, she turned to face her tormenter.

Dressed casually in a worn sweater and wool breeches, Marcus had never looked more virile, the roughness of his edges unblunted by any social veneer. His hair was tied back at his nape, but the salty breeze tugged the silken strands free and blew them softly across his handsome face.

Just looking at him made her feel like crying.

"You shouldn't have come," she told him.

"I had no choice."

"Yes, you did. If you had any sense you would allow this . . ." She gestured wildly. ". . . thing between us to die out gracefully, instead of dragging it out to its inevitable bad end."

"Damn you." A muscle in his jaw ticked as he took a step toward her. "Damn you to hell for throwing away what exists between us as if it does not signify. Risking your life—"

Her hands clenched into fists at his wounded tone. "I took the outriders with me."

"The only bit of sense you've shown since I met you."

"You are a bully! You have been from the first. Seducing, scheming, and manipulating me however you wish. Go back to London, Lord Westfield, and find another woman's life to ruin."

Turning from him, Elizabeth stalked toward the cliffs. Marcus caught her arm as she attempted to pass, pulling her to a stop. She struggled with a frightened cry, alarmed by the possessiveness of his gaze.

"I was content before you came along. My life was simple and orderly. I want that back. I don't want you."

He thrust her away with such force she stumbled. "Regardless, you have me."

She hurried toward the rope-lined path. "As you wish. *I shall leave.*"

"Craven," he drawled after her.

Eyes wide, Elizabeth turned to face him again. Like the time he'd asked her to dance at the Morelands', his emerald eyes sparkled with challenge. This time though, she would not be goaded into acting foolishly.

"Perhaps," she admitted, lifting her chin. "You frighten me. Your determination, your recklessness, your passion. Everything about you scares the wits from me. It's not how I wish to live my life."

His chest expanded on a deep breath. Behind him the waves continued to beat upon the shore, the relentless driving rhythm no longer soothing. It urged her to flee. *Run. Run far away.* She took a backward step.

"Give me a fortnight," he said quickly. "You and I alone, here in the guesthouse. Live with me, as my partner."

"Why?" she asked, startled.

His arms crossed his chest. "I intend to wed you."

"*What?*" Suddenly dizzy, Elizabeth backed away with hand to throat. Tripping on her skirts, she fell to her knees. "You've gone mad," she cried.

His mouth curved in a bitter smile. "It seems so, yes."

Her breath coming in unsteady pants, Elizabeth leaned forward, her fingers sinking into the damp sand. She didn't look at him. She couldn't. "Whatever made you conceive of such a ridiculous notion? You've no wish to marry, nor do I."

"Not true. I must wed. And you and I suit."

She swallowed hard, her stomach roiling. "Physically, perhaps. But lust fades. In no time at all you'll grow weary of a wife and seek your pleasures elsewhere."

"If you are equally bored, you won't be disturbed."

Furious, she grabbed handfuls of sand and threw them at his chest. "Go to hell!"

He laughed, shaking out his sweater with maddening nonchalance. "Jealousy is a possessive emotion, love. You'll have to wed me if you want the right to feel that way."

Elizabeth searched his face, looking for deceit and found nothing but cool impassivity. His face, so breathtaking, revealed nothing of his thoughts. The determined line of his jaw, however, was achingly familiar. "I don't wish to marry again."

"Consider the benefits." Marcus held out his hand and ticked off with his fingers. "Elevated rank. Great wealth. I will afford you the same independence you enjoyed with Hawthorne. And you'll have me in your bed, a prospect you should find vastly appealing."

"Conceited rogue. Allow us to discuss the negatives as well. You thrive on danger. You are eager to die. And you're too bloody damn arrogant."

Grinning, he held out his hand and helped her to her feet. "I ask for a fortnight to change your mind. If I cannot, I'll leave you in peace and never bother you again. I'll resign from this mission and another agent will protect you."

She shook her head. "The situation here is far different than our life would be under normal circumstances. There is little danger for you around here."

"True," he admitted. "But perhaps I can make the rest of your life so pleasant that my work with Eldridge will be of less consequence."

"Impossible!"

"A fortnight," he urged. "It's all I ask. You owe me that much, at least."

"No." The gleam in his eye could not be mistaken. "I know what you want."

Marcus met her gaze squarely. "I won't touch you. I swear it."

"You lie."

His brow rose. "You doubt I can restrain myself? I shared a bed with you last night and didn't make love to you. I assure you, I have control over my baser needs."

Elizabeth chewed her lower lip, weighing her options. To be free of him forever . . .

"You will find another room?" she asked.

"Yes."

"You promise not to make any advances?"

"I promise." His mouth curved wickedly. "When you want me, you'll have to ask me."

She bristled at his arrogance. "What do you hope to accomplish by this?"

He came toward her and when he spoke, his voice was tender. "We already know you enjoy me in your bed. I intend to prove you will enjoy having me in the rest of your life as well. I'm not always so tiresome. In fact, some would say I'm quite pleasant."

"Why me?" she asked plaintively, her hand sheltering her racing heart. "Why marriage?"

Marcus shrugged. "'The time is right' would be the simplest answer. I enjoy your company, despite how often you are obstinate and disagreeable."

When she shook her head, he frowned. "You said yes once before."

"That was before I knew about the agency."

His tone deepened, became cajoling. "Don't you wish to manage your own household again? Wouldn't you like to have children? Build a family? Surely you don't wish to be alone forever."

Startled, she stared at him with wide eyes. Marcus Ashford discussing children? The longing that washed over her so unexpectedly scared her to death.

"You want an heir." She looked away to hide her reaction.

"I want you. The heir and other progeny would be added delights."

Her eyes flew to meet his again. Flustered by his nearness and his determination, Elizabeth turned toward the path in the cliffs.

"Do we have an agreement?" he called after her, remaining behind.

"Yes," she threw over her shoulder, her voice carried by the wind. "A fortnight, then you are out of my life."

His satisfaction was a palpable thing and she ran from it.

Elizabeth reached the top of the cliff and fell to her knees. *Marriage.* The word choked her throat and made her dizzy, leaving her panting for air like a swimmer too long under water. Marcus's will was a force to be reckoned with. What the devil was she to do now that he'd set his mind on marriage again?

Lifting her head, she looked toward the livery with aching longing. It would be such a relief to go, to leave the turmoil behind.

But she discarded the idea. Marcus would come for her, he would track her down as long as she still wanted him. And no matter how hard she tried, she was unable to hide the depth and breadth of her attraction.

Therefore, the only way to be rid of his attentions was to accept the bargain he offered. Marcus would have to end his pursuit of his own accord. There was no other way the obstinate man would quit.

Wearily resolved, Elizabeth stood and made her way toward the guesthouse. She would have to move carefully. He knew her too well. The slightest intimation that she was uneasy and he would pounce, pressing his advantage with his customary ruthlessness. She would have to be relaxed and indifferent. It was the only solution.

Satisfied she had a reasonable plan of action, she quickened her pace.

Meanwhile, Marcus lingered on the beach and wondered at his sanity. God help him, he wanted her still. Wanted her more than before. He'd once hoped to satisfy his need and finally be done with her. Now he prayed his aching need would never end, the pleasure was too great to forfeit.

If only he'd known the trap that awaited him in her arms. But there had been no way to know. With all his experience, he still could never have imagined the searing rapture of Elizabeth's bed or the ever-growing need he had to tame her and pin her beneath him, as lost to his desire as he was.

Picking up a rock from the pile Elizabeth left behind, he tossed it into the water. He'd created quite a challenge for himself. Her one vulnerability had always been their desire for each other. Naked and sated, Elizabeth was soft and open to discussion. Now he was denied seduction to achieve his ends. He would have to woo her like a gentleman, something he'd never managed even the first time.

But should he succeed, he would thwart Eldridge's plan to replace him and prove to one and all that Elizabeth was his. There would be no doubt.

Marriage. He shuddered. It had finally happened. The woman had driven him insane.

"I want to see where you're taking me."

"No," Marcus whispered in her ear, steadying her with his hands on her shoulders. "It would not be a surprise if you knew."

"I'm not fond of surprises," Elizabeth complained.

"Well, you will have to become accustomed, sweet, because I am full of them."

She snorted and he laughed, his heart as light as the afternoon breeze. "Ah, love. Much as you wish it weren't so, you adore me."

Her lush mouth curved in a smile, the ends of her lips touching the underside of the blindfold that blocked her vision. "Your conceit knows no bounds."

She shrieked as he hefted her into the air, and then sank to his knees. He set her down on the blanket he'd spread earlier and removed her blindfold, watching expectantly as she blinked against the sudden bright light.

With the help of the duke's staff, he'd arranged a picnic, selecting a field of wild grass just over the rise from the main manor. She'd been unnaturally tense since their talk on the beach that morning and he knew something unexpected was warranted if he wished to make headway.

"This is lovely," she exclaimed, her eyes wide and filled with pleasure. Sans the assistance of an abigail and unwilling to let him help her dress, Elizabeth was forced to attire herself in a startlingly simple gown. With her hair uncoiffed and tied back from her face, there was nothing to compete with the singular beauty of her features.

Basking in the glow of her surprise, Marcus silently agreed with her sentiment. Elizabeth was breathtaking, her fine features lovingly shielded by the wide brim of her straw hat.

Smiling, he reached into the basket and withdrew a bottle of wine. He filled a glass and handed it to her, the touch of her fingers against his sending a frisson of awareness up his spine.

"I'm pleased you approve," he murmured. "It's only my second attempt at formal courtship." His gaze lifted to hers. "I'm a bit nervous, truth be told."

"You?" She arched a brow.

"Yes, love." Marcus lay on his back and stared up at the summer sky. "It's distressing to think I may be refused. I was more confident the first time around."

Elizabeth laughed, a soft joyful sound that brought a smile to his face. "You shall find another, far more suitable candidate. A young woman who will worship your remarkable handsomeness and charm, and be far more biddable."

"I would never marry a woman such as you describe. I much prefer passionate, uneven-tempered seductresses like yourself."

"I am not a seductress!" she protested, and he laughed with delight.

"You certainly were the other evening. The way you arched your brow and bit your lip before fucking me senseless. I vow, I've never seen anything as seductive. And the way you look when you—"

"Tell me about your family," she interrupted, her cheeks flushing. "How are Paul and Robert?"

He glanced sidelong at her, relishing the view of her against the natural backdrop, freed from the constraints of society. The tall grass around them flowed like waves of water in the gentle breeze, filling the air with the scent of warm earth and salty sea. "They are well. They inquire about you, as does my mother."

"Do they? I am surprised, but pleased they don't resent me overmuch. They should venture out more. It has been almost a fortnight since they arrived, and yet they've not attended one social function."

"Robert still has no interest whatsoever in social pursuits. Paul prefers his club. He spends most of his time there. And my mother has to order new gowns every Season, and refuses to be seen until they are finished." His grin was fond. "Heaven forbid that she be seen in a gown from last year."

She smiled. "Is Robert still the spitting image of you?"

"So I've been told."

"You don't think so?"

"No. The resemblance is there, but no more than one would expect. And Paul remains as different from me as you are from your brother." He reached for her hand and linked his fingers with hers, needing the physical connection. She tugged, but he held fast. "You will see for yourself soon enough."

She wrinkled her nose. "You seem quite confident in your ability to win my hand."

"I cannot think otherwise. Now tell me you wrote Barclay about your location."

"Yes, of course. He would be frantic, and unbearable company for Margaret if I had not."

They lapsed into silence and Marcus enjoyed their rare accord, content to experience the daylight hours with her.

"What are you contemplating so seriously?" he asked after a time.

"My mother." She sighed. "William says she loved the coast. We used to visit here often and play in the sand. He tells stories of her lifting the hem of her skirts and dancing across the beach with our father."

"You don't remember?"

Her fingers tightened fractionally on his and lifting her glass, she took a large swallow of wine. Her gaze moved to the distant cliffs and her voice, when it came, was soft and faraway. "Sometimes I think I recall her scent or the tone of her voice, but I cannot be certain."

"I'm sorry," he soothed, rubbing his thumb across the back of her hand.

She sighed. "Perhaps it's for the best that she's only a fleeting impression. William remembers her, and it saddens him. It's why he's so protective, I think. Her illness progressed so quickly, it took us all by surprise. My father especially."

There was an unusual edge to Elizabeth's voice when she referred to her father. Marcus rolled to his side and rested his head in his hand, maintaining his casual pose while studying her intently. "Your father never remarried."

She returned his gaze, a small frown marring the space between her brows. "He loved my mother too much to ever take another wife. He still loves her."

Marcus considered the Earl of Langston's libidinous reputation. This in turn led him to consider his own dislike of romantic entanglements.

"Tell me about your father," he urged, curious. "As often as I've spoken with him, I still know precious little about him."

"You are probably better acquainted with him than I. My resemblance to my mother is painful, so he avoids me. I often think he would have been best served by never falling in love. Lord knows the sentiment brought him precious little happiness and a lifetime of regret."

There was a sadness in her eyes and a firmness to her lips that betrayed her distress. He wanted to pull her into his arms and comfort her, so he did just that, rising to a seated position and pulling her against his chest. Tossing aside the obtrusive hat, he pressed a kiss to her neck and breathed in her scent. Together, they faced the ocean.

"I worried about my mother when my father passed on," Marcus murmured, his hands caressing the length of her arms. "I was not certain she could live without him. Like your parents, mine also had a love match. But she is a strong woman and she recovered. While she most likely won't marry again, my mother has found contentment without a spouse."

"So have I," Elizabeth said softly.

Reminders of how she didn't need him would not benefit his cause. He had to win her before she learned of Eldridge's decision. Reluctantly pulling away, Marcus removed her glass from stiff fingers and topped it up. "Are you hungry?"

Elizabeth nodded, obviously relieved. Then she gave him a dazzling smile that made his breath catch and his blood heat.

At that moment, he knew. She was his, and he would protect her. Whatever the cost.

A cold tingle crawled up his spine as he remembered the sight of her ransacked room. What would have happened if she'd been home? Clenching his jaw, he vowed to never find out.

Marriage seemed a small price to pay to keep her safe.

Chapter 12

"The servants from the main house brought supper."
Elizabeth looked up from Hawthorne's journal to see
Marcus lounging in the doorway. With a sigh, she snapped
the book closed and pushed aside the blanket she had wrapped
around her legs. Rising from the chaise, she took the arm he
offered her. Once they were seated in the small formal dining
room, he tucked into his veal with his usual fervor.

She watched him with a soft smile. Marcus's appetite for
life amazed her. He did nothing in half measure.

"I suppose the outriders told you my destination," she said
dryly.

"Which is another reason we should wed," he replied
around a bite. "You are a troublesome baggage. You require
a great deal of watching over."

"I am perfectly capable of taking care of myself."

He frowned, his gaze piercing beneath his drawn brows.
"Your room was ransacked after your departure, Elizabeth."

"Beg your pardon?" The color drained from her face.

His mouth twisted grimly. "You look as I felt when I saw
it. I thought you had been kidnapped." He lifted his knife
and shook it at her. "Don't ever scare me like that again."

Elizabeth barely registered his words. Her room. *Ransacked.*
"Was anything missing?" she whispered.

"I'm not certain." Marcus set aside his utensils. "If anything is amiss, I'll replace it."

Bristling at the offer, which was entirely too proprietary, Elizabeth was struck with a terrifying thought. "William? Margaret?"

"Everyone is well," he soothed, his features softening.

"William must know about the journal, then?"

"Your brother assumed it was your doing, that I had driven you into a rage. He knows nothing more."

Her hand to her chest, Elizabeth tried to imagine what the scene must have looked like. "All of my things sorted through." She shuddered. "Why did you not tell me earlier?"

"You were already distressed, love."

"Of course I'm distressed, it's too dreadful."

"You've every right to feel violated. I thank God you weren't home at the time. Although that's not encouragement for you to run off whenever the urge strikes you."

"Sometimes a respite is a necessity," she retorted, her palms damp with her unease and disquiet.

"How well I know it," he murmured, reminding her of how he'd left England after her marriage. "But I need to know where you are, every minute of every hour."

Flustered by his news and stung by guilt she snapped, "*You* are why I need respite!"

Marcus heaved a clearly frustrated breath. "Eat," he ordered.

She stuck her tongue out at him, then gulped down her wine in an effort to warm the chill within her.

They finished the rest of the meal in silence, both absorbed in their own thoughts. Afterwards, they retired to the front parlor. Elizabeth resumed perusing the journal while Marcus took off his boots and began to polish them.

Using the book to hide behind, she watched him engaged in his task, the light from the fireplace casting a golden halo around him. As the powerful muscles of his shoulders shifted with his exertions, Elizabeth felt a familiar longing spread

through her. She couldn't help but be reminded of his powerful body flexing over and inside hers, dissolving her will in
decadent pleasure. After years of equanimity, she was inun-
dated with feelings too strong to control.

With great effort, she returned her attention to the journal,
but the endless pages of code were unable to engage her mind.

Shifting in his chair, Marcus was achingly aware of Elizabeth's heated gaze. He wished he could lift his head and return it, but she would be embarrassed to be caught staring
and that would destroy the comfortable silence they were
sharing. Rubbing furiously over the worn leather of his boots,
he stealthily perused her.

Dressed like a peasant, she lay on the chaise with her legs
curled up beside her and covered with a blanket. Her hair was
unbound as it had been all day. He loved her hair. He loved to
touch it and wrap it around his fist. Soft and unfettered in clothing and demeanor, Elizabeth aroused him just by breathing.

He smiled in spite of himself. As always, he was both
soothed and excited by her presence. The world could go to
hell around them and he would pay no mind, tucked away
with no servants, no family. Just the two of them.

In separate beds.

Christ. He was certifiable.

Elizabeth shut the journal with a soft thump. Lifting his
head, he gazed at her expectantly. Desire coursed through his
veins when he saw her eyes, dark and melting. Hope welled.
She wanted him.

"I believe I'll retire," she told him, her voice husky.

He took a deep breath to hide his painful disappointment.
"So early?"

"I'm tired."

"Goodnight, then," he said, his voice studiously nonchalant as he returned his attention to his boots.

Elizabeth paused in the doorway, and watched Marcus for
a moment, hoping he would break his word and ravish her. But

he ignored her. His attention was fixed entirely on his task as it had been for the last hour. She might as well not have been there. "Goodnight," she said finally before drifting down the hallway to her room.

Pressing her back against the door, she closed it with a sharp click. She stripped and dressed in her night rail, then climbed into bed. Closing her eyes, she willed herself to sleep.

But oblivion was elusive. Her mind jumped from one lascivious thought to the next, remembering the coarseness of Marcus's callused palms as they caressed her skin, the feel of his strength over her, and the sound of his guttural cries as he reached his climax within her. Knowing he was hers for the asking and yet depriving herself was driving her mad.

Groaning into her pillow, she wished desperately for her body to cease its throbbing, but she couldn't forget Marcus, who sat by the fire, breathtakingly virile. Her skin became too tight, too hot . . . her breasts heavy and swollen, her nipples puckered tight and aching.

He'd come to her every night, sated her hunger long enough to make it through the brief hours until she could have him again. Now it had been two days and she was starved for his touch and the caress of his mouth. She tossed and turned, her movements making her hot. She threw back the covers, her skin and hair damp with sweat, her thighs squeezed tight in an attempt to dull the emptiness there.

Marriage. The man was mad. When he tired of her he would dally and she would lie at home, as she was doing now, and burn for him.

Damn him to perdition! She could do without him, didn't need him. She cupped her breasts in her hands and squeezed, a low moan escaping at the sudden flare of heat between her legs. Embarrassed and knowing it was wrong, she still couldn't prevent rolling her nipples between her fingertips and imagining it was Marcus. Her back arched, her legs spread against her will, her body desperate for the nightly fucking it had grown addicted to.

Near desperation, her hand moved down her torso and slipped between her legs. Her own juices coated her fingers as she found the source of her torment. Her head tilted back and she cried out softly, determined to find her own relief.

The door flew open with such force it slammed against the wall. Startled, she screamed and sat upright.

Marcus stood in the doorway in silent fury, a single taper held aloft in his hand. "Stubborn, contrary, maddening wench! I can hear you," he growled, striding into the room as if he had every right to. "You would punish us both rather than admit the truth."

"Get out!" she yelled, mortified to be caught in such a compromising position.

He set the taper on the nightstand and snatched up her hand, lifting it to his nose. His eyes closed and he breathed in the scent of her sex. Then he parted his lips and suckled her fingertips.

Eyes wide, Elizabeth whimpered as the hot velvet of his tongue swirled around and between her fingers, lapping her cream. Relief flooded her, making her limp and pliant. Thank God he'd come for her. She couldn't have borne another moment without his touch, his scent . . .

"Here." He shoved her wet fingers unceremoniously between her legs.

"Wh-what are you doing?" she asked breathlessly, yanking her hand to her waist to clutch at her night rail.

In the light of the candle and backlit by the fire in the grate, Marcus looked like Mephistopheles himself, austere and filled with a palpable dark energy. There was no softness to him, no seduction, just a silent irrefutable command. "Finding the relief you've refused me."

He tore open the placket of his breeches and pulled out the magnificent length of his cock. Elizabeth's mouth watered at the sight of it. Hard and thick, it pulsed with starkly etched veins. Her legs spread wider in invitation.

Marcus tilted his head arrogantly. "You shall have to ask

ASK FOR IT 151

me, if you want this." His hand gripped at the root and stroked to the tip.

She groaned her anguish. He was merciless. Why couldn't he simply take what he wanted?

"You want me to take you," he said hoarsely, all the while holding his cock out to her like a gift. "You want me to take the decision from you, so there will be no guilt. Well, I won't, love. You set the rules and I gave my word."

"Bastard!"

"Witch," he threw back at her. "Tempting me, offering me heaven with one hand while taking it away with the other." He pumped his hand and a drop of cum beaded the tip of his erection.

"Must you always have your way?" she whispered, trying to collect how she could want him and hate him with equal ardor.

"Must you always deny me?" he retorted, his voice low and deep, brushing across her skin like rough silk.

Elizabeth curled into a ball and turned away from him . . . and a second later was flipped onto her back and dragged to the end of the mattress, kicking and screaming. "You are a brute!"

He bent over her with hands on either side of her head, the silky smooth head of his erection pressing into her thigh. His emerald eyes narrowed and burned. "You will lie here with your legs spread while I take my pleasure." Thrusting along her thigh, Marcus teased her with what she desired, leaving a trail of wetness behind. "If you move or otherwise attempt to evade me, I will tie you down."

Furious, Elizabeth lifted her hips and almost caught him. He slipped into her for a moment, just the tip, and she gasped with relief.

He pulled away with a curse. "If my goal were less worthy, I'd fuck you properly. Lord knows you need it."

"I hate you!" Tears welled and slid down her temples, yet still her body ached for him. If her pride meant any less to her she'd be begging.

"I'm certain you wish you did."

With far from gentle hands, he arranged her to his liking on a pile of pillows. Elizabeth found her hips on the edge of the bed, her legs hanging down the side and spread as wide as comfort would allow. She was completely exposed from the waist down, her glistening sex displayed in the candlelight. As always, Marcus held all the power and left her with nothing.

Her gaze rose to his face, and then traveled the length of his body, watching the play of muscles across his powerful torso as he moved. Curling his long fingers around his cock, Marcus swirled his hand down the length of his shaft, his strokes fluid and graceful despite his obvious lust. His heavy sac was tight and hard, his gaze locked between her thighs.

She lay motionless, arrested by the sight of him. She'd never witnessed anything so erotic in her life, could never have imagined it. One would think a person would be vulnerable in such a pose, and yet Marcus stood proudly, his stance wide for support as he pleasured himself. In an effort to see him better she tried to sit up, but his hands stilled.

"Stay where you are," he ordered tersely as he squeezed the engorged head of his cock in his fist. "Put your heels on the mattress."

Elizabeth licked her lips and the gesture made him groan. She lifted her legs as he'd demanded and watched a flush creep over the crests of his cheekbones. His pupils dilated, the brilliant emerald retreating until it was only a faint rim around the black.

It was then she realized that the power was hers. She so often forgot how he craved her, how he had always craved her, taking his harsh words as the truth when his every action belied what he said. Filled with renewed confidence, she spread her legs wider. His lips parted on a hiss of air. She plucked her nipples and he moaned. All the while she watched his hands, pumping his cock with a strength that looked painful, but gave him obvious pleasure. Her hands wandered down her torso toward her sex and his motions became more urgent.

She felt the moisture leaking between her legs and she dipped her fingers inside. Marcus growled. Elizabeth wondered if he knew she was there or if she was merely an inspiring view.

"*Elizabeth.*"

Her name was a tormented cry from his lips as he spurted, his hot seed splashing in creamy bursts through her fingers and mingling with her own arousal. Startled by the stunning intimacy, she shivered and came, her neck arching back into the pillows with a gasping breath.

Feeling wicked and wonderful and some other warm emotion she couldn't name because she'd never felt it before, she slipped her fingers into her mouth and sucked the tangy saltiness of his release.

Marcus stood for a moment watching her with eyes so heated her cheeks flushed. Then he moved behind the screen and she heard him pour water from the pitcher and wash his hands. With breeches fastened he returned to her and cleansed his release from her stomach and thighs. She moaned at his touch, arching into his hand. He bent and pressed a firm, quick kiss to her forehead.

"I shall be next door, if you want me."

And he made his egress without another word or even a backward glance.

She stared at the closed portal with mouth agape and waited. Surely he would return? He couldn't be finished. The man was insatiable.

But he didn't return, and she refused to grovel for his attentions.

Sweating under the covers, but too cold without them, Elizabeth gave up trying to sleep a few hours before dawn. She pulled her cloak around her and returned to the parlor.

Marcus had banked the fire in the hearth, but the room was still warm. Tucking the chaise blanket around her feet, she picked up the journal, hoping it would bore her to sleep.

* * *

The sun was just beginning to light the sky when Marcus discovered Elizabeth fast asleep with Hawthorne's journal open on her lap. He shook his head and grimaced.

One sleepless night passed, thirteen left to survive.

Confused by his soul-deep disquiet, he tugged on his boots and left the small residence. He crossed the circular cobblestone drive that swung by both the main manse and the house he shared with Elizabeth, and headed toward the stables beyond. Below the cliff face he heard the rhythmic roaring of the waves upon the shore and felt the misty breeze as it swelled over the ledge and permeated his sweater. Once inside the warmth of the stables he sucked in the scent of sweet hay and horseflesh, such a stark contrast to the salty bite of the air outdoors.

He bridled one of his carriage bays and led the gelding out of the stall. With a singular determination to work himself to exhaustion so he could sleep at night, Marcus set to the task of grooming his horses. As the heat of his exertions made him sweat, he discarded his sweater in favor of comfort. Lost in thoughts of the night before and the remembrance of Elizabeth displayed erotically in the candlelight, he was startled by a gasp behind him.

Turning about swiftly, he faced the winsome lass who delivered their meals. "Milord," she said, dipping a quick curtsy.

Eyeing the groomsmen's quarters behind her, he quickly deduced her worry. "Don't fret," he assured her. "I've been known to be dumb and blind on occasion."

The servant studied him with obvious curiosity, her appreciative gaze taking in his bare chest. Surprised to find himself a bit flustered by a woman's sensual perusal, Marcus turned to retrieve his sweater. As his hand closed around the garment, which was slung over the nearest stall, the temperamental beast inside had the temerity to bite him.

Cursing, Marcus snatched back the injured appendage and glared at the duke's stallion.

"'e's a bit testy that one," the girl said with sympathy. She reached his side and held out a rag, which Marcus accepted quickly and wrapped around his hand to staunch the trickle of blood.

The girl was a pretty thing with soft brown curls and passion-flushed cheeks. Her dress was disheveled, betraying her recent activities, but her smile was genuine and filled with good humor. Marcus was about to return that smile when the stable door slammed open, startling his horse who then side-stepped anxiously, knocking Marcus into the servant and tumbling them both to the floor.

"You rutting beast!"

Marcus lifted his head from the girl's shoulder and met a violet gaze of such fury he couldn't breathe for a moment. Elizabeth stood with her hands on her hips in the stable doorway.

"I wouldn't wed you for any reason!" she shouted, before spinning in a swirl of skirts and running away.

"Christ." Marcus leapt to his feet and then yanked the servant girl to hers. Without another word, he was in pursuit, rushing past the gaping, sleep-mussed groomsman and out to the rapidly lightening dawn.

Elizabeth, a woman well accustomed to physical exertion, was several feet ahead of him and he lengthened his stride.

"Elizabeth!"

"To hell with you," she yelled back.

Her pace was frantic and her path too close to the cliff's edge for Marcus's comfort. His heart racing madly in his chest, he leapt, tackling her and twisting to land on his bare back. Small rocks and the coarse wild grass cut at his back as he slid some distance in the morning dew, Elizabeth's squirming body clutched tightly to his.

"Stop it," he growled, rolling to pin her beneath him and deflecting her flailing fists.

"Constancy is beyond you, you horrid man." Her face, so heartrendingly perfect, was flushed and tearstained.

"It's not what you think!"

"You were half dressed atop a woman!"

"A mishap, nothing more." He pinned her arms above her head to prevent sustaining any further injury. Despite the chill of the morning, the pain of his back and hand, and the consternation that drew his brows together, he was still intensely aware of the woman who thrashed beneath him.

"A mishap you were caught." Elizabeth turned her head and bit his bicep. Marcus roared and shoved his knee between her legs, sinking betwixt them intimately.

"Bite me again and I will turn you over my knee."

"Spank me again and I'll shoot you," she retorted.

Having no other notion of what to do, he lowered his head and captured her lips, his tongue slipping briefly inside before he yanked his head back from her snapping teeth.

He snarled. "If you worry so much about my fidelity you should ensure it."

Her mouth fell open. "Of all the arrogant utterances."

"Selfish wench. You don't want me, but God forbid if any other woman does."

"Another woman can have you, with my pity!"

He pressed his forehead to hers and muttered, "That chit is dallying with one of the groomsmen. You spooked my horse and caused a tumble."

"I don't believe you. Why was she standing so close to you?"

"I was injured." Marcus held her wrists with one hand and displayed his makeshift bandage. "She was attempting to assist me."

Frowning, but softening, Elizabeth asked, "Why are you bare-chested?"

"It was hot, love." Marcus shook his head at her disbelieving snort. "I'll present the libidinous parties to you for a confession."

A tear slid down her temple. "I will never trust you," she breathed.

He brushed his lips across hers. "More the reason to wed me. I vow marriage to you would exhaust any man into finding the female gender unappealing."

"That was cruel." She sniffled.

"I'm frustrated, Elizabeth," he admitted gruffly, the soft pressure of her curves under his only exacerbating his discomfort. "What more must I do to win you? Could you give me some clue? Some inkling of the length of the road left to travel?"

Her reddened eyes met his. "Why won't you cease? Lose interest? Seek the attentions of someone else?"

Marcus sighed, resigned to the miserable truth. "I cannot."

The fight left her tense body with a silent sob.

He hugged her tighter. She looked as he did—tired, unhappy. Neither one of them was getting any sleep, tossing and turning, craving each other. Physically they were so close, shut off from the world and alone together, and yet the distance between them seemed unending.

For the first time since he'd met her, Marcus conceded that perhaps they weren't meant for each other.

"Do you . . . Do you have a mistress?" she asked suddenly.

Stunned by the quick change of topic, he blurted, "Yes."

Her mouth quivered against his cheek. "I won't share you."

"I wouldn't make that request of you," he promised.

"You must rid yourself of her."

He pulled back. "I intend to make her my wife."

Elizabeth lifted her eyes to his.

"Vexing wench." He rubbed his nose against hers. "I've

barely the energy required to pursue you. Think you I have the wherewithal to chase other skirts?"

"I need time to think, Marcus."

"You have it," he promised quickly. The hope that was near dying flared again.

She pressed her lips to his throat and gave a shaky sigh. "Very well then. I'll consider your address."

Chapter 13

Elizabeth paced the length of her bed. The drapes at the windows were open, as they had been since the third night of her stay, and the pearlescent light of the moon lit the path she paced. There was no point in closing them. Dark or not, she couldn't sleep, snatching only an hour or two of rest a night.

She covered her face with her hands. If she didn't get some relief from this miserable aching for Marcus she would surely go mad.

Over the last ten days she had collected hundreds of images of him in her mind—Marcus lying on a blanket on the beach, Marcus sprawled in his shirtsleeves on the settee reading aloud, Marcus at the hearth lit by the light of the fire as he banked it for the night.

She had memorized his smiles and the way he rubbed the back of his neck when he was tense. She knew the way the overnight growth of beard darkened his face in the morning, and the way his eyes gleamed wickedly when he teased her, and then darkened when he wanted her.

And he did want her.

The look in his eyes and the timbre of his voice told her daily that he wished he were holding her, touching her, making love to her. But he kept his promise, making no overt attempts to seduce her.

Sighing, she stared at her hands clenched in front of her. The truth of it was, no effort was required on his part to make her desire him. It was instinctual, uncontrollable.

So why was she here, pacing her room in fevered anguish, when the relief she sought was just a door away?

Because he was wrong for her, she knew. The epitome of everything she had never wanted. A libertine of some renown, he'd proven again in the stables that he was not to be trusted. She wanted to lock him away, keep him to herself, share him with no one. Only then would she find some measure of peace. Only then could she catch her breath and not feel this clawing ache that she would lose him.

Jealousy is a possessive emotion, love, he'd said to her that first day on the beach. *You'll have to wed me if you want the right to feel that way.*

The right. The right to keep him, to claim him. She wanted that. Despite the torture she knew it would be.

There would be no pleasure in binding herself to a man like Marcus, a man whose appetite for life and adventure would make taming him impossible. There would be only heartache and endless disappointment. And the craving. The craving that would never go away.

She stilled and stared at the bed, remembering the depth of that hunger.

Were not a ring, his name, and the right to his body better than nothing at all?

Before she could consider it further, Elizabeth left her room and walked directly into Marcus's without bothering to knock.

Heading straight toward the bed, she slowed when she saw it was empty, the covers tossed back and wildly askew. Startled, she glanced around and found Marcus in front of the window.

Naked, he stood immobile, bathed in moonlight, watching her with an unblinking stare.

"Marcus?"

"What do you want, Elizabeth?" he asked harshly.

She clutched the sides of her gown with damp fists. "I haven't been able to sleep in over a week."

"You won't find sleep in this room."

She shifted restlessly. Now that she was with him and he was naked, she found her courage had been an ephemeral thing. "I had hoped you would say that," she admitted, her head down.

"So tell me what you want."

Unable to say the words, Elizabeth pulled her night rail over her head and dropped it to the floor.

Marcus reached her in two strides. Wrapping his arms around her waist with a low growl, he clasped her naked body firmly against his. He took her mouth with breath-stealing hunger, his tongue thrusting in blatant imitation of what was to come.

Holding her secure with one arm, he lifted and anchored her leg with the other, his knowledgeable fingers tracing the curve of her buttocks before delving into the crevice and the damp curls of her sex. Moaning her relief and pleasure, Elizabeth clung to his broad shoulders, her breasts held tight to his furred chest as he teased through the slickness of her desire, and then slid upwards into her heat.

His cock, hard and hot, burned the skin of her belly. She reached for it, wrapping trembling fingers around it, her other arm gripping his waist to keep her balance. He throbbed in her palm, groaned into her mouth, his powerful frame trembling against hers.

Elizabeth could barely breathe, couldn't move as his fingers fucked with the expertise of a man who knew his lover well. Hard and fast, he stroked her desire, making her mindless with need. She buried her face against his skin, gasping in his scent, imprinting it all over herself.

"Please," she begged.

"Please what?"

She groaned, her hips undulating to match the movements of his hand.

"Please what?" he demanded, removing his touch.

Sobbing at the sudden dearth of sensation, she pressed desperate kisses against his skin. "Please, take me. I want you."

"For how long, Elizabeth? One hour? One night?"

Her tongue tasted the flat point of his nipple and his breath hissed between his teeth.

"Every night," she breathed.

Marcus lifted her feet from the floor and took the two steps to the bed, sinking into its disheveled softness over her. Elizabeth opened her legs with blatant eagerness.

"Elizabeth . . ."

"Hurry," she begged.

Settling between her thighs, he thrust into her with consummate skill. He was harder, thicker than he had ever been before, stretching her completely and she tore her mouth from his, crying out as she climaxed immediately, primed for pleasure by days of longing and the mastery of his touch.

Marcus buried his face in Elizabeth's neck and groaned hoarsely as the endless spasms of her release milked his aching cock. Against his will, he came, flooding her grasping depths with his seed. It was too much, too fast. His toes curled and his spine arched with pleasure so intense it was almost painful. Lost for a breathless moment, he clutched her body to his with near desperation.

It could only have been moments, but it seemed like hours before he could roll his weight from her. He draped her body across his chest, her legs straddling his thighs, their bodies still joined. Whatever doubts he might have harbored about marriage were burned away by the shudders that still wracked his frame.

"Christ." He crushed her to his chest. Their coupling had lasted all of two minutes. He hadn't thrust at all, yet he had never experienced anything as powerfully fulfilling in his life.

Elizabeth had surrendered to him, acknowledged his claim. There would be no turning back now.

Her fingers stroked through the hair on his chest, soothing him. "I want you to resign your commission with the agency," she whispered softly.

He stilled and released a deep breath. "Ah love, you don't ask for much, do you?"

Elizabeth sighed, her breath warm against his skin. "How can you ask me to marry you, knowing the danger you court?"

"How could I not ask you?" he retorted. "I will never have enough of you, enough of this." He thrust gently, showing her the power of his interest in his renewed erection.

"Lust," she said scornfully.

"Lust I know well, Elizabeth. It does not come near to resembling this."

She moaned as he nudged deeper inside her. "What would you name this then?"

"Affinity, love. We simply suit very well in bed."

Elizabeth rose above him, pushing him deeper still, until the slick lips of her cunt hugged the root of his cock. She studied him with the narrowed-eyed glance that told him trouble was afoot. Then she clenched her inner muscles, hugging his cock in the most intimate of embraces.

His hands fisted in the disheveled sheets and he grit his teeth. Scant moments before he'd felt like he was dying. Already he was eager to feel that way again.

She lifted from him, his cock slipping free from swollen, wet tissues. "Promise me you will consider leaving Eldridge." She slid back onto him slowly.

Sweat beaded his brow. "Elizabeth . . ."

She lifted and lowered again, caressing his cock with her silken cunt. "Promise me you will be careful while considering."

His eyes slid closed on a groan. "Damn you."

Elizabeth rose, withdrawing from him.

His entire body tensed, waiting for the exquisiteness of her body to sink and clasp tightly around him. When she hesitated, he looked at her. She waited, one finely arched brow lifted in challenge. She would continue to wait until he capitulated, he knew.

Unable to do otherwise, Marcus surrendered immediately. "I promise."

And his reward was sweet indeed.

"Good God!"

Elizabeth jumped awake at the familiar, albeit horrified cry. Marcus's outstretched arm pushed her back down and she gasped at the sight of the wicked knife in his hand. She lifted her head and looked toward the door, gaping at the sight of the beloved figure there. *"William?"*

Her brother stood with a hand clasped over his eyes. "I will await"—he choked—"you both in the parlor. Please . . . dress."

With her brain still sleep muddled, Elizabeth slipped out of bed, shivering as her bare feet hit the cold floor. "I often tell myself that William cannot possibly become more outrageous and yet somehow he manages it."

"Elizabeth."

She ignored the soft query in Marcus's tone and moved swiftly to her discarded night rail at the foot of the bed. It was awkward, this moment, recalling the intimacy of the night before and the brazen way she'd elicited his promise. To wake to the sight of a blade in his hand was sobering. She'd agreed to marry this man, for no other reason than sexual *affinity* and misplaced possessiveness. She was daft.

"You can stay abed, love," he murmured. "I can speak with your brother."

Straightening with her garment in hand, Elizabeth paused at the sight him pulling on breeches. As he moved, the ripple of honed muscle along his arms, chest, and abdomen arrested her gaze.

He glanced up, caught her staring, and smiled. "You are a fetching sight, all sleep mussed and ravished."

"I'm certain I look a fright," she said.

"Impossible. I've yet to see you look anything but delectable."

He rounded the bed, took the night rail from her hands, and dropped it over her head. Then he kissed the tip of her nose. "Nowise did I plan for us to be rushed this morning." Shaking his head, he moved to the armoire and finished dressing. "Keep the bed warm and wait for me."

"It would be best if you learned now that I won't be ordered about. William is my brother. I will speak to him."

Marcus sighed internally at Elizabeth's stubbornness, acknowledging to himself that he would have to grow accustomed to it, and went to the door. "As you wish, love."

He raked her barely clad body with an affectionate glance before closing the portal behind him and traversing the length of the hall. He really shouldn't be surprised they'd been discovered, but he was, and disappointed. Their agreement was too new, the tie too tentative to set his mind at ease.

The first time he'd proposed he'd sat in the study of Chesterfield Hall and discussed the marital disbursements in cold, hard facts with her father. The banns had been read, and the papers notified. Teas and dinners had been held. He could not have expected she would bolt. He could not have anticipated she would marry another man. And at this moment he had far less than he'd had then. At this moment he had only her promise and she had proven that was not to be trusted.

Years of frustration and anger rose like bile in his throat. Until she made restitution for what she'd done to him he would never find peace.

He entered the parlor. "Barclay, your timing leaves much to be desired. You are—quite lamentably—*de trop*."

William paced before the fireplace, his hands clasped at his back. "I am scarred for life," he muttered.

"A knock would have been wise."

"The door was open."

"Well it's moot in any case; you shouldn't have come."

"Elizabeth had run off." William stopped and glared. "After the tantrum in her room, I had to find her and see if she was well."

Marcus ran his hands through his tumbled locks. He couldn't fault the man for caring. "She sent word. I suppose I should have as well."

"At the very least. Debauching someone else's sister would also be preferable."

"I am not debauching her. I'm marrying her."

William gaped. "*Again?*"

"We never quite finished the business the last time, if you recall."

"Damn you, Westfield." William's fists clenched until the knuckles were white. "If this has anything to do with that idiotic wager, I will call you out."

Rounding the settee, Marcus sat and bit back the harsh words that longed to be freed. "Your sterling estimation of my character is most uplifting."

"Why in hell would you want to wed Elizabeth after what transpired before?"

"We have an affinity," Elizabeth said from the doorway, studying the two men who held such important places in her life—both of them so obviously restless. "Or so he attests."

"An *affinity?*" William pierced her with a narrowed gaze. "What the devil does that have to do with anything?"

Then he paled and held up his hands. "On further consideration, I don't wish to hear the answer to that."

She didn't move, simply stood in the doorway trying to decide whether to enter or not. The tension in the room was as thick as fog. "Where is Margaret?"

"At home. The journey wouldn't be wise for her now. She becomes ill easily."

"You should be with her," she admonished.

"I was worried about you," he said defensively. "Especially when Westfield conveniently disappeared at the same time. Your missive told me nothing of your mind-set or your location. You are both damned fortunate that Lady Westfield saw fit to give me direction." He crossed the room to her and gripped her elbow. "Come outside with me."

"It's too cold," she protested.

William shrugged out of his coat and tossed it about her shoulders. Then he dragged her outside.

"Are you daft?" he growled when they were alone. The chilly bite of the coastal morning was rivaled by the chill of her brother's tone.

"I thought so earlier," she said dryly.

"I understand. You've had a taste of . . ." he choked, "carnal pleasure, one denied you before. It can be heady and unduly influencing for women."

"William—"

"It's hopeless to deny it. A man can discern these things. Women look different when they are content with their lovers. You lacked that appearance with Hawthorne."

"This is a very uncomfortable conversation," she muttered.

"I am enjoying this as much as I would a visit to the tooth drawers. But I must beg you to consider this engagement further. There was a reason why you didn't proceed with the marriage before."

Elizabeth looked at the sky, seeing soft blue peeking from the heavy morning clouds. She wondered if she could learn to look for brightness in a marriage that would be rife with cloudy issues.

"You could refuse," he suggested, softening his tone to match her mood.

"Even I am not that cruel." She sighed and leaned into him, accepting the strength he'd always provided.

"You don't wed to alleviate guilt. And I'm not so certain his intentions are honorable. He has much to hold against you. Once you wed him, I would have very little recourse should things deteriorate."

"You know Westfield better than to attribute such thoughts to him." She returned his scowl. "Honestly, there are many times I cannot abide the man. He's arrogant to a fault, stubborn, argumentive—"

"Yes, I agree, he has his faults, all of which I know well."

"If he recovers some of his lost dignity by wedding me, I won't hold it against him. At worst, should he lose interest, he'll simply treat me with the faultless, albeit distant charm for which he's known. He would never physically hurt me."

William blew out a frustrated breath and tilted his head back to look at the sky. "I still cannot find comfort in this. I wanted you to find love the second time. You are free to choose whomever you like. Why settle for 'affinity' when you can have true happiness?"

"You are becoming as much of a romantic as Margaret." Elizabeth shook her head and laughed. "There are times when Westfield's company is quite pleasant."

"So, enjoy a liaison," William suggested. "Much less messy all around."

Her smile was bittersweet. The fact was, Marcus was one of the very few individuals strong enough to stand up to William. She needed to show her brother she was in safekeeping with a man he could trust to be capable. Then perhaps he would worry about her less. Margaret needed him now, as would their child. If there had been any doubt about her forthcoming marriage, it was dispelled by her brother's presence here. He could not continue to leave his wife to care for his sister.

"I want to marry him, William. I don't think I'll be unhappy."

"You are using him to hide. If you choose a man who dislikes you, you have no worries about something more coming of the relationship. Our father has done you a grave injustice with his decline. You are still afraid."

She lifted her chin. "I understand you don't approve of my choice, but that's no reason to malign me."

"I'm speaking the truth, something perhaps it would have been best to do long before now."

"No one knows what the future will bring," she argued. "But Westfield and I are of like station and pedigree. He is wealthy and solicitous of my needs. When this affinity fades, we will still have that foundation. It is no less than any other marriage."

William's gaze narrowed. "You are set in this course."

"Yes." She was glad he'd come after her now. Secure in the knowledge that she was benefiting someone other than herself gave her a peace of mind she'd lacked upon waking. Whether William would admit it or not, this would be good for him, too.

"No elopement," he warned, his frown unabated but unable to diminish the beauty of his features.

"No elopement," she agreed.

"Am I allowed no say in the matter?" Marcus asked, coming up behind them.

"I think you've said quite enough," William retorted. "And I'm famished. I spoke to His Grace when I arrived and he said to drag you both up to the manse. He hasn't seen enough of you since you arrived."

"That was by design," Marcus said dryly. He held out his hand to her, an affectionate gesture they'd never shared in front of others. Sans gloves it was undeniably intimate. The look in his eyes dared her to refuse.

He was always daring her to refuse.

And just as she'd always done, she met the dare and placed her hand in his.

Chapter 14

By any estimation, their betrothal ball was a smashing success. The ballroom of Chesterfield Hall was filled to overflowing, as were the card and billiards rooms. Overwhelmed and overheated, Elizabeth was grateful when Marcus led her out to the garden to enjoy the cool night air.

Realizing the importance of the occasion, she had chosen a burgundy shot silk taffeta gown. Panniers widened the skirt, which was split in the front revealing an underskirt of white lace. Matching lace frothed from the elbows and surrounded the low square neckline. The gown had given her a surface shell of composure, but inside, her stomach was knotted.

She was an expert at the common social pleasantries, but tonight had been so different from the interactions she was accustomed to. The men had been dealt with easily. It was the women and their often catty, spiteful natures that caught her by surprise. After an hour, she'd resorted to smiling while relying on Marcus to carry them through the prying questions and snide comments disguised as congratulations. His skilful handling of women set her on edge, making her jaw ache from the unnaturalness of her outward mien. Not for the first time, she lamented the loss of the quiet she'd enjoyed on the coast.

After William departed Essex for London, Marcus had insisted they remain another three days in the guesthouse. They had lived those days in a state of deep intimacy. He had assisted her with her bath, and demanded she do the same for him. He had helped her to dress, and showed her how to undress him, patiently showing her where every button was and how best to free it until she was as skilled as any valet. He had reinforced those skills at every opportunity—on the beach, in the garden, in almost every room of the guesthouse. With every touch, every glance, every moment, Marcus had weakened her resolve until she had accepted without reservation that she no longer wanted to be free of him.

Resigned to their joined future, she made the effort to learn more about the issues that were important to him. She asked questions about his views of the Townsend Act repeal, and was secretly relieved when he showed no hesitation in sharing them with her. Discussing weighty topics with women was heavily discouraged, but then Marcus was not a man to follow convention.

Pleased with her interest, he debated a variety of topics with her, challenging and pushing her to explore all sides of a subject, then smiling with pride when she reached her own conclusions, even if they were in opposition to his own.

Elizabeth sighed. The simple fact was, she enjoyed his company and the times when business or Parliament kept him away, she found she missed him.

"That was a melancholy sigh if I ever heard one," he murmured.

Lifting her chin, she met his gaze, made more brilliant in contrast to the pure white of his wig. In a pale gold ensemble, Marcus outshone every other gentleman present.

"You look beautiful," she said.

His mouth tilted upward on one side. "I believe I am supposed to say that to you." The heat in his eyes left her no doubt as to what he was thinking.

William had forbade any further meetings in the guesthouse. She suspected Marcus had so readily agreed to that demand to ensure her continued cooperation. Achey and restless, her body craved his and the constant reminder of her need negated changing her mind about their approaching nuptials.

"You're flushed," he said. "And not for the reason I'd prefer."

"I'm thirsty," she admitted.

"We must find a drink for you then." With his hand over hers where it rested on his sleeve, he turned her back toward the manse.

She resisted. "I would rather await you out here." The thought of returning to the crush after so recently escaping was vastly unappealing.

Marcus began to protest. Then he spotted William and Margaret descending the stairs and led her to them. "I shall leave you in capable hands," he said with a kiss to the back of her hand. Moving away, he ascended the steps to the house with a grace she found hard to look away from.

Margaret linked arms with her and said, "The ball is an unequivocal triumph, as we all expected. Much more entertaining to gossip about you than any other topic."

William looked over their heads. "Where is Westfield going?"

Elizabeth hid a smile at his curt tone. "To the drink tables."

He frowned. "Wish he would have said something before he went in. I could use some libation myself. If you will excuse me, ladies, I believe I'll join him."

As William moved away, Margaret gestured toward the garden and they set off at a sedate stroll.

"You look well," Elizabeth said.

"Regardless, a clever modiste cannot hide this belly any longer, so this ball will be my last social event of the Season." Margaret smiled. "Lord Westfield seems quite taken with you. With luck, you will be having children of your own soon." Leaning closer, she asked, "Is he as skilled a lover as they say?"

Elizabeth blushed.

"Good for you." Margaret laughed, and then winced. "My back aches."

"You have been on your feet all day," Elizabeth scolded.

"A respite in the retiring room is long overdue," Margaret agreed.

"Then we must hasten to get you there."

Turning around, they headed away from the garden.

As they neared the house, they saw more guests filtering out into the cool night air. Elizabeth took a deep breath, and prayed for the patience she'd require to endure 'til morning.

"Yours will not be an easy pairing, you are aware of that?"

Marcus glanced at William as they descended the garden steps, drinks in hand. "Truly?" he drawled. "And here I'd been led to believe marriage was a tranquil institution."

William snorted. "Elizabeth is by nature quite feisty and downright argumentative, but around you, she is not herself. She's almost withdrawn. Lord only knows how you convinced her to accept your addresses, but I've taken note of her marked reticence around you."

"How obliging of you." Marcus clenched his jaw. He was a proud man. It did not sit well with him that Elizabeth appeared less than enthusiastic to wed him.

Margaret approached, her arched brows drawn tight with discomfort.

William rushed to her. "What pains you?" he asked gruffly.

She waved his concern away with a lift of her hand. "My back and feet ache is all. Nothing to worry yourself over."

"Where is Lady Hawthorne?" Marcus asked, searching the winding path behind her.

"Lady Grayton had an unfortunate mishap with an unruly climbing rose and needed more assistance than I." She wrinkled her nose. "Frankly, I think Elizabeth simply didn't want to return to the house yet."

Marcus opened his mouth to reply, but was silenced by a distant female scream.

William frowned. Marcus, however, was almost crippled with fear, his entire body tensing to the point of pain.

"Elizabeth," he whispered starkly, his well-trained senses telling him the danger that stalked her was right there in the garden. He dropped the glasses he held in his hands, paying no mind to the delicate flutes shattering on the stone pathway. With William fast on his heels, Marcus ran in the direction of the disturbing sound, his stomach clenched and frozen with dread.

He'd left her with family when he should never have left her at all. He knew his job, knew the rules, knew she was not safe anywhere after the ransacking of her room and he'd ignored all of it simply because she asked him to. He'd been a fool and now he could only hope fright from an overactive imagination would be the extent of his punishment.

Perhaps it was not Elizabeth. Perhaps it was a minor incident of a stolen kiss and a woman with a flair for dramatic outcries . . .

Just as panic began to overwhelm him, he saw her up ahead, sprawled on the pathway next to a rose-covered arbor in a flood of displaced panniers and endless skirts.

He dropped to his knees beside her, damning himself for lowering his guard. Lifting his head, he searched for her attacker, but the night was still and quiet except for her labored breathing.

William crouched on her other side. "Christ." His hands trembled as he reached for her.

Because the darkness made sight difficult, Marcus felt along her torso, searching for injury. Elizabeth groaned as his fingers lightly skimmed across her ribs, finding an object protruding from her hip. Moving her arm aside carefully, he exposed a small dagger.

"She's been stabbed," Marcus said gruffly, his throat tight.

Elizabeth opened her eyes at the sound of his voice. Her skin was pale beneath her powder, the rouge she wore unnatural in comparison. "Marcus." Her voice was a gasped whisper as her fingers curled weakly over the hand that touched the hilt. He gripped them tightly, willing some of his vitality into her, willing her to be strong.

This was his fault. And Elizabeth had paid the price. The extent of his failure was crushing, a brutal fall from the heights of satisfaction he'd felt when the evening started.

William stood, his body tense as he searched their surroundings much as Marcus had done a moment earlier. "We need to move her to the house."

Marcus lifted her, careful to avoid unduly jarring the knife. She cried out, then lost consciousness, her breathing slipping into a rapid but measured rhythm. "Where can I go?" he asked in near desperation. Through the ballroom was obviously not an option.

"Follow me."

Moving like shadows through the garden, they entered through the bustling kitchen. Then they took the cramped servants' staircase, which caused a laborious ascent hampered by Elizabeth's panniers.

Once safely in her room, Marcus shrugged out of his coat and reached into an inner pocket, withdrawing a small dagger not unlike the one lodged in Elizabeth's side. "Send for a doctor," Marcus ordered. "And ring for towels and heated water."

"I will instruct a servant on my departure. It will be faster if I collect the doctor myself." William left with reassuring haste.

With careful, tentative movements, Marcus used his knife to cut through the endless material that made up her dress, stays, and underskirts. The task was torturous, this sight of his blade next to precious ivory skin a nightmare, and he was drenched with sweat before she was free of the pile.

A steady steam of blood leaked from around the dagger.

She was still unconscious, but he whispered soothingly as he worked, trying to calm himself as well as her.

The door opened behind him, and he cast a quick glance over his shoulder to see the entry of Lord Langston and Lady Barclay. A maid entered directly behind, carrying a tray weighted with hot water and cloths.

The earl took one look at his daughter and shuddered violently. "Oh God," he breathed. He swayed unsteadily, his face a stark mask. "I cannot go through this again."

Marcus felt his stomach knot. The pain he witnessed on her father's face was what tormented Elizabeth so. That same pain had pushed Elizabeth away and every other woman who'd had the misfortune to care for the dashing, but endlessly grieving widower.

"Come. Let's get you settled somewhere quiet to wait, my lord," Margaret said softly.

Langston did not hesitate to agree, fleeing the room as if the hounds of hell were on his heels. Marcus cursed under his breath, fighting the urge to chase him and thrash some sense into him, to make the man care for his daughter.

Lady Barclay returned a quarter hour later. "I must apologize for Lord Langston."

"No need, Lady Barclay. It's long overdue that he answer for his own actions." He released a deep breath and rubbed the back of his neck.

"Tell me what to do," she said softly.

With silent efficiency, Margaret helped him clean the blood from Elizabeth's skin. As they were finishing, William returned with the doctor who removed the blade, examined the puncture, and announced the fine boning of her stays had deflected the dagger away from any vital organs, and into the fleshy part of her hip. Stitches and bed rest would be all that was required.

Nearly dizzy with relief, Marcus steadied himself against the post of the bed and tugged off his wig. Had Elizabeth been uncorseted, the wound might have been fatal, and his destruction assured.

He glanced at William and his wife. "I will remain with her, you both should return to the guests below. It's bad enough Elizabeth and I will be absent from our own betrothal celebration. Your absence will only worsen the situation."

"You should go below, Lord Westfield," Margaret said gently. "It would be less awkward if at least one of you were in attendance."

"No. Let them think what they like, I won't leave her."

Margaret nodded though her eyes were still troubled. "What tale should I relate to your family?"

Rubbing the back of his neck, he said, "Anything aside from the truth."

William turned to the maid. "Say nothing of this to anyone if you wish to remain employed."

"And ready the other bedroom in this suite for Lord Westfield," Margaret added, ignoring the glare from her husband. The maid left swiftly.

Margaret gestured William toward the door. "Come, dear. Lord Westfield has everything well in hand. I'm certain he will call for us if needed."

Still pale and clearly stricken, William nodded and followed Margaret out.

Elizabeth woke only a moment later, thrashing as the doctor began the first stitch. Marcus lay across the bed and held her down.

"Marcus!" she gasped, her eyes flying open. "It hurts."

She began to cry.

His throat aching with her pain, he bent low to kiss her forehead. "I know, love. But if you can find the strength to be still, it will be over all the sooner."

Marcus watched with much pride and admiration as Elizabeth did her best to remain unmoving while her wound was closed. She writhed slightly, but she did not cry out again. Fine beads of sweat dotted her brow and mingled with the steady flow of tears as she clung to his torso with bruising fingers. He was grateful when she lost consciousness again.

When the doctor finished, he cleaned his instruments carefully and returned them to his bag. "Keep an eye on that, my lord. If it festers, send for me again." He left as quickly as he'd come.

Marcus paced restlessly, his gaze never straying far from Elizabeth. An overwhelming well of protectiveness rose up within him. Someone had tried to take her away from him. And he had made that task too easy.

Far more than affinity was involved here. That relatively simple state could not account for the madness that threatened his sanity. To see her so pale and wounded, to think of what might have happened . . . He clutched his head in his hands.

For the rest of the night, he watched over her. When she stirred, he went to her, murmuring softly until she settled. He tended the fire in the hearth and checked her bandages regularly. He could not be still, could not sleep, feeling so helpless he wanted to howl and tear something apart.

Dawn lit the sky when the Earl of Langston returned to the room. Looking briefly at Elizabeth, his reddened eyes drifted to Marcus. Reeking of stiff drink and flowery perfume, the earl was disheveled, his wig askew as he stumbled in on his heels.

"Why don't you retire, Lord Langston?" Marcus asked with a disgusted shake of his head. "You look nigh as bad as she does."

Langston leaned heavily against a side table. "And you look far too collected for a man who nearly lost a bride."

"I prefer to be of sound mind," Marcus said dryly. "Rather than drowning in my cups."

"Were you aware that Elizabeth is the reflection of her mother? Rare beauties, the both of them."

Marcus released a weary breath and prayed for patience. "Yes, I am aware, my lord, and there are many things I wish to say to you, but now is not the time. If you don't mind, I have much to consider and would prefer to do it in silence."

Turning bleary eyes toward the bed, the earl winced at the sight of Elizabeth, the paleness of her skin making the heart-shaped patch on her cheek stand out in stark relief.

"Lady Langston gave you a family," Marcus felt compelled to say. "You do no honor to her memory by neglecting them as you have."

"You don't care for me, Westfield, I've known this. But then you fail to understand my situation. You cannot, since you don't love my daughter as I did my wife."

"Do not presume to say that Elizabeth is not important to me." The steel of Marcus's voice snapped through the tension like a whip crack.

"Why not? You think the same of me."

With that, the earl left Marcus to the silence he'd wanted, a silence he found deafening with its unyielding accusations.

Why had he not been there for her?

How could he have been so careless?

And would the fragile trust he'd worked so hard to build be shattered by his broken promise to protect her from harm?

His head fell back, and his eyes closed on a bitter moan.

He'd never allowed himself to consider losing her again and now, confronted with it like this, he realized what he hadn't before.

She'd become necessary to him. Far too necessary.

Chapter 15

Elizabeth jolted awake with a breathless gasp. Her heart racing, it took a moment to register the familiar canopy above her bed, and then a moment more before a heady floral scent teased her senses. She turned her head, her bleary gaze wandering and finding every flat surface in her room covered in a riotous display of hothouse roses. Amidst the flowery profusion, Marcus slumbered with careless grace in a chair beside her bed. He was dressed in a linen shirt open at the neck and soft tan breeches, his rich sable hair tied back at the nape. With his bare feet propped on a footstool, he looked very much at home.

Studying him in repose, Elizabeth felt a possessive pride that both alarmed and pleased her. A feeling so strong she was instantly comforted, the panic she'd felt upon waking dissipating with his proximity.

She raised her hands to rub gritty eyes, then attempted a seated position. She cried out at the pain that burned through her hip, and Marcus was instantly at her side.

"Wait." He pulled her up gently, propping pillows behind her. When she was comfortable, he sat next to her on the bed and poured her a glass of water from the nearby pitcher. With a grateful smile, she took a sip to clear her parched throat.

"How do you feel?" he asked.

She wrinkled her nose. "My hip throbs dreadfully."

"I expect it would." Marcus looked away.

Curious about his somber mood, she reached out to touch his hand. "Thank you for the flowers."

The curve of his mouth was intimately tender, though his thoughts were shuttered in a way she'd not seen in weeks. He looked very much like he had at the Moreland ball so many nights ago, remote and guarded.

"I'm sorry to have disturbed you," she said softly. "You looked very comfortable."

"With you, always." But the tone of his voice was practiced, far too smooth to be genuine, and he gently removed his hand from under hers.

She shifted nervously and pain lanced through her side.

"Stop that," he ordered with a chastising squeeze to her shin.

She shot him a narrowed glance, dismayed by the newly erected barrier between them.

The slight rap on the door broke the moment. Marcus bade the person to enter and Margaret walked in with William directly behind her.

"You're awake!" She greeted Elizabeth with a relieved smile. "How are you feeling?"

"Awful," Elizabeth admitted ruefully.

"Do you recall anything about what happened the other night?"

Everyone looked at her expectantly.

"The other night?" Her eyes widened. "How long have I been asleep?"

"Two days, and you needed every minute of that rest."

"Good heavens." Elizabeth shook her head. "I don't remember much. It all happened so quickly. Lady Grayton stalked off in a bit of a temper, blaming our slovenly gardeners for allowing the climbing rose to grow. Then I was accosted from behind and pulled away."

"How dreadful!" Margaret covered her mouth in horror.

"It was. Still, it could have been much worse."

"You were stabbed," William growled. "It does not get any worse."

She lifted her gaze to meet his. "I believe the assault was not meant to go that far. But the other man—"

Marcus stiffened at Elizabeth's words. *More than one.* He would expect as much from an organized effort, but the knowledge still struck a sharp blow. "What other man?"

Elizabeth sank back into the pillows, frowning at his harsh tone. "I could be mistaken, but I think the man who attacked me was frightened away by someone else."

"Most likely by Westfield and Barclay," Margaret suggested.

"No, someone else. There was a shout, a masculine voice, and then the . . . rest."

Margaret rounded the bed, and sat on the other side. William, however, strode purposefully toward the open door to the sitting room. "Westfield, a word, if you would."

Wanting to hear more of Elizabeth's recollection, Marcus shook his head. "I would rather—"

"If you please," William insisted.

With a curt nod, he rose and followed William, who shut the door behind them.

When William gestured to the nearest chair, Marcus realized this would not be a short conversation. "Barclay, I really must—"

"Elizabeth's stabbing is my fault."

Marcus stilled. "What are you talking about?"

William again gestured for him to sit as he moved to a nearby chair to do the same. "Hawthorne's death was not the result of highway robbery, as everyone has been led to believe."

Feigning surprise, Marcus sank onto the settee, and waited for more.

William hesitated a moment, studying him with disquieting intensity. "I cannot say much, I'm sorry. But since Elizabeth will soon be residing with you, I feel you should know something of what you will face as her husband." He paused for a deep breath, and then said, "Hawthorne was privy to sensitive information that led to his murder. It was not an accident."

Marcus kept his face impassive. "What information?"

"I cannot tell you that. I can only tell you that my own safety and the safety of my wife has been a point of tortuous care for the last four years, and with your marriage it will become likewise for you with Elizabeth. She and I are the only ones who knew Hawthorne well enough to be a danger to those who killed him."

"I can see that. However, I fail to see how her stabbing would be your fault."

"I knew of the danger and should have been more cautious."

Marcus sighed, knowing full well how the other man felt. William, however, had no knowledge of the journal or the attack in the park. Barclay's failure to foresee the events in the garden was excusable. Marcus's was not. "You have been dogged in your protection of her. You could not have done any more than you have."

"I don't believe the disarray we saw in her room was her doing," William continued. "Although she claims it was."

This time Marcus's shock was genuine. "You don't?"

"No. I think her room was ransacked. That is why I tracked her to Essex. I was terrified for her." William leaned his head back, and closed his eyes. Against the burgundy leather of the wingback chair the exhausted strain of his features was even more striking. "Those ten days were the worst of my life. When I found the two of you together, I wanted to thrash you both for allowing me to worry myself into an early graying."

"Barclay . . ." Marcus sighed, his guilt weighing heavily. "I am sorry."

William opened his eyes and scowled. "I have no notion how you found her before I did. I have connections—"

"A fortunate guess," Marcus said quickly.

"Yes, well, what she has in her possession that is so important I haven't a clue, though obviously Elizabeth does. I don't
know if they've threatened her in some manner or if she simply wants to protect me. She's been skittish since Hawthorne
passed on."

"It would be difficult to lose a spouse, I'm sure."

"Of course. I don't discount that." His voice lowered.
"Although Hawthorne was an odd fellow, he was a good
man."

Marcus leaned forward, resting his forearms on his knees.
"Odd?"

"Hawthorne was an excitable sort. One moment he'd be
as calm as you and I at this moment, then the next he'd be
pacing and muttering. The damnedest thing, I tell you.
Annoying at times."

"I know a few gentlemen such as you describe," Marcus
said dryly. "The king, for one."

"In any case." William's gaze narrowed. "You are taking
this rather well for a man discovering someone wishes to
harm his future wife."

"That discovery was made a few days ago. I've had time to
consider it. Of course this cannot be allowed to continue. No
one can live like this, reacting after the fact. The threat has to
be dealt with."

"I should have told you sooner." William grimaced. "I assumed I had some time to find the best way to present it.
What does one say in a situation such as this? Too many
questions and not enough answers. But things have been hec-
tic, and you both are so bloody popular. You are always in a
crowd. I thought the sheer volume of witnesses would keep
her safe, but she's not inviolable anywhere. A *ball* for Christ's
sake! One would have to be mad to attempt absconding with
the guest of honor at such a well attended event. And the
knife!"

Marcus stilled. "What of it?"

William flushed. "Nothing of importance, just—"

Rising, Marcus moved through the door to his chamber and retrieved the knife. He turned it over in his hands and examined it in the light of day. He'd meant to do this earlier, but the need to watch over Elizabeth was a lure he couldn't resist. The blade could wait, it was not going anywhere.

Now he studied it carefully. It was well made and costly. The gold handle was intricately designed with vines and leaves, which gave the hilt a textured grip. The base of the handle was monogrammed with the initials *NTM*. Nigel Terrance Moore, the late Viscount Hawthorne.

Marcus looked up as William entered the room. "Where has this been?"

"I assume whoever killed Hawthorne took all of his valuables. He always carried that, and it was with him the night he was killed."

Lost in thought, Marcus attempted to put the pieces of the puzzle together, but they didn't fit—no matter how many various ways he assembled it.

Christopher St. John had returned Elizabeth's brooch to her, the brooch Hawthorne had been carrying when he was killed. Now another item from that night had reappeared.

The clues laid blame at St. John's feet, but the attacks on Elizabeth were out of character. St. John was successful because of his cleverness and pinpoint precision. Both of the assaults against Elizabeth had resulted in failure, something the pirate would never have allowed to happen once, let alone twice. While it was possible St. John was the culprit, Marcus could not shake the feeling that something else was amiss.

Why take the risk of attacking Elizabeth at a ball where hundreds of people were in attendance? She would not be carrying the journal during such an event.

But if St. John was innocent, a possibility that infuriated Marcus, there was someone else who was aware of the journal, and desired it enough to kill for it. Acknowledging that his own efforts were not enough, he regretted he could not confide in William, but he would honor Elizabeth's wishes for the moment. In the end, her safety was paramount, and he would elicit all the help he needed to ensure it.

Elizabeth's gasp from the doorway startled them both. Dressed in a simple night rail and dressing robe, she stared at the dagger in shock, all color draining from her face. She looked so tiny, so childlike with her disheveled hair and fidgeting fingers.

His chest tightened, and Marcus shoved the feeling aside ruthlessly. His deepening affection for her could only bring more trouble, as had already been proven. Dropping the knife back into the drawer, he hurried to her side. "You should not be walking around yet."

"Where did you find that?" she asked in a barely audible whisper.

"It was the blade used to stab you."

Her knees buckled, and Marcus supported her gently in his arms, paying careful attention to her wounded hip. He walked her back to her room with William close on their heels.

"That was Hawthorne's," she whispered as he returned her to the bed.

"I know."

William moved to the other side. "I will explore this matter further, Elizabeth. Please don't worry, I—"

"You will do no such thing!" she cried.

He squared his shoulders. "I will do what is best."

"No, William. It is no longer your duty to protect me. You must look after your wife. How could I ever face Margaret were something to happen to you on my account?"

"What can Westfield do?" he scoffed. "I am in a much better position to acquire the information we need."

"Lord Westfield is a powerful and influential man," she argued. "I'm certain he has important connections as well. Leave this business to him. I will not have you involved in any way."

"You are being ridiculous," he grumbled, his hands on his hips.

"Stay out of this, William."

Leaving the side of the bed, he stalked toward the door. "I must do something or go mad. You would do no less for me." He slammed the door on his way out.

Elizabeth stared at the portal with mouth agape. When she lifted her gaze, she was crying. "Marcus, you must stop him."

"I will try my best, love." He stared grimly at the door, trying to ignore the way her tears tore at his conscience. "But your brother is as stubborn as you are."

After a light meal with Elizabeth, Marcus took his carriage and collected Avery James. Together, they traveled through town to meet with Lord Eldridge.

Staring pensively out the coach window, Marcus barely registered the bustle of the London streets or the calls of vendors to sample their wares. There was too much to consider, too much awry. He didn't say a word until they reached Lord Eldridge's office, and then he filled in the details he'd been unable to expand upon through the post.

"First of all, Westfield," Eldridge began when he'd finished, "I cannot leave you on this assignment. Your impending marriage destroys any hope for objectivity."

Marcus drummed his fingers on the carved wooden arm of his chair. "I maintain I am in the best position to protect her."

"At this point we know so little about the danger. The best protection would be to keep her locked away. But her safety is not our only aim. And before you protest, consider the alternatives. How else can we apprehend the culprit, other than to draw him out?"

"You want to use her as a lure." It was not a question.

"If need be." Eldridge moved his gaze to Avery. "What say you about the attack on Lady Hawthorne, James?"

"The reasoning eludes me," he admitted. "Why attack

Lady Hawthorne when she does not have the book with her? What purpose does that serve?"

Marcus stilled his fingers, and shared his conclusion. "Ransom. Lady Hawthorne for the journal. They know the agency is involved. The brooch and dagger suggest they were at the site where Hawthorne was murdered so they know Barclay is involved as well. The move against her was rash, yes. But it was truly the only time since Hawthorne's journal surfaced that she has been without escort."

"After the incident with the brooch I am certain St. John is involved," Eldridge said, rising from his seat and turning to take in the view of the thoroughfare. "The men assigned to watch him have a gap in their accounts of his whereabouts the evening of the betrothal ball, an hour of time close enough to the stabbing to be suspicious. Although underlings could have performed the deed, I would think something of this delicacy would be a task he would perform himself. He's a bold one."

"I agree," Marcus said gruffly. St. John was not averse to doing his own dirty work. In fact, he seemed to prefer it.

"There is one person who can help us," Avery suggested. "The individual who scared away Lady Hawthorne's attacker."

Marcus shook his head. "No one came forward at the ball, and I certainly cannot interview everyone on the guest list without revealing the nature of my inquiry."

Eldridge clasped his hands behind his back and rocked on his heels. "Troubling to be sure. I wish we understood the contents of that journal. The key to this whole affair is locked away in there." He fell silent a moment and then, casually, he mentioned, "Lord Barclay came by this morning."

Marcus stifled a groan. "I cannot say I'm surprised."

"He came looking for James."

Avery nodded. "I will speak with him when he comes to

me. Hopefully, he will allow me to research the matter on his behalf."

"Ha!" Marcus laughed. "Those Chesterfields are a stubborn lot. I would not count on his easy complacency."

"He was a good agent," Eldridge mused. "I lost him when he married. If this would bring him back into the fold—" He shot a pointed glance over his shoulder.

"You once told me that young, foolishly adventurous agents are easy to acquire," Marcus reminded.

"Ah, but there is no substitute for experience." Eldridge returned to his chair with a slight smile. "But it's just as well. Emotional detachment is necessary to put the mission first. Barclay would lack that. As, I suspect, do you, Westfield. It is extremely possible that your emotional involvement with Lady Hawthorne will jeopardize her life."

Avery shifted nervously in his seat.

Marcus smiled grimly. "It already has. But it won't happen again."

Eldridge's gaze never wavered. "You are certain about that, are you?"

"Yes." He'd forgotten, for a few brief weeks, how deeply she could hurt him. He'd thought himself beyond that. Now he knew he was not. It was best, for both of them, that he keep his distance. He refused to need her to survive. She'd already proven she did not need him. First, with her elopement, and then with her ease in ending their affair. There was no doubt he was expendable to her.

"All men succumb eventually, Westfield," Eldridge said dryly. "You are in great company."

Marcus stood, effectively cutting off the line of discussion. "I shall continue to work on the journal. The wedding is only a fortnight hence, and then she'll be in my home, where she'll be far better protected."

Avery stood as well. "I will speak with Lord Barclay and see what can be done to allay his concerns."

"Keep me advised," Eldridge ordered. "As it stands, unless we learn more about the journal we can only wait, or use Lady Hawthorne to draw out her attacker. It won't be long before we must decide which course to take."

Sunlight sparkled in the puddles left by the early morning's light rain. The day was momentous, the day of his wedding, and Marcus turned from the window to finish dressing. He had ordered the creation of a jacket and breeches in a pearl grey with a silver waistcoat heavily embroidered with silk thread. From the top of his wigged head down to his diamond-studded heels, his valet took great pains to make Marcus's appearance perfect, and the act of dressing took well over an hour.

Once finished, he walked through the adjoining sitting room, then beyond into the lady's chamber. Most of Elizabeth's personal belongings had already arrived, and he'd scattered them about the room in an effort to make her feel welcome and less alienated. Touching her things had seemed so intimate, he hadn't allowed the servants to do it. He would keep his emotional distance as he had the last fortnight, but he had rights now and after all he'd been through for her, he would damn well enjoy them.

Glancing around the room one last time, Marcus made certain everything was where it should be. His gaze came to rest on the escritoire, where a small likeness of Lord Hawthorne sat. Marcus picked it up, the image bothering him as it always did. Not because of jealousy or misplaced possessiveness: No, the image disturbed him because of the niggling sense that he should be seeing something he was missing.

As often happened in recent days, his mood turned pensive. How different his future would have been had the handsome viscount lived. When Elizabeth married, Marcus had thought she would be forever out of his reach. Seduction had crossed his mind. Despite the Hawthorne title, he'd always thought of her as his, but when he'd returned to England she was already widowed, negating that course of action.

He returned the image to the escritoire, where it joined likenesses of William, Margaret, and Randall Chesterfield. The past was gone and best forgotten. Today, a great injustice that had been done to him would be righted, and then his life would return to some semblance of the normalcy he'd known before Elizabeth.

Moving downstairs, Marcus collected his hat and gloves before vaulting into his coach. He was one of the first people to arrive at the church and he breathed a sigh of relief to learn Elizabeth was already in the bride's ready room preparing for the ceremony. Truth was, he'd half feared she would fail to appear. Until she spoke her vows, he couldn't quite allow himself the satisfaction he longed to revel in.

Smiling, he spoke with family, friends, and important members of society as they arrived. With safety paramount, agents were spread out liberally among the guests. Aside from Talbot and James, who sat together, he was unaware of who they were, he knew only that they were there.

A curious sort by nature, he couldn't help cataloging the personages in the pews, wondering who amongst them lived an agent's life like he did. He also noted the marked reticence between peers and their wives, and wished he also felt such detachment from Elizabeth.

Would they have lost their minds, as he nearly had, if their spouses had been threatened? Was their every breath contingent upon the safety of their wives? He doubted it. It was unnatural, this fascination. Without its curse, his failure to protect Elizabeth would never have occurred, and he would not feel as restless as a caged animal.

Oddly, the only way he could conceive of finding peace was to wed himself to his torment. For four years, the loss of Elizabeth had been the thorn in his side. Now, he could pull it free. Now, he would be rid of the ache that plagued him.

From this moment on, his mission and his own sanity could take precedence. Elizabeth would be his, and the world would know it. Those who thought to harm her would know it. *She* would know it.

There would be no more running, no more chasing, no more frustration. He'd wanted closure.

Today he would have it.

Chapter 16

"You're trembling," Margaret murmured.

"It's cold."

"Then why are you perspiring?"

Glaring, Elizabeth met her sister-in-law's sympathetic gaze in the mirror.

Unperturbed, Margaret smiled. "You look beautiful."

Lowering her eyes, Elizabeth examined her appearance in the mirror. She'd chosen pale blue silk taffeta with elbow-length sleeves, matching skirt and open overskirt. The result was serene, an emotion she wished she felt at the moment.

She sucked in a shuddering breath and grimaced. Having sworn this day would never come, she was completely unprepared for the reality of it.

"Your spirits will improve once you stand with him," Margaret promised.

"Perhaps I'll feel worse," she muttered.

But a quarter hour later, as Elizabeth walked down the aisle on her father's arm, the sight of Marcus arrested her, lifted her, just as Margaret had predicted. He was resplendent in his finery and gazed at her so intensely she could see the emerald color of his irises even from a substantial distance.

There was more between them than just this physical space. Marcus's reputation and his work with Eldridge were great obstacles she wondered if they could surmount. He'd hinted at fidelity and agreed to consider leaving the agency, but he'd made no promises. If he failed to change his course on either account, she could grow to detest him. And if he married her for revenge, their arrangement was doomed before starting. She couldn't help but worry, couldn't help but be very afraid of the future.

"Are you certain this is the path you choose to take?" her father asked in a low tone.

Startled, Elizabeth glanced at him with wide eyes. He stared straight ahead, as aloof as ever, in much the same way Marcus had adopted in the last few weeks. "Why?" was all she could manage to say.

His lips pursed as he stared at the altar and the man who waited there. "I had hoped you would consider marrying for happiness."

If not for the multitude of observers she might have gaped. "I would not have expected such a statement from you."

He sighed and shot her a sidelong glance. "I would gladly suffer a thousand torments for the privilege of having your mother as long as I did."

Her heart ached for him and the emptiness she glimpsed in his eyes. "Father—"

"We can turn about, Elizabeth," he said gruffly. "Westfield's motives concern me."

As the doubts began to churn her stomach, she turned her head to study her groom. Marcus's mouth curved with blatant charm, a silent encouragement, and her heart stopped.

"Think of the scandal," she whispered.

He slowed his steps. "I care for nothing other than your well-being."

Her breath caught for a moment and her steps faltered. How long had she waited for some sign that she mattered at all to her pater? Long enough that she'd thought it an impossible dream. The unexpected support for a hasty retreat was not only astonishing, but very tempting. She studied him and the occupants of the church, then she looked at Marcus again. She saw the tiny step forward he took and the clenching of his fists, barely noticeable warnings that he would give chase should she flee.

It should have frightened her further, that almost imperceptible threat. Instead, she remembered how the sound of his voice in the garden had filled her with relief. She remembered the way he'd held her after the stabbing, and how the trembling of his arms and voice had betrayed the depths of his concern. And the nights in his arms, how she craved them. Her heart started to race, but it was not the urge to run that moved her.

She lifted her chin. "Thank you, Father. But I'm certain of my course."

Marcus glanced at his younger brother, who stood with him at the altar. Paul grinned, his brow arching in silent query. *Any doubts?* his look seemed to ask.

Marcus opened his mouth to whisper back when the sudden hush in the church drew his attention. Elizabeth entered beside her father and the sight of her took his breath away. Paul's low whistle just before the music swelled said his unspoken question had been answered.

Marcus had never seen a more beautiful bride.

His bride.

Muffled weeping moved his attention to his mother who sat tearfully in the front row. His youngest brother, Robert, held her fragile hand carefully in his and gazed at Marcus through gold-rimmed spectacles with a reassuring smile.

The soon-to-be Dowager Countess of Westfield was beside herself with joy. She'd adored Elizabeth upon their first meeting so many years ago, and now said that any woman who could move her eldest son to matrimony must be extraordinary indeed. Marcus had never quite managed to explain that *he* was dragging his fiancée to the altar, and not the reverse.

Even as he thought it, Elizabeth's steady steps faltered. She glanced around the church like a frightened doe. He stepped forward. She would not run. Not again. His heart raced with something akin to panic. Then she met his gaze, lifted her chin, and continued to approach him.

The ceremony began. And it was long. Too bloody long.

Eager to hasten the process, he repeated his vows with strength and conviction, his deep voice carrying across the packed pews. Elizabeth repeated her vows slowly and with great care, as if she were afraid to stumble over the words. He could see her trembling, felt how cold her hand was in his, and knew she was terrified. He squeezed her hand gently, reassuringly, but with unmistakable claim.

And then the deed was finally done.

Pulling her close, he kissed her, and was surprised at the ardor with which she kissed him back. Her taste flooded his mouth, intoxicated his senses, made him mad with desire. His forced abstinence weighed heavily between his legs, demanding the rights that were now his alone.

It was horribly scandalous.

He didn't care.

Marcus felt an anxious, unrestrained emotion well up inside of him as he stared at his wife. It was almost too much.

So he crushed it and looked away.

Elizabeth tried not to think too much while she prepared for her wedding night. Taking her time with her toilette, she glanced around the room, content to be surrounded by her own things even in a strange place. The chamber was beautiful and expansive, the walls lined with soft pink damask. Only two doors separated her from the room where she'd first made love to Marcus. The remembrance made her skin hot and her stomach clench. It had been so long since he'd taken her, just thought of the night to come made her shiver in anticipation.

Despite the endless desire she'd become accustomed to, it

was still terrifying to have married a man whose will was greater than her own. A man so determined to achieve the realization of his goals that nothing was allowed to stand in his way. Could she influence such a man? Convince him to change his ways? Perhaps change was not even possible and she was foolish to hope.

When she finished bathing, she instructed Meg to leave her hair down, then she excused her abigail for the night. Elizabeth walked to her bed where her night rail and robe awaited her. Both garments had been especially ordered for her trousseau. Admiring them, she brushed her fingertips over the gossamer-thin fabric and costly lace.

She paused as her wedding ring caught the candlelight. It was so different from the much simpler set chosen by Hawthorne. Marcus had given her a massive diamond ring, the large center stone surrounded by a multitude of rubies. It was impossible to ignore, a blatant claim to her, and if that was not enough, the Westfield crest was etched upon the band.

There was a quick rap at her bedroom door and Elizabeth moved to pick up the night rail, then thought better of it. Her husband was a man of voracious sexual appetite and his interest lately had been less than warm. If she hoped to keep him engaged, she would have to be more daring. She didn't have the experience his many lovers had, but she had enthusiasm. One could only hope that would be enough.

Disregarding the garments, she called for him to enter. She took a fortifying breath and turned around. Marcus opened the door and then came to a halt just inside. Dressed in a thick black satin robe, his body visibly tensed at the sight of her. Frozen on the threshold, his emerald eyes smoldered and a tingling awareness flared over her skin. Elizabeth fought back the urge to cover herself with her hands, lifting her chin in a display of courage she didn't feel.

His low and husky voice brought goose bumps to her skin. "Wearing no more than my ring, you are beyond beautiful."

He stepped inside and closed the door, his movements deceptively casual. But she was not deceived. She sensed the fine, taut alertness about him. She watched in fascination as the front of his robe twitched and then rose with his erection. Her mouth watered, her nails digging into her palms as she waited for the halves of the robe to part and reveal that part of him she coveted.

"You're staring, love."

His robe swirled gently around his legs as he crossed the room to her, his body drawing close enough that she could feel the warmth radiating from him. His scent of sandalwood and citrus surrounded her, and her nipples peaked tight and hard, spreading sharp tendrils of desire from her breasts to her sex. She bit back a moan. Her desire for him increased by the day, aggravated by the forced celibacy of the last month.

When had she become such a wanton?

"I—I've missed you," she exhaled, waiting desperately for his touch.

"Have you?" He stared down at her with a rapt expression and she returned the scrutiny, noting the rigidness of his jaw that belied the heat of his gaze. He'd grown so distant, a charming stranger. Then his hand was between her legs, his long middle finger slipping through the lips of her sex to glide through her cream. "Yes, I see you have."

She whimpered when he pulled away and Marcus soothed her with a soft murmur.

His hands moved without haste to the belt of his robe. He tugged the trailing ends free and parted the edges, revealing the rippling power of his abdomen and the hard, pulsing length of his cock. Framed by the ebony lining of his robe, his lean body was stunning.

Elizabeth tore her gaze upward and met his. She said what she needed him to know, needed him to understand. "You belong to me."

Wanting to break through the sudden chill in his features,

she lifted her hand, her fingertips drifting along the side of his throat and farther down his chest. He sucked in a breath, his skin heating under her touch.

Her mouth curved as she relished the power she held over him. She'd never known it could be like this, had never really wanted it to be like this, but he was hers now. That fact altered everything.

Marcus lifted her by the waist and took the one step to the bed. "Lady Westfield," he growled, setting her down on the very lip and surging forward, his cock piercing deep into her with a single heavy thrust.

Elizabeth cried out, writhing away from the unexpected and painful intrusion, but he held her fast. He forced himself over her, pressing her into the bed, his robe a silken cage around their joined bodies. His mouth captured hers in a devastating kiss, his tongue thrusting in a blatant rhythm that robbed her of her senses.

This was no careful, coaxing seduction, as their previous encounters had been. This was a claiming of the basest kind, one that left her momentarily stunned and confused. She knew his touch, her senses recognized his scent and the feel of his body, but the man himself was a stranger to her. So intent and brutally possessive, throbbing hot and hard inside her.

One large hand found her breast and squeezed roughly, breaking her temporary paralysis. His thighs tightened against hers as he slid a fraction deeper. She struggled beneath him, turning her head to gasp for air. His lips moved on, trailing down her cheek, his teeth nipping sharply at her earlobe.

"*You* belong to *me*," he said gruffly.

A threat. She stilled as realization hit.

He wanted her submission. The ring, his name, her desire . . . it was not enough to soothe him.

"Why take what I would give freely?" she whispered, wondering if perhaps it was the only way he could have her,

the only way she'd ever given herself. She thought back, trying to remember a time when she'd tendered herself without
duress.

He groaned and buried his face in her neck. "You've given
me nothing freely. I've paid with blood for all that I have of
you."

Elizabeth's hands slipped beneath his robe and caressed
the rippling cords of his back. He arched into her touch,
sweating in his need, grinding his hips desperately against
hers until she soothed him with her voice. "Let me give you
what you want."

Marcus clasped Elizabeth to his chest with a crushing grip,
biting the top of her shoulder as her cunt rippled along his
cock in a teasing caress. "Witch," he whispered, laving the
indentions left by his teeth.

He'd come to her room with a singular purpose, to slake
their mutual need and consummate the marriage so long in
coming. It was meant to be a dance, one of which he knew all
the steps, a carefully planned encounter without the unwanted
abandoned intimacy. But she'd met him naked, gilded by firelight, hair tumbled about her shoulders and chin lifted with a
Jezebel's pride. She'd stood there and said he belonged to her.
All these years she'd cared nothing for him, and now, *now*,
after all he'd suffered, she claimed the victory.

And she *had* won. He was ensnared, gripped tight by her
lithe thighs and creamy depths, her fingers kneading and
drifting across his back.

Lost in her embrace, he arched his spine upward and kissed
a fiery trail down her throat to her breasts. He licked and savored the pale skin, stroking the sides with his hands, cup-
ping their weight as they become heavy and taut. Her nipples
peaked tight, an irresistible lure, and he bit one crest, worry-
ing it with his teeth before laving the hardened flesh with
leisurely laps of his tongue. Marking her. As he would mark
her everywhere.

Only when she begged did his mouth open and engulf her completely. He suckled her with slow, deep, rhythmic pulls of his tongue and lips, shuddering as the sensation traveled through her body to milk his cock. He could come like this, just from the measured clench and release of her silky tissues. Enflamed by the thought, he hollowed his cheeks, increasing the suction. His eyes drifted closed, his body shuddered as his sac drew up. He swiveled his hips, rubbing her clitoris, and then groaned with her orgasm, releasing his need in burning hot streams of semen.

Gasping and only partially sated, he released her breast and rested his head upon it, wondering if he would ever have enough of her.

Her fingers drifted into his hair. "Marcus . . ."

He rose above her, his arms on either side of her shoulders, and Elizabeth stared up at her husband, attempting to gauge his odd mood. His handsome face was so austere, his eyes searching hers. And she quivered, almost afraid. He looked angry, with his narrowed emerald gaze and harshly drawn mouth. Then he pulled away, the warmth of his body leaving hers, and she was bereft. How could he be equally absorbed and distant?

Marcus stood above his wife, taking in the sight of her sprawled and flushed pink, her thighs spread wantonly, revealing all that he coveted. His erection, covered in her cream, grew cold, but didn't diminish. He watched, arrested, as his seed dribbled from between her legs. His hand reached forward, collected it on his fingertips, and spread it around the lips of her cunt, massaging the clitoris that peeped from its hood.

Mine, mine, mine . . . all mine . . .

Half mad with relief and pleasure and desire, he spread his semen around her sex, watching her arch and writhe, listening to her beg and plead with a detachment that was not detached at all.

Every inch of satin skin belonged to him, every raven hair on her head, every breath she took. For the rest of their lives he could touch her like this, own her like this.

All mine . . .

The thought made him hard as stone, swollen and heavy as if he hadn't just spent himself in her. He stepped forward again, took his cock in hand, and massaged her with the tip. "Take me inside you."

Half expecting her reticence, he groaned when she lifted her hips immediately, engulfing the sensitive head of his cock in liquid, burning heat. He arched his hips and filled her, falling onto his outstretched arms as he sank into the heart of her. It was heaven, the blazing clasp of her cunt around his cooled shaft. If only he could remain like this forever. But he couldn't. Despite how right it felt, it was all wrong.

Gripping her shoulders to pin her in place, Marcus pressed his face against the side of her neck and began to fuck her, his strokes fierce with his hunger, skin slapping against skin. Wrapping her legs around his hips, she rose to meet his every thrust, returning his ardor, holding nothing in reserve, shamelessly crying out on every downward plunge. He battered her with his lust, and she took it, accepted it as she'd promised she would.

"Yes," she cried, her nails in his back. "Marcus . . . Yes!"

It was like drowning, being sucked into a whirlpool, and he grit his teeth and fought against it. Yanking out of her encircling arms, he stood, feet flat on the rugged floor. One hand gripping the bed post, he withdrew from her body until only the tip remained encased, every nerve ending in his body screaming its protest.

Elizabeth burned. Everything burned—her skin, her sex, the roots of her hair. Frustrated tears wept from her eyes. "Don't deny me!"

"I should," he bit out. "For years I was denied."

Rising to brace on her elbows, she stared at the place where they joined, where she ached. She had no power in this, none.

And she would acknowledge that if she must. "You feel so good," she choked out. "I will do anything—"

"Anything?" He rewarded her with a scant inch.

"Yes. For God's sake, Marcus."

He thrust deep and withdrew. Swiveled his hips and plunged. A shallow dip and then gone. Teasing her. And she watched the erotic display, the rippling of his abdomen as he fucked with such skill, the tensing of his thighs as he used his thick, beautiful cock to drive her mad.

She wanted to scream. Her skin was damp with sweat, her limbs trembling, her sex weeping. "What do you want from me?"

Continuing to vary the pace and depth of his fucking, his eyes never left her face. "Everything."

"You have it! I have nothing left."

He took her then, like a ravening beast, gripping the bedpost with white-knuckled force for leverage, the thrusts powerful enough to move her up the bed. He followed, pumping hard and deep with little care for her comfort.

Unable and unwilling to deny him, Elizabeth gave herself up to the turbulence of her husband's passion, her orgasm breaking with a cry of relief.

Marcus held himself above her, watching her abandon, absorbing her trembling, feeling her body tighten exquisitely around him even as he continued to take her.

He could not remember any time when he had been more caught up in the sexual act. His entire body was covered in a slick sheen of sweat, his hips working tirelessly to prolong her pleasure and hurtle himself toward his own. He growled with the sheer animal enjoyment of making love to his wife, a fiercely passionate woman who goaded his desire and then met it with her own.

Feeling, emotion, need—they both worked together to take him to a level of sensation he had never experienced before. His heart aching, he gasped her name as he poured himself into her, wishing desperately for it to be enough, but knowing it would never be. The bottomless well of his need was terrifying. Even now, spewing into her, clutching her desperately, gritting his teeth until his jaw ached, he still wanted more.

Would always want more, even when there was no more to be had.

He rolled from her as if she burned him. His chest heaving, he stared at the canopy, waiting for his eyes to focus, waiting for the room to cease its spinning. The moment it did, he left his wife's bed.

Her scent on his skin, her soft protest behind him, Marcus belted his robe and left her room.

He didn't look back.

Chapter 17

Elizabeth woke to a bright ray of sunshine that snuck between the tiny gap in the curtains and slanted across her face. Stretching, she became aware of the soreness between her legs, a pressing reminder of her husband's rough lovemaking and even rougher departure.

She slid out of bed slowly and stood for a moment contemplating what she now knew to be true. Marcus had married her for his vengeance and he'd gotten it from her tenfold, because some time between the horrendous evening in the Chesterfield garden and yesterday, she'd grown to care for him. A foolish, painful error.

Resigned to the fate she'd walked into with eyes wide open, she called for Meg and the footmen to bring up hot water for her bath, determined to scrub her husband's scent from her skin.

She'd cried the first and last time over Marcus Ashford. Why she'd thought their marriage would be a deeper union was something she couldn't recollect in the bright light of day. She imagined it was the sex. Too many orgasms had rattled her brain. In all fairness, his boredom had been obvious for weeks. Marcus had made no effort to hide it. Still, he'd been solicitous and courteous up until the night previous, and she had no expectation that he would change now that he'd exacted his revenge. She would afford him the same courtesy in return. So her second marriage would be much like her first, distant personages sharing a name and roof. It was not unusual.

Despite these mental reassurances, she felt ill and weepy, and her chest ached badly. The thought of facing Marcus nauseated her. When she finished with her toilette, she looked in the mirror, further distraught to see the faint shadows under her eyes that betrayed her lack of sleep and hours spent crying. It was best she leave the house for a while. This was not home yet, it was very much Marcus's bastion, and the memories she'd made in her history with the house were not pleasant. She took a deep breath and headed down to the foyer.

Passing through the hall, she looked at the clock and saw it was still early morning. Because of the hour, she was surprised to find Marcus's family at breakfast. She felt dwarfed as her tall brothers-in-law rose at her entry. They were a pleasant lot, the Ashfords, but at the moment she wished only to be alone to lick her wounds.

"Good morning, Elizabeth," greeted the lovely Dowager Countess of Westfield.

"Good morning," she returned with the best smile she could manage.

Elaine Ashford was a beautiful and gracious woman with golden hair the color of fresh butter and eyes of emerald green that became translucent when she smiled. "You are up early this morning."

Paul grinned. "Is Marcus still abed?" When Elizabeth nodded, he tossed his head back and laughed aloud. "He's upstairs sleeping off his wedding night, and you are down here dressed flawlessly and ready to go out, unless I miss my guess."

Elizabeth blushed and smoothed her skirts.

Smiling affectionately, Paul said, "Now we see how our

beautiful new sister has led our bachelor brother to the altar. Twice."

Robert choked on his eggs.

"Paul," Elaine admonished, her eyes lit with reluctant amusement. "You are embarrassing Elizabeth."

Shaking her head, Elizabeth was unable to hide her smile. Due to her injury, and the need to hide the knowledge of it, she'd had precious little time to become reacquainted with Marcus's family. But she knew from her earlier association that they were a light-hearted, mirthful group with a wicked sense of humor, due considerably to Paul's penchant for good-natured teasing. That he chose to tease her so informally made her feel accepted into their tight circle, and relieved some of the tension that made her shoulders ache.

Although physically of the same height and breadth of shoulder as Marcus, Paul had black hair and warm, chocolate brown eyes. Three years younger than Marcus and equally handsome, Paul could take Society, and its eager debutantes, by storm if he wished, which he didn't. Instead, he preferred to remain in Westfield. Elizabeth had yet to discern why he chose to isolate himself in the country, but it was a mystery she intended to unravel at some point.

Robert, the youngest, was nearly the spitting image of Marcus with the same rich sable hair and emerald green eyes, which were charmingly enhanced by spectacles. He was an extremely quiet and studious fellow, physically just as tall as his brothers, but much leaner and less muscular due to his bookish nature. Robert was interested in all things scientific and mechanical. He could wax poetic about any number of dull and boring topics, but all of the Ashfords indulged him when he took his nose out of his books and deigned to speak with them. At the present moment, that nose was buried in the newspaper.

Paul stood. "If you will excuse me, ladies. I have an appointment with the tailor this morn. Since I rarely come to

Town, I must exploit the opportunity to keep abreast of the latest fashions." He glanced at Robert, still engrossed in the paper. "Robert. Come along. You require new clothes more than I."

Robert glanced up, eyes blinking. "For what purpose would I dress in the latest fashions?"

Shaking his head, Paul muttered, "Never met a more handsome chap who could care less about his appearance." He walked over to Robert's chair and slid it back easily. "You are coming with me, brother, whether you like it or not."

With a long suffering sigh and a covetous glance at the newspaper, Robert followed Paul out of the house.

Elizabeth watched the exchange with affectionate amusement, liking both of her new brothers immensely.

Elaine arched her brows as she lifted her teacup. "Don't let his surliness disturb you overmuch."

"Paul's?"

"No, Marcus's. Marriage is an adjustment, that's all. I still wish you would consider going away. Allow yourselves to settle in without the pressures you'll find here in Town."

"We intend to, once the Parliamentary session is over." It was the excuse Marcus had suggested they supply. With the journal a hanging weight over her head, they couldn't afford to leave London. Waiting until the end of the Season seemed the reply least likely to raise suspicion.

"But you are unhappy with this decision, are you not?"

"Why would you say that?"

Offering a sad smile, Elaine said, "You've been crying."

Aghast to have her torment known, Elizabeth took a step back. "A bit tired, but I'm certain a drive in the crisp morning air will cure that."

"A lovely idea. I'll join you." Elaine pushed back from the table.

Stuck in a position where refusal would be rude, Elizabeth released a deep breath and nodded. With a strict warning to the staff to leave the lord of the house undisturbed, Elizabeth and Elaine departed.

As the town coach lurched into motion, Elaine noted, "You have a fair number of outriders to accompany you. I believe you are more heavily guarded than the king."

"Westfield is a bit overprotective."

"How like him to be so concerned."

Elizabeth seized the opportunity to learn more about her husband. "I've wondered, is Marcus much like his father?"

"No. Paul is most like the late earl, in appearance and disposition. Robert is a bit of an anomaly, God love him. And Marcus is by far the most charming, but the more reserved of the lot. Always has been difficult to collect his aim until after he's achieved it. He hides his thoughts well behind that polished façade. I've yet to witness him losing his temper, but he has one I'm certain. He is, after all, his father's son and Westfield was a man of high passion."

Sighing inwardly, Elizabeth acknowledged the truth in the words spoken to her. Despite hours of physical intimacy, she knew little about the man she'd wed, an exquisite creature who drawled when he spoke and shared few of his thoughts. Only when they were alone did she see the passion in him, both his fury and desire. In her own way, she felt blessed to know those sides of him, when his beloved family did not.

Elaine leaned across the carriage and captured one of Elizabeth's hands with her own. "I knew the moment I saw you together how perfect you would be for him. Marcus has never appeared so engaged."

Elizabeth flushed. "I would not have thought you would endorse me after what transpired four years ago."

"I subscribe to the 'reason for everything' school of thought, my dear. Life has always come too easily for Marcus. I'd prefer to think your . . . *delay* contributed to his grounding these last few years."

"You are too kind."

"You wouldn't think so if you knew the things I said about you four years ago. When Marcus left the country I was devastated."

Riddled with guilt, Elizabeth squeezed Elaine's hand and was touched when her hand was squeezed in return.

"Yet you married him anyway and he has grown much from the man who first offered for you. I hold no ill will toward you, Elizabeth, none at all."

I wish Marcus felt the same, Elizabeth thought silently, and not a little sadly.

The coach slowed to a halt. Before they had the opportunity to alight from the carriage, the employees of the shops lined the curb to greet them. Having spied the crest emblazoned on the door, they were anxious to assist the new Countess of Westfield and reap the rewards of her husband's largesse.

The morning passed swiftly, and Elizabeth found a respite from her melancholy with Elaine, appreciating the older woman's suggestions and advice while relishing the maternal companionship she'd lacked all her life.

Elaine paused in front of a milliner's window and sighed at a lovely creation displayed in the window.

"You should try it on," Elizabeth urged.

Elaine blushed and confessed, "I have a fondness for millinery."

Waving her mother-in-law inside, Elizabeth strolled to the neighboring perfumery, leaving the two outriders who followed her at the door.

Once inside, she stopped before a display of bath oils and removed the stopper from a bottle to sample the fragrance. Disliking the scent, she put it down and picked up another.

"I hear congratulations are in order, Lady Westfield," rasped a masculine voice behind her.

Startled, she almost dropped the fragile bottle, her stomach tightening in recognition of the unique voice. She spun to face Christopher St. John, her heart racing and eyes wide.

In the light of day, without a mask or wig to hide his features, he was a splendid looking specimen, angelic in appearance with his dark blond hair and vivid blue eyes.

Arrested at first by his exceptional handsomeness, she quickly came to her senses and changed her mind. Fallen angel was a more apt description. The signs of hard living were etched on his countenance. Shadows marred the skin beneath those amazing eyes, betraying a life that had no place for restful slumber.

His lips curved derisively. "Has no one told you it's not polite to stare?"

"Do you intend to stab me again?" she asked curtly, taking a step back and bumping against the display. "If so, get on with it."

St. John threw his head back and laughed, drawing the attention of the clerk behind the counter who gazed at him with blatant admiration. "Feisty, aren't you? I can see why Nigel liked you so well."

Her eyes widened as the familiar address. "And how would you know how my husband felt?"

"I know a great many things," he replied arrogantly.

"Ah yes, I forgot." She was frustrated by his confidence in the face of her fear. "You somehow learned of Hawthorne's journal and have been threatening me for it ever since." Elizabeth gripped the bottle of bath oil so tightly her hands ached.

St. John glanced down. "Put the bottle aside before you hurt yourself."

"Don't worry about me. It's *you* who most stands to be hurt by it." She hefted the bottle in warning before dropping it carelessly onto the shelf, ignoring the roiling in her stomach. "What do you want?"

St. John stared at her, his face reflecting an odd mixture of emotions. "It took me all morning to lose those lackeys Westfield has hounding me."

Through the glass front of the store she saw the backs of the two outriders who stood guard. "How did you get in here?"

"Through the rear entrance. It has been extremely difficult to approach you with those damned outriders and Westfield guarding you at all times."

"That is the point."

He scowled. "The first time we met, I had only a few moments to speak with you. I couldn't explain."

"Explain now."

"First, you must know I would never hurt you." His jaw tightened. "I'm attempting to assist you."

"Why would you wish to do that?" she scoffed. "I am married to a man who would see you hanged if he could."

"You are my brother's widow," he said quietly. "That is all that matters to me."

"*What?*" Physically thrown off balance by his statement, Elizabeth reached behind her in an effort to steady herself and instead knocked over several bottles, which crashed to the floor and shattered, filling the room with the cloying scent of flowers and musk.

"You lie!" But the moment she denied it, she knew it was true.

Upon closer examination, the similarities were obvious. Nigel's hair had been the same dark wheat color and his eyes had been blue although not as brilliant as St. John's. The nose was the same, the shape of the jaw and chin, the placement of the ears.

"Why would I?" he asked simply.

She examined the pirate in greater detail. His mouth was not the same. Nigel's had been less wide, the lips thinner, and his skin had been softer, more pampered. Nigel had sported a mustache and Van Dyke. Christopher's face was clean-shaven. But the differences were minor. Had she known to look, she would have caught the resemblance earlier.

Brothers.

The color drained from her face.

Her lungs sought air, but the restriction of her corset made it difficult to breathe. She felt dizzy and her legs gave way, but St. John caught her to him before she fell. He dipped her over a steely arm, his hand tilting her head back to better open her airway. "Easy," he soothed in his raspy voice. "Take a breath. Now another."

"Damn you," she gasped. "Have you no tact? No sense to know better than to spring such news on me with no warning?"

"Ah, your charm is once again in evidence." He smiled and looked for a moment very much like Nigel. "Keep breathing as deeply as you can. I have no notion of how you women suffer your corsets."

The bells above the door chimed merrily.

"The dowager has arrived," he murmured in warning.

"Elizabeth!" Elaine cried, her voice growing louder as she rushed closer. "Unhand her immediately, sir!"

"I apologize, my lady," St. John replied with a smile that was charming even from Elizabeth's underside view. "But I am unable to oblige you. If I release Lady Westfield she will certainly collapse to the floor."

"Oh," said the shop girl as she joined the muddle. "Christopher St. John."

"St. John?" murmured Elaine, trying to place the name.

" 'E's famous," supplied the girl.

"You mean infamous," grumbled Elizabeth as she struggled to right herself.

Christopher laughed.

Elaine frowned. Uncertain of how to handle the situation she fell back on her manners. "Thank you, Mr. St. John, for your assistance. I'm certain The Earl will be most appreciative."

The full lips curved with wry amusement. "I sincerely doubt that, my lady."

Elizabeth struggled against his thickly muscled chest. "Release me," she hissed.

He chuckled as he straightened her, making certain she was steady on her feet before dropping his arms away. Then he turned and paid the besotted shop girl for the broken items.

"Elizabeth, are you unwell?" Elaine asked with obvious concern. "Perhaps it is too soon after your illness for you to be out."

"I should have eaten this morning. I felt faint for a moment, but it's passed now."

St. John returned to their sides, gave a courtly bow, and made his excuses.

"Wait!" Elizabeth hurried after him. "You cannot simply walk away after telling me something like that."

Christopher lowered his voice, glancing over her head at the dowager countess. "Does your mother-in-law know of this affair?"

"Of course not."

"Then it's not wise to discuss this now." He collected his hat from atop the bin near the rear hallway where he'd left it. "I will find you again soon. In the meantime, please be careful and trust no one. I would never forgive myself if something untoward happened to you."

It was shortly before luncheon when Elizabeth and Elaine returned home. They parted on the second floor landing, both retreating to their rooms to change their gowns. Elizabeth was exhausted, hungry, and totally confused by St. John's revelations, a combination that gave her a splitting headache.

What was she to do now?

She couldn't share St. John's claims of kinship until she knew them to be true. And if they were, her marriage would be a disaster. Marcus truly hated St. John and had wed her for reasons best left unconsidered. What would he do if he knew? Despite how she wished it, she couldn't see him considering it of no consequence. Certainly it would mean something to him, and Eldridge as well, that the man they pursued with a vengeance was connected to her in so personal a way. And William. All these years it was St. John who bore the blame for nearly killing him. But was that true? Was the pirate so cold and calloused as she'd been led to believe? And Nigel . . . *Dear God, Nigel.* Working for Eldridge to hunt his own brother. Or perhaps he'd assisted St. John in his activities, which made him a traitor.

She needed time to think and contemplate the ramifications of what she'd learned today. As it was, she was barely able to walk, her steps dragging and her stomach growling. Later, once she was of firmer mind, she would reason out how to share the news with her husband.

Entering her room, she closed the door. She moved to collapse in the large wingback chair by the fireplace and started in surprise to find Marcus sitting there.

"Good heavens, Marcus! You gave me a fright."

He rose from the chair and Elizabeth wondered if it was her lack of sleep that made him appear taller and more menacing. "Surely not so much of a fright as I received when I discovered you had left the house," he drawled.

Her chin lifted in response to the sudden leap of her heart. Dressed for riding, he was impossibly handsome and she hated to discover that she still wanted him, even after crying over him all night. "Such care for my well-being. Unfortunate that you had none for me last night."

When she attempted to pass him, his hand whipped out and caught her upper arm, dragging her to him. "I heard no complaints," he growled.

"Perhaps if you'd stayed longer you would have."

"If I'd stayed longer, there would be no complaints at all."

She yanked free of his grip, her chin quivering at his words, which betrayed his understanding of the pain he inflicted. "Leave me and take your arrogance with you. I must change for luncheon."

"Despite being *de trop*, I believe I'll stay," he said softly, though the challenge in his eyes was hard.

"I don't want you here." His presence renewed the unhappiness she'd spent all morning trying to forget.

"And I did not want you venturing out without me. Sometimes we don't attain the things we desire."

"How well I know it," she muttered, ringing for her abigail.

He released a breath that could only be described as frustrated. "Why must you deliberately ignore the danger?"

"I took the outriders with me and as you can see, I am home and all in one piece. You didn't mind when I went out before. Am I to be a prisoner now that we're wed?"

"You have not been out since the stabbing. The danger is greater now, and well you know it."

Elizabeth dropped into her gilt vanity chair and gazed at his angry reflection in the mirror.

Marcus eyed her closely before resting his large hands on her shoulders and squeezing so tightly she flinched. He opened his mouth as if to speak and then a soft rap came at the door.

For the next half hour he watched as her abigail helped her to dress. He said nothing, but his stifling presence made both her and the servant uncomfortable. By the time she finished changing she was certain she was about to expire from hunger and the thick tension radiating from her husband. She was greatly relieved when they reached the main floor and joined his family for the meal. She settled into her seat and ate with as much decorum as she could manage considering how long she'd gone without food.

"I am relieved to see you feeling better, Elizabeth," Elaine said. "I thank the Lord you were caught by that St. John fellow before you fell to injury, although he did seem—"

"Could you repeat that, Mother?" Marcus said with dangerous softness.

Elizabeth winced and ate with greater haste.

"Surely your wife mentioned her near faint this morn?" Elaine shot a questioning glance down the table.

"As a matter of fact, she did not." Setting his knife and fork down with unnatural care, he offered a grim smile and asked, "Did you say St. John?"

Elaine blinked in obvious confusion.

Elizabeth's stomach clenched in apprehension. She should say something, she knew, but her throat was so tight she couldn't manage even one word.

The sudden pounding of Marcus's fist on the table startled everyone. Only the plates rattling sharply together broke the ensuing stunned silence. He slid his chair back and stood, placing his palms flat on the table. His glowering face had Elizabeth quaking in her chair. She held her breath.

"At what point did you intend to share this with me?" he roared.

The Ashfords sat with mouths agape, utensils paused in mid-air.

Galvanized by their horror, Elizabeth pushed back from the table and stood. Paul and Robert leapt to their feet.

"My lord," she began. "If you would prefer to—"

"Do not try to sway me with sudden docility, Lady Westfield." He walked around the table. "What did he want? By God, I'll kill him!"

She tried again. "Might I suggest the study?"

Paul sidestepped neatly into his path. Marcus glared, then moved to the sideboard and poured a hefty ration of brandy.

"I didn't mention it directly, because I knew it would upset you."

Marcus stared at her as if she'd grown two heads, then he downed his drink in one gulp and left the room, his handsome face set in harsh, unyielding lines. She heard the front door slam behind him.

Paul whistled softly.

"Good heavens," gasped Elaine, collapsing backwards in her chair. "He was *angry*."

Robert shook his head. "I would not believe it if I hadn't seen it with my own eyes. Can hardly believe it now."

All eyes turned, awestruck, to look at Elizabeth who stood trembling. She inhaled a shaky breath. "I apologize. I realize you are unaccustomed to seeing him in such a state. I regret you had to witness it today."

Robert frowned. "St. John. The name sounds familiar."

"I should explain." She sighed. "Marcus suspects St. John is responsible for the attacks on vessels belonging to Ashford Shipping, but there is no evidence to support that."

"Was it simply unfortunate that he happened to be in such close proximity to you?" asked Elaine. "I thought it odd for him to be perusing soaps and bath oils."

Elizabeth searched for an explanation. "He was a close friend of Hawthorne's. When our paths cross, he pays his respects."

Robert removed his spectacles and began to polish the lenses. "Is St. John aware of Marcus's suspicions about him?"

"Yes."

"Then he should bloody well stay away from you and keep his respects to himself," Paul growled.

Elaine tapped her fingers against her water glass. "You did not appear to care much for him yourself, Elizabeth."

"He is a stranger to me."

"And for Marcus to be goaded into such a temper over the whole affair," Elaine continued, "well, I've never seen the like."

"He was very angry," Elizabeth agreed, crestfallen. She'd never seen him so furious. That his fury had driven him to leave the house made her sick to her stomach. Certainly she was angry at him as well, but this gulf between them seemed as wide as when she'd been married to Hawthorne. She stepped away from the table. "I pray you will excuse me."

Climbing the stairs, Elizabeth considered the events of the

day with a heavy heart. Marcus was important to her. She'd known that when she chose to marry him, and though she'd tried to discount it when he'd treated her so coldly, it remained immutable. Now that their bond, as tentative as it was, was threatened, she understood the depth of her attachment.

This morning the distance between them had been entirely her husband's doing. Now she too contributed to their estrangement. Perhaps if he cared for her they could meet in the middle, but she'd destroyed whatever tenderness he'd felt for her four years ago.

And she finally understood just how much she had lost.

Chapter 18

Elizabeth woke to damp skin at her back and warm hands on her body, one wrapped in her hair and the other stroking her thigh. Her toes were curled, her nipples hard, her body already aware, even though her mind was not.

She whimpered. Marcus had been gone for hours, all through the afternoon and late into the night. She had cried herself to sleep again, after she'd sworn she wouldn't, and the feel and smell of him against her was both a balm and a barb. His cock, hard and hot, snuggled in the valley between her buttocks, a silent promise of his amorous intent.

"Hush," he said softly, his mouth nuzzling her throat, his wet hair cooling her suddenly feverish skin. Gripping her inner thigh, he lifted her leg and anchored it on his own, his fingers drifting to the curls between her legs. His touch was gentle, coaxing, once again the lover she craved and not the fiercely possessive husband who'd claimed her the night before.

With skill born of much practice and intimate knowledge, Marcus parted the lips of her sex with reverent fingers and dipped inside, swirling around her clitoris and the opening to her body with a callused fingertip, the roughness of which heightened her pleasure almost unbearably. Desperate, she undulated helplessly against his hard body. "Please . . ."

"My wife," he exclaimed, his tongue swirling around the

shell of her ear, his breath hot against the newly damp flesh. "Always on fire. Naked in her bed, and waiting for my attentions."

He stroked through her cream and then slipped inside her, thrusting into the drenched walls of her sex with maddening leisure. *In and out.* Just that one digit, not nearly enough to satisfy, but enough to make her beg for more.

"Marcus!" She struggled to turn, to move, to take what she wanted, but his arm tightened and pinned her still.

"Relax, and I'll let you come."

Elizabeth stilled a tremor shaking her body as his single finger was joined by another, the deep plunge and withdrawal sounding wetly over her panting breaths. She hitched her leg higher, opening herself wider, and he fisted his hand in her hair and arched her neck back.

Turning her head, she met his avid mouth with her own, her tongue thrusting along his in a frenzy of desire. Her eagerness goaded him, broke his rigid control. The shift was tangible, his frame tensing behind her, his cock swelling even further between them, his hips grinding forward.

She gasped as his thumb rubbed her clitoris, the barely-there pressure increasing her thrashing. At her back she felt the rapid rise and fall of his chest, in her mouth she caught his harsh exhalation. Her skin was coated with a fine sheen of sweat and she rode his thrusting fingers with greater and greater urgency.

"Please!" she cried, clenching around his fingers in her quest to orgasm. "I need you."

Marcus shifted, his fingers sliding free to reach for his cock. Then he was there, the wide flared head breaching her and pushing inside. His hand, drenched in her cream, cupped her breast, pinched her nipple. And deeper he slid, a thick pulsing possession.

"Yes," she hissed struggling to meet him, to hurry him, to take the long length of him.

His groan in her ear enflamed her. That she could bring him such pleasure while lost in her own was an intoxicating power.

And still he pressed into her.

But it was not enough. The curve of her buttocks kept him from the full depths she craved, and she wanted *him*, all of him. Not just his cock and his hand at her breast, but his body over hers, his eyes locked on hers. The gulf between them was there, widened by the hours he'd spent away from her today, but in this there was no division. In this, they could be one.

"You're not deep enough," she complained, wiggling her bottom against his pelvis, crushing the curls at the base of his shaft.

He growled. "Greedy vixen."

"You made me this way." She cupped her hand over his, kneading her breast with his hand, bearing down on his rigid cock with her hips. "Roll me over," she urged, her voice husky with want. "Fuck me deeply. Let me hold you."

It was the last that moved him. He yanked free of her with a curse, pulling her onto her back so he could loom over her. Elizabeth spread her legs wide in welcome and moaned aloud when he sank to the hilt inside of her.

He stilled then, staring down at her in the faint light from the banked fire. Backlit as he was, she couldn't see his features, but his eyes glittered with an unmistakable hunger.

Her heart ached with longing. Marcus Ashford belonged to her, and yet he would never truly be hers.

At least she had this. His passion, his desire. It would have to be enough since it was all he would give her. The feeling of his cock stroking in deep inner caresses, the clenching of his hard, muscular buttocks as he propelled himself into her, the scent of his skin, heated and damp with sweat, the sound of his guttural cries of pleasure.

She wrapped her arms around him and held him as if she would never let go, absorbing what she could of him, until finally, with silent tears, she sank into blissful relief with him.

*   *   *

Flat on his back, Marcus stared up through the darkness to the canopy above. Against his side Elizabeth curled, her thigh atop his, her arm across his waist. The warm, soft feel of her curves was heaven after the loneliness of their wedding night. Dawn had arrived without him sleeping a wink. He'd paced for hours, fighting the urge to return to her, to hold her, as he had during the nights of their affair. He'd thought the physical distance would help him find objectivity, but when he awoke to find her gone, he'd realized how hopeless that endeavor was.

Their row, and the gulf it created, had shown him the folly in pushing her away. Damn it, she was his *wife*! He'd waited all these years to have her, only to turn away from her once she was his.

Elizabeth stirred, and then sat up. Heedless of her nakedness, she settled back on her heels. She presented such a vision of loveliness Marcus almost forgot to breathe. Wanting to see her in all her glory, he slid from the bed to light the bedside taper.

"If you walk out that door, don't visit me again," she said coldly.

He stilled, fighting the urge to snap back. While her threat to bar him from her bed was not one he would accept, *ever*, he understood it was his own churlish behavior that prompted her to throw down the gauntlet.

"I simply wish to throw some light on the situation."

She made no sound, but he could sense her sudden relief and closed his eyes. He had every right to protect her, and his goal had been worthy, but the execution had been a terrible mistake. How much damage had he inflicted? *She said nothing of St. John to him . . . she didn't trust him . . .*

"Are you still angry?" she asked hesitantly.

He sighed aloud. "I haven't yet decided. What happened today? Tell me everything."

Behind him, she shifted uncomfortably and his hackles

rose. "St. John approached me. H-he claims to want to help me. I believe he—"

"In what way did he offer to help?"

"He didn't say. Your mother arrived. He was unable to finish speaking."

"Dear God," he exclaimed, horrified at the thought of St. John in such close proximity to his wife and his mother.

"He knows who desires Hawthorne's journal."

"Of course he does." His voice was gritty with renewed anger. He should have killed the pirate.

Leaving the bed, Marcus took a moment to stoke the fire and relight the extinguished taper. Then he returned to Elizabeth and eyed her suspiciously. "You are not the type of woman who succumbs to fits of vapors. You forget I have seen you shoot a man without a qualm. You are hiding something from me." He arched a brow in silent query.

Her gaze met his.

"Why didn't you tell me earlier, Elizabeth?"

"I was feeling cross."

Marcus narrowed his gaze. He knew she could be spiteful when angered, but she was not stupid. Anger alone would not prevent her from protecting herself. Something was amiss, he could feel it. She was attempting to conceal information and he considered all possibilities. Perhaps the pirate had threatened her in some manner. If so, he intended to discern the cause and attend to it directly. More than he already had.

"Where did you go?" she asked when the silence stretched out.

"To locate St. John, of course."

Her eyes widened and then dropped to his torso. She gaped. "Look at you! You've been hurt."

"He revealed even less information than you, dear wife. But I'm certain he now understands the foolishness of approaching you again."

"What did you do?" Her fingertips drifted with heartening concern to the spreading bruise that marred his ribs.

He shrugged, completely unaffected by her horrified gaze. "St. John and I simply engaged in casual discourse."

She poked brutally into the swelling and he winced. "*That* does not come from talking," she argued. "And look at your hand." She examined his swollen knuckles and shot him a chastising glance.

Marcus grinned. "Better you should look at St. John's face."

"Ridiculous. I want you to stay away from him, Marcus."

"I will," he agreed, "If he stays away from you."

"Aren't you curious as to what manner of help he's offering?"

Marcus grunted. "He made no offer of assistance to me. He is deceiving you, love. Attempting to win your trust so you will give the book to him."

Elizabeth opened her mouth to argue further, then thought better of it. It was best if Marcus didn't dig too far into Christopher St. John. It was miraculous that nothing more than blows were exchanged. She marveled at her husband's restraint. That the pirate continued his activities chafed Marcus, she had no doubt, but he forced himself to wait. For what, she was not certain. There must be something Eldridge wanted with St. John, or they would have disposed of him long ago.

She was startled when Marcus reached for her hand and tugged her face-first onto the bed. He rolled over her, caging her to the mattress. It was then she noted his erection, the tip of it pressing into the curve of her derriere.

"You are my wife," he growled in her ear. "I expect you to tell me of the things that happen in your life, to share things with me, even if they seem inconsequential, but most especially when the matter is so dire. I will not tolerate your lying to me or withholding things from me. Do I make myself clear?"

She pursed her lips. The brute.

He thrust his hips forward and his cock glided through the valley between her buttocks, his path eased by the weeping head. "I will not have you putting your life in danger. You

should never leave the house without me. Can you understand how worried I was? Wondering if you were in danger . . .
wondering if you needed me."

"You are aroused," she replied, surprised.

"You are naked," he said simply, as if only that was
enough. "You must learn to trust me, Elizabeth." His lips
moved against her shoulder as he stroked himself with her
prone body. "I will try to be worthy of it."

Elizabeth's hands fisted in the sheets and she hid her sudden tears. "I'm sorry I made you angry."

Marcus nuzzled her throat. "I apologize to you, as well."

"I accept, on the condition you share my bed." Elizabeth
moaned as he thrust again, a slow deliberate glide that left a
damp trail behind. Heat blossomed instantly. With a forlorn
sigh, she closed her eyes. She should have told him the truth
when she had the chance. Now he would always wonder
why she hid it from him.

"My bed is bigger," he drawled, slightly breathless.

Her heart swelled with tenderness. The urge to tell him
about her kinship with St. John was nearly overwhelming.
But now was not the time.

She arched her hips upward impatiently. "If we switched
locations, would you hurry?"

Lifting enough to allow her to her knees, he entered her
from behind with a single powerful stroke.

"Sweet Elizabeth," he groaned, his cheek to her back. "We
can switch rooms tomorrow."

Elizabeth waited in the far reaches of the garden. Pacing
with impatience, she spun about quickly as she heard approaching footsteps.

"Mr. James! Thank God, you've come."

Avery stopped before her, frowning. "Why have you sent
for me?" He glanced around. "Where is Lord Westfield?"

She took his arm and tugged him behind a tree. "I require
your assistance and Westfield must not know of it."

"I beg your pardon? Your husband is the agent assigned to assist you."

She gripped his arm tighter to convey her urgency. "Christopher St. John approached me yesterday. He claims to be brother to Hawthorne. I must know the truth."

Avery was stunned into silence.

Looking over his shoulder, she watched the path behind him. "Westfield was furious when he learned of the meeting. He left the house to search for St. John." She lowered her voice. "They exchanged blows."

Avery's mouth quirked with a rare smile. "Well, then. All was well."

"How can you say that?" she cried.

"Lord Westfield was merely making a point. And releasing some steam in the process."

"How can you condone such rash behavior?"

"I do not condone it, Lady Westfield, but I can understand his motivation. Your husband is an excellent agent. I am certain he did not go into the encounter without careful planning. He would never have allowed emotion to rule his actions."

Elizabeth snorted. "I assure you, he was highly strung when he departed."

Avery tried to look reassuring. "I believe Lord Westfield is more than capable of handling this matter, if you will just trust him to do so."

"I cannot go to him with conjecture." She clasped her hands together imploringly.

"What is it you would ask of me that you would not ask of your husband?"

"I need you to research St. John's story. If what he says is true, we must wonder at the irony of two brothers working on opposite sides of the law. Hawthorne was killed and my brother wounded while investigating St. John. That cannot be a coincidence." She clutched his hand. "And Lord Eldridge must remain ignorant of this development."

"Why?"

"Because he would certainly tell Westfield. I'm not certain how my husband will take the news. I need some time to sort this out."

"You sound as if you believe."

Elizabeth nodded miserably. "I have no reason not to. The resemblance between St. John and Hawthorne is startling, and the tale is so fantastic how can it not be true?"

"I fear you may be doing a disservice to his lordship."

"A little more time," she begged. "It's all I ask. I promise to tell him everything you discover."

He released a long-suffering sigh. "Very well. I will investigate, and keep my silence in the interval."

Elizabeth's heart gave a tiny leap of grateful relief. "Thank you, Mr. James. You have always been a dear friend to me."

Flushing a dull red, he said, "Don't thank me just yet. We may both end up regretting that I agreed to this business."

Over the next few weeks, Elizabeth accustomed herself to married life with Marcus. The Ashfords remained in residence at his insistence. He rested easier knowing she was not alone and Elizabeth appreciated the company while he attended to his affairs.

At Eldridge's insistence, they attended the occasional Society event, ones most likely to attract St. John. The pirate had managed to throw off the agents tracking his whereabouts and hadn't been seen in London since the afternoon he'd spoken with her. His sudden departure was a mystery that set them all on edge.

The threat to her was always on Marcus's mind. Guards were stationed in and around the house, dressed in Westfield livery to avoid arousing the suspicions of his family. The endless waiting made her husband as restless as a caged animal. She'd known from their very first dance together that he was a man who held a tight rein on his passions. He unleashed them fully on her.

He held nothing back. When he was angry, he yelled. When he was pleased, he laughed. When he was aroused, he made love to her, regardless of what time of day it was or where they were at the moment. Twice he left the Lords in the middle of the afternoon to seduce her. She had never felt so important to someone, so necessary. Blatantly possessive, he showed no hesitation in speaking harshly to any man who acted too familiarly with her.

For her own part, Elizabeth found that her jealousy did not ease with her new ownership. It was a miserable personality flaw to be cursed with in a society where dalliance was not only widespread, but expected. Marriage only increased Marcus's appeal to other women. His vibrant energy was now mellowed to the slow, languid grace of a man who was well-loved often by a passionate woman. It made him irresistible.

One evening, during a masked ball, Elizabeth's jealousy finally got the better of her. As Marcus moved toward the beverage tables, she noticed several women choosing the same moment to replenish their own glasses. Looking away in disgust, Elizabeth spied the Dowager Duchess of Ravensend coming toward her.

"Do you see the way women follow my husband?" she complained, rising from a quick curtsy.

Her Grace shrugged. "Masked events give license to cast off what little restraint Society clings to. Note the shaking palm tree in the far right corner? Lady Grenville and Lord Sackton have abandoned their spouses in favor of some exhibitionist sport. And Claire Milton returned from the garden with twigs in her hair. You should not be surprised they sniff after Westfield like mongrel bitches."

"I'm not," she announced curtly. "But I won't tolerate it. Excuse me, Your Grace." With rapid strides, she moved into the next room to find her husband.

She located him near the refreshment tables, a glass in each hand and surrounded by women. He shrugged innocently when he saw her, his lips curving wickedly beneath the edge of his half mask. Pushing through the small crowd, Elizabeth claimed one of the glasses, and then linked her arm with his. Her spine stiff, she led Marcus back to the ballroom, all enjoyment in the evening gone.

The duchess took one look at her face, and excused herself with a smile.

Marcus chuckled. "Thank you, Lady Westfield. To my recollection that is the first time I have ever been rescued."

"You have never wanted to be rescued," she snapped, hating that he could be so nonchalant in the face of her upset.

He lifted a hand to caress a powdered curl. "You're jealous!" he crowed.

She turned away, wondering, as she often did, how many women in the room knew him carnally as she did.

Marcus stepped around until he faced her. "What is it, love?"

"None of your affair."

Uncaring of their audience, Marcus traced the bottom curve of her lip with his gloved thumb. "Tell me what's wrong, or I cannot fix it."

"I detest every woman who knew you before." Blushing, she lowered her head and waited for his laughter.

Instead, his deep, velvety voice swirled around her, encasing her in warmth. "Do you remember when I said intimacy and sex can be mutually exclusive?" His head lowered to hers, his mouth brushing her ear as he whispered, "You are the only woman I have ever been intimate with."

A tear escaped. Marcus brushed it away.

"I want to take you home," he murmured, his emerald gaze hot behind the mask. "And be intimate with you."

She left with him, desperate to have him all to herself. That night he was so tender in his lovemaking, adoring her with his body, giving her everything she asked. His gentle ardor brought tears to her eyes and afterward he held her in his arms as if she were the most precious thing in the world.

Every day brought her closer to him. She was beginning to need him, not just with sensual craving but for so much more. It was a passion that would take a lifetime to sate.

She could only pray fate would give her that chance.

Chapter 19

"You should not have come to my home."
Christopher St. John vaulted into the unmarked Westfield town coach. The pirate's overwhelming presence dominated the interior and added a palpable energy to the air, forcing Elizabeth to retreat into the squabs. Glancing out the window, she remained surprised at the elegance of the small townhouse he resided in. It was conspicuous in the unfashionable part of town where it was located. However the two burly henchmen at the door betrayed the seediness of the goings-on within.

He took the seat opposite her. "It's not a fit place for a lady and this ostentatious equipage is attracting the kind of dangerous attention you don't want."

"You know I had no choice. As soon as I learned your direction, I had to come. I have no other way of reaching you." She arched a brow. "You, Mr. St. John, have questions to answer."

His full mouth curved wryly, as he leaned back and adjusted his coat. "No need to be so formal. We are related, after all."

"As if I could forget."

"So you believe me then."

"I had your claim investigated."

St. John glanced around, taking in the opulence of the dark

leather interior with one sweeping glance. "Such a shame you married Westfield. Looks as if the man could use a lightening of his purse."

"I strongly suggest you find other sport, if you don't wish to anger me. I am not pleasant when I'm cross."

St. John blinked, then threw his head back and laughed. "By God, I do like you. Rest assured, I am loyal to members of my family and Westfield is something of a family member, is he not?"

Rubbing between her brows in a vain effort to ward off a headache, she muttered, "Westfield knows nothing of this and I prefer to keep it that way."

St. John reached over and opened the small compartment door by his seat. Withdrawing a glass, he poured two fingers of brandy, which he then offered to her. When she refused, he put the decanter away. "I realized you hadn't told him about us when he came to see me. However, I did think you would have told him since then."

Studying him more closely, she noted the faint yellow of a healing bruise around his left eye and the small scab on his lip. "Are your injuries from Westfield?"

"No other man would dare."

She winced. "I apologize. I had no intention of telling him about our meeting, but I neglected to tell my mother-in-law to keep quiet about it."

St. John waved his hand in a dismissive gesture. "No lasting harm done. Quite stimulating, actually. After years of doing nothing more strenuous than exchanging barbs, it was time for us to get to business. I was glad he found me. I was curious to see how he felt about you. The man has never had a weakness in his life. I regret you are one I cannot exploit."

"What is your grievance with Westfield?"

"The man is too arrogant, too titled, too wealthy, too pretty—too everything. He's as rich as Croesus and yet he cries foul when I take a tiny bit of his blunt."

She snorted. "As if you would have a party should someone steal from you."

He choked on his brandy.

"I must know about Hawthorne," she asked, leaning forward. "It's driving me mad not knowing who he was."

St. John removed his hat and ruffled his wavy blond locks with a large hand. "Nigel was your spouse. I prefer you to remember the man you spent a year of your life with."

"But I don't understand. If you were close to one another, how could he work with Eldridge without harming you or . . . or . . ."

"Acting as traitor?" he finished softly. "Elizabeth, I pray you leave such concerns outside the scope of your recollections. He was a good husband to you, was he not?"

"So I should only cling to the facets I knew and discard the others?"

He sighed and set his hat on the seat next to him. "Did your investigation reveal information about our father?"

Elizabeth sat back and bit her lip.

"Ah, I see it did. Touched, they call it. A bit off, half mad—"

"I understand."

"Do you?" He looked down and examined his jeweled heels with unnecessary focus. "Did you hear of the violence? The ravings? No? That's for the best. Suffice it to say that no steward would work for him and he was too daft to manage his finances properly. When he passed, Nigel discovered the title was bankrupt."

"How? We never wanted for anything."

"We met when I was ten. My mother had been raised in the village and when her condition became obvious, she was released from her position as scullery maid and returned to her family in shame. Nigel was two years younger than I, but even as children we knew. We looked too much alike, had certain mannerisms that were the same. Nigel would find ways to see me. I'm certain it must have been difficult living with our pater. He needed the escape of friendship and brother-hood.

"So when I learned of his financial difficulties, I came to London and learned what I needed to. I became friends with the people I had to, I did the things they asked me to do, I went to the places they told me to go. Whatever it took to make money, I did it."

There was no pride in his voice. In fact, his tone held no inflection at all.

"Nigel asked me how I was able to pay off his debts, which, I assure you, were exorbitant. When he learned of my activities, he was furious. He said he could not stand by and enjoy his newfound wealth and stability while I placed myself in danger. Later, when I realized I was being investigated, Nigel went to Lord Eldridge and—"

"—became an agent," she finished, her heart sinking as her worst fears were realized. "My brother was assigned to track you. Hawthorne used me to ingratiate himself with Barclay."

St. John leaned forward, but when she shrank away, he withdrew. "It's true that information learned through the agency allowed me to elude Westfield, but Nigel cared for you, don't doubt that. He would have offered for you re-gardless of your brother. He admired and respected you. He spoke of you often and was adamant that I continue to look after you if something should happen to him."

"The irony," she muttered. "Westfield prefers I not use my widow's pension and yet some of that settlement rightfully belongs to him, does it not?"

"In a way," he conceded. "Proceeds from the sale of Ashford cargos were used to pay off the Hawthorne debt."

Elizabeth felt the color drain from her face. This was worse than she could have ever possibly imagined. "There is so much I don't understand. How did you come to have my brooch?"

"I was nearby when Barclay and Hawthorne were attacked," he said sadly. "It was I who sent men to find help for your brother. I took the brooch because I was not certain I could trust anyone else to care for it and see it returned to you."

"Why were you there? Was his death because of you?"

He flinched. "Perhaps. In the end we must all pay for our sins."

"What is in the journal that makes it so important? Who wants it?"

"I cannot say, Elizabeth, for reasons I cannot explain."

"Why?" she cried. "I deserve to know."

"I'm sorry. For your protection, you must not know."

"He tried to kill me."

"Give the book to me," he urged. "It's the only way to spare you."

She shook her head. "Westfield has it locked away. I don't have access to it. It contains maps of various waterways in addition to the coded writings. He thinks the book may have detailed information about Nigel's missions. If I were to give the book to you, a known pirate, it would be considered treasonous. He would question me, discover our kinship, Eldridge would learn of it—"

"Westfield would protect you. I would manage Eldridge."

She swallowed hard. She couldn't lose Marcus. Not now. "After what transpired four years ago, my husband does not trust me. If I were to betray him this way he would never forgive me."

St. John cursed under his breath. "The book is worthless without Nigel. No one will be able to decipher it. If I take it off your hands, you can go away, have a honeymoon. Then I can draw the man out with it and end this."

"You know more about the journal than you are telling me," she accused. "If it were worthless, my life wouldn't be in danger."

"The man is mad," he growled. "Mad, I tell you. Think of

the attack on your person at your betrothal ball. Were those the actions of a rational person?"

Her lips pursed. "How did you learn of the stabbing?"

"I've had men watching out for you. One of them was there at your betrothal ball."

"I knew it!" There *had* been someone else in the garden, someone who chased away her assailant.

"I am doing my best to assist you—"

"You've been absent for weeks," she scoffed.

"On your behalf," he corrected. "I have been searching."

"Find him! Leave me out of this mess."

He dropped his glass carelessly inside the door panel. "I have been scouring England, and during those times you have been assaulted on two occasions. He knows me too well. He plans his attacks when I am out of Town." St. John grabbed her hands and held them tightly within his own. "Find a way to give me the book and this can all be over."

Shaking her head, Elizabeth pulled her hands away. "Tell me truthfully: Does the book have anything to do with Nigel's murder?"

St. John remained bent over, his elbows resting on his knees as he stared at her with clear eyes. "In a way."

"What does that mean?"

"Elizabeth, you already know too much."

Frustrated tears filled her eyes. There was no way to know if St. John was sincere or simply very cunning. She strongly suspected the information in the journal had something to do with him. If she were correct, her husband would want to use the information to bring the pirate to trial. For Marcus, it could be the chance for justice he'd waited years for.

"I must think about this. It is too much to absorb at once." She sighed wearily. "I have had little enough happiness in my life. My husband has been my one true joy. You and your brother's machinations could be the end of that."

"I am truly sorry, Elizabeth," he said, his sapphire gaze

dark with regret. "I have hurt a great many people in my life, but to have hurt you is a sincere lament of mine."

St. John opened the carriage door and began to descend. Suddenly he turned about. Hunching in the doorway, he kissed her on the cheek, his lips warm and gentle. Then he leapt from the carriage and reached for her hand. "You now know my direction. Come to me if you need anything. Anything at all. And trust no one but Westfield. Promise me that."

She gave a jerky nod and he backed away.

The footman waited patiently, too well trained to show any emotion.

"Return to the house," she ordered, her head throbbing painfully and her stomach twisting with dread.

She couldn't help feeling that St. John would be the end of her happiness.

Marcus studied Elizabeth from the doorway of his bedroom. She slept, her beautiful face innocent in slumber. Despite her betrayal, his heart swelled at the sight of her cuddled peacefully in bed. Next to her, on the small table, sat two open packets of headache powder and a glass of water, half full.

Slowly she stirred, the force of his presence and the heat of his gaze penetrating her sleep. She opened her eyes and focused on him, the instant tenderness of her gaze quickly shielded by guilt-heavy lids. He knew in that instant the reports were true. He held himself upright by will alone, when all he wanted to do was crawl to her and bury his pain in her arms.

"Marcus," she called in the soft, throaty voice that never failed to arouse him. Despite his anger and torment, he felt his cock stir. "Come to bed, darling. I want you to hold me."

Traitorously, his feet moved toward her. By the time he reached her, he had removed his coat and waistcoat. He stopped at the edge of the bed. "How was your day?" he asked, his voice carefully neutral.

She stretched, the movement of her legs pulling down the sheet so that her torso was exposed through the thin shift she'd worn to sleep. He grew hard, and hated himself for it when his thoughts drifted to the secrets she kept. Nothing could temper his response to her. Even now, his heart struggled to forgive her.

Wrinkling her nose, she said, "Truthfully? It was one of the most horrid days of my life." Her mouth curved seductively. "But you can change that."

"What happened?"

She shook her head. "I don't want to talk about it. Tell me about your day instead. It was certainly better than mine." Pulling back the covers, she silently invited him to join her. "Can we have dinner in our rooms tonight? I don't feel like getting dressed again."

Of course not. How many times would she want to dress and undress in one day? Maybe she hadn't undressed at all. Maybe St. John had merely pushed her skirts up and . . .

Marcus clenched his jaw and willed the image away.

Sitting on the bed, he yanked off his shoes. Then he turned to her. "Did you enjoy your trip into town?" he asked casually, but it didn't fool her.

Elizabeth knew him too well.

She made a great show of sitting up in the bed and fluffing the pillows into a comfortable pile. "Why don't you simply say what you mean?"

He tore his shirt over his head, then stood to remove his breeches. "Did your lover not bring you to orgasm, love? Are you anxious for me to finish what he started?" He slid into bed next to her, but found himself alone. She had slipped out the other side and stood at the foot of the bed.

With hands on her hips, she glared at him. "What are you talking about?"

Marcus leaned back against the pillows she had so recently arranged. "I was told you spent some time with Christopher St. John today, in my carriage with the curtains closed. He gave you a touching kiss goodbye and an open welcome to call on him for *anything* you might need."

The violet eyes sparked dangerously. As always, she was magnificent in her fury. He could barely breathe from the sight of her.

"Ah so," she murmured, her lush mouth drawn tight. "Of course. Despite your insatiable appetite for me, which often leaves me sore and exhausted, I find I still require further sexual congress. Perhaps you should commit me?"

Turning on her bare heel, she left.

Marcus stared after her, agape. He waited to see if she would return and when she did not, he pulled on his robe and followed her to her room.

She stood by the hall door in her dressing gown, telling a maid to bring up dinner and more headache powder. After sending the servant away, she slipped into her bed without looking at him.

"Deny it," he growled.

"I see no need. You are decided."

He stalked over to her, caught her by the shoulders, and shook her roughly. "Tell me what happened! Tell me it's false."

"But it's not," she said with arched brow, so damn collected and unruffled he wanted to scream. "Your men related the events exactly."

He stared at her in shock, his hands on her shoulders beginning to shake. Afraid to do violence, Marcus released her and clasped his hands behind his back. "You have been meeting with St. John and yet you won't tell me why. What reason would you have for seeing him?" His voice hardened ruthlessly. "For allowing him to kiss you?"

Elizabeth didn't answer his questions. Instead, she asked one of her own. "Will you forgive me, Marcus?"

"Forgive you for what?" he yelled. "Tell me what you've

done! Have you taken a fancy to him? Has he seduced you into trusting him?"

"And if he has?" she asked softly. "If I've strayed, but want you back, would you have me?"

His pride so revolted at the thought of her in the arms of another man that, for a moment, he thought he would be violently sick. Turning away, his fists clenched convulsively at his sides. "What are you asking?" he bit out.

"You know very well what I'm asking. Now that you are aware of my duplicity, will you discard me? Perhaps now you'll send me away. Now that you no longer want me."

"*Not want you*? I never cease wanting you. Every damned moment. Sleeping. Waking." He spun about. "And you want me too."

She said nothing, her lovely face a mask of indifference.

He could send her to the country with his family. Distance himself from her . . .

But the mere thought of her absence made him crazy. His ache for her was a physical pain. His pride crumbled beneath the demands of his heart.

"You will stay with me."

"Why? To warm your bed? Any woman can do that for you."

She was only an arm's reach away and yet her icy demeanor had her miles from him.

"You are my wife. You will serve my needs."

"Is that all I am to you? A convenience? Nothing more?"

"I wish you were nothing to me," he said harshly. "God, how I wish you were nothing."

To his amazement, her lovely face crumpled before his eyes. She slipped from the bed and sank to the floor. "Marcus," she sobbed, her head bowing low.

He stood frozen.

She wrapped her arms around his legs, her head resting on his feet, her tears slipping between his toes. "I was with St. John today, but I didn't stray from you. I could never."

Near dizzy with confusion, he lowered himself slowly to the floor and took her in his arms. "Christ . . . Elizabeth . . ."

"I need you. I need you to breathe, to think, to *be*." Her eyes, overflowing with tears, never left his face. Her hand moved to cup his cheek and he nuzzled into her touch, breathing in her scent.

"What is happening?" he asked, his voice hoarse from his clenched throat. "I don't understand."

She pressed her fingertips to his mouth. "I will explain."

And she did, her voice breaking and faltering. When she fell silent, Marcus sat stunned.

"Why didn't you confide in me before?"

"I didn't know the whole of the story until this afternoon. And when I did know it, I couldn't be certain how you would react. I was afraid."

"You and I, we are bound." He caught her hand and held it to his heart. "Whether we will it or no, we are in this together—our life, our marriage. You may not have wanted me, but you have me all the same."

There was a rap at the door. Marcus cursed, then stood, pulling her up with him. Opening the portal, he accepted the dinner tray. "Tell the housekeeper to make preparations to pack."

The servant bowed stiffly and left.

Elizabeth frowned at him, her porcelain skin pinked from crying. "What are you about?"

Setting the tray aside, he grabbed her hand and pulled her through the sitting room to his room. "We are retiring to the country with my family. I want you out of London and tucked away for a while until I can make sense of this muddle." He closed the door behind them. "We have been concentrating on St. John. I felt secure enough staying in Town when he was the only perceived threat. Now I have no notion of whom to suspect. You are not safe here. It could be anyone. Someone we invited to our betrothal ball. An acquaintance who comes to call." He rubbed the back of his neck.

"But what of Parliament?" she asked.

He shot her an incredulous glance as he shrugged out of his robe. "Do you think I care more about Parliament than I do about you?"

"It is important to you, I know that."

"You are important to me." Moving to her, he loosened her dressing gown and pushed it to the floor, then divested her of her shift.

"I'm hungry," she protested.

"So am I," he murmured as he picked her up and carried her to the bed.

"I agree, leaving London would be wise." Eldridge paced in front of the windows, his hands clasped behind his back, his tone low and distracted.

"There was no way to know," Marcus said softly, understanding how difficult it must be to learn of a traitor in their midst.

"I should have seen the signs. St. John could not have eluded justice all these years without some assistance. I simply didn't want to credit it. My pride wouldn't allow it. And now, perhaps there is another among us, maybe more."

"I say the time has come for us to be more persuasive with St. John. So far, he is the only individual who seems to know anything about Hawthorne or the bloody journal."

Eldridge nodded. "Talbot and James can see to him. You see to Lady Westfield."

"Send for me if there's a need."

"I probably shall." Eldridge sank into his chair and sighed. "At the present moment, you are one of the few men I can trust."

For Marcus, there was only one man he could trust to care first and foremost for Elizabeth, and when he left Eldridge, he went straight to him, and told him everything.

William stared down at Hawthorne's book in his hands, and shook his head. "I never knew of this. I was not even aware that Hawthorne kept journals. And you." He raised his gaze. "Working for Eldridge . . . How alike we are, you and I."

"I suppose that is why we were once good friends," Marcus said without inflection. His gaze drifted around the study, remembering when he had sat in this very room and arranged marriage settlements. So long ago. He stood, and prepared to depart. "Thank you for guarding the journal."

"Westfield. Wait a moment."

"Yes?" He paused midstep, and turned about.

"I owe you an apology."

Every muscle in Marcus's body stiffened.

"I should have heard your version of events before passing judgment." Setting the book aside, William rose to his feet. "Explanations are perhaps worthless at this point, and in the end they are just excuses for why I failed you as a friend."

Marcus's anger and resentment ran deep, but it was a tiny spark of hope that prompted him to say, "I would like to hear them, in any case."

William tugged at his cravat. "I had no notion of how to feel when Elizabeth first mentioned her interest in you. You were my friend, and I knew you were inherently a good man, but you were also a scoundrel. Knowing my sister's fears, I thought you two would be a bad fit." He shrugged, a sign not of nonchalance, but of sheepishness. "You've no idea what it is like to have a sister. How you worry for them, and want to protect them. And Elizabeth is more fragile than most."

"I know." Marcus watched his old friend begin to pace nervously, and knew from experience that when William moved so restlessly, he was in deadly earnest.

"She was mad for you, you know."

"Was she?"

Snorting, William said, "Bloody hell, yes. She went on and on about you. And your eyes, and your blasted smiles, and a hundred other things I did not care to hear about. That is why, when I woke to her tearstained missive about your in-discretion, I took it to be true. A woman in love will believe anything her lover tells her. I assumed you were beyond re-demption for her to run off as she did." He stilled, and faced him. "I am sorry I assumed. I am sorry I did not go after her, and talk some sense into her. I am sorry that later, when I knew I had done you an injustice, I did not come to you and make amends. I allowed my pride to dictate my actions, and I lost you, the only brother I have ever known. I am most sorry about that."

Marcus sighed inwardly, and walked to the window. He stared out at nothing, wishing he could give some glib rejoin-der to defuse the tension. Instead, he gave the moment the at-tention it deserved.

"You are not entirely to blame, Barclay. Neither is Elizabeth. If I had told her about the agency, none of this would have happened. Instead, knowing how she longed for stability, I hid it from her. I wanted to have everything. I did not realize until too late that what I wanted and what I needed were two different things."

"I know it is my commitment to Elizabeth that brought you here today, Westfield, but I want you to know that I am equally committed to you. If you ever require a second, I will not fail you again."

Marcus turned, nodded, and welcomed the chance pre-sented to him. "Very well, then," he drawled, "we can call it even, *if* you forgive me for stealing Lady Patricia from you, although I think we both agree that your offense was greater."

"You stole Janice Fleming, too," William complained. Then he smiled. "Although I thrashed you for that one."

"Your memory is faulty, old chap. It was you who ended up in the trough."

"Good God, I forgot about that."

Marcus twirled his quizzing glass by its ribbon. "You once took a dunking in the Serpentine, too."

"You fell in first! I was attempting to assist you when you pulled me in."

"You would not have wanted me to drown alone. What are friends for, if not to suffer together?"

William laughed. Then they shared a grin, and an unspoken agreement to truce. "Truly. What are friends for?"

Chapter 20

It was late afternoon on the second day of travel when they arrived at the ancestral home of the Ashford family. The compelling castle-like appearance of the massive mansion gave mute testimony to the perseverance of Marcus's lineage. Turrets rose at varying heights across the great expanse of the stone exterior that sprawled for some distance to the left and right of the front door.

The three carriages and luggage cart slowed to a stop. Instantly the front door of the mansion flew open and a multitude of servants in Westfield livery descended the steps.

Alighting from the carriage, Elizabeth stared in awe. Marcus set his hand at her waist and stood beside her. His voice was low and intimate in her ear. "Welcome home."

He kissed the sensitive part of her neck where her shoulder met her throat. "Wait until you see the inside," he said with obvious pride.

As they entered the foyer, Elizabeth sucked in her breath with wonder. The ceiling vaulted away from them to dizzying heights, where a large crystalline chandelier hung from an impossibly long chain. Tapers gently lit alcoves located along the walls on either side, and the stone floor was covered in several immense Aubusson rugs.

Elizabeth set the pace for the group, walking slowly as she struggled to take in her surroundings. The sound of their muffled footsteps echoed hollowly through the vast space. In front of them, at the other end of the foyer, was a wall of French doors. When opened, they led out onto the large expanse of lawn just beyond.

But the focal point of the room was the immense split staircase curving gracefully along either wall to join at a massive landing above. From there the ascent branched off to hallways on the left and right, which led to the east and west wings.

Paul looked at her with a proud smile. "It is impressive, isn't it?"

Elizabeth nodded with eyes wide. "To call it impressive wouldn't do it justice."

They made their way up the dual staircase on the left side while servants hauled up trunks on the right. Marcus drew to a halt in front of an open doorway and held out his hand to urge Elizabeth inside. Paul and Robert excused themselves, promising to see them at the evening meal.

The room she entered was massive and beautifully decorated in soft shades of light taupe and creamy blue. Striped silk curtains framed wide windows that overlooked the front circular drive. Two doorways flanked the sides of the room. Through the open door to the left she could see a sitting room and a decidedly masculine bedroom beyond that, and on the right, a nursery.

Marcus stood directly behind her. "Do you like it?"

"It's perfect," she acknowledged.

With a caressing smile and a mischievous wink, he left through the sitting room and headed to his room beyond.

Alone, Elizabeth took in the contents of the room with greater care, this time noting the little details. The small bookcase built into the bottom of the window seat held copies of her favorite books. The vanity drawers held her customary toiletries.

As he had for the nights they'd spent in the guesthouse, Marcus had thought of almost everything.

Removing her hat and gloves, she went in search of her husband. Stepping through the open double doors that led to his room, she found Marcus at the desk, sans coat and waistcoat. She approached him with a smile.

"Marcus," she started gently. "Must you charm me every day?"

Rounding the desk, he wrapped her tightly in his arms, his mouth pressing a hard kiss to her forehead. "Of course."

She hugged him back almost desperately, so grateful she couldn't help telling him so.

"I'm relieved the house pleases you," he said gruffly, his mouth nuzzling her skin. "I will give you a full tour before supper and in the morning the staff will line up for your inspection."

"It is not so much the house that pleases me, as your thoughtfulness and care for my comfort." Elizabeth kissed the sharp line of his jaw.

He squeezed her brutally close, and then set her away. Returning to his desk, he bent his head to the papers he pulled from a drawer.

Sighing at the loss of his embrace, she sank into a chair in front of the fireplace. "What are you doing?"

His gaze remained on the desktop. "Gathering my ledgers and notifying my steward that I'm in residence. I usually handle expenditures after the Season, but since we are here, I may as well begin now."

"You are not decoding the journal?"

He glanced up and hesitated a moment before answering. "Keeping you and the journal in one location is foolhardy."

She stilled, surprised. "Where is it? With Eldridge?"

"No." He took a deep breath. "I placed it in Barclay's care."

"What?" she asked, shooting to her feet. "Why?"

"Because he is the only person besides St. John to have worked with Hawthorne closely on matters regarding the agency. And, at this moment, he's one of the few people I can trust."

"What about Mr. James?"

"I would have preferred Avery, but Eldridge has him occupied at the moment."

Elizabeth's stomach dropped. "St. John."

Marcus's eyes narrowed. "Yes. We must know everything he knows."

"What of Margaret? And the baby? The time draws near, William cannot be embroiled in this now." Her hand lifted to shelter her racing heart. "What if they should be attacked, as I was? How could you do this, when I begged you not to?"

"Barclay has been prepared for attacks against himself and his wife since Hawthorne's death." He rounded the desk.

"And that is why my room was ransacked?" she snapped.

"Elizabeth—"

"Damn you. I trusted you."

His voice came low and angry. "You entrusted me with your safety and I am seeing to it."

"You don't care about me," she argued. "If you did, you would not have done something guaranteed to hurt me. They are all I have, to risk them this way—"

"They are not all that you have! You have me."

She shook her head rapidly. "No. You belong to the agency. Everything you do is for them."

"That's not true, and well you know it."

"I know I was wrong about you, wrong to trust you." She brushed aside a tear with the back of her hand. "You deliberately said nothing to me."

"Because I knew it would upset you. I knew you would not understand at first."

"You lie. You failed to tell me because you knew it was *wrong*. And I will never understand. Never."

Elizabeth swept around the settee toward the door.

"I am not done speaking, madam."

"Then continue, my lord," she threw over her shoulder, nearly running to her room to hide the tears that flowed freely. "I no longer wish to listen."

*   *   *

William paced the length of his sitting room.

Margaret sighed, squirming into the pillows on the chaise, trying to find comfort for her aching back. "You knew nothing of this journal?"

"No." He scowled. "But Hawthorne was an odd fellow. I'm not surprised to learn his father was mad. I'm certain Hawthorne was a bit touched as well."

"How does that pertain?"

"There is something odd about this. I've gone over Westfield's notes. He has already dedicated a great deal of his time to the study of the journal and all we've learned is some spotty descriptions of remote locations with no explanation. I cannot understand the purpose."

Margaret rested her hands on her protruding stomach and smiled at the feel of her child moving in response to her touch. "So let's set aside the contents of the book for the moment and concentrate on Hawthorne himself. How did he come to be your partner?"

"He was assigned to me by Eldridge."

"Did he ask for you in particular?"

"I don't believe so. If I recall correctly, he gave some tale about a grievance against St. John."

"So he could just as easily have been assigned to Westfield, who was also investigating St. John."

William plunged both hands into his golden hair. "Perhaps, but Westfield was frequently paired with Mr. James. I had not yet built a strong rapport with any other agents."

"And you and Westfield never knew of one another's activities, even though you were fast friends?"

"Eldridge does not—"

"—share such information, in case you are captured or tortured for information." Margaret shuddered. "I thank God you no longer amuse yourself in that manner. Heaven only knows how Elizabeth manages. But then she's far stronger than I. Is it possible Hawthorne married Elizabeth in the hopes he would learn something of Westfield's activities?"

"No." William sat next to her and placed his hand over hers. "He would not have known about Westfield. Just as I did not. I believe he married her to ensure he would remain my partner."

"Ah, yes, that would have been wise. So we have Hawthorne, working with you to investigate St. John, but all the while his aim is to thwart you. He is married to Elizabeth and keeping a journal of cryptic text that so far has been revealed to be nothing of import. But in fact, it must be important enough to kill for."

"Yes."

"I'd say the best option would be to capture St. John and pair him with the journal, make him tell you what it says."

His mouth curved ruefully. "According to Elizabeth, St. John claims only Hawthorne can decode it. But obviously that cannot be true, so Avery is tracking the pirate, who most inconveniently has fled London again. He is the key."

"I worry for Elizabeth, you know I do, but I cannot help but wish Westfield had taken the journal elsewhere."

"I know, love. If there had been another choice, I would have suggested it. But truly, despite his long-standing association with James and Eldridge, I am the only man he knows who can be trusted to care more for Elizabeth than the agency. And you and I have been cautious for so long. I couldn't bear for our children to live in fear. We must end this." His gaze pled for her understanding.

She cupped his cheek with her hand. "I'm glad you now know the truth about Hawthorne and St. John, to ease the guilt you've felt all these years. Perhaps Hawthorne's death was inevitable, with his life so deeply entrenched in the criminal." She moved her hand to place his against her belly and smiled as his blue eyes widened with awed pleasure at the feeling of a strong kick against his palm.

"Can you forgive me for accepting this task while you carry my child?" he asked hoarsely, bending to press an ardent kiss to her powdered forehead.

"Of course, my love," she soothed. "You could not have done otherwise. And truly, in light of your lost friendship, I think it is a hopeful sign that Westfield came to you for help. We shall solve this puzzle together. Maybe then we can all find some peace."

"Pray, tell me what is the matter, Elizabeth," Elaine asked with concern. "It pains me to see you so distressed."

"I should be in London now, not here."

Elizabeth moaned as they sat in the family parlor, her thoughts filled with worry for William and Margaret. Marcus may have done what he thought was best, but he should have discussed it with her, allowed her to come to terms with it. He should have given her the opportunity to speak to William and thank him for his assistance. Her chest tightened as she thought of her brother, who loved her so much.

"I'm so sorry you are not happy here—"

"No, it's not that," she assured quickly. "I love it here. But there are . . . things that require my attention."

Frowning, Elaine said, "I don't understand."

"I asked Westfield to do something important for me and he disregarded my wishes."

"He must have had good reason," Elaine soothed. "He adores you."

Paul entered the parlor. "Why so glum?" he asked. Taking one look at Elizabeth's tear-streaked face, he scowled. "Is it Marcus? Has he yelled at you again, Beth?"

Despite her misery, Paul's use of a pet name brought a reluctant smile to her face. No one had ever called her anything besides Elizabeth.

"No. I almost wish he would," she admitted. "He's been so civil toward me this last week I can barely stand it. A good row would do much to improve my spirits."

Paul laughed. "Well, reserved civility is what Marcus does best. I take it you've had a lovers' quarrel?"

"That's a rather tame description, but I suppose it is something similar."

His brown eyes lit with mischief. "I happen to be somewhat of an expert on lovers' quarrels. The best way to recover is not to mope. You'll find greater satisfaction in exacting a little revenge."

Elizabeth shook her head. She'd already denied Marcus her bed for the last six nights. Every night he tested the locked door to her chamber. Every night he turned away without a word. During the day, he was his customary charming self, polite and solicitous.

What was lacking were the heated looks and the familiar stolen caresses that told her he wanted her. The message was clear. He would not be the only one denied.

"I think I've gone as far as I dare to incite a response," she said.

"Cheer up then, Beth. Lovers' quarrels never last long."

But Elizabeth couldn't agree with that. She'd hold her own until Marcus apologized. He couldn't just run roughshod over her. Decisions of this magnitude had to be discussed.

And quite frankly, she could be as stubborn as he.

The coals in the hearth shifted and Elizabeth jumped, every muscle in her body tense with expectation. She waited almost breathlessly for Marcus to test the brass knob. Once he did so, she could relax and attempt sleep.

If he kept to his routine, she'd have only a few more moments to wait. Sitting upright in bed, she clutched the edges of the sheet in her lap with nervous fingers. The lace throat of her night rail seemed too tight, making it difficult to swallow.

Then the knob began a slow turn to the right.

She couldn't take her eyes from it, couldn't even blink.

It made a soft click as it reached the barrier of the lock.

Her jaw clenched until it ached.

The knob released, turning rapidly back to its previous position.

She closed her eyes and sighed with a confusing mixture of both disappointment and relief. She didn't get to appreciate the dichotomy, however, because a heartbeat later the door opened and Marcus walked in, spinning a looped ribbon around his index finger, the end of which dangled the key.

Biting her lower lip, she seethed, but held her tongue. She should have known not to expect fair play from a man used to gaining whatever he desired. At any cost.

He strolled to the nearest chair and turned it about to face the bed, rather than the grate. Then he sat, crossing one ankle over the opposite knee and adjusting his heavy silk robe with studious leisure. The traitorous key was slipped into his pocket.

"You are the most arrogant man I have ever met."

"You are welcome to discuss my perceived flaws at a later date. At the present moment, let's keep to the topic of why you've been barring me from your bed."

She crossed her arms beneath her breasts. "You know why."

"Do I? Well then I appear to have forgotten. Would you be so kind as to remind me? And be quick about it, if you please. I've done my best to allow you time to set aside your pique, but a sennight of waiting has stretched my patience."

Elizabeth growled. "I am not merely a cunt to rut in. If you need sex so badly, take yourself in hand."

His harshly indrawn breath was the only sign she'd struck effectively. "If all I needed was sexual release, I would have done just that. Now, the reason for the locked door?"

She sat there for a long time, thinking it would be best if he determined what was wrong on his own. But finally the pregnant silence was too much to bear. "You owe me an apology."

"I do?"

"Yes."

"For what, pray tell?"

"You know why. It was wrong to involve William when I asked you not to."

"I will not apologize for that." His large hands, with their long, elegant fingers, curled over the carved wooden arms of the chair.

She lifted her chin. "Then we have nothing more to discuss."

"Ah but we do," he drawled softly. "Because I'm sharing your bed tonight, my lovely wife, and I prefer it to be a pleasurable experience."

"I have feelings, Marcus, and a mind. You cannot just trample over those things and expect me to welcome you with open arms."

"I covet your feelings, Elizabeth, and I respect your mind. I could not have married you otherwise."

Her head tilted as she considered him, so tall and broad he dwarfed the chair he occupied. "If you speak the truth, why didn't you discuss your intent with me and allow me to offer my opinion? You belittle me by acting without my knowledge and then concealing your actions."

"I concealed nothing. When you asked, I told you. And your opinion was known to me. I am fairly clever," he said dryly. "You can tell me something once and I'll retain it."

"Then my opinion is of so little consequence it does not bear considering?"

He stood. "I will always consider your opinion, and give it as much weight as my own, but your safety will always come first. Always."

Feeling on unequal footing, Elizabeth slid from the bed. Although Marcus was far taller than she, it gave her some comfort to stand tall against him. "And what of William's safety? And his family?"

Marcus crossed to her, and lifting a hand, brushed the back of his fingers along her cheekbone. His eyes closed, as if he savored the touch of her. For her part, she shivered at the smell of him, that warm scent of sandalwood and citrus she knew and loved so well.

"I worry for him, yes. And I regret I was forced to involve him. Should something happen to him or his wife I would be forever wracked with guilt and I would mourn the loss of a man who was once, and hopefully will be again, as close to me as my brothers." His voice lowered, became almost wistful. "But I would survive. I could not say the same were I to lose you."

"Marcus . . ." Stunned by his words, her hand came up to catch his and hold it to her cheek.

"I don't know how I lived those four years without you. Looking back now, remembering the endlessness of days, the aching longing, the sense I was missing something vital . . ." He shook his head. "I couldn't go through that again. And that was before. Before I knew the many facets of your smiles, the warmth of your skin, the sounds of your pleasure, feeling you next to me both in public and private."

Suddenly, she felt overwhelmed and she gasped for breath.

He tugged her closer and embraced her within gentle arms. "I am sorry you are hurt by my decision, but I would make it again, a hundred times over. This is difficult for you, I know, and I understand you cannot collect how I feel. I would sacrifice my own life to protect yours, because none of it would be worth anything without you. And so I am resigning my commission, because my work jeopardizes you."

"Wh-why . . ." She swallowed hard and held him tight. "I never expected you would say such things to me. I-I don't know how to reply . . ."

"A week without you was enough to realize it was best to explain myself plainly, so there would be no doubt."

"I never thought you would love me. Not after all that I've done."

His cheek rested atop her head. "I used to wonder why it had to be you. I've met beautiful women, smart women, funny and bold women. Why Elizabeth? Why not someone who could open her heart to me? Perhaps it was the chase. Perhaps it's that you are wounded and I wish to heal you." He shrugged. "The Lord only knows."

"I still cannot help but wish you would have told me your intent," she grumbled, even though her upset was immeasurably soothed by his declaration of her importance.

"In the future, I hope I have more time to convince you of the merits of my opinion, but in this case I didn't have that luxury."

She leaned against his arms and narrowed her eyes. "How long could it have possibly taken?"

He laughed. "A sennight it seems, and we didn't have that."

Looking up at him, seeing the warmth in his eyes and the loving curve of his mouth, she wanted to sigh like a besotted schoolgirl. Time and intimate familiarity did not lessen the effect of his masculine beauty. She didn't have the words to say things like he did, so plainly and with such courage. But she would do the best she could.

Her hands slipped between them and parted the front of his robe, revealing the body that made her mouth dry and her sex clench in eagerness. Her fingertips drifted over taut, warm skin, across his abdomen, and down to his thighs.

"Feel what you do to me?" he asked, his eyes drifting shut as he quivered beneath her touch. He licked his lips and clutched her waist, the crests of his cheekbones flushing with arousal. "I ache for this, Elizabeth, burn for it." Reaching for her hand, he brought it to his cock, already hard and throbbing. He drew in his breath sharply when she curled her hands around it.

Awed, her gaze roamed the length of his body, helpless in the grip of only exploratory caresses.

Trust, he'd said to her once. *This is trust*.

She would have to trust that he would always do what was

best for her, even if she did not agree with his methods. Would she not do the same to protect him?

Filled with feelings that had no outlet, she sank to her knees and opened her mouth, giving him the pleasure she knew he desired.

Ahhh . . . how she loved it as well. The silky feel of him, his ravished gasp, those long fingers clenched in her hair.

"Yes," he cried as he thrust his hips gently, his buttocks like stone within her palms. "I would die for this."

A moment later he lifted her and carried her to the bed, her night rail drifting over her head to be cast aside. She sank into softness, covered by hardness and everything melted as he lifted her thigh and slid deep within her.

The strength of him, the hard length of his thrusting cock, the damp skin, the near unbearable intimacy, was diminished by the intensity of his gaze.

Awash in heat and consumed by the memory of his words, she wrapped her arms around his straining body and cried with joy. Her tears wet his shoulder, mixed with his sweat, bound them together. Her body seized beneath his, suspended in orgasm, held there by the steady plunge and withdrawal Marcus knew would prolong her pleasure.

And when he joined her, when he shuddered against her and cried out her name, she set her mouth to his ear and spoke her heart.

Chapter 21

"Mr. Christopher St. John has come to call, my lady."
Elizabeth looked up from her novel and stared at the butler with mouth agape. She dropped the book on the settee next to her and rose. "Where did you put him?"

"In the lower parlor, my lady."

Marcus had departed with the steward to survey some tenant properties that required repair. Elaine had retired for an afternoon nap, and Robert and Paul had gone to the village only an hour past. She was alone, but unafraid, nodding at the two guards who stood on either side of the parlor door.

Taking a deep breath, she swept into the room. St. John rose when she entered, splendidly attired and angelically handsome. He smiled and the brief reminiscence of Nigel momentarily disconcerted her.

As she drew closer, she noted he appeared leaner, the ever-present shadows under his eyes were darker, and while his bearing was as proud as ever, she could sense the weariness beneath the façade.

"Rather daring of you to come calling here."

He shrugged. "I half expected to see Westfield charging through that door. I'm relieved it's you instead. I'm not worthy of a fight right now." He glanced over her head. "Where is his lordship?"

"Near enough."

His blond brows lifted, and his lips curved. "As long as he gives me a wide berth, I'll manage."

"Eldridge is searching for you."

Immediately the smile left Christopher's face. "I know."

"You say you want to help me, but you place my life in jeopardy by maintaining your silence."

He spun away, moving toward the window to brush aside the curtain and stare at the front circular drive. "I never wanted to involve you. I knew the man was vile, but to use you, to threaten you . . ." He growled. "I wish to God that bloody journal had remained hidden."

"I cannot say I feel the same. Perhaps if it had not arrived, Marcus and I would not have found each other again."

Facing her, he offered a sad smile. He looked around, taking note of the liveried guards who stood conspicuously by the doorway. "I see Westfield has you well-guarded. That eases my mind somewhat."

"I see you look worn," she retorted bluntly.

"Thank you for noticing," he grumbled, "after I took such pains to make myself presentable. I must remember to discharge my valet."

"The best valet in the world cannot hide the signs of hard-living," she retorted. "Have you ever considered a change of occupation? The way you live is sapping the life from you."

His full mouth thinned with displeasure. "I am not here to discuss my way of life."

Taking a seat, she waited for him to do the same. "Very well then. I no longer have the journal."

St. John cursed so foully Elizabeth blushed. "Is it in Eldridge's possession?"

She hesitated a moment, wondering how wise it would be to tell him anything further. "No," she said finally, the restlessness of her fingers was the only betraying sign of her unease.

"Thank God. Keep it from him."

"He has been content to allow Westfield to work on it. At the moment, he seems most interested in finding you."

"Yes, he would be. I'm surprised he waited this long, truth be told. I would venture to say he wanted all of his agents in a lather before he released them on me. He's nothing if not meticulous."

Elizabeth studied St. John carefully. "Why did you come?"

"Once I learned Eldridge was looking for me I understood how delicate this situation has become. I don't know what to do. In the end there is only one solution and yet it's nearly impossible to implement."

She opened her mouth to speak when a sudden disturbance outside drew their attention. Leaping to her feet, she ran with St. John to the window. Out front, a village cart tottered precariously on three wheels. "Stay here," she ordered, knowing Marcus would wish to speak with the pirate, perhaps even detain him.

Elizabeth took only a moment to ensure assistance was being offered and then turned back to the room. It was empty. She stood blinking.

"Where did he go?" she asked the two guards.

They rushed in and quickly searched the space.

St. John was gone.

Marcus leaned his shoulders against the headboard and adjusted the weight of his wife's sated body, which draped over his own. Even her grumbled protest failed to make him smile. He stroked his hand down the length of her spine, soothing her back to sleep, while finding his own elusive.

Why had St. John come? If his aim had been the journal, he would want more than just Elizabeth's verbal confirmation that it was no longer with her. And yet he'd learned no more than that before dropping out the window and fleeing. To have arranged the distraction of the broken cart in advance was typical. To have known the house was emptied of Ashford men meant he'd been watching them.

His arms tightened around Elizabeth and her face nuzzled his chest in response. The pirate's warning was clear, *You are not safe. Even in your own domain.*

Even as he thought it, Marcus stilled. He cocked his head, his ears straining to hear over the soft crackling coming from the grate. He was greeted by silence, but he couldn't relax. The hairs on his nape stood on end.

He'd long ago learned to trust his instincts, so he slid down to his back and rolled, settling Elizabeth into the pillows. Her arms surrounded him, accustomed to his habit of waking her for sex. Pressing a quick kiss to her mouth, Marcus disentangled himself and withdrew from the warmth of the bed.

"What are you doing?" she complained, blinking.

Her pout was flattering and he took a moment to relish it. There had been a time when he could only dream of having her in his bed, eager for him. His ring on her finger caught what remained of the firelight and his jaw tightened. He'd be damned if anyone or anything jeopardized her now.

Tugging on his discarded breeches, he whispered, "Hold that thought for a moment, love." He grabbed his small sword, which rested conveniently against a nearby chair, and withdrew the blade from its scabbard. Elizabeth's head came up from the pillow. With a finger to his lips, he warned her to silence, and then padded across the room on bare feet. Marcus took a deep breath before cracking open the door that led to the sitting room.

Through the tiny space between the door jamb he could see across to Elizabeth's chamber. From the gap beneath her door, candlelight was clearly visible. Once again, his instincts had stood him in good stead. Someone was in there. Marcus rolled his shoulders and slipped out of his bedroom. St. John hadn't given up. He'd come back, as Marcus had suspected he would.

He'd wanted to position a guard in the sitting room, but Elizabeth had been horrified that someone would be so close while they made love. She'd been adamant and, doubting his restraint, he'd acceded. Now he could only shake his head at his fascination for his wife, which overruled every other consideration. Moving rapidly, he reached the door and tested the knob. It was locked. Cursing himself, he returned to his room for the key.

Elizabeth was slipping on her dressing gown.

Marcus shook head and scowled. *Stay here*, he mouthed.

What is it? she replied.

For his answer he held up the key, and then he returned to the sitting room. Immediately he noted the light under her door was gone. Hindered by darkness, it took him a moment to reach it. The chill breeze that flowed from the gap over his bare feet betrayed the open window on the other side. He was not fool enough to enter an unlighted room. Stepping out to the dimly lit hallway, Marcus grabbed the taper from the alcove and lit the candelabra on the console.

When he turned about, he saw the hallway door to Elizabeth's room was ajar. He kicked it open with his foot, candelabra in one hand, small sword in the other. The drapes were spread wide, allowing the pale light of the moon to cast shadows. The sheers fluttered in the soft evening breeze, a ghostly presence that made his fists clench tight. High as they were on the second floor, he doubted anyone would make the effort to enter or exit from that venue. Which meant they were either still in the room, or had slipped down the hallway while he'd gone for the key.

Elizabeth.

All was quiet, but still his nerves sizzled with awareness.

"My lord?" murmured a deep voice behind him. "What is amiss?"

Marcus turned, and faced one of the guards. Behind him stood Elizabeth, who worried her bottom lip with her teeth. For a moment, his throat clenched tight at the thought of her traversing the unsafe galleries. But there was naught else she could have done and once again his heart swelled with admiration. She was a practical woman, and a brave one. He took a moment to collect himself and then answered, "Someone was trespassing in her ladyship's room. Wait with her until I can be certain the intruder is gone."

The guard gave a quick nod, and Marcus made a thorough sweep. The room was empty, but the sense of unease remained with him. "Wake the other guards," he ordered as he returned to the hall. "Search the vacant rooms and exits. Discover how he gained entry. And from this night on, I want one of you to stay in my sitting room."

Passing the candelabra to the grim-faced guard, Marcus caught Elizabeth's elbow and led her back to the bedroom.

"It's time to come out of hiding, Marcus."

"No."

"You know I must." She stopped abruptly to face him.

His jaw tightened, and he shook his head. "It's too dangerous."

"What else can we do? Look at the risk to your family, to your home."

Marcus took her face in his hands. "You are my family, my home."

"Please don't be obstinate."

"You ask too much, Elizabeth."

"I ask for freedom." Her eyes glittered up at him. "I weary of this. We make no progress with this endless waiting. We must take the initiative and force his hand. End this."

He opened his mouth, and she placed her fingers over his lips. "Don't argue further. I understand your position. Just consider it. That's all I ask of you."

Knowing she was correct did not ease his torment and when they returned to the bed he held her too closely, needing her physical proximity to warm the icy fear that tightened his chest.

"Please don't worry," she whispered, her soft lips moving

against the skin of his chest just before she drifted back to sleep. "I trust you."

He held her close, loving her for believing in him enough to propose such peril. She'd once said she would never trust him, and he had believed that without question. To discover he'd reached her so deeply was a soothing balm to the festering wounds that were healing with every day that passed.

But he had nothing but contempt for himself, unable to understand how she could display such unwavering faith when he continued to fail her at every turn.

For Elizabeth, the three days following the incident in her room were fraught with tension. Marcus withdrew to his study, where he worked tirelessly to find all vulnerabilities in his defense of her. The nights were worse. Because of the guard positioned on the other side of the bedroom door, she could not relax enough to enjoy lovemaking and Marcus refused to take her when she was so reluctant.

"I hate to see you so glum, dear Beth," Paul said one afternoon, as she gathered together the meal plans scattered across the dining table.

"I am not glum."

He arched a brow. "Are you bored then? I wouldn't blame you. You have been penned up for days."

Wrinkling her nose, she almost confessed how she missed Marcus, but that would not have been appropriate so she simply shook her head.

"Would you like to go to the village?" he asked.

"No. Thank you." Marcus wouldn't allow her out of the manse, but that was not her only consideration. Luncheon would be served shortly and that seemed to be the only time lately when she had a few moments of his charming discourse. She told herself it was silly to miss him when they were so physically close, but she could not change how she felt, and quite surprisingly, would not want to. She'd once dreaded needing him so much. It was now a bond she relished.

"Are you certain?" Paul pressed.

Waving him off with a reassuring smile, Elizabeth moved out to the foyer. A few moments more and then she could call Marcus away. Her step lightened as she thought of her husband and the smile he would bestow upon her when she called his name from the study doorway. Lost in the thought, she missed seeing the arm that reached out and snatched her into the space beneath the left side curving staircase. Her meal plans, which she'd been carrying to the kitchen to discuss with the cook, scattered across the marble floor.

Her startled protest was cut off by a passionate kiss, her husband's large body crowding her to the wall. Her hands, lifted to push her attacker away, slipped around his neck and held him close.

"Sweet wife," he breathed, his lips pressed to hers.

Her heart racing at the sudden fright, she gasped to catch her breath. "Wh-what are you about?"

"I need you." He nibbled at her throat. "It's been three damned days."

Eyes closed, she breathed him in. The warmth of his skin, the obviously aroused length of his frame, the large hands that moved feverishly over her curves . . .

"Why can you not remain naked?" he complained. "Too much material separates my touch from you."

Elizabeth noted their surroundings. The sunlight from the rear lawn poured in from the French doors displaying their ardor to any hapless passerby. Only from the foyer were they hidden from view. "You must stop."

"I cannot."

She gave a breathless laugh, so enamored with his attentions she wished she were naked as well. Her blood thrummed in her veins, her body softening and relaxing into his. "What are you doing?"

"Making up for my lack." Marcus pulled away only slightly, his hands occupied, one at her waist, the other fighting uselessly to feel her breast through her corset.

"We'll be seen," she cautioned.

"You cannot dissuade me." He licked her lips.

"You cannot mean to ravish me here."

"Can I not?" He tugged at her silk bodice and the threads popped in protest. "I'm nigh desperate."

"Marcus." She swatted his hands away.

"I want you." The look in his eyes gave proof to that statement.

"Now?" She bit her lower lip, pleased that he had no control over his desire. "I don't understand your mood. Can you not wait?"

He shook his head and the simple denial filled her heart with joy.

"I want you, too," she confessed.

His grip tightened and the scorching heat of his gaze made her blush. "I never thought you would, not truly." His voice lowered. "But you do, don't you?"

Nodding, Elizabeth pressed her lips to his chin. "I ache for you. I've missed you so much."

"I have been here." He drew her as close as her skirts would allow.

"I'm selfish, Marcus. I want the entirety of your attention."

"You have it." His smile was wicked. "Now, would you like the rest of me as well? We can slip away, find somewhere private."

"Can I bind you? Tie you down? Keep you to myself for hours, days?"

Marcus drew back with widened eyes. "Are you serious?" He couldn't hide the sensual interest that deepened the curve of his smile.

The image in her mind made her wet. "Oh yes."

"You have five minutes with which to find a bed and disrobe. Any longer and I will cut that dress from you with my blade."

"You wouldn't," she protested, laughing. "I adore this gown."

"Four and three-quarters."

Elizabeth turned and fled. "Don't forget to collect my papers," she called over her shoulder.

Lifting her hem, she hurried up the stairs. Halfway to the top, she saw the butler emerge from the upper floor gallery. He descended to meet her.

"My lady, the post has arrived."

She reached for the missive on the silver salver, recognizing the familiar Langston crest stamped in the wax. "Thank you."

Breaking the seal, Elizabeth scanned the brief contents, and then reread them.

"Margaret has had the baby early," she cried. "A boy!"

"Two minutes," Marcus drawled, his deep voice coming from just below her.

She stilled instantly. "Did you hear? I must go to them."

"Come here, Lady Westfield." His purr was ominous as he ascended the staircase with predatory grace. "You wanted my attention. I vow, you have it. Your nephew will have to wait."

Elizabeth laughed aloud. "You will have to catch me first," she challenged as she flew up the stairs. She gained the landing and ran down the hallway, the precious letter in one hand and her skirts held in the other. Marcus was fast on her heels.

Elaine watched the antics from the lower parlor doorway. She spoke to Paul who stood next to her. "I have never seen him so happy. Marriage has done wonders for him."

"So it has," he agreed.

She looked up with an affectionate smile. "You, dear son, are next."

Chapter 22

Because of the need for secrecy, it was after midnight when the hired hackney arrived at Chesterfield Hall. Exiting the carriage at the rear of the mansion, Elizabeth and Marcus then entered through the delivery door.

"Is this level of prudence truly necessary?" Elizabeth complained as she shivered in the chill night air.

Marcus tossed his cloak over hers and wrapped his arms around her, sharing his warmth. "I refuse to take chances with your life. You are too precious to me."

They made their way up to Elizabeth's former room by way of the servants' staircase. "How precious am I?" she asked softly, preceding him down the hallway.

"Priceless."

Closing the door behind them, Marcus removed both cloaks from her shoulders before turning her to face him. He lowered his head, his eyes staring deeply into hers. His kiss was soft and generous, his lips clinging with obvious affection.

"Do you love me, Marcus?"

She had promised herself never to ask him how he felt about her. He showed her in a hundred different ways every day how much she meant to him. But somehow the need to hear the words could not be denied.

His mouth smiled against hers. "Do you even have to ask?"

Elizabeth pulled back to search his face. "Would it pain you so greatly to say it?"

His mouth parted to speak just as a soft rap came at the door. "Come in," he called out, unable to hide his relief.

William poked his tousled blond head inside. "Lady Barclay heard you arrive. She would like Elizabeth to meet her nephew now. You will have to wait until morning, Westfield."

"Of course I'll come now." Elizabeth stood on tiptoe and waited until Marcus lowered his lips to hers. "I am not finished with this conversation, my lord."

He nuzzled his nose against hers. "I await your pleasure, Lady Westfield."

As Elizabeth left the room, William stayed behind.

Marcus regarded his brother-in-law carefully, noting the dark shadows under his eyes. "You look exhausted."

"The future Earl of Langston has a voracious appetite and Lady Barclay has refused a wet nurse. I attempted to dissuade her, but to no avail. She stands firm."

"Congratulations." Marcus extended his hand and William clasped it firmly. "You are a most fortunate man."

William ran his hands through his hair. "You should not have returned to London."

"I agree, but like your wife, Elizabeth could not be discouraged. Unfortunately, she has reached the point where she's willing to make herself a target to bring the situation to a head." Marcus sighed. "The woman shows a deplorable lack of fear."

"Yes, she always has. Don't look so grim, Westfield. I can see you are not in accord with her decision by way of your early morning arrival and avoidance of returning to your own residence. You don't want anyone to be aware of her return."

"Do you fault me for that? She is my wife. You must know how I feel. Have you not lived with the same fear these last four years?"

"It was not like this," William admitted. "There was no journal to worry over and no knowledge of a spy within the agency. The danger is greater now, I'm not blind to it or nonchalant. I love Elizabeth, as you well know, but I have a son. The time has come to conclude this chapter of our lives so we can all proceed."

"And what of my children? Should something befall Elizabeth I will be left with nothing. You both beg the impossible from me."

"Westfield . . ." William sighed heavily. "You and I will be prepared when the time comes."

"When the time comes for what?" Elizabeth asked from the doorway.

"For you to be *enceinte*," William said with a smile that hid the true nature of their exchange.

Elizabeth's eyes widened. "You were discussing children?" She looked at Marcus. "*Our* children?"

He smiled at the thought. Every day he forced himself to believe she was his. It was a gift he continued to marvel over.

William engulfed her in a quick hug.

"Your son is beautiful," she said with a soft smile. "He'd fallen asleep by the time I arrived. I look forward to holding him when we are both less weary."

Kissing her forehead, he yawned before making his egress. "'Til morning then."

The door shut with a quiet click and Elizabeth faced Marcus with shoulders squared. "We have never discussed children."

"There is no need." He moved toward her. "They'll come when they come, and not a moment sooner."

She looked away, biting her lower lip.

He frowned at the sudden chill of her features. "What pains you, love?"

"I don't wish to discuss it."

Chuckling softly, he ran a fingertip over her collarbone, feeling the flare of awareness flow from his touch to her skin.

"You often say that, and then force me to pry your thoughts from you. But the hour is late, so I pray you'll spare me."

Her eyes closed. "Can we not just retire? I'm tired."

"Tell me," he urged, his lips to her brow. He dropped his voice seductively. "There are ways I can make you. Would you like that?"

"Perhaps . . ." Her chin lowered, as did her volume. "Perhaps I'm barren."

He pulled away, stunned. "Where do you find these ridiculous notions?"

"Think of it. I was married a year to Hawthorne and—"

"He didn't put any effort into it," Marcus dismissed with a snort.

"You have put more than enough effort into it these last months," she argued. "And still my courses come with clockwork regularity."

Frowning, Marcus stared at Elizabeth's downcast head. Her tangible sadness caught his breath. "Ah, sweet." He reached behind her and began to loosen her garments. "You worry without cause."

"With every month that passes I fear I've failed you." She rested her cheek against the velvet of his coat.

"How odd. With every month that passes I'm thankful I can have you to myself for a little while longer."

"Please don't jest."

"Never. I have two brothers. The Ashford line is in no danger."

"Surely you want your own offspring and it is my duty to provide them."

"Enough." He spun her around to facilitate undressing her. "I only want you. In all my life, I've only ever wanted you."

"Marcus—" Her voice broke, as did his heart to hear it.

"I love you," he said gruffly, his throat tight. "I always have." Beneath his hands he felt her crying. "If it is meant to be just you and I alone, I would die the happiest man. Never doubt it."

She turned and caught him, tugging his mouth down to hers, pressing tear-covered lips to his. "I don't deserve you," she sobbed, her fingers frantic in his hair.

Marcus absorbed her assault with a crushing embrace, unable to speak now that he'd said the words he'd once sworn not to say, not to even think. She pressed forward, her movements so wild he stumbled backward. Her hands slipped into his coat, shoved it from his shoulders, tore at the ivory buttons of his waistcoat.

"Elizabeth."

She was everywhere, clawing at the many layers of his clothing and the placket of his breeches until all he could do was help her. He understood her, perhaps better than she understood herself. She was cornered, trapped by feelings she had run from since she'd met him, and she was running again, only this time it was *to* him, rather than *away* from him. And he would give her the solace she needed, and take what she offered in return, because he loved her with every breath in his body.

"Take this off," she cried, ripping at her bodice. "Get this off me."

He gripped the loosened back flaps, and rent the gown open. She stepped out of the remnants, then with corset and chemise and a pile of underskirts, his wife tugged him to the floor, pressed him down, and tossed her leg over his hips. Marcus laughed, adoring her in her concentration and near brutal need of him. Then he gasped, and arched upward as she took him in hand, and then took him inside her, clasping his cock in slick, silky tissues.

"Christ," he groaned, wondering, as he did every time he fucked her, if the pleasure would ever subside to where it was at least bearable. If this was all there was, if his seed never took root, he could live with that. He knew it in his soul.

Elizabeth stilled, panting, her waist and breasts squeezed tight by her undergarments. She gazed down at her husband, sprawled beneath her, so gorgeous in his disarray. Marcus Ashford, known for his unshakable implacability, was flushed, his eyes bright, his sensual mouth parted. Unable to resist, she cupped his nape in her hand and lowered her lips to his. The taste of him, dark and dangerous, and the feeling of his tongue, silken and hot, made her shiver and clench tight around the shaft that throbbed within her.

He moaned into her mouth, and wrapped gentle arms around her. He thrust his hips upward in deep lunges, stroking her depths with the broad head of his cock.

"Marcus . . ." Filled with heated, voluptuous yearning, she rose and swiveled her hips, then bore down as he pumped upward, taking him so deeply she writhed with the pleasure of it. Every touch, every growl from his throat told her how much he loved her and accepted her, how much he needed her. Despite all her faults.

The intensity of his gaze was a tactile caress. He loved to watch her, she knew. Loved to hear her cries, and feel her need. Her body undulated over his, a thing separate from her mind, lost to her desire. The unyielding grip of her corset altered the experience, made her both achingly aware and dreamily dizzy.

"Yes," he urged hoarsely. "Take what you need. Let me give it to you."

Her fingertips rested on his abdomen and beneath his linen shirt she felt the tight, hard lacing of muscles flex with his exertions. Her eyes locked with his. "Hold me."

He pulled her down, pressed his lips to hers, his tongue driving into her mouth in rhythm with the long, deep plunges of his cock. She was so wet, so aroused, every upward thrust sounded wetly through the room.

I would die for this, he'd said, and she knew it was true, because there in his arms, she did.

And was reborn.

*   *   *

Elizabeth woke late in the morning, and found herself alone. She bathed and dressed, eager to find Marcus before she spent the rest of the day with Margaret and the baby.

As she descended the main stairs, she spied Lord Eldridge and Avery standing with her husband in the visitors' foyer. She paused a moment, composing herself for whatever was ahead, and then proceeded.

Seeing her approach, Marcus met her at the bottom of the staircase. "Good morning, my love." His gaze, both warm and appreciative, spoke volumes.

"Has something transpired?" she asked.

"I must leave with Eldridge. St. John has been seen in London, and there are other things that need to be attended to."

She smiled briefly at Lord Eldridge and Avery. "Good morning, my lord. Mr. James," she called out.

Both gentlemen bowed in greeting.

Turning her attention back to Marcus, she searched his face, and noted the taut lines that etched his lips. "Is there something else? Something you are withholding from me?"

He shook his head. "I simply worry about leaving you. Avery will remain, but I would much prefer to guard you myself. Whenever I turn my back, something untoward happens and—"

Setting her fingers to his lips, Elizabeth silenced him. "Hush, I will be fine with Mr. James. And William is here."

"Even the King's guards could not ease my mind."

"So stay," she said simply. "Send Mr. James with Eldridge."

"I cannot. I have resigned my commission, and there are things I must resolve before I can be free."

Elizabeth covered her mouth with her hand, tears filling her eyes and threatening to fall from her lashes. He'd kept his promise.

"Tell me those are happy tears."

"I love you," she breathed.

His mouth curved in an intimate smile. "I shall return at my soonest. Stay out of trouble in the meantime. Please."

Making their egress from Chesterfield Hall, Marcus and Eldridge retrieved the reins from the waiting groomsmen and mounted their horses.

"Did you say anything to Lady Westfield?" Eldridge asked once they'd reached the road.

"No. It would only serve to unduly worry her."

"You don't believe a threat against your life is worth the worry?"

Marcus snorted. "St. John would have killed me before, if that was his true intent," he said dismissively. "He is aware that threats to Lady Westfield carry the greater weight. Still, the possibility exists that I would lower my guard of her to raise my own. A foolish attempt, but it costs him nothing more than the missive he sent you to try."

Marcus was so confident in his assessment that when the shot rang out and burning pain tore through his shoulder, he was caught completely unaware.

The horses reared, Eldridge yelled, and Marcus was thrown with stunning force to the ground. Dazed, he could not defend himself against the half dozen men who swarmed toward him in ambush. He could only realize, with horrified clarity, how far he had erred when Talbot loomed over him with small sword in hand. *He works well with Avery James,* Eldridge had said. Blind to the perfidy, he'd left Elizabeth in the care of the very man who wished her harm.

Now he lay on his back and noted that the trees, which shielded the lane, were a verdant backdrop to the steel of the blade swooping toward him with deadly precision.

But in the end, his greatest fear came not from his approaching death, but for his beloved wife, who needed him. And he would not be there.

Chapter 23

"You look beautiful."

Margaret blushed. "Good heavens, Elizabeth. How can you say such a thing? I must look a fright. I've not had a full night of rest since the birth, my hair is ever in disarray, I am—"

"Glowing," Elizabeth interjected.

Gazing with adoration at her infant son, Margaret smiled, "I did not believe it was possible to love someone as much as I do this child." She glanced at Elizabeth who stood by the door. "You shall see when you and Westfield have children of your own."

Elizabeth nodded sadly, and reached for the doorknob. "I will leave you to feed my nephew."

"It's not necessary for you to go," Margaret protested.

"We arrived so late yesterday, I find myself still weary. A small nap, and then I'll return."

"Where is Lord Westfield?"

"Attending to some matters. I expect he'll return shortly."

"Very well, then." Margaret nodded. "Come back to me refreshed. I miss female companionship."

Yawning, Elizabeth retreated to her room, her heart heavy with worry. Marcus was disturbed. Despite his denials to the contrary, she couldn't shake the feeling that something was terribly wrong.

She paused in the gallery outside her chamber, frowning when she noted the door was ajar. Entering cautiously, she saw the familiar figure digging in her escritoire drawers. He turned to face her.

It was then she saw the knife in his hand.

She froze, and swallowed hard. "What are you about, Mr. James?"

Inwardly steeled for the pain of being run through, Marcus jolted in surprise at the sound of gunfire. Talbot jerked, his eyes widening in horror. Deep crimson soaked through his waistcoat, spreading from the hole that bored through his chest. The downward swing of his sword arm faltered and he stumbled, forcing Marcus to roll away as he fell to the ground. Dead.

Surrounded by a grisly melee, Marcus leapt to his feet, staring at the battle that raged around him. A dozen men, none of whom he recognized, fought with deadly intent. Dust rose from the dry lane, choking his throat and gritting his eyes. Steel clashed in a macabre cacophony, and while his left arm was nigh useless, his right was serviceable. He withdrew his sword with lightning speed, prepared to defend himself.

"Stand down."

Spinning about with blade raised, he faced St. John.

"You are in no condition to fight," the pirate said dryly, tossing aside a now useless smoking pistol.

"How long have James and Talbot been in your employ?"

St. John continued to approach him. "They haven't been. That's not to say I lack eyes and ears within the agency. However, the men you mention are not associates of mine."

Marcus stilled, his thoughts quickly catching up to the reality he faced. He turned, searching for Eldridge, and found him nowhere. He did, however, note Talbot again, and came to the only conceivable conclusion. Nothing was as it seemed.

Snorting, St. John said, "So now you see the truth. I would have told you. However, you would not have believed me."

A man fell at their feet, and they both leapt quickly out of the way.

"Allow my men to handle this, Westfield. We must bind your wound, ere you bleed to death, and find Lady Westfield."

It was galling, the thought of working with St. John, and Marcus spit out the bile that coated his tongue. All this time, all these years . . .

Gradually the lane grew quiet, but Marcus's blood raged, drowning his hearing in roaring sound. He shrugged out of his coat, discarding the ruined garment in the blood-spattered dirt. St. John worked quickly and efficiently at binding his damaged shoulder while Marcus watched the pirate's lackeys drag the proliferation of bodies away with frightening nonchalance.

"How long have you been aware of this?" he asked gruffly.

"Years."

"And the journal?"

Tightening the binding until Marcus winced, St. John nodded at his handiwork and stepped back. "Can you seat a horse?"

"I have been shot, I'm not an invalid."

"Right. Let's go. I can explain on the way."

"Where is the journal, my lady?" Avery asked.

Elizabeth kept her gaze trained on the knife. "Safe."

"None of us are safe."

"What are you talking about?"

He came toward her quickly, and she recoiled. "Now is not the time to be skittish. I need you to think quickly and trust me implicitly, or you will not survive."

"I don't understand."

"I don't know that I do either. I watched several men approach from the rear garden and fan around the manse."

"A siege?" she cried in horror. "There are servants here, Lord and Lady Barclay . . . Oh God. The baby."

Avery gripped her elbow and led her toward the door. "Lord Langston is gone, as is Westfield and Eldridge. If there are enough of the brigands, they could take you with little effort. They've ransacked your room before, they know the way in."

"Who would be so daring?"

A trusted bewigged figure filled the doorway, blocking their egress.

Avery paused, his jaw tightening grimly. He jerked his chin toward door. "*He* would."

Marcus peered through the cover of bushes, and cursed under his breath. His heart raced in a panicked rhythm as he thought of his wife. In all of his near death encounters, had he ever been so afraid?

He counted four men at the front and three at the rear. If he were well, it would be a simple matter, but he had only one arm. Weakened by both blood loss and near crippling fear for Elizabeth, he knew he would be unable to fight them all. So he watched in frustrated helplessness as St. John's men tended to the distasteful matter, creeping stealthily along the perimeter, waiting for an opening to strike.

"Eldridge knew almost from the first moment," St. John said quietly, drawing Marcus's attention. "He noted the resemblance between Hawthorne and me immediately. He confirmed his suspicions and confronted Hawthorne, threatening to reveal his treasonous intent for joining the agency."

"Unless . . . ?"

"Unless we worked with him. He would provide the information, we would make use of it, and he would collect half the proceeds."

"Jesus." Marcus returned his gaze to Chesterfield Hall, barely registering the brick exterior with its climbing vines. Four years of his life had been dedicated to a lie. "I trusted him," he said grimly.

"Hawthorne didn't. Hence the creation of the journal."

"Which contains . . . ?"

"Nothing." St. John shrugged at his glare. "Hawthorne knew we were expendable, so he bartered with the journal, which was said to be an account of witnesses to Eldridge's guilt and locations of booty we'd hidden from him. In truth, we had nothing, but the book ensured our safety. If something befell us, Eldridge's perfidy would be revealed and he would lose what he thinks to be a fortune."

"You saved yourself, but risked my wife?" Marcus growled. "Look at all she has suffered, what she is suffering now."

"I am responsible for the search of her rooms. The attacks, however, were not my doing. They were a warning to me. I would have killed Eldridge long ago, but he swore Lady Westfield would pay with her life if his death came by my hand. He also threatened to reveal Hawthorne's treason. I could not allow that to happen. So we have waited, he and I, for the day when the balance would tip and free one of us to kill the other."

Standing from his low crouch, Marcus watched as the last of Eldridge's men were eliminated, their throats slit so that no sound was made. With the same precision they'd shown on the lane, St. John's lackeys quietly dragged the bodies away from the manse and into the nearby coppice. "Why not kill you when the journal surfaced? Once it was in his grasp, what use did he have for you?"

"He fears I am the only man alive who can decipher Hawthorne's code." St. John gave a mirthless laugh. "He has allowed you to try. I imagine if you had succeeded, he would have killed you and laid blame on me. He cannot simply do away with me, the people would riot."

They left the cover of the bushes, and ran toward the manse. "It's too quiet," Marcus muttered as they entered through the front door. Chills coursed down his spine, along with the sweat that dampened his skin and clothing. They moved cautiously, unsure of what traps awaited them.

"*Westfield.*"

Both men paused midstep. Turning their heads, they met the intense aqua gaze of Viscount Barclay who stood frozen in a nearby doorway.

"Is there something you wish to tell me?" he asked, but his casual words could not hide the tension that stiffened his frame or the pure hatred he directed at St. John with a scathing glance.

Swiveling to face his brother-in-law, Marcus revealed his injury.

"Good God. What happened to you?"

"Eldridge."

William's eyes widened, and he took the news with a visible shudder. "*What?* I cannot . . . *Eldridge?*"

Marcus moved not at all, but William knew him well enough to be answered. He released a deep breath, composing himself, setting aside questions that could wait in deference to matters that couldn't. "You cannot continue. You need a surgeon."

"I need my wife. Eldridge is here, Barclay. In this house."

"No!" William shot a horrified glance up the stairs, then he pointed at St. John. "And you think him worthy of your trust?"

"I don't know whom to trust, but he just spared my life. That will have to suffice for the time being."

Pale and obviously confused, William took a moment to collect his thoughts, but for Marcus it was a moment too long. Too much time had passed. Eldridge was ahead of them by some lead. Elizabeth was endangered, and he was nearly mad with the agony of it. Leaving the others behind, he threw caution to the wind and raced up the stairs.

"Lord Eldridge?" Elizabeth frowned in confusion as she looked past him. "Where is Westfield?"

"Lord Westfield is otherwise occupied. If you wish to be reunited, you will retrieve the journal and come with me."

She stared, attempting to make sense of what he was

about. Then she noted the tiny dark spatters on the gray velvet of his coat. The sick sense of foreboding intensified. Her
hands clenched into fists, and she stepped forward. "What—
have—you—done?"

Eldridge shifted, startled, and Avery took that slight advantage to launch himself the short distance and tackle him
to the ground.

The two men hit the floor with a sickening thud and rolled
out to the hallway, crashing into the opposite wall. Her mind
dazed and her chest tight, Elizabeth wondered briefly if the
noise would wake the baby. It was that thought which galvanized her.

She searched the room desperately with her eyes, seeking
something, anything that could be used as a weapon.

"Run!" Avery grunted, his hands occupied with holding at
bay the knife Eldridge wielded.

That single word forced her to move. Lifting her skirts,
Elizabeth ran past the men locked in deadly combat and fled
down the hall toward Margaret's rooms. She rounded the
corner and rammed headfirst into a unyielding barrier. With
a scream of terror, she fell, clutching desperately at the hard
body that fell with her.

"Elizabeth."

The breath left her lungs as they hit floor.

Sprawled atop her husband, she lifted her head and caught
sight of William's shoes as he ran to his rooms.

"Leave Eldridge to me," St. John rasped softly, as he
stepped past them.

Elizabeth returned her gaze to her husband, but had trouble seeing him with the tears that streamed from her eyes.
With gentle hands, Marcus rolled her from him. He was
frighteningly pale, his mouth drawn, but the warmth and relief in his gaze was undeniable.

"He said you were captured!" she cried.

"I was very nearly killed."

She noted the blood-soaked bandage that wrapped his torso and shoulder. "Oh dear God, you've been hurt!"

"Are you well?" he asked gruffly, rising to his feet and then pulling her to hers.

She nodded, the tears flowing unchecked. "Mr. James saved my life by holding off Eldridge until I could escape, but I found him searching my room. He wanted the journal, Marcus. He had a knife . . ."

Marcus pulled her closer, absorbing her trembling with a one-armed embrace. "Hush. Go to your brother, love. Do not leave his side until I come for you. Do you understand?"

"Where are you going?" She gripped the waistband of his breeches in nerveless fists. "You need help. You're bleeding." Elizabeth straightened her spine. "Let me see you to William, then I can consider—"

His mouth took hers in a hard, quick kiss. "I do adore you, my fearless bride. But indulge me, if you will. Allow me to finish this. My masculine pride begs it of you."

"Don't be arrogant now! You are in no condition to chase criminals, and I can aim a pistol better than most men."

"I will not disagree." His voice firmed. "However, in this instance I'm afraid I must exert my husbandly right of command, despite the row I know that will cause. Go, my love. Do as I say. I will return to you shortly, and then you may both harangue and fuss over me to your heart's content."

"I do not harangue."

Steel clashed in the nearby hallway, and the look in his eyes hardened enough to make her shiver. Following the urging of the gentle shove he gave her, Elizabeth moved with shaky legs down the hall.

"Be careful," she admonished. But when she looked behind her, he was already gone.

Marcus watched Elizabeth retreat, and thanked God for her. Everything he'd believed in, everyone he'd thought solid and immutable had shattered in one fell blow. Except for her. Wanting desperately to take shelter in her, but needing to end this first, he turned about, running toward the sounds of conflict.

He rounded the corner, his jaw locked with grim resignation and discovered St. John, his body moving with loose-limbed grace, his sword arm thrusting so quickly it was difficult to track it. Eldridge opposed him, his wig lost, his hair wild, his face reddened from exertion. It was a losing battle he fought, but the agency leader was not Marcus's concern. Certainly Marcus had his grievances, but his wife was alive, and St. John's brother was not.

His attention was instead on Avery, who stood to the side with dagger in hand. Marcus waited, unobserved, wanting to give Avery the opportunity to do what was right. They had worked together for years, and Marcus had, up until an hour ago, thought of the agent as a friend. He couldn't prevent the tiny hope that his trust had not been completely misplaced.

St. John feinted, and then lunged forward on his right foot. A winded Eldridge could not move swiftly enough to deflect the hit, and Marcus watched as the blade sank home in his thigh and he fell to his knees.

The pirate loomed over the vanquished Eldridge with teeth clenched, his hand fisted around the other man's throat.

"You cannot kill me," Eldridge croaked. "You need me."

It was then that Avery made his move, approaching the distracted St. John from behind with his arm raised and knife ready to fall.

"Avery," Marcus growled.

Avery spun about and threw himself forward, forcing Marcus to return. Parrying the flashing dagger with his small sword, Marcus leapt back a step. "Don't do this," he grunted. But Avery would not desist.

"I have no choice."

Marcus attempted to draw out the confrontation, praying Avery would break through his panic and cease. He aimed his blade at less vulnerable areas, striking to wound and not to kill. Finally, however, exhausted by his own injury and depleted of options, he made a fatal thrust.

Panting, Avery sank to the floor, his back to the wall, blood drizzling from the corner of his lips. His hands were stained crimson, pressing against the spot on his chest where Marcus had impaled him. Eldridge lay at his feet, St. John's sword sunk so deep into his heart it gouged into the wood floor beneath.

Sighing, Marcus dropped into a crouch. "Ah, Avery. Why?"

"My lord," Avery gasped, sweat dripping from his brow. "You know the answer to that. Prison is not for the likes of me."

"You spared my wife, I might have helped you."

A translucent red bubble formed between Avery's lips and burst as he spoke. "I grew . . . I grew quite fond of her."

"And she of you." Marcus withdrew a handkerchief and wiped the sweat from Avery's brow. The agent's eyes closed at the touch of the cloth.

Marcus glanced at Eldridge. The scene was surreal, and heartrending.

"There were more . . . men," Avery wheezed. "Is she safe?"

"Yes, she's safe."

Avery nodded, his breath rattling in his lungs, and then he stilled, his body slumping into death's embrace.

Marcus stumbled to his feet, weary and disheartened. He glanced at St. John who said softly, "You saved my life."

"Consider my debt paid for your like service to me. What do you intend to do with Eldridge?"

"The poor man was a victim of highway robbery." St. John yanked his sword free. "My men will make certain he is found at the appropriate time and in the appropriate manner. If we are done here, I shall see to it."

Marcus could not prevent the twinge of guilt and sorrow he felt. He'd admired Eldridge, and would mourn the man he'd once thought him to be.

"Take the journal with you," he said gruffly. "If I never see the blasted thing again it will be too soon."

"My men will manage these two," the pirate said, gesturing over the bodies with the bloody tip of his sword. "We are liberated, Westfield. I trust the king will believe the tale when told to him by both you and Barclay. Then the bad seeds will be routed from the agency and Eldridge's threat to haunt me after death will be negated."

"Yes, I suppose that is true." But Marcus found little comfort in the ending. He knew he'd be haunted by this day forever.

"Marcus?"

He turned at the tentative sound of his wife's voice. Elizabeth stood a few feet away, a pistol weighting her arm and dangling at her side. The sight of her, so small but determined, eased the tightness in his chest, and he left the ugliness behind to find solace in her arms.

EPILOGUE

London, April 1771

The weather was perfect for a ride in the Park, and Marcus relished the day. His mount was spirited and pranced impatiently, but nevertheless, he managed the reins with one hand, while touching the brim of his hat in greeting with the other. It was the start of a new Season, his first complete Season with Elizabeth as his wife, and he could only call his mood elated.

"Good afternoon, Lord Westfield."

Marcus turned his head toward the landaulet that drew up beside him. "Lady Barclay." He smiled.

"May I inquire after Lady Westfield?"

"You may. She's presently napping, I am sorry to say. I pine for her company."

"She's not ill, is she?" Margaret asked, her brows drawn into a frown beneath her wide-brimmed hat.

"No, she's well. Weary and a bit achy at the moment, but then we just returned to Town, as you know. The journey can be tiring." Of course, he hadn't allowed her much sleep at the inn.

Elizabeth grew more beautiful by the day, and more irresistible. He often thought of the portrait of her mother, the one that hung above the fireplace in the formal parlor of Chesterfield Hall. He'd once wished to see such happiness reflected in Elizabeth's countenance. Now he would say her contentment far surpassed it.

To think that a year ago he'd thought to sate his lust and end his torment. The former would never happen, not while he breathed, but the later was a distant memory. He thanked the Lord daily that he'd managed to slay her demons as well. Together, they'd found peace, and it was a state of being he cherished.

"I am relieved to hear it's nothing serious. My son is quite eager to see his aunt again, and she promised to call this week."

"Then I'm certain she shall."

They spoke for a few moments longer, but when his horse grew agitated, Marcus bade his farewell. He took a less traveled path than the Row, and freed his mount to run, then he turned toward Grosvenor Square, hoping he'd given Elizabeth enough time to sleep, but too impatient to dally any more, regardless.

As he rode up to the steps of his house, he caught sight of the man who departed and a heavy uneasiness settled over him.

He tossed the reins to the waiting groomsman and hurried inside.

"Good afternoon, my lord," the servant greeted as Marcus handed over his hat and gloves.

"Apparently not, since the doctor was here."

"Lady Westfield is ill, my lord."

"The dowager?" But he knew that was not the case. His mother had looked the picture of health at breakfast while Elizabeth had been out of sorts for over a sennight. Worried beyond measure, he took the stairs two at a time. Her mother had fallen ill and never recovered, a fact he could not forget since the scars from that loss had kept them apart for years.

He entered their rooms cautiously, hesitantly. Pausing on the threshold of Elizabeth's boudoir, he caught the scent of illness, which lingered, defying the windows which were flung wide open to entice the air to circulate. His wife lay still as death on the couch with unhealthy pallor, her skin lightly misted with sweat despite the fact she wore only her negligee and the temperature was more cold than warm.

The doctor was an idiot. Despite his lack of medical knowledge, it was obvious to Marcus that Elizabeth was gravely ill.

A maid bustled around the room, arranging flowers in an effort to scent the room with something pleasant. One look from Marcus, however, and she curtsied and hurried away.

"My love." He fell to his knees beside the couch and brushed the damp tendrils of Elizabeth's hair off her forehead. Her skin was clammy, and he fought the urge to snatch her to him and hold her close.

Elizabeth moaned softly at the touch of her husband's hand. Opening her eyes, she stared at Marcus, acknowledging, as she often did, that she would never tire of looking at him.

"What ails you?" he asked softly, his low velvety voice a soothing caress.

"I was just thinking of you. Where did you go?"

"For a ride in the Park."

"You wicked man. Tormenting all the women in London with the sight of you." The harsh cynicism that had once etched his features was gone, revealing a face of breathtaking masculine beauty. "I'm certain you set every female heart aflutter."

He made a valiant effort to smile through his worried frown. "You never become jealous anymore. I'm not certain how I should feel about that."

"You arrogant man. I trust you to behave yourself. Especially in the near future when I cannot be with you."

"Cannot be with . . . Dear God." He tugged her from the sofa into his arms. "Please spare me," he begged. "Tell me what's wrong. I am wretched over your illness. I will find the best specialists, research every medical volume, call upon—"

She pressed cool fingertips to his lips. "A midwife will suffice."

"A midwife?" His eyes widened and then shot to her belly. "*A midwife?*"

"You certainly put enough effort into it," she teased, adoring the wonder that slowly filled his eyes. "You should not be quite so startled."

"Elizabeth." He squeezed her gently. "Speech fails me."

"Tell me you are happy. That is all I ask."

"Happy? Bloody hell, I was beyond happy when it was just you and I. And content. Now . . . now there are no words for how I feel."

Elizabeth buried her face in her husband's throat and breathed him in, finding instant comfort just from the feel of him next to her. She had suspected pregnancy for weeks, as her breasts had grown more tender and her body had been plagued by weariness. Hiding her morning illness had not been easy, but she'd managed until today. She finally called for the doctor when she'd been inwardly certain she would hear the news she desired above anything.

"I know precisely what you mean to convey," she murmured against his skin. "I will never be able to tell you how it touches me that you loved me, even when it seemed we would not have children."

Settling more comfortably into his lap, Elizabeth thought of how different her life was now from how it had been only a year ago. She'd said she wanted equanimity, but what she had truly wanted was numbness, a respite from the knowledge that she was missing something vital. To have been so afraid, so sure that loving Marcus would weaken her, rather than strengthen her . . . She couldn't fathom it now.

"I love you," she murmured, perfectly happy for the first time since she was a child. Secure in his arms, she drifted to sleep and dreamed of the future.

Don't miss "Love Potion #9" by JoAnn Ross in
BAD BOYS SOUTHERN STYLE.
Available now from Brava!

The Swansea Inn had begun its life as an antebellum mansion belonging to a cotton broker. Three stories tall, created of the local gray Savannah brick that turned a dusky pink when bathed in the red glow of sunset, it overlooked the Polaski Monument in Monterey Square, which Roxi considered the prettiest of the city's twenty-four lush green squares.

She'd heard rumors that the inn had, for several decades prior to the War Between the States, been a house of prostitution, where wealthy planters and merchants had kept a bevy of women for their shared pleasure. There was even one bit of local lore that had General Sherman, after deciding not to torch the city but to give it to President Lincoln as a Christmas present instead, paying a visit to the house to celebrate having concluded his devastating march across Georgia to the sea.

Like so many stories about the city, the tales were couched in mystery and wrapped in sensuality, and had been told and retold so many times that it was impossible to know how much was true and how much was the product of Savannahians' vivid imaginations.

She'd never been inside before, partly because she knew she'd never be able to afford the prices, but mostly because it was a private club. A place, more rumors persisted, of assignations. Even, she'd heard whispered, the occasional orgy.

She might have a liberal view of sex, but if Sloan Hawthorne had plans along those lines for tonight, he was going to be disappointed.

The moment the black car glided to a stop at the curb, the Inn's glass door opened and a man came down the stone steps.

A sudden, white-hot sexual craving zigzagged through her like a bolt of lightning from a clear blue summer sky, sending every hormone in her body into red alert.

Roxi recognized him immediately. She'd Googled him yesterday after talking with Emma on the Internet, and while on all those Web sites she'd visited he'd definitely appeared to be a hunk, up close and personal he was downright lethal.

His hair was warm chestnut streaked with gold she suspected was a result of time spent beneath the California sun, rather than some trendy Beverly Hills salon. He was conservatively dressed in a crisp white shirt, muted gray striped tie, and a dark suit, which looked Italian and probably cost more than her first car.

He opened the back passenger door. His eyes, which were as green as newly minted money, lit up with masculine appreciation as they swept over her.

"Wow. And here I thought the woman was fictional," he murmured.

"Excuse me?" Her body wasn't the only thing that had gone into meltdown. Sexual images of Sloan Hawthorne and herself writhed in her smoke-filled mind.

She told herself the only reason she was taking the hand he'd extended was that the car was low, her skirt tight, and her heels high.

Liar. Not only wasn't she sure she could stand on her own, she was actually desperate for his touch. Not just on her hand, but all the other tingling places on her body.

"I'm sorry." He shook his head. Sheepishly rubbed the bridge of his nose. "I tend to talk to myself when I'm bewitched."

"I see." He wasn't just drop-dead gorgeous. He was cute. It also helped to know that she wasn't the only one who'd been momentarily mesmerized.

The butterflies settled, allowing Roxi to pick up a bit of her own scattered senses. "Does that happen often?" she asked.

"This is the first time." His gaze swept over her—from the top of her head down to her Revved up and Red-y toenails, then back up to her face again. "That is one helluva dress."

"Thank you." It was a basic black dinner dress. That was, if anything that was strapless and fit like a second skin could be called basic.

"Did you wear it to bring me to my knees?"

"Absolutely."

"Well, then." He flashed a grin that would've dropped a lesser woman to *her* knees. As it was, it had moisture pooling hotly between Roxi's thighs. "You'll be glad to know that it's working like a charm."

Like so many of the fine old homes in Savannah's historic district, the Inn had several steps originally designed to keep the dust and mud from the unpaved dirt streets outside the house.

Sloan put a hand on her back as they started walking up the five stone steps, hip to hip. Although the gesture seemed as natural to him as breathing, Roxi's knees were feeling a bit wobbly as a doorman in a burgundy uniform with snazzy gold epaulets swept the door open for them.

Here's a look at Amy J. Fetzer's
HIT HARD,
available now from Brava!

Viva inched closer to the American, staring down at Half Ear guy. "Is he dead? He really *really* looks dead," she said, horrified and curious.

Sam pushed her behind him and cocked his rifle with one hand. "Now would be a good time to run, lady."

He fired a warning shot into the air, and she bolted into the jungle. At least she had the cuff, and put it on before jumping over a low stream and splashing up the other side.

Then she heard the heavy thump of footsteps, the thrashing. Oh God. Bad guys. *Bad guys.* She pushed faster. Her legs burned with the strain, her body weeping sweat. Anything in her path sliced at her legs, her arms; then through the trees, she saw the rise in terrain, and headed toward it.

She hadn't taken ten steps when it hit her, the hard impact to the back of her legs. Strong arms clamped around her knees and she went down. Her chin hit the ground, her teeth clicking. The collision pushed air from her lungs and she collapsed, dizzy, gasping for air and wondering how this day turned so bad so fast. She inhaled dirt, blew it out, then pushed up.

She twisted. Jungle guy. He was breathing hard and had lost his hat somewhere.

"You make it really hard to help you, lady." He backed off her.

"Thank you for your assistance, but did I ask for you to butt in?" God, the sheer idiocy of that hit her and she faced him, her head ringing too much to stand yet.

"You can go back. I'm sure they'll be interested in a little payback."

"I won't dignify that with a response." She sent him a brittle smile as she brushed off leaves. "I'm quite done with adventure for the day, thank you very much."

Sam shifted back on his haunches, then pulled the bandanna from his throat and wiped his face. Shapely, red haired, and a nutcase, he decided. Anyone who'd take on the Thai mafia without a weapon was two jacks short of a full deck.

Then she eased back like a crab.

Aware of her intentions, Sam grabbed her ankle, yanking her close. "They're still out there, along with tigers, snakes—" *whoever shot that dart.*

"And you."

"I'm not going to hurt you, for crissake." Sam let her go and stood, dusting off his clothes.

"I appreciate your interception, really, but I have to go to Bangkok."

He gave her a tight glance that said, *we'll just see about that.*

She saw right through it. "Who made you king of the jungle? While you look real cool with that rifle and whip, I'm sure you can see the wisdom in a hasty departure. And I'm not about to join your little band." She motioned behind him as another man walked up. Jungle guy didn't take his gaze from her as the other handed over the hat.

"Ma'am, I'm Max Renfield." Max held out his hand to help her up.

She didn't budge, and glanced between the two. "Where were you when all that was going on?"

He patted the gun at his side. "Backup."

"Effective, was it?" Viva brushed her hair back and took a

deep cleansing breath, but the tension refused to leave her body. All my fault, she thought, and wondered where her sanity went to play this morning to antagonize all the wrong people. She fingered the gold cuff that hadn't been worn in a few thousand years, and knew it was worth it. She wore history on her wrist, though she hadn't planned to be a part of it today.

"I'm going to look for Phan," Sam said to Max. "Stay with her."

"I don't need a guard."

"No, you need a brain."

Her smile was nothing short of acidic. "Chivalry isn't your strong suit, I see. If it were, you'd at least be seeing to the wounds you made." She modeled her bloody knees.

They were a mess, but considering the bandits wanted to put two bullets in her head, she shouldn't be complaining. "Sorry, lady, no medical supplies."

"I have something to fix that," Max said.

"Figures."

As Sam walked away, Max moved forward, and knelt. "Don't mind him, he's in a rotten mood."

"I couldn't tell, his effervescent personality just blew me away." Max ripped open a packet and started to clean her knees. "Oh, it's not that bad," she said, taking the antiseptic towel.

He frowned.

"Well—" She flushed. "He knocked me down when a 'hey you, wait' would have done the trick. That man is *extreme* in every sense of the word."

Max sat back, grinning. She had Sam pegged from the get-go. Interesting. She finished cleaning her knees, pulling her leg up to her face like a dancer to blow off the sting. Great legs.

"Thank you, Max."

He frowned, glanced the way the other had gone. "Come on."

"Shouldn't we wait for him?" She really didn't want to trek through the jungle. The dart had to come from somewhere.

"He's been gone too long."

"Well, that can't be good."

He helped her off the ground and she followed him as they moved into the forest. Max hacked their way through the jungle for a considerable distance when he stopped, and called out softly.

Viva peered around him and she saw his partner.

He waved Max on. "You stay there," he said, pointing.

"Anyone ever mention you have control issues?"

And finally, take a peek at HelenKay Dimon's
"Player's Club"
in her upcoming anthology,
VIVA LAS BAD BOYS,
coming next month from Brava!

"Nothing to see. The lights are off. I don't hear the air-conditioning so I'm guessing we blew a circuit breaker or something."

"You're trying to say your kisses were so good that we blew a fuse? Try again, stud."

His chuckle rumbled against her chest. He flicked back the edge of the curtain and let the light from the Strip stream into the room. "Probably from the construction. 'Tho think how impressive the kiss thing would be."

Dumb didn't begin to describe how she felt at the moment. She made every professional misstep imaginable. Lose control? Check. Let her desires overwhelm her good sense? Check. Let her consulting client go one step too far on the floor of her office? That was new, but still a check.

Damn hormones.

What she needed was a little decorum. Getting off the floor and out from under him would be a good start. "Okay, fun time is over."

"Most people would look at the lights being out as a message."

He felt so right there with her body curved into his. "Right. The message being to get up."

He frowned at her and managed to look adorable doing it. "I was thinking more like the opposite conclusion."

She tried to concentrate on his argument, lame as it was, but his firm body kept dragging her attention away. From the impressive bulge pressing against her thigh to his hard-as-granite everything else, she wanted him.

His pretty boy face and easy charm attracted her from the beginning. With every day that passed she wanted him more.

"Shouldn't you get back to your kitchen?" she asked.

"Sam has it under control. He's my second in command. He could run his own kitchen and is totally qualified to take over in my absence."

Commonsense didn't seem to be working, but she tried again. "Yeah, well, we should be out there checking on the guests."

"Unless you plan to hand out flashlights, I'm not sure what you could do."

"I could . . ." Something?

"We can't do any work. We're all alone. It's dark. I'm on top of you."

"I notice you're not getting up," she muttered under her breath.

"Think of the darkness as the universe's sign we should keep on doing what we're doing." His hand rested on her breast and showed no sign of moving, so it wasn't hard to figure out what the "what" was.

"We need to go," she insisted.

"Most people wouldn't view the lights going out as a reason to stop having fun."

Then it hit her. She was having sex with Zach. On her floor. In her office. She'd even touched his ass. So much for professionalism. Nothing prepared her for Zach.

"Zach, I'm serious." More like embarrassed, but he didn't need to know that.

He lowered his head until his forehead touched her breasts. The move sent an ache spinning from her chest to the damp space between her thighs.

"You're actually going to do it." He mumbled into the thin material separating them.

Her breath caught in her throat. "Do what?"

He skimmed his finger under the edge of her camisole and flimsy bra and outlined her nipple until it puckered. "Call a halt. Go right to the edge and pull back."

"I didn't—" She gasped when he slipped the two layers of silk down, exposing her breast.

Then he palmed her, his hand warm against her chilled skin. "Man, you're beautiful."

She couldn't speak.

"I wanted time to do this." He licked her nipple, flicking his tongue across the tight bud.

She tried to remember her name. Bartholomew something . . .

"And this." He placed his hot mouth over the tip and suckled her. Twirling his tongue over her and wetting her skin.

Someone moaned. She feared it came from deep inside of her.

"So pretty." His reverent whisper tickled against her breast.

Two more seconds and her skirt would be over her head. "Stop!"

"You still want that clipboard?"

"Yeah, so I can beat you with it."

"Well, honey, I'm not usually into that, but I'm game."

She couldn't handle his cuteness. Not now. She needed him angry. Pissed. Whatever it took to get him off of her.

"Your Performance Plan is getting longer by the second."